THE GRAND SCHEME OF THINGS

THE GRAND SCHEME OF THINGS

WARONA JAY

First published in the UK in 2024 by
Footnote Press

www.footnotepress.com

Footnote Press Limited
4th Floor, Victoria House, Bloomsbury Square, London WC1B 4DA

Distributed by Bonnier Books UK, a division of Bonnier Books
Sveavägen 56, Stockholm, Sweden

First printing
1 3 5 7 9 10 8 6 4 2

A CIP catalogue record for this book is available from the British Library.

ISBN (hardback): 978 1 804 44123 7
ISBN (trade paperback): 978 1 804 44124 4
ISBN (ebook): 978 1 804 44125 1

Printed and bound in Great Britain
by Clays Ltd, Elcograf S.p.A.

MIX
Paper | Supporting
responsible forestry
FSC
www.fsc.org   FSC® C018072

To Waz, circa 2013. Don't stress! You'll be just fine.

It takes time to reject the most important lie: that black people can't do the same things that white people do unless a white person helps them.

—*BlacKkKlansman* (2018), dir. Spike Lee

EDDIE

The Man in the Café

October 2015

In your defence, it was really busy on the day we met.

You probably felt that you had no choice but to sit at the empty spot beside me. Nobody ever chooses the tables that face the windows, the ones with the stools too high off the ground, where if you place your belongings beneath you, it's a whole manoeuvre just to reach down and grab them. It's usually only if they have no other choice. Of course, I'm generalising preferences, and I'm excluding myself from the generalisation. I love window tables in cafés. This particular spot had been mine for weeks before the fateful day we met. I would sit right where the bustling street in Holborn worked as a foreground, hammering away at my laptop in either focused ferocity or erratic desperation, with a piping-hot mocha to the left of me, every weekday for a few hours, in the same chair, in the same café, like clockwork. I'd often have a chair left between me and the next stranger, so I would have preferred it if you had scanned the room for a little longer so you could find a free spot elsewhere, or anywhere to give me space for myself. But this one day, nobody was giving up space. The café was getting busier and busier, with activity climbing towards its lunchtime summit just as you came in. I wouldn't have given you a second glance if you had walked past, but you stopped after you entered, hesitated, and then walked to the seat right next to me. I moved my tote bag out of the way, and you smiled instinctively, harmlessly. I kept my eyes glued to my laptop screen as you set up your things, but I was very much aware that you were there, floating, hovering, bobbing around in my periphery.

Art is a stressful game, Hugo. I know you know that now. But it was consuming me that day. I was trawling through the script for the play I was working on, so, so close to the end, yet so far away. I had the passion for it, but not the discipline. I had the dream, but not always the drive. I was excited, but I was also stressed. And to thwart the stress, I would take a smoke break every hour, to the hour. I'd start rolling up Golden Virginia tobacco into a Rizla paper, stick in a menthol filter, and then step outside, directly ahead of the window, where I could keep an eye on my things. I found myself turning to you after I licked the cigarette closed. I politely asked you to watch my belongings while I stepped out to degenerate my lungs, and you politely obliged. You were a faceless stranger. Sometimes I cherish that first hour we sat together, with no knowledge of one another. It was peace, for us to blend into the café, become a part of everything else, all consumed by our own lives and worries. It was peace before your life became mine, before mine became yours.

"I'm sorry, I shouldn't have pried, but I couldn't help but notice that you're working on something interesting," you said to me around five minutes after my return. I turned to look at you properly for the first time. I was slightly intimidated, wondering what on earth compelled this man to have an ounce of interest in me. I was self-conscious, knowing I smelled like a fresh ashtray, so I internally tensed at the sound of your introductory apology. I thought you were going to bring up my disgraceful habit. British people have a way of using an apology to convey opposing things; it represents 50 percent regret, and 50 percent inconvenience. I relaxed once I realised you were just being deferential. "Is that . . . a script for a play, or a show, or something?" you asked. Unlike me, you did not smell like a fresh ashtray. I remember thinking, *I bet his cologne is the most expensive recommended retail price Hugo Boss, or a limited-edition Abercrombie & Fitch fragrance or some shit like that.* Of course, I didn't know the retail prices of men's cologne, and you'd later come to tell me that those brands were on the modest end of the price scale: "Creed Aventus is my go-to, typically." But it wasn't really money I could smell. It was just whatever I couldn't afford.

"Umm, it's just a personal project. A play." I tried not to say too much. You nodded, still looking over at my laptop. I thought, *Should I have locked my screen when I went outside? Closed the laptop?* But I didn't think you'd care. Strangers aren't usually that interested in other strangers.

"A play? That's amazing. Sorry, I just saw a page from the corner of my eye. I didn't touch anything, I promise. But the script, it sounds interesting. What's the play called?"

"It's called *The Worthy*," I said. "It's this kind of . . . near-future dystopia."

"Oh wow. A dystopia. What's it about? If you don't mind me asking."

"It's about a lot of things, really. Mainly national identity, citizenship, capitalism, that sort of thing. I'm still working on it, so the specifics aren't all quite there yet."

"That's very impressive. When did you start it?" I quickly glanced over at your screen, where I could see an application form for something. The page had expired due to a lack of activity, so you would have had to refresh it. I guess getting swept into the sweet embrace of procrastination was at least one thing we had in common.

"I've been working on it since the late summer. I started it around August, and I'm nearly done. Hopefully by next month, or December. I think I'll spend the Christmas holiday tweaking it."

"That's great. I'm quite into theatre myself." You took a sip of your coffee. "I love the West End. I love drama in general. Films, TV. Do you work for anybody? Should I expect to see this anywhere?"

"Uhhh, no." I shook my head. "It's just a personal project. I'll try and get it out there myself, but we'll see. It's a long road to stardom." I chuckled uneasily. I had completely lost my creative train of thought at this point; it was going to be a ball ache to try to get back into the script. "I graduated from Kingston University in drama and creative writing, which was not exactly in my parents' life plans for me."

"Really? Wow." You frowned in surprise, and then your expression softened as you stared through the window, out at the busy road ahead. "Chasing your dreams is always worth a shot every now and then, isn't it?"

"Sure. Well, what do *you* do, then?" I rallied a question back, somewhat intrigued by your response.

"Oh, uhhh, I'm a master's student. LSE. Law. Fun stuff."

"You don't sound too convinced."

"Like I said, I have a great love for theatre. But law runs in the family, so the road has been somewhat paved for me," you said, shrugging lightly. You didn't need to expand on that point. As I looked you up and down, it all made sense. What struck me, however, was that your assurance towards obtaining a career in what I thought must be an extremely competitive profession didn't necessarily read as enthusiasm or pride. I was quick to wonder whether most people with privilege felt resigned to it, or whether you were something of an outlier.

"I guess sometimes we know what our destinies have in store for us." I smiled, closed my laptop, and jumped off the stool to collect my bag. I had to leave; I was getting too stressed out, thinking about where my life was going, terrified at not knowing. But you were set for life. I knew that from the moment I saw you.

"What's your name, by the way?" you asked, once you realised I was making a run for it. "I'd love to see the finished product at some point. I'm sure it'll be out there in the world one day."

"My name's Eddie. You can add me on Facebook if you want," I found myself saying, taking my phone out of my pocket. "What's your name? I can add you now."

"My name's Hugo," you said. "Hugo Lawrence Smith. Lawrence with an *A-W*, not an *A-U*. But I'm just Hu to most."

"Nice. I'll see you around, Hu." I had no intention of seeing you around.

You nodded and smiled courteously as I turned away. I laughed internally at the revelation of your name. You weren't *wearing* Hugo, you *were* Hugo. You were a living, breathing embodiment of splendour. It was etched into your linen shirt, your crisp trousers, your charcoal-grey overcoat, your hazel eyes, your diplomatic smile, your attention-commanding posture. Even though you were a coward at heart, your outward form was a hiding place from that truth.

◆ ◆ ◆

See, Relebogile Naledi Mpho Moruakgomo is quite a mouthful of a name if you've never heard it before, I'll admit. My mother couldn't decide which name she liked best, so she took all three she was considering, scooped them up into her hands in Gaborone's Princess Marina maternity ward, and stuck them onto my birth certificate without a second thought. My father had no say whatsoever; they had this idiosyncratic deal that if I came out a boy, he could pick my name. My mother was elated that I was a girl. I had my father's surname, anyway—that should be enough, she'd huffed. When we moved to England, Naledi ended up winning the space where Relebogile stood, just to make things easier for everyone else, and that was the name I'd hold from there on. But even a name that was easier for everyone else wasn't going to be *easy* for *everyone*. I'd be lying through my teeth if I said I had always hated my name, because there was a time—a blissful moment—where I would assertively correct my peers on its pronunciation. No, it's not Nail-dee, it's not NAR-leh-dee, it's not Nah-leh-DIE, it doesn't rhyme with Malachi, it rhymes with Eddie, it's *Naledi*. You'd think the English language would be more accommodating to the arrangement of the letters, you'd think it would be easier, but it has its trials and tribulations on the British tongue. And don't even get me started on the rest of my names.

It didn't help that as I sauntered into my teenage years, social standing and appearance became everything, and I had a name that was practically oral acrobatics, a name that had me growing tired of racking up three times the number of introductions to strangers than the average local, a name that received a predictable scroll of questions about the meaning. A suggestion that "Eddie" might be easier. It didn't help that in my weariness, by the time I started university, I gave in to that request.

So that was naturally how I introduced myself to you. I was Eddie. No, it wasn't short for anything, yes, my parents knew what they were doing giving me a boy's name, it just added to the flair, the zaniness of my character, it built me up for the judgemental world around me, they thought it would get me further in life, that's why they did it. I told you a year after we'd first met that it wasn't actually Eddie, it was short for Naledi. You looked at me funny and asked me why I went on that faux spiel about my name's origin, and I told you it's the same reason that when someone asks me where I'm *really* from, I'll have a different genesis, because they don't really care, it doesn't really matter. My name is Relebogile Naledi Mpho Moruakgomo, but my name is Eddie. You thought Naledi sounded cooler, more unique, but I could only translate that as it sounded more Other, and I was tired of that kind of attention.

I'll never truly know now if you genuinely understood where I was coming from, considering the sequence of events that have occurred thus far, but I think that was the beauty of it. You never truly understood, and you never really cared, and your name was easy on the ears, your face was easy on the eyes, your smile was easy on the heartstrings, and that was why I chose you.

She Comes with Rain

July 2015

My mother must have known I wasn't straight.

Of course, it can be difficult to discern one's sexuality, but there was a hint in the fact that I had never shown any interest in boys growing up, and the very first person I ever loved, who I would have died for, was female. I say my mother must have known because I didn't exactly try to hide it. I'd always mention Blue to her, and she had met her a handful of times. But the way the patriarchy is built, it can be easy to conclude that two girls kissing are just besties who love pillow fights and comparing each other's labia for the hell of it. It can be easy to conclude that two girls kissing are just openly sexual while being emotionally platonic. Unless one of us proposed to the other in broad daylight in front of the general public to witness, even just holding hands could harbour some heterosexual clarification. I hadn't officially told my mother I had a real-life, living, breathing girlfriend until the summer I completed my studies at Kingston. I came out to her a few weeks before my graduation, which was roughly three months before I met you.

• • •

The news wasn't exactly digestible to an African woman born and raised in a devout Christian African world (a colonial conundrum, in my eyes). I had to tell her eventually, and the fear and danger I felt, the bile that rose up my throat, the tremor I could feel in the core of my being, making its way to my dewy palms, was always going to be a part of pushing that closet door open.

"You have a *girlfriend*? *Ao*. Since when?" She didn't break her gaze from the dinner she'd made us. I had just moved out of campus, and I was back at home. We'd take turns making dinner because it was basically just the two of us; my brother also lived here, but as a fresher, he spent most of his time crashing at his friends' uni accommodation. This evening, it was my mother's turn to cook. She scooped a madombi dumpling into her hand, dipped it into the vegetable gravy, and bit into it ferociously.

"It's Blue." My throat was incredibly dry, no matter how many times I took a sip of the drink beside me.

"*Waitseee...*" She shook her head, still chewing. "This is ridiculous. She is your friend, no? *Wa re* your *girlfriend*? *Wa tshameka*. You are pulling my leg. She is your friend."

"We've been together since last year, around Christmas. She's more than my friend, Mum. I'm not joking. *Ga ke tshameke.*" I could have thrown up, right there, right then. Instead, I swallowed. My food had turned cold at this point.

My mother continued. "Do you know what job you are getting after you graduate?"

"I'm not sure yet, I'm still looking—"

"Was that degree worth it? The arty-farty dancing onstage pretending to be the next Shakespeare? Have you got job prospects? *That* is my main concern."

Shakespeare didn't dance onstage, I wanted to say. *He was a playwright. That's what I am. That's what I want to be.* "I'm still working on it, Mum. You can't expect me to have a job the second I leave university."

"If you had just done law, or business like Nicholas, we wouldn't be having this conversation. There are jobs everywhere for those professions. Theatre? Unless you are a descendant of Shakespeare, forget about it."

"These things take time. And you're changing the subject. I told you, I'm in a relationship. Blue is my girlfriend."

"We are going to Botswana this summer, right after your graduation. The tickets have already been booked. Your family want to congratulate you on being the first of us to finish schooling in the UK. There will be a graduation party in Gaborone. Then you are going to visit your grandmother in Lobatse. Your father also wants to see you. The two of you can arrange something, you can visit him in Francistown for a week or so."

"Are you joking? I just told you I'm gay. Do you have nothing to say?"

"Don't mention that stupid word in this house again, Naledi," she said more assertively. I was crying silently, having lost my appetite. "And don't mention any of this when we get to Bots. *Se bue jalo. Tswee-tswee.* Especially not to your father. *Wa utlwa?* Am I clear?"

• • •

I stayed over at Blue's house the night before my graduation, as she was set to join me at the ceremony for support. With her was where I'd always felt most comfortable. I loved to fall asleep to her heartbeat at night, and her arms had always been the softest. It was the only thing that made me happy; a reminder that she was a living human being like me, that she felt just as happy with me too.

I knew my mother was going to see her the next day, which had me feeling stubborn and embarrassed at the same time. It had been a few weeks since our pointed conversation and she had since kept our talks minimal, only bringing up graduation plans and the like. I remember telling Blue everything the night I came out to my mother, crying over the phone and telling her that my relationship with my family was probably over and done with, and that the trip back to my home country was going to be more of a trial and tribulation than a wholesome return. I knew spending time with Blue and her family before my big day was something of a *Fuck you*, but it wasn't a welcome one. Although nothing could make me ever compromise my love for Blue, it didn't mean that it was a carefree decision and not a mortifying one in the face of my family's potential disdain. I just couldn't stand the judgement.

"You're so fucking beautiful, do you know that?" Blue said to me the next morning. My ceremony was in the early afternoon, and I had texted my mother and younger brother Nick to meet me near the venue an hour beforehand. Until then, I was getting myself prepped, hiding out with Blue in her bathroom—the only place we could find a semblance of privacy from her hovering, overenthusiastic parents. She kissed me and smiled with pride before I put my lipstick on.

"You always say I'm beautiful," I responded.

"I mean it. You're stunning."

I kissed her, sliding my fingers through her night-coloured coils of hair. "Look at you. You put just as much effort into today as I have." I gazed at her outfit: an off-white ruched blouse paired with peach-coloured cropped trousers. She was wearing the gold-plated amazonite chain necklace I had bought her for her birthday a few months prior. It sat so gloriously on her chest. I really, really did love her.

"You mean how you always put in so much effort when you turn up to any of my gigs, no matter how big or small?" she chuckled. "It means the world to me."

"I wouldn't have it any other way." I smiled.

"I'll be in your position next year. Getting ready to put my graduation hat on and all that."

"You mean mortarboard?"

"Okay, I get it. You know fancy words. Let's have breakfast before we start running late." She kissed me on the cheek before opening the bathroom door, and we walked down into the kitchen, where her parents were making food for us. Her father was playing Alton Ellis's rendition of "Workin' on a Groovy Thing" while her mother bopped along, flipping pancakes. I remember how I felt that day: so happy. But I was also in so, so much pain. I never knew rejection could feel so visceral until this point. In an alternate universe, I was dancing around to music with my mother, but not in this one. This pain—the pain of rejection, the pain that came with being turned away for just being exactly who I was—holy shit, Hugo.

There was more to come.

◆ ◆ ◆

When Queen Elizabeth made a visit to Botswana in 1995, it was raining. The locals saw it as a sign; the rain was something the queen brought on. They nicknamed her Motlalepula, which means "she comes with rain." On my first visit to the country in nearly three years, the rain was torrential, which was quite an eyebrow raiser for a semidesert in the winter. An uncommon occurrence. I'm not leaping to any conclusions, but one could assume that I brought the rain on. Of course, nobody would think that. I'm not British royalty.

We were greeted by my aunty Yarona and my cousin Tshiamo outside Sir Seretse Khama Airport, before hurrying into their car under the shelter of semi-functioning umbrellas we clutched tightly with our free hands. We were lucky our suitcases weren't more soaked through by the time we thrust them into the boot and slid into the backseats.

I had felt so uneasy on the whole journey from England, knowing that my mother was sitting on a Pandora's box of information that she was either ready to open up to chaos and familial scrutiny, or keep sealed shut. I'd had no time to delve into searching for theatre work between leaving university and flying to Botswana, so I wasn't sure what I was going to tell my relatives when they hounded me with questions. I definitely wasn't sure what I was going to say when they asked me if I was any closer to walking down the aisle. Nosy aunts always think they have a stake in the workings of your private life, like a listener's commitment to a podcast conversation. I didn't need a dissection of my life, a poking and prodding at my goals and aspirations. Being the first child in my mother's family to be raised outside the country meant that every return was like Neil Armstrong bringing remnants of the moon back with him, with everyone clambering for a piece. Only, I wasn't so sure they'd be as impressed with the remnants of my truth.

"So how is London treating you?" Tshiamo asked as we took a long walk around the block after the rain had passed in the late evening. We had stopped at a tuckshop, where she bought us some Fizz-Pop sweets and bartered for some cheap cigarettes for us to smoke on our walk. She had perfume in her handbag to cover ourselves with once we'd finished smoking. It brought me back to the summers I used to spend with her, when she took me under her wing once she noticed I was the outcast cousin who others were reluctant to interact with. Naturally, I started sharing less and less in common with my distant family as time went on, but she'd make sure to bring me along to house parties and car-park functions so I could get a piece of the fun. We'd stagger home exhausted, sneaking into the yard in a mask of body spray to cover the smells of debauchery that clung to our skin and hair.

"London's okay," I sighed. "I'm sure you know I've just graduated."

"Arts, right?" She sucked in the nicotine. "Congrats."

"Playwriting. Thanks."

"Nicholas has just finished his freshman year, *akere*? I forgot what he studies. Why didn't he come with you guys?"

"He's Interrailing around Europe with his friends. And yeah, he finished his first year. Business and management at Queen Mary."

"Queen this, Queen that." She laughed. "Who even is that? I didn't know there was a Queen Mary."

"She was King George V's wife, so she wasn't an actual queen."

"*Eish*, it's too complicated, man. Anyways. Are you looking forward to your grad party next week?"

"No," I answered honestly. "I'd rather be anywhere but here." She was oddly silent after my admission. I sensed she knew something she wasn't supposed to disclose, so I elbowed her lightly, asking her what was up. *"Ke eng?"*

"I overheard my mother on the phone a week ago. I think she was talking to your mother. *Wa re*, something about . . . I don't know, I couldn't fully make out everything they were saying. But I think they were talking about you."

My heart stopped. "What could you hear?"

"*Ba re*, they expected you to marry a *lekgoa* at the most, but they weren't expecting you to be with a *kgarebe*."

"They thought I'd marry an English man before I got with a girl?" I repeated, breaking out into a nervous chuckle.

"*Eeh.* My mother said it's just a phase. Maybe you'll snap out of it."

"Do you know the girl I always post on my Instagram? That's the *kgarebe*."

"The yellowbone? *Ke a itse.* I thought she was just your best friend."

"No. She's the girl I love. She's not a 'phase.' She's the only person in this world who I can be around and be myself." I stubbed out the butt of my cigarette, suddenly feeling nauseous. A stray dog trotted along the red sand, blanketed in night, on the side of the road.

"*O seka wa bolelela ope* that I told you. You haven't heard anything from me, okay?"

"I won't tell anyone."

Tshiamo turned to me. "My mother said that England must have corrupted you. Your family went there for a better life, and this is how you respond, by falling into the wrong circles."

"*Bathong*! I'm not exactly moving blow around the boroughs. I'm not part of a gang. Why do people think they know me? Nobody knows me. Nobody gets me."

"*Ga gona mathata*, Naledi. Don't worry. It's just elders being elders. Parents being parents. Speaking of parents, when are you seeing Uncle Karabo?"

"Ideally, never. Realistically, in a few days. I'm absolutely dreading it, though. Especially with all this . . . newfound information."

I knew that visiting my father would be a stressful ordeal. He moved back to Botswana when I was ten and had since been running his own trucking company there. To my dismay, he was still a devoted member of a religious sect called God's Living Angels (a cult, to put it frankly). He'd ended up falling into it during our annual trips to Botswana, and my parents divorced shortly after, having different ideas about where Nick and I should be raised. My father had wished to return to his roots and live out his life as a committed man of God, away from the corruption of secular society. But my mother had been reluctant to follow suit. *It will hinder Naledi's and Nicholas's studies,* she had told him. *It will stunt their chances for better opportunities.* So she'd decided to stay in England with me and my brother, fraying the tethers that held her to my father. At the time, I had a vague understanding that there had been a gradual clash of religious beliefs, but I knew now it had been more than that.

Before my father left the UK for good, he had been made redundant from his third job, and he was struggling to find a new one. A better one. My mother's jobs as a nurse and hairdresser were comfortable enough, but my father wanted to be hired into a position of authority, or at the very least a job in an office. He was tired of working as a taxi driver, a bus driver, a warehouse worker. He wanted to wear a white collar. But no matter how many applications he put in, no matter how much education and work experience he had, he got nothing back. It was Radio Silence. Mr. Karabo Moruakgomo was stumped. From the bottom of my heart, I believe that was the real reason he'd moved back to Botswana, although he would never admit it.

Tshiamo took out her perfume and gave us both a spritz. "Can I come back to London with you? Life is too simple here. *Ke batla go live my best life.*"

"I'm not even sure I'm living mine." I huffed. "Seriously, though . . . an English man? They really thought that? I'll be dead before I even associate with *any* kind of man. End of story."

I think back a lot to that statement I made, Hugo. I'm sure you can see the irony in it now.

◆ ◆ ◆

When I eventually went to visit my father in Francistown, I wasn't shocked to find out he was still steadfast in his belief that my mother had made the wrong decision by keeping us in the UK. He ranted on about how Nick was the saving grace, the one who could prove her right. He'd become the potential moneymaker, the one worthy of the citizenship we held. My father made this loud and clear, harping on about how I'd abused my chances in a better world. I'd followed the corrupted, the hippies, the artists, the kind of lifestyle that only a *lekgoa* could afford to live. I had sabotaged my citizenship, according to him. I didn't deserve the opportunities I had been given abroad. I was not worthy of them.

But this time, I didn't feel as dejected as I usually would during his degrading, irrational, holier-than-thou, condescending lecture. Instead, it actually gave me a second wind. Then and there, the accumulating pressure to make my family less ashamed of me became the inspiration for a new script idea. I was going to write a play, and I knew exactly what it was going to be about. I was going to title it *The Worthy*, and it was going to be a near-future dystopia that explored national identity, citizenship, and capitalism. I needn't say any more because you know the play very well. But that was where the idea stemmed from, how the script blossomed. It was birthed from a rant my father showered over me, two months before I met you. A rant that concerned my supposed lack of belonging, my lack of worth, in the only place I called home.

The Worthy

January 2016

As per my prediction, I completed my first draft of the script in early January, three months after my conversation with you in the café. Every now and then I'd think back to the kind words of a stranger who saw potential in my work before I had even finished it. Remembering that I had you on social media, I searched through my friends list on Facebook and scrolled through your profile, finding nothing surprising. Photos at the Royal Ascot; a fancy date night at the Berkeley with a blonde-haired, cobalt-blue-eyed woman who I assumed was your girlfriend; UCL graduation pictures; a family trip to Hong Kong. *Cheers for the well-wishing,* I thought to myself as I sat in the suffocatingly tiny bedroom of my childhood home.

Though I had completed my play, I kept the entire plot to myself. I told nobody—not Blue, not my university friends, not anybody. I wanted to surprise everyone with a viewing of the play in person, whenever that might be. *If* ever that might be. But I guess I also believed in the superstition of the evil eye—that the less I spoke of what I was aiming to achieve, the better the chance I had of achieving it. I didn't really have strong connections to the theatre world, despite my degree, though one of my lecturers had been an actor in the West End before he turned to teaching, and I built up enough of a rapport with him that I could use him as leverage once I began sending my play off to agencies and contests. I thought that might have helped, as well as my first-class degree from one of the best drama schools in the country; and the collegiate creative writing award in my second year, in which I won third place; and the local script-writing prize for BAME applicants that I won halfway through my third year, after handing in one of my assignments on a whim. I had the credentials. I had what it took to break through. There was just something missing, and it hurt to consider what that something might be. The nagging notion that it might have had nothing to do with my credentials or how hard I worked, and more to do with everything I couldn't change, was never lost on me. I just had to hope for the best in my situation; I couldn't succumb to the frustration. The road to success is slippery, you see. It's a nebulous wonder. A pain in the arse.

I had secured a Christmas temp position at Lush near Monument Station, and my contract had expired in the first week of the new year. There was an interview scheduled at a Byron Burgers restaurant near the Cutty Sark in Greenwich a few days later. The hours would be enough to allow me to travel around the city and contribute towards the bills and the groceries. My mother was getting older; her hands were starting to ache due to the repetitive strain she had endured from years of hair-braiding, so she couldn't take on as many clients anymore. Nurses wouldn't be given pay rises anytime soon, and I didn't want to be another financial burden she had to consider. Though she might have been ashamed that I hadn't found full-time work, I know she secretly didn't want me to move out. If I were to break out of the nest, she'd be left with nothing but cable TV and her own thoughts. She seemed to have warmed up to the concept of Blue being more than just my friend, though it pained her to admit it. She knew Blue was a good person who had shown nothing but respect for my family, despite their reservations. Still, I started spending more of my time at Blue's house, and Blue started spending less time at mine.

"Why won't you just tell me what it's about?" Blue moaned one evening as we sat smoking a joint in her bedroom. The perks of living in a liberal household meant that she could consume as much weed as she wanted, and her parents would chip in on the dealer's offers instead of kicking her out of the house.

"I just don't want to. Don't ask me again. Just wait and see."

"Fuck's sake. *Fine.*"

"Let's stop talking about me. How's the band going?"

"It's not doing too bad." She shrugged. "We've bumped practice from two to three times a week now. My Sundays aren't as free as they used to be." She was in her final year of music at Guildhall. Two years earlier, she had joined a five-piece jazz fusion band called Ego Birth, assembled by some of her uni mates. In the time they'd been active, her band had cultivated a following in London's underground music scene. We had met through a mutual friend at one of her shows at the Windmill in Brixton, and from the moment we locked eyes, the rest was history. From that day forward, I was Ego Birth's most devoted groupie, attending nearly every show and some studio rehearsals. The mastering of their second EP, *Learn to Swim*, was finalised, and they had an upcoming gig in Kentish Town to celebrate the release. The evening she'd tried quizzing me on my secret play, she was nonchalantly practicing one of her band's songs on her bedroom keyboard in preparation for the show. Eventually, she had got so high she gave up playing and put on Anderson. Paak's new album. She lay next to me on her bed as we sank into the soft melody of "The Bird", the opening track.

"You're going to be famous one day. I can feel it in my bones," I whispered to her, running my thumb across her cheek. "You're going to go on world tours with Ego Birth and win all the Grammys, all the Ivor Novellos, you name it."

"I'm not striving for fame, Eddie."

"It doesn't matter. It's about getting the recognition you deserve. Your music is amazing. You're amazing. I know you're going to make it out there."

"How do you know?" she whispered, looking at me.

"*A bird with the word came to me.*" I smiled, repeating the lyrics of the song that was playing. I looked right into her eyes. She had her mother's—big, brown, and angular, with enviously thick lashes that curled out from under her soft hooded eyelids. She had a button-shaped nose and full lips with a sharp Cupid's bow. Her smile was the warmest. When I first met her, I could never quite tell if she was Southeast Asian or black. Her hair texture and skin tone said one thing, and her facial features said another. It turned out she was both.

She switched her position on the bed, propping her elbows on the pillow, and looked down at me as I stared longingly at the ceiling. "What does your name mean in English, Ed?" she asked.

"Naledi? You already know. I've told you before."

"I know. I just want you to say it."

I sighed. "It means 'star.'"

"So your name literally means 'star,' and you're telling me I'm the one who's destined for fame?"

• • •

I wanted to believe Blue so badly, but after twelve weeks of pitching my play to different agencies and competitions, I wasn't getting any responses. It was disheartening because I was so, so sure I had hit the jackpot with this play. It was the third one I had ever written, and I knew that it was a thought-provoking, intense, and heartfelt manifestation of all the blood, sweat, and tears (and qualifications and credentials, for fuck's sake) it had taken me to get there. I didn't need anybody to tell me that. But paradoxically, I *did* need someone to tell me that. I needed someone to tell me, and then tell everyone else. I needed someone to give it a chance. There was only one problem: the Brexit referendum was slowly creeping closer, and it had ripped an invisible chasm through the country. A play about immigration and national identity might have been a *bit* too on the nose at the time. A little too sensitive for a Divided Kingdom.

In *The Worthy*, it wasn't birthright or naturalisation that determined citizenship. Instead, there was a points-based system, which meant that *anyone* could be exiled if they could not contribute towards the economy or the fabric of society. Of course, in real life, these are arbitrary concepts, and this was quite a far-fetched idea. But in this world, it would tear families apart, leaving hundreds of thousands of people displaced. Families would all be awaiting the National Sweep: an annual interview that every individual had with citizenship officers, determining whether or not they would be forced to leave the country and seek asylum elsewhere. In the wake of the turn politics took that year, it might not have been the most appropriate premise for a play. But fiction is fiction is fiction, is life, is art, is life, and life imitates art imitates life.

Sometime in April, I had a panic attack. I had just finished shopping around for more literary agencies to send my work to. As I did my research, scrolling through the websites, figuring out who to contact, I noticed something: the majority of these agencies' clients looked nothing like me. Though there were a few, they were few and far between. When it came to the agents themselves, I'd be extremely lucky to find anyone I saw myself in. In all honesty, I had always known this, but on this one particular night at three in the morning, after my fifth cup of coffee and my nth query submission, the realisation became daunting. One could argue, what did I expect when people with skin like mine made up only 3 percent of the population? When people like me, people who were born outside the UK, made up 13 percent of the population? What did I expect when I was just a pinch of pepper grains in a bucket of salt? I began to spiral, asking myself, what did I expect? What did I expect? What did I expect?

I was sure my name must have been a drawback. They must have seen a name like Relebogile Naledi Moruakgomo and concluded that they knew my whole life story. I googled black British writers to see how many of us were out there, and I stumbled upon an A-Z list on Wikipedia. I sighed, heart sinking. That's how I knew I didn't stand a chance. We could all be reduced to an exhaustive list. To make matters worse, I found a list specifically promoting female black British writers on another website, and I scrolled to the comments section, where one particular comment stood out to me: *Thank you for including me in this! But I would just like to point out that the photo you chose is not a photo of me! Please let me send in a correct image.*

These agencies, they must have seen a name like Relebogile Naledi Moruakgomo and thought, we've already got Yrsa Daley-Ward, we've already got Chimamanda Ngozi Adichie, Chioma Okereke, Cecile Emeke, Sade Adeniran, Patience Agbabi, Yaba Badoe, Theresa Ikoko, Oonya Kempadoo, Sarah Ladipo Manyika, Irenosen Okojie, Kadija Sesay, we can hold off on another ethnic woman for now. My heart rate catapulted and my palms began to sweat; my armpits tingled and my eyes blurred into tunnel vision. I realised that I was just going to be an indecipherable, indistinguishable artist, shoved into a box. An exhaustive list. Another name to hurdle over, another face to memorise. The chance of exposure came and went as often as a panda's fertility window. This probably wasn't my time, but I had no way of knowing when it would be. People like me don't have the luxury of time, Hugo. Maybe we're not worthy of it.

The Evolution of a Name

April 2016

Billy Andromeda, a middle-grade sci-fi space opera comprising six books, had sold nearly half a billion copies since its debut in the mid-nineties. It had been adapted into a film series that racked up millions of fans and just as much revenue. Collections, merchandise, theatre franchises, theme-park attractions, video games, fan fiction, fan clubs and conventions, recognisable catchphrases, had proliferated from the birth of *Billy Andromeda*. It had become marinated in the cultural fabric of our society. There were BuzzFeed quizzes that could tell you which intergalactic *Andromeda* fleet you belonged to based on whatever kind of breakfast you prefer; I'd consider that an indicator of success, if you asked me. The author, C. H. Edmonds, is one of the most successful and influential writers alive. But things might have been different if she'd chosen to go by Charlotte Edmonton-Smith—her full name.

Things might have been different had her publishers not recommended that she shave down her name in an attempt to appeal to the target market of her books—young boys who may not have gravitated towards a book written by a woman. It's a ridiculous thing to have to do, to have your work judged on something you can't change about yourself, as opposed to the merits of the work itself. It's a sad reality, but it happens. George Eliot, one of the most influential writers of the nineteenth century, had no other choice but to divorce her real identity from her work. Charlotte, Emily, and Anne Brontë may have never stood a chance at the beginning of their careers if they hadn't gone by Currer, Ellis, and Acton Bell.

Interestingly enough, after Edmonds catapulted into fame and couldn't hide the fact that she was born with a vagina, she decided to publish more books under a male pseudonym: Harold Danforth. It was done secretly, but soon enough it was front-page news that the gripping new adult crime novel, *White Silver*, had not been written by a man, but in fact a woman we already knew and loved. When interviewed, Edmonds said she did it for her work. She wanted it to stand out on its own merits. She already had the power of exposure, but then it became about how closely her public perception tied into what she wrote. Her book was critically acclaimed without anyone knowing it was she who had written it, and that was all that mattered. I mean, it's not like having a colossal industry backing basically astroturfed her anonymous publication, but hey ho. Even after everyone found out, she decided that she would continue to write under the moniker, because she loved the idea of having a persona. I may have not stood a chance as Naledi Moruakgomo, even if I should have. Even if it was 2016.

In the theatre world, the latest play to win the Laurence Olivier was written by Martin McDonagh, and before that it was Mike Bartlett, and before that it was Lucy Kirkwood, a white woman, but before that it was Simon Stephens, it was John Hodge, it was Bruce Norris, but hey, before him it was Katori Hall, a black woman, but before her it was Gregory Burke, it was Simon McBurney, it was David Harrower, it was Simon Stephens, it was Alan Bennett, it was Martin McDonagh, it was Nicholas Wright, but hey, before that it was August Wilson, a black man! But before that it was Joe Penhall, it was Richard Nelson, it was Conor McPherson, it was Patrick Marber, but hey, before that it was Pam Gems, a white woman! But before that it was David Hare, it was Arthur Miller, it was Tom Stoppard, it was John Guare, it was Ariel Dorfman, it was Brian Friel, it was David Hare, but hey, before that it was Timberlake Wertenbaker, a white woman, and before that it was Caryl Churchill, a white woman! But before that it was Christopher Hampton, it was Peter Barnes, Michael

Frayn, David Mamet, Julian Mitchell, Mark Medoff, Charles Dickens and David Edgar, Harold Pinter, Brian Clark, Henry de Motherlant, Vivian Cox and Bernard Miles, it was Denis Cannan. Just like that, Naledi Moruakgomo became Edward Moore. It read like a winner's name, in more ways than one.

• • •

"D'you reckon that's going to work, like? Just changing your name like that?" my coworker Lydia asked me as we lounged on the grass in Greenwich Park. We had just finished a hectic lunchtime shift at the burger restaurant, where I'd now been working for three months. We'd been hired at the same time, and to celebrate passing our probation period, we grabbed a couple of cans of beer from a nearby Tesco Express and made our way to the patch of grass beneath the Royal Observatory, overlooking the metallic metropolis skyline that is Canary Wharf. I had formed a new friendship with Lydia, a bubbly second-year art history student at the School of Oriental and African Studies, who was originally from Liverpool. I found myself divulging my life story to her in increments, during work smoke breaks, and eventually once we began scheduling hangouts outside of our shifts. Her thick Scouse lilt and penchant for ending every other sentence with the word *like* particularly took some getting used to, but I eventually saw them as part of her charm. During our conversations, I'd tell her about Thomas Swindon, a former university classmate of mine whose play had just been picked up by a major agency, or of Christen Winn, another budding playwright who had just announced her debut at London's Regium Theatre. I'd tell her that even though we graduated from the same school with the same grades (I'm pretty sure I actually did better than them, but alas) I always had this nagging feeling there was just something everyone else had that I apparently didn't. When I told her of my plan to go under a pen name, she wasn't so convinced.

"It's worth a try. My name's a bit of a mouthful. Maybe it puts all the agents off. They're probably too afraid to misspell it, even though they could just copy and paste my email signature." I took a swig of my Red Stripe.

"I think you should stick to your *real* name. It's more authentic, you know? I don't know, if I were an agent and I saw a name like yours, it'd probably pique my interest."

"That's my point—I don't *want* my name to pique interest. I want my play to do that. So maybe it's worth muting my profile a little." I looked down the hill, observing the sprawl of people and families enjoying their day in the park. "It shouldn't even matter what my name is, but I know it does."

"Bollocks," Lydia said. "So many writers have names that are difficult to pronounce. So what? We just learn them."

"You're talking about the 0.002 percent of writers with difficult-to-pronounce names that even make it in the industry," I responded. I had plucked that statistic out of my arse, but it hadn't come from a complete vacuum. I wanted to mention how C. H. Edmonds's real name wasn't difficult to pronounce at all, but she *still* had to change it. There were too many layers to consider here. Questions surrounding writer authenticity and name phonetics were just the tip of the iceberg. Lydia seemed fairly aware of concepts like white privilege, the patriarchy, late-stage capitalism, but it was one thing to be aware of these things, and another thing to feel them weighing you down as you tried to stay afloat.

"All I'm saying is that shit takes time," Lydia said, running a hand through her dark red hair. Her cropped bangs fluttered in the subtle breeze. "I'm sure your work is great enough for you to not have to jump through hoops to get recognition." She looked at me sympathetically. *Thank you, Lydia Flagstaff,* I thought to myself. *Yours sincerely, woman with a foreign name that's constantly being misspelled in emails, even though they could have just copied and pasted my email signature.*

A couple of drinks and a shared joint later, Lydia had to make it to a cousin's engagement party in Muswell Hill. Despite knowing she'd probably be the first person to turn up already drunk, she assured me it was the only way she thought she'd be able to endure a night of saccharine revelries encompassing patriarchal ideals of romance. As we parted ways, I realised that I was tipsy enough not to call it a day, but instead make it a night. The sun started to dip below the city when

I rang up my brother Nick and asked if he was free. I'd usually text my uni friends, like Sinead, or Ellen, or Kristian, but the last thing I wanted to do was entrap myself into overlapping conversations about theatre since graduation. It had been nine months since we threw our mortarboards in the air, but I barely had anything to show for it.

My closest uni friend, Amanda, had picked up on my ever-growing distance from the uni crew about a month ago, but this was also a week before her one-way flight to the USA to take on a Broadway acting role she'd auditioned for over Skype. We'd bonded over the hardships of being a pair in the miniature handful of black female creatives in our academic field, even though we played different roles. She was a passionate stage actress with a hypnotic presence. It was no wonder she'd made her break so soon—even if it meant being cast as a seventeenth-century runaway slave for a primarily middle-class New York audience. She'd asked me why I'd become distant in recent months, and I didn't have the heart to tell her it was because, once we'd all graduated, there was that one fewer thing holding us together: the uncertainty of our futures.

We were all students doing what we could to get by, and now that we'd transitioned into just *adults* doing what we could to get by, the margins of uncertainty wavered at the same time as they shrank. I was working at a fucking burger place, for crying out loud. Neither Sinead, nor Ellen, nor Kristian needed the scoop on that. Amanda was abandoning me for her success. I spent way too much time with Blue for it to be the first port of call every time I found myself with nowhere to go on a weekday evening. There was nowhere else to turn but to my brother.

I'm saying that like he was a last resort. He wasn't. From the moment my brain could put together images and sounds and recognise faces and voices, Nick had been there. I was a toddler when he was born, but I threw myself into a maternal position from the beginning: fawning over him, performing overprotectiveness and a domineering persona to a near-concerning level. Even with my neuroticism and obsession with control, Nick never seemed to be too fazed. We're polar opposites in that way; he's cool as a cucumber growing in a nursery on the Arctic tundra, whereas the only thing about me that had ever been relaxed was my hair, courtesy of the chemical straighteners I had spent my formative years taking advantage of.

When I met Nick at the pub about an hour after waving Lydia goodbye, I was on my fourth cigarette, standing outside the Bethnal Green Tavern, feeling both skittish and lethargic at the same time. Nick approached, and I stubbed out the remainder of my butt before dodging his incoming embrace.

"So it's like that, yeah?" Nick shook his head as we made our way inside the pub.

"I stink. I'm sorry," I responded, instantly picking up on a shadow of the molasses-like slur oozing from my voice. I was already four beers and half a joint down at this point, so it made sense. The feeling that the night was still young had ended abruptly after the second cigarette, but knowing my brother was now en route, I had to see it through. It had been a while since we'd hung out anyway.

"D'you plan on quitting the cigs anytime soon?" Nick asked once we were sitting down. The dim lighting, accompanied by the moderate murmur of other patrons, the occasional clink of glasses, and the sounds of the nostalgic rock playlist permeating the air, had me holding my chin up with my hands on the table as a crutch for my dip in energy.

"I plan on quitting when I quit," I said, looking down at the drinks menu. "Do you know what you want?"

"I think I'll just get a rum and Coke," Nick said, leaning forwards to briefly scan the menu after he'd already made his declaration. Then he leaned back in his chair and tapped his fingers on the table. "Why does this feel like a date?" He chuckled.

"What the fuck, Nick? Don't be so weird," I started.

"Mate, you're gay. I just meant, like, this is so formal. Also, I think this is the first time you've ever got drinks with me."

"That's not true. The grad party, remember?"

"I mean just *you*. It's always you and Blue."

"Touché. How's life?" I said, picking my bag up from the floor to look for my purse. "Actually, hold that question while I go get our drinks. Rum and Coke, right?"

"Uhhh . . . yeah. I think I'll just have one drink tonight."

"Big fat loser," I sighed, leaving the table. Though I'd always been something of a motherly figure to my brother, there was a point where he'd matured and I must have regressed, and it was all coming to the fore. I returned with my pint of Camden Pale Ale and his poison of choice, and asked him why he wasn't down for a rager.

"Exam season, sis," he responded. "It's intense. I can't deal with a hangover until this shit is over and done with. Then I'll go fucking crazy."

"So that's your life at the moment?" I took a liberal swig of beer. "Just uni?"

"Mainly, yeah. I'm still hunting for a job placement too. It's a lot of pressure."

"You'll be fine." I shrugged. "Anything else going on?"

It was like I'd given him an opening to veer somewhere personal; a place we barely ever traversed together. Back when I first started seeing Blue, introducing her to my brother had been much less of a hassle and happened way sooner than coming out to my mother, in part due to his easygoing nature. He got on well with her and promised to keep our relationship quiet until I was ready to reveal it. He was one of the few people I could trust, and I hoped that it went both ways. Though he was well aware of my sexuality and relationship status, I wouldn't say we were on equal grounds. I always wondered what his social life was like.

"I'm dating someone," he said. "Still early days, though."

"Go on. Tell me more. *Divulge*."

"Man, I don't want to jinx anything."

"I don't think you're putting a hex on your relationship by telling me her name, at the least."

He paused. "She's called Deborah. Debs for short. We're on the same course."

"Wow. That's lovely. What is she?"

"What do you mean?" Nick narrowed his eyes.

"You know what I mean. *Lekgoa*? Not *lekgoa*?"

"She's French, actually. Her dad's Algerian. Mum's from Bordeaux."

"Your summers are gonna be lovely." I sighed. "Wine and charcuterie boards galore."

"Let's not get too hopeful. How's your play stuff going? You getting somewhere?" Nick asked, sucking me back into the reality of my situation.

"Let's not get too hopeful," I said with a grimace, parroting him. "I'm still doing the rounds."

Nick looked at me soberly. "It's tough out there, isn't it?"

"Dog eat dog." I took another swig. "But let's not talk about it. Let's cheers to your new girlfriend, Debs. Maybe we can go on a double date one of these days! After your exams, of course."

"Stop dashing the topic."

"Ugh. I don't want to disappoint Mum," I finally lamented. "I can't let her know I'm struggling. *You* can't tell her I am."

"You know I won't," Nick replied, sounding slightly stung, as if I wouldn't put it past him. "There's obviously no point in telling her anything that isn't a success story. I know that just as much as you do."

"I know. I know. I can just *feel* the tension sometimes. I come back from work and she'll ask me how it was, and then she'll ask me if I'm looking for other jobs, and I'll respond with 'work was fine' and 'yes, I am,' and the cycle continues. I know she thinks I'm a huge disappointment."

"Far from the truth, Naledi," Nick responded. To this day, he's one of the few people who has never called me by anything other than my real name. Every time he does, it's like an existential anchor that drops me into a small crevice outside the multitudes of my identity. "You're not a disappointment. Maybe to your own expectations, but nobody else's."

"Shut up. You're nineteen. Stop being a wise man," I responded, with the sudden urge to cry. Instead, I finished my drink.

"It's true, though. I went to your final year showcase. It was sick, man. Something I ain't ever seen before. It's not a surprise you left with the highest grade."

I wanted to say something cynical about how your final uni grades didn't matter once you graduated, but then I remembered I was talking to a uni student. "I'm a theatre kid at the end of the day," I said instead. "I'm not a Canary Wharf briefcase wanker. I'm not a hashtag-girlboss-building-my-empire. Just a theatre grad."

"Negative Naledi." Nick shook his head. "You've got something special. Everybody knows it. No matter what it takes, you're gonna make it."

He was right. Emphasis on the "no matter what it takes." If anyone knows exactly what it took, it's you, Hugo.

• • •

Come June, two responses peeked out of the small mound of rejections, which meant I had piqued some interest. However, after the first round of requests to send in the entire play, I was told by both agencies that my work was not *quite* what they were looking for.

I remember where I was when I got the second rejection email, taking a smoke break at work, heart sinking. My thumbs moved autonomously straight to Facebook so I could distract myself by doomscrolling through the endless cycle of Brexit news articles as the referendum crawled closer. I remember being stopped in my tracks, my jaw hanging open, at a headline I couldn't believe was real: in broad daylight, Jo Cox, a Labour MP, had been shot with a modified hunting rifle, then stabbed to death, in West Yorkshire. Two days later, the terrorist told Westminster Magistrates' Court, "My name is death to traitors, freedom for Britain." He was declared sane by a psychiatrist after his arrest.

I was at Blue's house on the morning of the referendum. The margin between the opposing sides was so slim, it felt even more hopeless than if it had been a landslide victory. It was essentially fifty-fifty, but the Leave's fifty was bigger. Democracy is supposed to be this precious thing, a hallmark of a thriving, functioning society, but what happens when the proletariat's choices are funnelled through the ideals of the ivory tower elite? What happens when the prime minister has too much faith in a world from which he is so far removed?

I couldn't help but sink into my seat, as my heart sank into my stomach, Blue utilising every swear word under the sun next to me, when I realised we were severing ourselves from the union we had built as a pact to stick together after the Second World War. I thought back to a conversation I had had with Sam, a coworker I despised with a passion, a few weeks earlier. He told me he had voted Leave, in his unmistakable Essex drawl, and when I asked him why, he told me it was because he didn't want any more Arabs coming into the country. Instead of telling him that the last time I heard, Arabs weren't from Europe, I told him that Molly, the effervescent blonde who only did weekend shifts, the same girl whose DMs he'd slid into on multiple occasions, was Syrian. All he could do was shrug. Now I sat staring dumbfounded and bitter at the television, and all I could see was Sam's idiotic face, his fist probably in the air as he yelled, "Come on then!" like he was watching the football.

The pound plummeted that day. I remember people saying it was just the initial stock market reaction to the results, but I just thought to myself how amazing it was that we functioned under an economy tenuous enough to collapse because hundreds of thousands of Sams had ticked a box on a piece of paper.

• • •

I was still holding close to my chest my mini social experiment regarding my playwright moniker in July. I'm not sure if it was a coincidence, but a couple of weeks after the referendum, I received a response from the Wentworth Agency, which I'd submitted to under Edward Moore. They said they were very interested in the subject matter of the play and would love to read the rest, so I immediately sent it to them. I was at Blue's house when I'd got the email, and she poured us glasses of red wine to celebrate the little beam of progress, of hope, in my creative journey. I'd been telling her about each enquiry rejection and acceptance—she'd been there with me every step of the way. The one thing I didn't mention to her was the name change, as I was sure I'd get the same kind of response from her that I'd got from Lydia or Nick, but even more impassioned, even more demanding. She always had too much faith in me, Hugo. Too much faith to let me give my play away to an Edward Moore, a nonexistent abstraction, a reflection instead of a transgression of the world we lived in. If she knew what I'd done, she'd be so disappointed in me.

Seven days after I'd sent the entirety of *The Worthy* off to the Wentworth Agency, I received an email to arrange a meeting for the coming week. I'd been leaning on my bedroom windowsill with my head poking awkwardly out of my open window as I blew a puff of smoke as far out into the ether as I could muster. My mother was somewhere earning extra cash doing braids for a regular in Plumstead, and I took advantage of the empty house and my ever-increasing adolescent bravery to risk the smell of cigarette smoke permeating the flat. It was around five in the afternoon when I got the invitation, and I froze with elation. *It's really happening,* I thought to myself. *An agency wants to take on my work. Six gruelling months later, my dreams are coming true!*

• • •

I thought long and hard about what to wear on the day of the meeting. Did it matter if I looked as presentable as possible, dress suit and heels, red lips, heat-combed hair? Did it matter if I came as my usual self, standing in aged trainers and thrifted attire, zany jewellery from Brixton market, waist-length box braids bundled into a misshapen top bun, no makeup, septum piercing on show? I knew it didn't make a damn difference what I wore. As far as they were concerned, they were negotiating a potential production deal with a man. After calling in sick to Byron Burgers, I hopped onto public transport and headed to the agency's offices in Bloomsbury. As soon as I entered the building, my adrenaline started to kick in. I was all too aware of my brown skin, of my feminine form, of how I didn't look like an Edward Moore at all. It wasn't exactly a foolproof plan. Maybe in an alternate universe, in which I lived in a visually impaired society, I'd get away with it. But I guess if I wanted to get canonical with that line of thought, even in a blind world there'd be a way to separate the Naledis from the Edwards.

"It's a pseudonym," I told the puzzled receptionist, whose eyes were flitting back and forth between my face and the name on the sign-in sheet. "My playwright name."

"I'm afraid I'd need some form of identification to verify that this is you, madam," the woman responded pitifully.

"My name's Eddie. Well, it's Naledi. I can show you my license. I shortened it to Eddie, and that's how I came up with Edward. It's a bit of a stretch, I know. But it's the truth." I pulled out my ID in the hopes that it'd work, my heart stammering in my chest. Though I presented myself with a sturdy impatience, I was shitting a house of bricks.

The receptionist stared at it for a while, as if she was trying to put the pieces together. Then she frowned and looked up at me. "You're here to see Helen Hunter, right?"

"Yes, and I'm going to be late to the meeting. Please, just let me in."

"Let me just call up to her office. If she can verify your real name, then I can let you in."

"Fuck," I hissed quietly, but loud enough for her to hear. "Hold on. Don't tell her my name. Tell her I'm here for *The Worthy*. That's the name of my script."

I could see the cogs whirring in the receptionist's brain as she tried to figure out if Helen even knew my real identity, if it was worth enquiring any further. She picked up the phone on her desk and tentatively dialled the agent's office. "Hi, sorry to bother you—you have a meeting with Edward Moore at half past one? There's a woman in the lobby here. I'm not sure, but she's claiming—yes, a woman. She's claiming to be Edward. She said it's a pseudonym. Hold on—" She moved the phone away briefly, covering the microphone with her hand. "What's your play's name again? Sorry."

"*The Worthy*. That's what I told you to say."

"*The . . . Worthy*?" she repeated back into the phone. "Yes. Right. Okay, will do. Thanks, bye." She hung the phone up in a quick clunk before straightening herself out. Handing me the sign-in sheet on a clipboard, she told me to write my name and the time I entered, then she handed me a guest lanyard to get through the turnstiles. I thanked her, hiding my exasperation and making my way to the elevators, to the tenth floor of the building that overlooked the city. I could probably swim in the sweat that had accumulated between my armpits. Once I found the door to Helen's office, I took a deep breath, then knocked lightly. I heard her voice on the other side, beckoning me in with an authoritative pull.

• • •

The Wentworth Agency had been founded in the early nineties by Richard Wentworth, an esteemed playwright from Bristol who had struck gold in the West End a decade earlier. He wanted to curate a house of like-minded writers and artists, and boy did he do just that. By the time I put in my submission, it was one of the most fruitful agencies on the market, home to dozens of award-winning and award-nominated plays. For the last three years in a row, the winners of the Marston B. Greaves Awards for Theatre (the MBG Awards for short), the most prestigious competition for emerging theatre hopefuls, had been swept into contracts at Wentworth. Richard had died suddenly of a heart attack in 2000, and in his honour, his agency was renamed after him (it had originally been called the Blue Swan Agency, an ode to one of his most successful plays, and in my opinion, a much more creative name). Helen Hunter was an assistant agent working there at the time of his death, and over time had climbed the rungs to become the most intimidatingly revered agent in Wentworth's roster. She was known to be a no-nonsense curator of talent, and I wasn't ready to fumble my chances with her.

I sensed the bemusement in the air the second I walked in. There sat Helen at her wide glass desk, and next to her was a man I didn't recognise. The office was spectacularly modern and minimalist, brightly illuminated by daylight that poured through the floor-to-ceiling window ahead. There was so much glass everywhere. The transparency of the room made me feel like a prisoner in a literary panopticon.

"Hello. Edward?" Helen greeted me with caution, one eyebrow slightly raised. "Or did we get the timings mixed up?" She was leaning forwards over the desk, twiddling a pen between her thumb and forefinger. I looked down and saw what looked like the script for my play, a pile of paper. In between the pages was a rainbow of small sticky tabs. It dawned on me that I had made it in, my work was worth considering, all the way down to a detailed annotation. But judging from the body language of the agents, the gut feeling that I had maybe messed up was already forming, bubbling up inside of me.

"Edward's my playwright name. Stage name, if you will." I chuckled, ambling towards Helen as I held out my hand. She looked at it before pulling her own hand out and giving mine a firm shake. She never moved from her seat—I almost had to bend right over the table to reach her. "Lovely to meet you! This is so exciting."

"The feeling's mutual," she said. "This is my assistant agent, Tony. He helps me sieve through submissions."

"Nice to meet you, Tony," I said, beaming, and the young man sprang from his seat to shake my hand.

"Pleasure's all mine," he replied, nodding with a pursed smile. You know, the classic white-people smile. I sat down in front of the pair, observing the grey sky behind them.

"This script . . . it's wonderful, it really is. Hits the nail on the head, I think. Especially with what's happening in our political climate at the moment," Helen said, picking up the annotated script and straightening it out. I thought it was an odd thing to do, as the papers were already aligned. She put them back down and leaned back in her chair, crossing her arms. "Where did the inspiration for this come from? This idea of a cutthroat dystopia, indiscriminate in some ways, discriminate in others?"

"Well . . . it's largely influenced by my own upbringing, actually. I'm a first-generation immigrant, and my parents divorced when I was young. My dad struggled to find work here, so he moved back. My mother chose to stay, so me and my brother could have access to better opportunities. But better opportunities, to me, is having a respectable career," I said, noting their incessant subtle nods. "But what kind of career is deemed respectable? Usually something corporate, something white-collar. Where would an artist fit in a world like that? You know, I just had all these questions floating around in my head, so I found a way to conceptualise them."

"Wow. Fascinating." Helen nodded. "Where did you study again?"

"Kingston. Drama and creative writing. I graduated at the top of the class, by the way." I chuckled. I realised that I was still sweating, probably more than I had been before. I didn't get a breather between the stressful reception encounter and pitching myself to one of the most established agents in the country. I'd never wished for air-conditioning more than I did in that moment. "I have my playwriting CV in my bag, if you want to see more?"

"Hold that thought." Helen shook her head. "This play sounds promising. I'm very interested in it. We'll need to start looking into budgets, directors, producers, that sort of thing, but we can go into more detail at a later date. I tell you what, we'll set up another meeting sometime this month, to iron everything out. I'm actually running late for something, so I can't be too long today."

"Oh, okay." I nodded. "So is this just more of a preliminary meeting?"

"Something of the sort, yes. Just to get a clearer picture, and to put a face to the name." Both Helen and Tony looked at each other, then at me. "Which reminds me, why the pen name? You don't look like an Edward Moore to me."

"I suppose that's the point of pen names, no?"

"What's your actual name?"

I paused, shifting in my seat. "Naledi. Naledi Moruakgomo. Bit of a mouthful, isn't it?" I let out an awful nervous wheeze laugh, and the feeling hit me like a ton of bricks, that embarrassment. I couldn't tell if I was embarrassed about my name, or the fact that I'd omitted it, or both.

"It would have been lovely to know your real name during our correspondence, Naledi. You know—to get a real sense of where you're coming from. I mean with the play, of course."

"Is it that important?" I found myself saying. There was a defensive lilt to my tone I immediately regretted. I didn't want to tell her that the furthest I'd got in my creative endeavours had been when I lied about myself.

"For the purpose of representation, it's always important." She smiled at me pityingly, as if she knew more about representation than I ever could. Smarmy bitch.

◆ ◆ ◆

I left that meeting feeling out of place, as uncomfortable as putting on twisted tights. There was something about the way Helen and Tony had looked at me when I entered the room, like they had been *Punk'd*. There was something so condescending about Helen's demeanour, though I did feel like she liked the play. I wouldn't have got as far as I did if she didn't. But the week following the meeting was the longest week of my life, and Blue had to practically pry the millionth cigarette out of my mouth. She didn't understand that my fingers were either going to check my emails or grip onto Rizla tobacco tubes, and nothing in between. I was even a buzzkill in bed, losing my mojo every time Smarmy Helen's face popped into my head as Blue and I tussled under the sheets. No matter how much Blue tried to reassure me that

I was just looking at things negatively to protect myself, it would never suffice. She didn't know the half of it.

Twelve days later, the Wentworth Agency contacted me. The email was short and sweet. They said that due to extenuating circumstances, they'd had to cut their production budget and sign on fewer playwrights than they had initially wished. They said *The Worthy* had promise, but might be too politically sensitive. I sat on my bed, sighing, closing my laptop. I was floating somewhere, in a space between the beginning and the end. It was all over for me; it had only just begun.

Baby Blue

August 2016

Tanya Victoria Phan was born in St. Thomas's Hospital on a bitter February morning in 1995. She was in distress during the first few days of her life; she was difficult to feed, her pulse was weak, and she spent most of her time sleeping. Her tiny heart would pound intensely, and her skin had a pallid blue hue to it. It was soon discovered that she had a congenital defect, truncus arteriosus, in which the heart was formed with only one valve instead of two. It meant that her lungs were being fed too much blood, and her body not enough, causing her heart to overcompensate. Her condition was monitored and regulated for a few months, and once it was deemed safe enough, she underwent corrective heart surgery, which was successful. In no time, there was rosiness in her cheeks, a light in her eyes, her appetite in full swing, and she was as vivacious as ever. From the moment she was born, her parents never called her Tanya. She was Baby Blue, the colour of her deoxygenated skin and lips. Once she recovered, the name stuck. Even at school, since reception, she made sure that was how she was addressed. If anyone was to call her Tanya, I don't think she'd even turn her head.

In a lot of ways, the colour blue suits her perfectly. I couldn't imagine associating her with green, or pink, or any shade outside of cerulean, turquoise, azure, cobalt, sapphire, baby. She leaned into that persona a lot, getting blue highlights as soon as her mother let her dye her hair as a teenager; making sure that at any given time, at least one item of clothing she wore was blue. You'd *never* guess it, but her favourite children's show growing up was *Blue's Clues*. I know that blue can have negative connotations—despair, sadness—but when I saw my girlfriend, I just saw a fresh breeze. I saw the Caribbean Sea. Water flowing freely and fluidly, like time. The past, present, and future.

◆ ◆ ◆

I melted into a creeping depression after the disastrous meeting with Smarmy Helen at the Shitworth Agency. I felt the energy seep out of my bones. My vision dimmed, and I could only think about the future as far as my arm could stretch out in front of me. The fights with my mother at home were getting worse, too. With each passing day that I appeared to have nothing substantial to show for myself, I was more irritable, she was more irritable, and we just couldn't connect. After nights of slamming the flat door and fleeing to Blue's house in a huff came the alluring invitation of a temporary change in my living situation. It was the nth argument with my mother when Blue suggested I just move in with her and her parents while I got myself together. She could see me struggling, and how I sought a reprieve from my inner turmoil. She always knew my family had never been the most supportive towards my artistic exploits, and unlike mine, her parents encouraged creativity. All I knew was that I was fighting myself to get out of bed in the mornings, to make it to work, to even attempt writing any new plays. I was falling into a limbo, and I needed something to change in my life.

With both desperation and reluctance, I told my mother I was moving out for a while. When she asked me for how long, I couldn't give her a definitive answer. She didn't have much to say in return, though it's safe to presume there was an element of pride in that. She wasn't going to beg for me to stay, of course not. I wouldn't have wanted her to. Still, her acceptance of my absence only served to stick the knife in deeper. Maybe I was right to leave.

It was Blue's parents, Ritchie and Mai, who helped me move my things out one weekend in mid-August. I think they could sympathise with my situation, being familiar with the need to leave home. Blue's mother was the daughter of Vietnamese refugees who had fled to the UK after the end of the war in 1975, and her father was a second-generation Windrush immigrant whose parents had moved to London from Jamaica in the early fifties. (It's funny how you can apparently inherit immigration; my feelings against this sentiment grew stronger as time went on, as Brexit campaigns were starting to take flight. The idea that you could be considered an immigrant purely based on where your mum's mum had had your mum had always got on my tits. If we're going on the basis that a woman is born with every egg she'll ever have, and somehow those eggs have not only a presumptive claim to life but land, then . . . sure. Otherwise, generational immigration is just a way to draw a line between legitimate and illegitimate, authentic and inauthentic. Where my grandmother or great-grandmother got pregnant had nothing to do with me, at the end of the day. I had no say in it. I attempted to throw this concept out the window in *The Worthy*, because migration was fair game in my reimagined Britain. But nothing really is fair game. There'll always be a different reason to draw a line, be it through capitalism or diplomacy, or whatever else. So if immigration was fair game, would it really be? Who knows? But I digress.) Mai and Ritchie met as teens in Lewisham, and it wasn't long before Mai's parents had shown disapproval towards her relationship with a black man. Aged nineteen, Mai packed her things up and moved to Brixton, where she had lived ever since. A year later, Blue was born.

The morning I moved out, my mother was on call at work, and there was a terrible silence in the flat. Though she knew I was leaving, a part of me was preemptively broken inside with the knowledge that by the time she came back from work, she'd be alone. I just knew that it was the best thing for both of us at the time.

Blue and her parents cooked up a welcome meal for me upon my arrival: pho and spring rolls. I'd had it plenty of times before at their house, but every time felt like the first. It was funny seeing how many experimental new Vietnamese restaurants were popping up like whack-a-moles in pockets of Brixton, most likely owned by affluent gap-year students who had once had a moment of enlightenment in

Hanoi. The latest one was called Pho Real, and Blue and I couldn't help but scowl at the building every time we walked past it. Most of the workers were of Asian descent, but with a little digging, we found out the owner definitely wasn't. Typical.

• • •

Blue's graduation was five days after I moved in. She'd managed solid results in her final grade and had bagged a job in marketing for a record label based in Shoreditch. On her big day, she shone in a deep red sheer chiffon dress, embroidered with pink and blue flowers. Her hair was sleek and straight, a rare occurrence. Most of her paternal family attended, including an array of the black and biracial cousins she had grown up with. All her bandmates were there, and they promised that as soon as the formal festivities were over, we were getting fucked up.

Filly, the bass player, held an intimate gathering in Camberwell that evening, abundant in the supply of alcohol. Mary Jane, Mandy, and Charlie were also in attendance, if you know what I mean. At around eleven in the evening, a group of us were sitting in Filly's living room at varying levels of inebriation. Blue was on the higher end, coupled with the fact that she'd taken trips to the bathroom with her set of keys every half an hour since she'd arrived at the party.

"Daffodils" by Mark Ronson was playing in the background as Filly and Quentin, the drummer, got into a heated debate near the kitchen door about which of Miles Davis's albums was his magnum opus. On one of the sofas, I was making small talk with Arianna, the saxophonist, who I'd always had a hard time connecting with. I found her slightly pretentious, but I had a feeling that it was mutual. Malcolm, the lead vocalist and the guitarist of the band, was sitting opposite Arianna and me on the sofa, whispering something into Blue's ear as he balanced a drink on his knee. I saw Blue break into a big grin before saying something back to him. Then Malcolm turned the music down, grabbing everyone's attention. All the other partygoers, people I barely knew as they were part of Blue's music scene, turned their heads to the centre of the room.

"Hello, everyone. Thank you all so much for being here to celebrate Bluey's grad day. I know Filly's yard isn't the biggest, so I hope it ain't too cramped for your liking."

"Go on, show us your mansion then," Filly retorted jokingly, pulling a laugh out of half the crowd.

Malcolm grinned before continuing. "All right, all right. Anyway, I just wanted to congratulate this girl on everything she's doing at the moment, as I feel we sometimes just go through life letting things happen and not appreciating them, you know?" I could detect a faint slur in his voice, and I was worried his toast might turn into a digressive speech too long to bear. "But I also wanted to make a lovely announcement: Ego Birth is supporting our *first* big act on tour this autumn." The room erupted into whoops and hollers before he could even finish his sentence, and Blue jumped from the sofa, clapping profusely before embracing Malcolm. "All right, all right, settle down," he continued over the fading noise. "We have Blue to thank for this—if she didn't campaign for us at Brava Records, I don't know how soon something like this would've happened. She's an amazing cheerleader. No wonder you're working in marketing." He laughed, and Blue laughed along with him.

"Are you gonna tell us who you're supporting, then?" a voice piped up.

"We're keeping it quiet until it's public. You know, until it's official and the act shares it everywhere. We don't need the evil eye."

"We're halfway there, I suppose," Quentin said.

"Shush, Q. Bluey, got any words?" Malcolm turned to her.

"I'm so speechless, you guys. Thanks so much for being here. It's blessings on blessings on blessings, man!" Blue hollered, holding her drink in the air, and everyone let out another small whoop. "Ain't got much to say besides the cheesy shit. I'm grateful for everything. Just twenty-one, and all my dreams are coming true. It's madness. Mal, Q, Filly, Ari . . . I couldn't appreciate you lot any more than I already do. And I have to shout out my beautiful, talented, supportive girlfriend, Eddie," she said, looking right at me. I could feel my heart swell in that moment. "She's been my rock since day dot. I love you lots." She blew me a kiss from across the room, and a wave of warmth rushed over me. "Oh, by the way, guys—Eddie's a *wonderful* writer. Writes sick plays like she's writing a shopping list, it's just that easy."

"So much talent in this room," Arianna said, smiling. "You should invite us to one of your plays." She turned to me.

"Thank you, Blue. I love you too," I said quietly, before looking down at the floor, suddenly aware of all the eyes on me. "Plays aren't that easy to make. It might take a while, but when I get there, I'll let you know. But honestly, Blue. Congratulations. You're amazing. Can someone turn the music back on?" I picked up the glass of red wine next to me and swallowed it all in three gulps.

Though everyone went back to their little circles of conversation, I could sense a shift in Blue's energy. This was more evident around twenty minutes later, when she essentially ambushed me on my way out of the bathroom. I flounced down the stairs back into the busy lounge and she followed behind me, holding on to my elbow. I hated it when she got lost-puppy drunk sometimes, but it was usually a sign that we'd be calling it a night soon. She plopped beside me on the sofa in the corner of the room and leaned her head on my shoulder. "Why are you so shy?" she asked me. "You've written this project, and you won't show me any of it. It's kind of annoying, if I'm honest. I want to read it! I've read all your others. I want to be there for you. I want to help you in any way I can."

"I'm just working behind the scenes, that's all. It's a very private process for me," I responded. I wished she would just melt back into the party. But I could see it in her eyes, slightly glazed, her need to campaign. Her inherent talent for it.

"It's all right to ask for a second opinion, you know. I always run Ego Birth's demos by you." She straightened herself up to look at me.

"I know you do, and I'm grateful that you value my opinion. I'm just working a little differently with this project." I couldn't tell her that my desperate hope for success was the same thing in my way. I couldn't let anyone see what I had to offer until it was already the world's. And if I'm honest, I was still embarrassed about the whole Edward Moore thing, though she didn't know about it. It was clear to me now that she was feeling shut out. She wanted access to every single part of me, and

I guess that was only fair. Especially considering she'd given me food and shelter. I often think back to the way she looked at me when she swiftly stood up to leave the room, and I think that's when I often ask myself why I didn't just let her in. Why I let *you* in first.

• • •

August turned to September turned to October, and before I knew it, the leaves were a burnt orange, spread across the concrete walkways. The air was yet to hold a crispness to it, but the autumn breeze blew, and the rain would come and go. Two months into living with Blue, I was still working at Byron, and I'd picked up a freelance copyediting and proofreading job from a woman who'd approached me on LinkedIn. Ego Birth were about to kick-start their UK tour supporting Renée Sinclair, the current breakout star in R&B. Her debut album scooped up a bunch of awards that year, and her first-ever UK tour was sold out in most cities. Their first date was up in Manchester, and they were going to be on the road for six weeks, touching back down in London on their last leg. I'd already been seeing less and less of Blue post-graduation as the band locked themselves away for rehearsals. I felt her gaping absence grow bigger. Ritchie and Mai were lovely to live with, treating me like a stand-in daughter and occasionally rotating a spliff with me on a quiet evening. Sometimes I'd go and visit my mother somewhere for lunch, but it felt silly every time, like we were on visitation or something. Ultimately, life became a new slog, a new rinse-and-repeat. It just felt embarrassing to be alive.

On Blue's last evening before her departure, I cried after sex. I didn't know where it came from, but it was like there was a broken tap in my head, in my throat, and I was spluttering and blubbering like a little child. Blue didn't say anything and instead just held me. The last thing I wanted to do was rain on her parade. I wanted to be her proud partner, wishing her well on her amazing new journey, but the excitement was buried under gallons of sadness. I didn't want her to think it was jealousy or resentfulness, because *I* didn't want to think it was. I was just . . . going through it. Sometimes when you're going through it, all you can do is cry. If she understood anything, she understood that.

I felt so boxed in, Hugo. Even though I'd stopped trying, I felt like

I was *being* stopped. It's hard to explain. I didn't *want* to explain it to anyone. I felt like my time was up, and I was a nobody, and I'd remain a nobody for years to come. And my girlfriend was going to be a star while I continued to sit on the sidelines and praise her, and all the other people in my life were doing better than me. Failure is a funny feeling, because it doesn't have to be real; you give yourself an expiration date, and you find yourself there, thinking you've missed your chance. The irony in naming my play *The Worthy*, when that was the last thing I felt.

I couldn't sleep at all that night, so I wasted time on my phone instead, the bright light beaming on my face in the darkness of the room. Blue was out cold, and I was scrolling through sensationalist BBC news article headlines and posts on obscure private groups I had joined on Facebook. It was around midnight when I got a notification. It was one of those friendship anniversary reminders. It had been exactly one year since I met you at that café in Holborn. Curiously, I stalked your profile to see what else you had been up to. By the looks of it, you were on some gap-year shit: adventuring in South America as recently as a few weeks before. I saw that the same skinny blonde girl had joined you, and I clicked on her name, tagged in photos. Annabelle Griffiths. In her profile bio, she had plugged her Instagram account, which I decided to take a scroll through. She had tens of thousands of followers, and picturesque influencer-like shots of your vacations took up a hefty portion of her feed. You were in every other photo; the two of you, this happy, pretty, rich white couple, beaming down at everyone. I'd be lying if I said I wasn't jealous, because your life looked so fucking easy, man.

A few posts down, there was a picture of you and your girlfriend posing with a woman I recognised instantly. It was what looked like a premiere of *Billy Andromeda*'s West End feature, and the woman was none other than C. H. Edmonds, the richest female author in the Western Hemisphere. I furrowed my brows as I read the caption: *my fella's cousin's cooler than yours!!!*

Ahhh, I thought. *Right.*

Charlotte Edmonton-Smith.

Hugo Lawrence Smith.

Smith.

The most unassuming, run-of-the-mill name you could ever imagine, that *you* had, turned out to be from the same lineage as a billionaire author.

Typical, I thought to myself before sighing and resuming my doomscrolling. Fires had been set at the Calais Jungle refugee camp, just as the French authorities were planning to demolish it and relocate its inhabitants; Donald Trump's star on the Hollywood Walk of Fame was smashed with a hammer; ISIL had executed nearly three hundred people in Iraq. These news articles were sandwiched in between posts from groups like *Previously Unseen Images in Human History*, *A Group Where We Speak Gibberish and Pretend to Understand Each Other*, and my personal favourite, *Depression Meals: Gone Wild*. Before I knew it, I had fallen asleep, phone still in hand, mouth probably agape, at three in the morning. When daylight came around, the sound of Blue's electric toothbrush roused me from unconsciousness, and I sat up, stretching my limbs. Instinctively checking my phone, I saw I had a message:

> [08:47] **Hugo Lawrence Smith:** Hi, Eddie! Apologies if you don't remember me, but I met you a year ago—got a nice reminder from FB. It's our friendiversary haha! Just curious, how's everything going? Will I see your name in flashing lights anytime soon? Would love to meet over coffee again and have a catch-up if you're feeling social. :)

I'd call it romantic, if this was a true romance. I remember letting out a laugh from somewhere within me, a place I couldn't source. It was like the universe was amused, long before I knew what it was doing to me.

The Party

"This is gonna be so bants." Lydia giggled as we sat in Blue's bedroom on Halloween night. "So much free booze, I reckon. We're gonna get sloshed."

"I don't want to embarrass myself in front of a bunch of posh twats, so I hope that doesn't happen, actually," I responded, sitting in front of the mirror as I applied my makeup. There was a joint leaning out of a clay ramekin on my left. Lydia picked it up after shimmying into the angel costume she'd ordered off Amazon Prime a few days earlier and took a long toke.

"I couldn't give a toss about embarrassing myself around a bunch of Tories, like," she said between inhales. "I'm there for the food and the booze, and quite frankly, to take photos of me having fun that'll make Declan jealous as fuck." She laughed, and I laughed with her.

"Exes care a lot less than you think they do. God, where *is* your integrity, Lydia Flagstaff?" I trilled with a comically dramatic tone.

"Integrity? I'm not the one going for walks in the park with the likes of *them*," she responded.

"Oh, don't try and make me look bad, it doesn't mean that I was going to take him up on the invite to the party! It was *your* idea to go." I stopped and turned to face her, holding in another laugh.

"Why did you even meet the lad in the first place? I thought you were a steaming lesbo."

I shrugged. "Bored." At least that was an honest answer. Since Blue's departure, I was more willing to do things I wouldn't normally do. It was either that or wallow in my self-pitying melancholy. When I'd decided to respond to your Facebook message a few weeks earlier, I thought, *Fuck it*. There's no harm in making a new friend.

• • •

We met on a strangely warm late morning at the foot of Primrose Hill a week after our message exchange. There was a small church across the street, and within its garden perimeters was a van selling coffee and pastries. The brown and orange leaves were unavoidable, littering the cobblestones. You offered to pay for both our coffees—my mocha, your espresso—and you picked up two almond croissants. I said you didn't have to, and you shook your head and swatted your hand like I'd offered to give you a penny in change.

I could admit that you were good-looking. Your hair had grown since I first saw you; it was a caramel mop that ended just below the ear, with a centre-parting that kept the curled forelocks out of your eyes. Your skin had a bronze-pink hue that I gathered was a tan from months in the South American sun. You were well-dressed, wearing a black Saint Laurent half-zip fleece sweatshirt, dark blue jeans, and brown leather boots. But God, that smile. That glorious smile. It took the cake.

We started off with small talk. You know, how our respective days were going, how the weather was, that kind of mind-numbing back-and-forth that you have with strangers. Once we'd set off up the hill, you fell into more detail. You'd just completed your master's degree with top marks, and you had a legal practice course set for the following autumn, giving you a year to do whatever you wanted before entering into the corporate world. You told me how shortly after your final exam, you got on a plane to Brazil with your girlfriend, then made your way through to Venezuela, Colombia, and Chile with just a backpack, a wallet, a camera, and your passport. Your return to London was more of an intermission before heading out to Southeast Asia the next spring. I listened with intent, trying my best to cloak my awe at how you said everything with such ease. There were times when I'd be jolted with a feeling of inadequacy, staring down at my worn-out New Balances, trudging up the earthy terrain as the cityscape slowly came into view.

You told me you were a middle child: you had a brother nearly twenty years older than you, settling into middle age while you were a few years shy of quarter life. He was a successful international arbitration lawyer at White & Case. You also had a half sister six years your junior, born to a Hong Kongese businesswoman who your father married after his divorce from your mother when you were five. He was now retired, living in the Surrey countryside and renting out his London properties. You had the keys to his Hammersmith abode in between your travels. I wanted so badly to bring C. H. Edmonds into the conversation, just to hear you say, *I know her, she's my cousin!* But I couldn't yet gauge whether that was information you were happy to divulge, and in all honesty, it wasn't necessary. I think it was halfway through our walk, once the coffees had cooled and the croissants were long consumed, when I began to wonder to myself what I was doing here.

We soon sat down on a bench, where our conversation continued. You asked me whereabouts I was based.

"Why does this feel like a date?" I chuckled. I saw your face briefly contort, trying to figure out if I was flirting or joking.

"Don't say that. My girlfriend will probably hear you." You shook your head, grinning.

"Yeah. I don't think mine would be too happy either." I could see you freeze from the corner of my eye, mouth half-open like you were about to say something. Then you relaxed, nodding slowly.

"So you're . . . not of the heterosexual persuasion, then?" you asked, finishing the last dregs in your coffee cup.

"Nope. So your girlfriend needn't worry about anything." I turned to you, smiling in amusement. Then I reached into my jacket pocket and got out my tobacco, a filter, and some Rizla. As I rolled, I gave a brief summary of my life: I was a native of Woolwich, but I was currently living in Brixton, working as a freelance editor. I omitted the whole burger-restaurant-waitress thing, as well as the fact that I was lodging in my girlfriend's house while she toured the country playing live gigs. I would have omitted the play, but I knew you were bound to bring it up again. And when you did ask me how it was going, I winced internally. But I guess there was a reason we were sitting next to each other, right there, right then, breathing in the early noon warmth as we watched the world go on around us. It was like the gods could sense my unease, my pregnant pause at your loaded question, because your phone began to ring. You took it out, and I saw your face deflate a little bit.

"Speak of the devil," you said. "One second. Hey, babe. What's up? I'm in Camden. No, I'm just getting some fresh air. No, no. Of course. Sure. What time? Yeah, no. Just tell me where. All right, babe. See you in a bit. Love you too."

The duration of the call was probably less than a minute, and I stared out at the clear sky as I eavesdropped, inhaling the last of my roll-up. I sensed your change in demeanour; it was like you were a soldier who had been called to action. You turned to me, telling me that your girlfriend wanted to meet for lunch in Maida Vale, so it'd probably be best to cut our hangout prematurely short. Little did you know, it was perfect timing; my social battery was running low.

"We can always rearrange," I said as we both rose from the bench. Did I mean that, or was I being polite?

"No, we should. And I think we ought to have a good sit-down and talk theatre at some point. What d'you think?"

"I mean, I guess it's the only reason we know each other." I shrugged.

"True. We'll meet again, Eddie."

"We will." I nodded.

Before you walked away, you hesitated. "Actually, are you free on Halloween? I'm throwing a party, and you're more than welcome to come."

"Are you sure? Won't I be, like, some random?" *Some random black girl*, I wanted to specify.

"Trust me, there'll be a lot of randoms there. Half the guest list is full of plus-ones. You can bring one too, if you like." You put your hands in your jean pockets, looking at me.

"I'll let you know. See you later."

I had no intention of letting you know. But when I told Lydia in passing at one of our shared work shifts, her eyes lit up. She saw it as a golden opportunity to see how the other side lived. I'd given her a synopsis of how I'd met you and what I already knew, and she was probably even more fascinated than I was at the thought of infiltrating your lifestyle, even if just for one night. So that's how we ended up pre-drinking and beating our faces as we got into our costumes, blasting "Beam Me Up" by Midnight Magic on the speaker. Lydia was dressed as an angel, and I was the devil, donning a red jumpsuit and a devil horn headband. I could feel myself loosening up, hyping myself for an evening of extravagance.

I got Lydia to check your girlfriend's Instagram story instead of me, as if that would somehow absolve me of being the stalker. The party was supposed to have started at around eight, and it was half past nine. Judging from the videos Annabelle posted, things were already in full swing. She was dressed up as Marilyn Monroe, the ultimate Hollywood bimbo, and I must admit, she looked pretty damn good. Lydia and I finished our joint and we downed the Absolut and lemonade pitcher we were glugging between a card game of higher/lower. Soon we were trotting down the road to Brixton Station, hand in hand, giddy and cross-faded. We eventually stepped out of Barons Court Station, and Lydia lamented over her bursting bladder. Once I'd figured out which direction we were headed, she concealed herself behind the gates of a cemetery and dropped into a squatting position to relieve herself. I stood and watched, and we both burst into laughter. Oh, the irony of an angel practically pissing atop a grave.

When we arrived at the front door of your Hammersmith town house, we could hear the muffled revelry and the thrumming bass of the music. It was Annabelle who opened the door to us, with a huge smile that froze in place as she tried to hide her confusion.

"Hi! You're here for the party?" She stood under the doorframe, clutching a glass of rosé. *No, we're here to fix your sink*, I thought.

"Hi. Yes. Hugo invited us. Is this . . . the right address?" I responded.

"Yes, you've come to the right place! You must be one of his *many* friends." She relaxed, realising that we at least knew the host's name and weren't just opportunistic crashers. I doubt she'd expected an alternative tattooed woman with a third-wave feminist haircut and a black woman with box braids and a nose piercing to turn up. "I'm Belle, by the way. Hugo's girlfriend. Come on in, he's just in the kitchen somewhere."

Your home was exactly what I had expected it to be: a grandiose amalgamation of rococo old money and minimalist contemporary design. Lydia and I gawked at the spaciousness of the hallway and the sublimeness of the chandelier hanging above. As Belle led us through the house, I couldn't help but notice how many doors I'd spotted on the ground floor. The kitchen was full of partygoers in ridiculous costumes, and most people were already drunk at this point. There was a game of beer pong on the other side of the room, adjacent to the buffet table. An array of fancy finger foods, wines, and sliced steak was being topped up by what looked like a pair of butlers. I felt like I had just walked right into a Tory fever dream. I was genuinely expecting to be swallowed up by a sea of inebriated affluent Caucasians, but I was relieved to spot a couple of non-whites dotted around. Of course, they were probably just as rich as you were, so it didn't necessarily mean we were cut from the same cloth.

Belle interrupted a conversation you were having with someone to alert you to our presence. Your eyes instantly lit up, and you grinned, moving in for a hug.

"Eddie! I'm so glad you could make it," you cheered. On your head sat a wreath made not of bay laurel or olive leaves, but fake romaine lettuce, croutons, garlic cloves, and miniature bottles of olive oil. You were draped in an ancient Roman toga, and there were rich red bloodstains dotted all over your body. Funny.

"Thanks for having us. This is my mate Lydia," I responded.

"Fucking class costume, that." Lydia cackled.

"I try," you said, feigning modesty. "Let's just hope nobody in this house is conspiring against me. Help yourselves to the bar, guys, it's open. And have as much food as you want, it's all on the house. Or should I say, *in* the house? Haha!"

"God, stop with the dad jokes, Hu," Belle huffed. "So, Eddie, how do you know each other?" She wrapped an arm around your waist, looking up at you.

"Honestly, I'm more of a stranger. It was nice of him to invite me," I said.

"Not at all. Sorry—no problem, I meant. Ha." You took a generous swig from your bottle of Desperados.

"He'd invite all of London if he could. It's the Libra in him," Belle tittered. "Totally random, but is Eddie your real name, or a nickname? Sorry, I was just wondering, 'cause it's usually . . . you know . . . for men," Belle said. "Wait, are you, like, nonbinary or something? I apologise if you are!" She grimaced, quickly joining her hands together in a penitent praying position.

"No, I'm not. My parents just really loved Eddie Murphy." I shrugged.

"Oh. That's hilarious!" Belle squeaked, and you gave me that look again, the one where you were trying to discern my level of sincerity.

"That's not true, is it?" Lydia screwed up her eyebrows.

"Of course it's not true," I scoffed. "It's just Eddie. It's not short for anything. My parents just gave me a boy's name. Just because."

"That's so cool." Belle nodded slowly. "Well. I'll leave you guys to chat, I've got to top up my glass!" She beamed before trotting away. Then it was just you, Lydia, and me standing in a triangle, feeling the awkward silence between us in a room full of commotion.

You drank your beer again, probably more as a filler action than with an intent to drink in that moment at all. "So, how do you two know each other?" you asked us.

"We're work buddies," I responded.

"Ahhh. I take it you work for the same editors?"

"Eh? We wait tables," Lydia said, bemused. "The only thing I edit is an order when someone suddenly remembers they only eat gluten-free."

I felt heat rise to my face. "Uh . . . I also do restaurant work on the side. I told him I edit." I turned to Lydia. "I'm juggling quite a bit at the moment. Anything to pay the rent."

"Oh. That's fair," you replied. I was expecting judgement from you, but there was a twinkle of sympathy behind your irises. "I did a bit of waiting myself, back in Colombia. This lovely family in Medellín let us stay with them for a few weeks and we helped out at their restaurant. I just about managed with my IB-level European Spanish."

For a split second, I had the intrusive urge to punch you. Instead, we carried on our three-way conversation, exchanging a lot of nothing between one another. My weed high was wearing off, and I was becoming desperate to make use of the free bar. Soon enough, that's exactly what Lydia and I did. We avoided eye contact with strangers, beelining for the Grey Goose and grabbing a disposable plate to share a roster of cured hams and cheeses. Eventually we loosened up again, bloated from the finger food and fuzzy from our second round of drinking.

"Let's explore," Lydia said to me in one of the bathrooms a while later. She was sitting hunched on the toilet, her underwear heaped at her feet on the floor. "If we nick something, he'd probably not even notice it's gone, like." She was slurring a lot more now, and I knew we were both one more drink or substance away from the point of no return. I was just relieved that I'd not yet done something mortifyingly stupid in front of the dozens of partygoers.

"Let's maybe *not* steal something from him? He seems nice," I said, leaning over the sink, examining my melting red face paint.

"I think we should've switched costumes. Clearly you're the real voice of reason here."

"Clearly. What do you think of him, though? He's all right, right?" As I asked, I whipped out my phone and texted Blue.

[23:03] **Eddie:** I'm in some random rich white guy's bathroom rn lol

"He's fit, I'll give him that. But he's proper rah. That's all I'm gonna say," Lydia responded, flushing the toilet and then pulling her knickers back up. "The lad has butlers, for fuck's sake. We're out of our element here."

[23:04] **Blue:** now that's a scary way to spend ur halloween!

I chuckled.

[23:04] **Eddie:** Hahaha.
[23:04] **Eddie:** I miss you.

[23:05] **Blue:** I fuckin miss you too! Don't have too much fun
without me x

[23:05] **Eddie:** Impossible.

"Get off your phone and let's *explore!*" Lydia prompted, snapping me away from my screen.

"Fine, fine. Jeez. Did you bring any of that Charlie?" I looked at her.

"Oh my God! I forgot about that." She fished inside her bra and pulled out a small transparent baggie half-full of white powder. "Let's fuckin' 'ave it," she said, her Liverpudlian accent coming through stronger than ever. We took turns taking a bump, and that was my last clear memory.

I woke up on her sofa in Mile End the next day, dazed and discombobulated. She was fast asleep, snoring lightly on the sofa adjacent to mine. We were both still in our costumes, and there was a mop bucket on the floor between us. Every bone in my body ached, and my stomach felt like a tumble dryer full of charcuteries, bile, and hydrochloric acid. I sat up, scrambling to check if I still had all my belongings. My bag was on the coffee table, and I painstakingly got up, loped towards it, and opened it up. Thank God my phone was still there. There was a string of texts, some from Blue, some from you. *Shit,* I thought. *It's two in the afternoon?*

[09:12] **Hugo Lawrence Smith:** Hey, did you get home safe? Is your
friend still alive?

[09:13] Missed Audio Call

[09:15] **Hugo Lawrence Smith:** Call me back when you get this.

[09:20] **Hugo Lawrence Smith:** By the way, I'm so sorry to hear you're
struggling with your script. I'm more than happy to read it
and see what I can do to help.

[09:21] **Hugo Lawrence Smith:** And I like your real name, I think it
sounds cooler. More unique.

It took me a while to wrap my head around the messages. There were so many gaps in my memory. It was like rummaging through a database of jumbled images and sounds. Vague vignettes flashed through my mind: Lydia vomiting, me crying, blurred streetlights, you and I locked into an uncomfortable conversation, a garden hedge, a handful of salami, a sliver of the crescent moon in the night sky. What I definitely knew was that I must have broken at some point. I turned on a tap of vulnerability, and you bore witness to it. After reading the messages, I slowly put my phone down on the table and quickly reached for the mop bucket to vomit. I placed it back on the floor, wiped my mouth with the back of my hand, and sighed.

You said my name was more unique. What you meant was more Other. But I appreciated the euphemism. You coated your words with sugar, like the endearing sweetheart you were. After I swiftly replied to your messages, I sent you an attachment of *The Worthy* upon your subsequent request. Looking back was no longer an option.

HUGO

The Woman in the Café

I think it was around one in the morning when my carefree demeanour began to melt away. I know I said that plus-ones were allowed to come, but I didn't expect them to become plus-twos and-threes—a party guest mitosis of sorts. I'd made my speeches and downed my shots, and eventually, I was sucking on the last dregs of my hosting virtuosity. All I wanted was a nap, even if just for five minutes, even if those five minutes would probably turn into a sharp dawn.

I clambered up the stairs, definitely not sober, but not drunk enough to be a story on someone's lips the next day: Julius Caesar, stabbed in the back by his lack of inhibition. With each step I took, I thought of my father, and how this wasn't even my house, it was his. Not that he'd even set foot in it more than three times that whole year, but it didn't stop me from feeling like the teenage Hugo, ready to spring into action when one of my parents made their sudden appearance at the driveway. I opened my bedroom door, letting out a long sigh as I entered into the dark silence. I could feel the bass of the music from downstairs tapping at the soles of my feet. *Thank fuck nobody's in here,* I thought to myself. I felt for the light switch on the wall and flicked it on. My next thought hit me like a freight train, overlapping with the sound of yelps—both mine and yours. *Oh fuck, somebody* is *in here.*

You jolted from my bed, tumbling ungracefully onto the wood-panelled floor with a thump. Your friend stirred slightly next to you, but she stayed unconscious. There were smudges of red face paint on the pillow and bits of uneaten salami and cheese strewn on the duvet cover, some of which you were gripping in your hand. You looked up at me like a bewildered baby deer.

"Oh my God, oh my God," you muttered, fixing your jumpsuit. "What the fuck, I'm so sorry." You scrambled to your feet, wobbling. "We just . . . went into the first room we saw."

"It's mine," I said. "Don't be sorry. Do . . . d'you want me to call you an Uber or something? I'm wrapping the party up soon," I lied, knowing full well it was probably going to continue until someone, I don't know, maybe the sod in the lobster costume, finally found the front door. I'm not great at telling people when to fuck off.

You sat back on the bed, looking blankly ahead. Then you mumbled something.

"Sorry? I didn't make that out." I stood awkwardly in the corner of my own room, the same way Belle would whenever there was a spider that'd temporarily won the turf war over the area by the wardrobe.

"Relebogile . . . Naledi . . . Mpho. Is my name." You looked at me. "Naledi. Eddie. Not Eddie Murphy. Haha. Eddie Murphy? No. Not at all. Haha. Fuck."

"Oh," I said, not sure how else to respond. "Umm. Is your friend all right? Should I get you an Uber?"

"I'm sorry, why am I even here? Just taking up space. So fucking random, L-O-L, I'm in a Tory's house, haha. What's my life."

I was stung by the truth that tumbled out of your mullered tongue. A fucking *Tory*? Me? Did I . . . did I *really* seem like a Tory? Did I have to specify that I wasn't?

"Eddie. Honestly, I don't mind getting you a cab home. You seem tired. So's your friend. Leah?"

"Lydia," you mumbled in a low tone. "Not Leah. A name is a *very* important thing, you know. *I'd* know. Like *Hugo*." You overpronounced my name, saying it in slow motion. To say I felt uncomfortable would be an understatement; however drunk I was coming up the stairs, I was metaphorically going back down them again now. I hoped Belle wouldn't suddenly realise I'd been missing for more than five minutes and go on a quest to find me in my bedroom with two other women, so I kept my distance, as she did with the spiders.

"Do you want to know how my *play* is going, Hugo? The one you saw one fucking page of and decided you liked? Well, it's not going anywhere, *Huuuugo*. Nobody gives a shit about it," you said, and that was when the first tear fell. "Nobody cares about my work. I've tried everything. I've worked so fucking hard"—you sniffed—"and nothing's happening. I got an interview with a good fucking agency, but they turned me down because I wasn't Edward Moore, because I'm a black!" You sobbed. In that moment, uncomfortable was no longer an understatement, but a word without any conveyance. I didn't even think to ask who Edward Moore was.

"All these playwrights . . . they're all . . ." You didn't finish the sentence, instead careening into a maudlin rant that took me by surprise. "I never read *Billy Andromeda* as a kid. Not into sci-fi fantasy. But I'll give the author some props, I s'pose. Must be nice to be related to a literary billionaire! What's she like in real life? Can I get her autograph? Can she pull some strings for me? I know she's got a play at Palace Theatre, how cool! Lucky her! Tell Charlotte I said hi." The thing is, you didn't even sound splenetic, or resentful. Just sad. I could feel the sadness, pulsating through the air. I had no words.

The Uber arrived half an hour later, after I'd finally convinced you to let me order one on your behalf. It was a bit of a ball-ache trying to get an address out of an inebriated she-devil and a barely conscious messenger of God, but I managed in the end. Belle helped me help the both of you out of the house, manoeuvring through a throng of costumed hot messes on the way out. With fate-fuelled timing, Lydia vomited into the front hedge just as the Uber pulled up, but the leaves concealed her from the driver, who I'd doubted would've let her in the car if he saw. Belle huffed under her breath at me about how I "just invite anyone, for God's sake," and I had the compulsion to tell her that you weren't just anyone, you were my friend.

Once Lydia had finished her projectile streaming of stomach contents into the privet leaves, I held her shoulder and escorted her out onto the pavement where you stood, looking up at the sky. I scampered to the driver's window to tell him your name, and he nodded impatiently. I told you to call me when you made it home, and waved goodbye with the sheen of the car's back window between us. Belle grabbed my arm and lured me back into the noise of the party. I took one look at the crescent moon that had caught your eye before going back inside.

• • •

In my defence, it was really busy on the day we met.

I didn't have much of a choice in terms of seating arrangements, and besides, nobody chooses the tables that face the windows. Not actively, anyway. I'm personally more of a booth kid. But there I was, stumped on where to sit at the apex of noon, as that Holborn café swarmed with coffee and sandwich fiends. I usually tended to work in a different café, somewhere west, but I thought I'd branch out a little bit. I wasn't particularly drawn to the study spaces on the university campus. I guess maybe it's because, that way, I could just pretend I wasn't a law student, you know? If I studied in a café, there was an amorphousness to my purpose. On the day I met you, I was looking for something else in my life. Something I'd be happier to face. Not the corporate pipeline nor the rat race, nor all the familiar faces at whichever Magic Circle firm I'd end up working for, watching and waiting to see if my father's and brother's legal prowess had trickled down, if there was a genealogical advantage to becoming a lawyer. I could see my training contract play out already, clear as day. Conversations like, *You're Graham's boy, aren't you? My dad worked with him! Are you a bulldog like him? Are you more of an arbitration guy, like your brother? Dom's been doing some high-profile work in the ICC! You've got some big shoes to fill!*

I saw you move your tote bag off the free seat next to you, and I acknowledged your ceding of territory. I kept my eyes ahead as I set up my things, but I was very much aware that you were there, floating, hovering, bobbing around my periphery.

Law is a stressful game, Eddie. It consumed me that day. I was doing my rounds for vacation schemes at firms, something I should have been more proactive about in my second year of uni. Now I was a master's student, scrambling for my next opening. My last resort would be to try to get a position at the firm where my father used to work, if all else failed. I had an understanding of the law, but not the passion, nor the discipline. Procrastination was my modus operandi; I'd fill in applications just to end up refreshing the expired screen due to a lack of activity. I'd eventually got to that point as I sat next to you, and when you asked if I could watch over your things, it had snapped me out of my fog. To make matters worse, I was the kind of restless where everything else around you is ten times more fascinating than whatever is right in front of you. So when I turned my head to an angle and my eyes fell onto your unlocked computer screen, they wandered in and out of the words on the page until my fingers itched to keep reading, to keep scrolling.

It was a script for a play, or a show, or something. I glanced outside to watch you smoking, looking down at your phone as you slowly paced along the pavement. Then I looked back at your laptop screen, and the urge for me to talk to you came full-force. Of course I was hesitant, because I felt like I'd probably be a nuisance, and you'd lose your writing streak. But then I thought, maybe seeing that a stranger showed interest in what looked like a work in progress could serve as motivation, or fuel to your inspiration. I went back and forth in my head between *nuisance* and *encouragement*, and then I settled somewhere along the lines of, *Ah, well, fuck it.* So I asked you about your play when you returned. You looked cautiously at me, and I wondered if I'd made a mistake, overstepped my boundaries. I could feel your reluctance to open up, but it was already too late.

I was slightly intimidated by you for a multitude of reasons. Firstly, you seemed too cool. Second of all, you just seemed . . . free. You were dressed like an experimental artist, your braids tied messily and your opal septum piercing glinting in the sunlight. There was conviction and focus in your eyes, but you also seemed spontaneous. Maybe that was just the perk of being an artist. Maybe that was something I wanted for myself. I needed not to know what I was destined for, or what my day would look like tomorrow, or the day after, or the day after that. So even though I could tell you weren't interested in conversing with me, once I started, I couldn't stop.

• • •

You texted me back in the afternoon after my party. Though I hadn't been hammered, I was still recovering, and Belle and I had to deal with the cleanup efforts from the wreckage that was red Solo cups, spilled food and drink, and scuff marks from the wankers who'd ignored the NO SHOES sign in the hallway. I knew you probably would've assumed that I had a maid who did all the cleaning, but I didn't. I hadn't since my parents' divorce, anyway.

It was around two in the afternoon when you responded to my messages and I knew that you were still alive. While Belle was losing her mind over the bits of food you'd left strewn over my bedroom the night prior, I was memorising your real name, rolling it around my tongue like a hard candy. *Naledi, Naledi, Naledi.*

[14:16] **Eddie:** God, please don't remind me what I said last night. I don't wanna know. Apologies in advance.

[14:16] **Eddie:** I told you my real name? Thanks for the compliment, but it's a very common name where I'm from. It's not unique at all.

[14:19] **Hugo:** Oh, I see. I just meant that it's unique here. I know way more Eddies than I know Naledis. So it's cool to me. You shouldn't change it.

[14:19] **Hugo:** And honestly, you were fine last night. You were just reasonably upset about your script. So please feel free to send the final product over. I've been waiting on this for a year now!

[14:20] **Eddie:** Haha are you sure?

[14:23] **Hugo:** Of course! I wanna see what all these agents are missing out on.

[14:26] **Eddie:** Yeh, but then what? You're not in the theatre industry. How could you possibly help? No offence

[14:28] **Hugo:** I don't know. We'll cross that bridge when we get there I spose. Just send it over! Pleeaseee

[14:28] **Eddie:** Bloody hell, all right I will.

[14:30] **Eddie:** the_worthy.docx

I called you up later that evening after I'd finished reading the script. I was sitting in the study staring at the pages on my laptop, and I was in awe of how insanely good it was. I had to let you know that it wasn't just a fluke. It was worth something. It could go places.

You could go places. You sounded despondent over the phone, like I was rather telling you something you didn't want to hear instead of singing your praises. You tried to change the subject and asked me if you had said anything super embarrassing the night before. I told you that embarrassment was subjective.

"Don't give me that," you sighed. "I said something pitiful, didn't I? That's why you're here licking my arse. You feel bad for me."

I broke into a smile, leaning back in my desk chair. "You've got it all wrong, Naledi. I'm quite the opposite. One might say . . . jealous of you. Of your talent."

"Umm. Thanks."

"Do you really think that people would care more about the play if a white person wrote it?" I mustered up the courage to ask.

"Is that what I said at the party?"

"Something to that effect, yes."

"Ugh. I guess drunken words really are sober thoughts, aren't they?" you responded.

I knew it wasn't a question for me to answer, but I did anyway. "You shouldn't think that way, that people would care more in that case. It's not like *I* care."

"Don't start," you responded flatly, but with enough conviction to put me in my place. "You don't know what you're talking about."

"I'm sorry. I'm just optimistic."

"You just came out of the right vagina is what happened."

I scoffed. "Is that what you think?"

"Yes."

I didn't want to believe you, of course. To truly believe our fates were all sealed for us was a tragedy. But there it was, a tiny thread that you started to pull. I wanted to see where it would lead. I wanted to get to the bottom of your line of thought, to meet you eye to eye. So when I invited you over that night, that was my initial plan. Things took a bit of a left turn, obviously.

"Are you free tonight, by any chance?" I asked. "I've finally finished cleaning, and I think we could maybe keep this conversation going. I just can't get your play out of my head. There's so much for us to talk about."

"I might be. Where's your girlfriend?"

"She's at her mum's in Holland Park. She won't be back until tomorrow. I'm meeting them for brunch."

"Okay. Should I bring red or white wine?"

I raised an eyebrow. "You're already back on it, are you?"

"I'm just putting the dog's hair to use."

"Funny. Let's go for red. You decide the label. When am I expecting you?"

"Give me an hour-ish."

We sat on opposite ends of the living room sofa around ninety minutes later, clutching our glasses of rouge in between our fingers. You were curled up, periodically looking out the window. I had my laptop on the coffee table in front of us, ranting about the brilliance of your work. Despite the fact that we'd drunk copious amounts the night before, the wine was still hitting us quickly. We'd both failed to eat as much as we should have, and you didn't seem to be listening to me much. It was hard to tell. But it was somewhere in the middle of our one-sided conversation that you suddenly shot up, placing your wineglass on the table before grabbing your stuff from your bag. "Right, I need a cig. Give me five."

When you came back, you were swaying. Alcohol melded with a nicotine rush. The first thing you asked me upon your return was about my law degree, and if I enjoyed it. It took me a moment to respond. Even then, all I could muster was an *I don't know*. Because it was true, I didn't. I *had* enjoyed my degree, but could I have enjoyed something else more? Had I really found the one thing that I was put on this planet to do? Existential, I know. Not everyone needs a calling or a purpose in life, I get that. But there was a sinking feeling I couldn't shake in the pit of my stomach once I realised I might be one of those people, and I didn't want to be. I wanted to stand out from the crowd, from the suits, from the run-of-the-mill. I wanted to be somebody.

You proceeded to ask me what it was I loved so much about theatre, and I told you, again, that I didn't know. That there was a time when I wanted to become an actor, but I wasn't so sure of myself. I was set for life with law. It was what my father had done. It was what my brother did. It was what I was going to do.

"What the fuck do you mean by that? If you want to be an actor, go for it," you demanded, slurring slightly.

"Look, I don't want to get into my life choices right now."

"But you're okay getting into mine? I'm supposed to follow my dreams, but you're not supposed to follow yours? Even though this world is made for people like you to be able to?"

"It's important for you to try, though. To break through."

"Break through what, Hugo?"

"You know . . . barriers."

You let out a startling laugh. Heat prickled across my skin.

"You said you could help me. How? Who do you know? What can you do?"

I cupped my chin between my thumb and forefinger, stumped. "I want to help you. I really do."

You stayed silent for a while, clearly thinking over our options. Then you turned to face me.

"This is how you're going to help me," you said. "It's a bit of a mad one. So, just hear me out."

Great Belonging

July 2017

"It's okay. You're okay. You've got this." I had my hands on your shoulders, crouching to your level as you sat on the toilet, taking laboured breaths.

"I don't know. I don't know. I feel weird." You closed your eyes.

"No, no. You're fine. I can assure you of that."

You shot up and paced around the accessible bathroom like a caged tiger. There wasn't much I could do to calm you. We had already made it this far.

It was nine months later, in July of the following year. We stood side by side in formal attire: my crisp royal-blue shirt and dark-grey trouser suit, your purple satin dress with an asymmetric neckline, your black clutch, your marvellously braided hair, your painted nails and colourful eyelids and dark red lips, your slip-on kitten heels. You were shaking, learning how to breathe again, probably trying not to throw up—and deep down, I was doing the same. I guess I was trying to act as the mediator for both our racing emotions.

"I promise you it'll all be fine. Just think of it as . . . a fun night out."

"A fun night out?" you snapped. "I think my heart's about to fall out of my arse."

"Just don't make too much eye contact with anyone. Smile at all times. Stay right next to me. We'll be out of here before you know it."

"And then what? What if we really do it?" you asked me.

"I mean . . . we've discussed what we'll do if it happens, haven't we? Remember?"

You nodded and took one more long breath. We both looked in the mirror at ourselves, standing in a silence that was eventually split by a loud knock at the door. Someone needed the toilet. We stayed quiet, quickly sprucing each other up and patting down our outfits. I hoped that the person knocking would have gone elsewhere upon their realisation that the toilet was occupied, but we were met with a middle-aged woman in a wheelchair instead, looking up at us with disapproval as we slinked through the sliding door. Welp. I guess a panic attack is somewhat crippling, right? Anything to go where we don't belong.

By the time we got to our seats, the place was relatively packed. It was a sold-out venue in Marylebone, bustling with just under two hundred people. Photographers littered the room, and the small stage was lit with rotating spotlights. On the big screen was the title of the evening beaming down at us. We kept to ourselves, although people did try to make small talk with us. We'd gone to town on the finger food and taken advantage of the free champagne, all in an effort to keep our hands and mouths too occupied to converse with strangers. And then the moment came for us to all be seated, and for the night to properly begin.

"Hello, and welcome, everyone, to the thirty-eighth annual Marston B. Greaves Awards for Theatre. This is the evening where we celebrate fresh talent from all across the United Kingdom, and have been doing so since 1979. I'm your host, Phoebe Egan, and it is my honour to be here, sharing a new generation of talent with you all." She stood tall in front of the podium, adjusting her microphone before she continued. "This has been our biggest year to date, with over ten *thousand* entries in twelve categories that span all facets of theatre. And somehow, we have managed to whittle it down to just *seventy-two* nominees across all our awards tonight. It was definitely not easy; months of rigorous analysis and judging went into this monumental feat, but here we all are. So, without further ado, let's get started, shall we?"

• • •

The first thing we did was change the title. It would have been too obvious to the agents who'd considered it before. It wasn't easy, but we brainstormed. I didn't know how much of my opinion actually mattered, but it seemed like right from the jump, we worked as a team. For weeks after the party, you'd find yourself over at my house at least one evening a week as we threw ideas back and forth for our plan of action. You knew how terribly reluctant I was, right from the moment you proposed your outlandish idea. A part of me didn't expect much. Success is improbable, after all. We both knew that. I think failure, in this instance, was something we were probably more open to. Because if we succeeded, it told us something tragic. It's a paradox, of course, but it's true.

The Worthy was eventually changed to *Great Belonging*. It was a title that gave the same sort of ambience as the original, sticking to the sentiment of a dystopian Britain that could throw anyone out at its own monstrous will. What *did* it mean to belong in a world like that? What did nationalism become? What did *the country* become? Those were the questions you wanted to answer. Also, *Great Belonging* sounded similar to Great Britain, so phonetically, it just worked. I still to this day can't remember who came up with the new title, but if it was me, I must say, maybe there was some creative potential inside me after all.

Then we started to brainstorm a new moniker. That was when we sat down in my dining room over a dinner of lamb, squash, and apricot tagine, and a bottle of Château d'Angludet, and you embarrassedly opened up to me about the evolution of your names in the last year. How you went from Naledi Moruakgomo to Edward Moore in an interesting experiment-slash-desperate ploy. Your drunken rant at my Halloween party began to make more and more sense, and with each word you spoke, my heart broke for you even more. After we'd finished eating and drinking, we put our heads down and discussed the implications of a name, and what it could do; how it represented the work, and whether it was an extension of the work itself. I wasn't sure I was truly convinced, but then you made a good point:

"You walk down Times Square, and on the fuck-off screen you see a model doing a campaign for Prada. She's absolutely stunning. Like, she looks sculpted by some sort of multidimensional alien. She's *objectively* gorgeous. She was plucked off the street outside an orphanage, and she becomes an overnight sensation, doing runways and fashion shows left, right, and centre. She wins fashion awards and begins to dabble in acting. Turns out she's an incredible actress, too. Only problem is, she's called . . . Keith. You could argue that it doesn't matter what her name is—she's beautiful regardless. 'What's in a name? That which we call a rose / By any other name would smell as sweet.'" You intoned the Shakespeare quote with flair. "But I'm telling you, they're changing her name. The world won't know her as Keith. It's just not happening. Now, imagine you don't even have a face. You're just a name. That's what a writer sells. A name. A face, too, but that part's a bit complicated. The name comes first. My name just isn't enough. Wentworth made that abundantly clear."

We didn't know at first whether to go with my full name, Hugo Lawrence Smith, or just Hugo Lawrence. Or Hugo Smith. Or H. L. Smith. Or even switch it around a bit—Lawrence Smith, maybe? Lawrence Hugo Smith? Hugo Smith Lawrence? God, the possibilities were endless. There was even a fleeting suggestion to go with Hugo Edmonds in order to prompt the association with my cousin—despite the fact that we were related by Smith, which was my maternal name, and her paternal. My mother was her father's sister, and her mother, Lynette Edmonton, was not related to me. The final suggestion was to go with my father's surname: Hugo Murray, which did have a ring to it, to be honest. But we ended up circling all the way back to the beginning. Hugo Lawrence Smith was not broken, and it didn't need fixing. So Hugo Lawrence Smith it was.

We didn't send the script off to all the same agencies as before. Some of them, but not all. We didn't want to rouse suspicion from the outset, especially considering this was now probably the third iteration of pitches under the third name. It was also a test to see which agencies had even properly read the script the first time, seeing as it was only the title and author name we'd changed. As the year was coming to a close, the competition deadlines for the next year were all cropping up, so we thought to focus our efforts there as well. The MBGs were an obvious contender, being the biggest award in the market, but you were reluctant from the start. You didn't specify why, but I could only assume it was due to your being rejected by Wentworth the first time around. I told you it didn't matter—this was a new start. A new opening. They were missing out on something special if you didn't try, and it was worth the shot.

The deadline was in February, so there was still time to mull it over. November switched to December, and the ball had started to roll. We had a plan for the new year, for how things were going to go once January came. All the while, I'd started slacking even harder on law firm applications, just as the rejections were staggering through, one by one. I'd tell my parents, and they'd tell me to keep my head up, to keep trying. But I felt I couldn't have half of me in one endeavour and the other half in the other. If I were to really discover if the arts were my true passion, I had to be all in. So come December, I decided to tell my parents about my newfound love for something else: playwriting.

"Since when?" my father said to me as we sat at his dining table for Christmas dinner.

"Writing plays is something I've been thinking about doing for a long time, actually," I responded.

It was a bit later in the day at his abode in Cobham, Surrey, and I had driven the one-hour journey from my mother's place in Sevenoaks in the afternoon, splitting the holiday between both parents. Every year I'd act as messenger, arranging who would be going full Monty on the Christmas dinner so that there wasn't waste at either end. The previous year it had been my mother, so this year I just shared a modest serving of roast duck breast with figs, rosemary, and garlic fried potatoes with her at lunch. Her homemade raspberry jam was sandwiched between freshly baked scones for dessert, and I packed the rest with me in the car, along with her gift to me. Now, in front of me lay full servings of roast potatoes, sprouts, parsnips and carrots, Yorkshire puddings, pigs in blankets, boats of gravy and cranberry sauce. The turkey sat in the centre, glistening golden brown. My father may have just turned seventy, but his enthusiasm for out-cooking my mother was still as sprightly as ever.

"Writing plays? Sure thing," my half sister Luna interjected, slouched in her chair next to me. "Totally on-brand, and not random at all." She was on her annual holiday visit from Hong Kong, where she had resided all her life. When she was around ten, my father divorced her mother and moved back to England. The arrangement was that she'd continue her education at a private international school, thriving with expats and wanting of locals. It meant that she could have very easily been from North America, judging from the way she spoke, but she did look primarily Asian, and she was fluent in Cantonese at her mother's behest. The only giveaway that she wasn't entirely Hong Kongese were her eyes, which were the same shade of hazel as mine. She lived with her mother in an apartment on the thirtieth floor of a block in Jardine's Lookout near Mid-Levels, where for just over a decade my father had also lived. That was until the harmony of his second marriage eventually unfolded into dissonance. I couldn't blame my sister for thinking my venture of the arts was completely out of the blue; being raised six thousand miles apart comes with its blind spots.

"It isn't random at all," I responded to her defensively. "I've been focusing on it as a side hobby. You know, reading up on the greats. Arthur Miller, Alan Bennett, all of them. This past year—since my master's—it's just grown on me. I think it's something I could try to pursue."

"Are vacation scheme applications going that awry for you, Hu?" My father looked at me with investigative regard. He picked up his mulled wine and took a swig, never once breaking eye contact with me. "You know you always have Pointon & Sumner as a viable option."

"It's not about the vacation schemes. It's about me trying something else I enjoy before . . . you know, locking myself into a career."

"You've finished your postgrad. You've been travelling. You've had plenty of time to think about these things."

"Well, I wrote something in South America," I lied. "I'm quite proud of it. I think it could go places. If it doesn't, then I'll happily walk with my tail between my legs. Just give me until the end of 2017. Then I'll go back to law."

"Have you told your mother?" He cut into the turkey and lifted a hefty chunk onto his plate. "I'm sure she'll be supportive. Seems like you're leaning more towards her side of the family, I s'pose."

"No, I haven't told her yet. I just wanted to let you know."

"It's your life. This is your gap year, of course, but that's what it is. A *gap*. You've got to think about where it is you want to be."

"I understand." I swallowed.

"If I were you, I'd probably not rush into the arts so haphazardly. It's always worth having the credentials first. Writing a story in Colombia doesn't really count," he said flippantly in between bites. I felt slighted by his lack of faith in me, but I shouldn't have. He never *hoped* I'd succeed at anything. He just expected me to. I never saw the wonder and intrigue in his eyes like I'd always wished. Maybe that's why I wanted to shatter his expectations. I wanted to show him I wasn't who he thought I was going to be.

I studied the play intensely, like I was taking an Oxford-level final exam on it. I had three paper copies, all highlighted and annotated to the point that they looked more graffitied than Lisbon. You and I spent a lot of free time together, going over the politics of the work, how you interpreted it, and in turn, how I should. The least I could be was a vessel for your mind.

Belle and I had planned to leave for Southeast Asia in May of the following year. We had it all scheduled: we'd start off in Vietnam before hopping through Laos, then Thailand, then Cambodia. From there, we'd go to Indonesia, then the Philippines, and end our trip in Hong Kong, where I would visit Luna and her mother. I'd be back in the UK in time for my legal practice course and to carry on with the rest of my life. But when the short list for the MBG Awards was announced a month before the trip was meant to start, *Great Belonging* had made it to the finals.

Belle had known about my newfound venture and was somewhat supportive, but she was also just as confused as everyone else in my life. Of course, I didn't tell her the same thing I told my father—that I'd written it during our last travels—because she could obviously fact-check that. I made something up about how I wrote it in my spare time over a scattered period and it had all come together by the time we'd got back from South America. I told her that I wanted to one day surprise everyone with a viewing of the play in person, whenever that might be. She still wanted to go to Asia, so she found a friend of hers who was happy to take my place. I was invited to the awards ceremony in July, and I could bring a plus-one. I was the real plus-one, of course. Or, in truth, you and I were just two halves of one guest. And that's how we found ourselves in this predicament, sitting side by side in an audience of budding theatre hopefuls, palms sweating and hearts running.

• • •

"And now, we move to the award for Best New Playwright," Phoebe began, around forty minutes in. Our eyes shot up, almost in sync. I instinctively grabbed your hand in anticipation, and you looked at me quickly before casting your eyes back downwards. I could see your left knee bouncing skittishly. "In this category, we waded through nearly three thousand entries, which showcased a wide range of work, from romances, to thrillers, one-man shows, comedies, and more. In the end, there were six plays that jumped out at us. Spanning different genres, these writers all came in with their own unique points of view, and in doing so, taught us something new about the limitless boundaries of art and culture. So, without further ado, the nominees are:

"Nelson Brewer, for his dramatic comedy set one hundred years into the future, *The Turn of a Century*; Ross Tulloch, for his suspenseful drama consisting mainly of a dialogue between two characters, *Me, You, Me*; Felix Rodwell, for his gripping story about post–World War II Coventry, *The Cathedral* . . ." Phoebe listed the names and titles, pausing briefly in between each as they appeared on the screen in succession. "Ian Hurst, for his romantic tragedy set during the AIDS epidemic, *All I Didn't Say*; Hugo Lawrence Smith, for his adventurous dystopia tackling citizenship and meritocracy, *Great Belonging*; and finally, Maisie Paulson, for her twist-filled interactive whodunnit, *Clifford Hangor*. It wasn't easy deciding on the outcome here, as they are all so deserving of recognition and stage adaptations. But after gruelling deliberations, we can now proudly announce the results."

Hearing my name read aloud over the microphone was a brief out-of-body experience. I couldn't even imagine how it must have felt for you. The whole time, you had not looked up once. We were sitting within the first two rows, along with the other nominees and their plus-ones. The Felix Rodwell chap was to my right, and he gave me a nudge of support when my name was called out. I nodded back, just as I felt your hand grip tighter onto mine as you white-knuckled the arm of your chair.

"In third place as our second runner-up and the recipient of three thousand pounds, we have"—Phoebe opened up the small envelope on her podium—"Ian Hurst."

The crowd erupted into applause as Ian went up to the stage to collect his bronze trophy, extended to him by a stagehand. He nodded and beamed at the crowd before quickly returning to his seat.

"Now for our first runner-up. In second place, and the recipient of five thousand pounds and a year's access to playwriting classes as part of our prestigious writing programme, we have . . . Felix Rodwell!" The same process was repeated once my seat neighbour shot up. He went to collect his trophy and did a small bow as he briefly revelled in his success.

"Finally, it's time to announce the winner, who will receive fifteen thousand pounds and a contract offer from the renowned Wentworth Agency to develop their work into a stage production at the Regium Theatre. All the nominees' work was such a pleasure to read, but this one really shone. Its creativity simply astounded the judges' panel. So let's give a huge round of applause to this individual." My chest tightened. I turned to you, and you to me. "I'm here for you, Naledi," I half mouthed, half whispered, and you nodded quickly.

"So, the recipient of the Best New Playwright is"—Phoebe pulled out the square of paper from inside the final envelope—"Hugo Lawrence Smith!"

Oh shit. I won. We won.

You won.

We both shot up, and I swathed you in a tight embrace, nestling my chin in the dip of your shoulder.

"You're amazing," I said.

"Go, go, go," you prompted, swiftly prying yourself out of my grasp and urging me to collect the award.

The applause was deafening; was it louder than the previous applauses? It was hard to tell. The lights onstage were brighter than I thought they would be from my vantage point in the audience. Phoebe Egan shook my hand before the stagehand gave her the winner's trophy: a glass sculpture of the Greek comedy and tragedy masks of Thalia and Melpomene overlapping one another. She handed it to me, and it was alarmingly heavy in my hands. I scanned the crowd, trying to recalibrate everything and find your face among the others. Usually, all nominees were recommended to have a speech prepared in case they won, and it was something we had considered. "Keep it short and sweet," you had told me. "Don't overstate yourself. You'll look humble." As I stood there with the trophy in my hand, I was overtaken by a funny kind of shame. I looked out into the hall and saw nothing but a sea of faces like my own. Although I was hyperaware of the fact that I didn't belong here, I fit in perfectly. Nothing seemed amiss. Proportionally, of course there would be more white people in this room, at this awards show, getting nominated, winning. Even then, this wasn't exactly proportional. Had *Great Belonging* rightfully been nominated under your name, you would have been the first non-white person in years to even get that chance. But it wasn't. And you weren't.

Blood rushed through my ears as I stood onstage, gearing up to make my winning speech. I felt like a deer in headlights. A part of me wanted to blurt out the truth, declare that this was a social experiment and that my plus-one was the actual deserving winner and that everyone in this room should be ashamed of their apparent unconscious biases, considering all but three of the previous recipients of this award had been white men, and I, a white man, was joining this legacy of unconscious bias, despite the fact that all I had really done up until this point was just be a white man—but I couldn't do that. At least not yet. It was too soon. Nominees were immediately disqualified upon any indication that their work was in fact not theirs. This wasn't something you were willing to throw away. "It's not about you," you had told me at some point a few weeks before. "It's about the play. The play is winning. The play is getting exposure. It's the model in Times Square. You're just her new name."

The winners and runners-up in all the categories were rounded together after the ceremony for pictures against a backdrop in the reception area. Thirty-six of us all huddled for a big photo with our awards in hand, followed by the twelve winners getting their own. Ian, Felix, and I were later pulled aside for separate snaps of the victors in the playwright category. All the while, you were hanging about, sipping on the champagne and mingling with the other guests.

"How lovely that you brought your missus with you," Felix said to me once we broke away from the hold of the cameramen. "I came alone because I was too afraid to lose in front of mine." He laughed. "I sort of regret it now." He looked at his trophy. "She'd have liked to see this." He was probably in his early forties, by the looks of it; his salt-and-pepper hair and crow's feet gave it away. It dawned on me that most of the nominees were considerably older than me—there were maybe a handful who were still in their twenties. I wouldn't have been surprised if I was one of the youngest people there. That meant you were, too. Another amazing feat.

"Oh, she's . . . she's not my girlfriend," I corrected Felix. "We're good friends. She's my biggest supporter."

"Ahhh, apologies. Still, it's lovely. Big congrats on the prize, my boy." He patted my shoulder before walking away. After rallying a congratulations back to him, I immediately sought you out, feeling drained from the adrenaline of the night, wanting to make a quick exit. When I scoped out the reception hall, you were nowhere to be found. I fished for my phone in my trouser pocket to call you. You told me you had gone outside for a smoke. We weren't supposed to take the trophies home with us that night; they were more for show. They had to be handed back to the event organisers and would be shipped to our houses in the near future. I desperately wanted to leave the building with it, so you could feel the weight of your victory in your own hands, but I guess I knew that time would eventually come. I gave it to someone I recognised as a handler, thanked them, and swiftly exited the venue.

The evening air was biting, and I could see the goose bumps on your bare arms. I went in to hug you, and you stepped back, holding your cigarette away from you.

"I stink."

"I don't care. Come here." I pulled you in again. You eventually threw the cigarette aside and wrapped both arms around me. "Congratulations, Naledi."

When we pulled apart, I could see a wetness in your eyes. You were crying. "No, congrats to *you*." You sniffed, wiping away a tear.

"I'm sorry. It's so fucking unfair. You deserve your flowers. You really do. Honestly, if you want, we can scrap the whole thing. I'll come clean as soon as possible," I replied.

"Absolutely not." You shook your head, regaining your composure. "We can't blow our cover this soon. I need to see this play. I *need* to. I don't want any more obstacles. That's the least I could ask for. At some point down the line, we'll tell everyone, but we'll cross that bridge when we get there. Okay?"

I nodded. "Okay. I've got you."

"Great," you said, smiling. "So, how heavy was the trophy? I've always been curious."

"Well, I'm not keeping it, so you'll find out. It's not mine, remember? Either I give it to you, or we give it back to them. There's no other option." I placed a hand on your shoulder. "Look. You've got to celebrate this as *your* win, whether you want to or not, or whether the play goes through to production, or everything goes tits up after this. You're a winner, Naledi."

You looked at me, smiling, before speaking. "I've never met anyone like you. You're nothing like the rest. And shit, you really are an amazing actor. You were so convincing on that stage. Even *I* was proud of your win for a second." You chuckled.

The deluge of praise I was subjected to after the MBGs paled in comparison to what you said to me that night. Knowing that someone saw potential in me was all I needed to hear. I could break away from the confines of the corporate world, finally! I could forge my own path. You and I, we could be stars.

Typical

DOES IT RUN IN THE FAMILY? MBG AWARDS' BEST NEW PLAYWRIGHT IS C. H. EDMONDS'S COUSIN

One surprising, or maybe not so surprising, newcomer to the theatre scene is twenty-two-year-old Hugo Lawrence Smith, who snatched the Best New Playwright prize. Not much is known about the writer, who has apparently swivelled from a law degree to follow his dreams in theatre production. One wonders if he had any help from his English literature professor mother, or his illustrious author cousin, C. H. Edmonds, who has a string of *Billy Andromeda* spin-offs onstage. It will be exciting to see where Smith ends up in the industry, and if he will be able to make a name for himself in the competitive world of the West End. "I'm very grateful for this opportunity that I've been granted, and I plan on embracing it to all extremes," the winner stated in his acceptance speech. "This play is much bigger than me. In fact, it can and should be seen as something completely divorced from me. It's almost like I didn't even write it. That's how it feels."

• • •

I was sitting in the kitchen the next morning, eating an omelette at the island counter, flicking through web articles about the awards ceremony, when I came across this one. I was shocked at how quickly the journalistic Powers That Be had been able to spin nepotism into the narrative. A part of me wondered if I was the best conduit to perform this experiment. Superficially, I was, but if a first cousin I didn't communicate with on a regular basis was already somehow getting the credit for my success, then was the hypothesis of our experiment compromised, or was it further validated?

"Naledi. Come and see this," I called out to you, unsure if you had awoken yet. After the ceremony, we thought it easier if you just crashed at mine.

You sauntered down the steps, and you took a seat next to me, yawning before looking closely at my laptop screen. Then you sighed, rolling your eyes. "Typical," you murmured. "But it's fine. I don't care. Whatever will catapult my art into the world, I'm okay with. Even if it happens to be little old *Billy Andro*. As long as the truth doesn't come out anytime soon, it's all good."

"I suppose you're right." I nodded. "Let's just keep playing it by ear."

"Shit. Your phone's been going off nonstop," you said, lifting it up from next to me. "So many people wishing you congrats." You took the fork out of my hand and bit into my omelette. "I'll just pretend they're all for me," you snickered, before standing up. "Right, I'm gonna take a shower, if that's all right? Then I'll be out. I'm meeting Blue for brunch."

"No worries. The bathroom is yours—go to town. Then you can go to town."

"An angel loses its wings with every pun you make," you said.

• • •

A few days later, my mother came to visit me. She brought a bouquet of flowers and some champagne. We sat and chatted about everything, and of course, the win was the main topic. I'd eventually told her about my new endeavour sometime after telling my father, and she took it much better than he did. She was never the condescending type—in fact, the complete opposite. She'd always been supportive of me, even if she wasn't sure I was supportive of myself. As a child, being raised by my parents was like being forced to pick a side, even before they eventually went their separate ways. If my father was a "should," my mother was a "could"—I wasn't tethered to any particular future in her eyes. I could do whatever I wanted, and that was the best way to make use of the safety net I'd always have. Her finding out about the MBG award I received must have vindicated her. Of course it was under false pretences, but there was still some truth to everything. It was my mother who campaigned to keep me in drama classes as a child when my father thought it a useless pastime. Sometime after my fifth birthday and during their pending divorce, my mother gave me the option to continue playing extracurricular football or to rejoin the local kids' theatre group, a year after my father pulled me out of it. I was cast as Joseph in my school's nativity not long after, and the high of my pride had not yet worn off. I wanted to chase it as far as it went. It was once I reached high school that I put down the script and eventually picked up a ball, exchanging whimsical artistry for being one of the lads. So in a way, none of this was a surprise to my mother. She remembered the beaming cherub of a Joseph, waving out to her in the audience, and she had always held on to him.

"I saw you in the papers, Laurie. I'm not sure if I'm just no longer in the loop with your life, but . . . who is that young lady you went to the ceremony with? I saw her in one of the photos. She doesn't look familiar to me. She's . . . different . . . from your usual friends," my mother enquired as we sat in the garden.

"Oh, that's Na—that's Eddie," I corrected myself. "She also writes plays. We met on this online writing course I was doing in the evenings for a while."

"Ahhh, I see. How lovely."

"Indeed. Sometimes we'd have to work collaboratively with other people on the course, and eventually we met in real life. I got to know her more. We'd have these little writing sessions in cafés, and the rest is history." This was the lie we agreed to tell about the way we met. It was something that was genuinely believable, and it didn't necessarily overstate our connection.

"Ahhh. Well, it's nice to see you making new friends. Speaking of friends, how're all your other pals doing? Damian, Andrew, everyone?"

"They're all good," I responded. "Same old. Damian's just got a new job. I think Andrew's applying for a PhD. Life just keeps going on."

"Have they said anything to you about . . . all of this?" She waved her hands in front of her, signalling the hot topic at hand.

"Yeah, they have. Damian's throwing me a little celebratory get-together at some point. Most of the uni lot will be there, too. You know—Olivia, Johan, Lucas. I think Emmy's coming, too."

"Splendid." She smiled at me. "It's a shame Belle's not here to celebrate with you. I bet it feels a bit odd, doesn't it?"

"I don't think living your best life in Indonesia is exactly the worst of compromises, Mummy," I answered. Judging from Belle's Instagram feed, she was documenting a trip that was enough to make anyone green with envy. The weirdest part was that I wasn't envious at all. I wasn't sure I even missed her. That realisation scared me more than I cared to admit.

"I guess so. But I find it interesting that you didn't tell your girlfriend about *any* of this," she rebutted.

"This was something for me to figure out on my own. I didn't need any outside influence. That's all."

"I take it that your writing friend knew?"

"Well, she was at the ceremony, wasn't she?" I said, more defensively than intended.

"It's all right, darling. I was just wondering." She shrugged, raising an eyebrow and sipping on her cup of tea like she was swallowing a secret.

• • •

I came to know all about Helen Hunter, courtesy of a history lesson from you. Winning the MBGs meant complicating things—that was what you told me three weeks after the awards, when the Wentworth Agency eventually reached out to me. If the script ended up on Helen's desk again under a new title, author name, and person, more questions would be raised. *Besides, that smarmy bitch doesn't deserve one penny from my work,* you told me with gritted teeth after I'd forwarded you the introductory email she sent. You hoped that even if word got around that this wasn't the first time the script had ended up inside the walls of the Bloomsbury high-rise offices, it wouldn't necessarily be back in Helen's hands. Unfortunately for you, it was.

I entered her office on a dewy August afternoon, flustered from the suffusion of the summer air. I'd barely thought about what to wear to the meeting; as long as it was light enough for me not to drown in my own sweat, all was good. I'd thrown on a cornflower-blue linen shirt and a pair of stone-coloured tapered trousers and slid into burgundy loafers. Initially glued to her laptop, feigning productivity or succumbing to the opposite, the receptionist straightened up at her cognisance of my arrival. Not once did she break eye contact with me or let up her welcoming demeanour. After she handed me my guest lanyard and as I strolled towards the turnstiles, she complimented me on the scent of my cologne. I thanked her, wondering if she was this congenial to every person who walked through these revolving doors. It should have made me feel more relaxed, but I was shitting a house of bricks. *I'm an intruder,* I thought. *I'm breaking and entering and leaving a trail of Creed Aventus behind me.*

"Hello, Hugo," Helen greeted me, standing up from behind her desk and leaning over to shake my hand as I got closer. "It's a pleasure to finally meet you. Congratulations on the win," she added, nodding. I looked down and saw what was most likely a paper copy of the play, annotated to the same degree as my own copies, if not slightly less.

"Hi, Helen. It's a pleasure to meet you, too. Thank you," I said, seating myself across from her.

"Right. Let's cut past the niceties," she said as she sat back down, leaning in her office chair. "I think we both know about the elephant in the room, don't we?"

I froze, wondering which way to go with a response. "Uhhh . . . yes, we do?" I searched for a tweak in her facial expression and found nothing.

"There's no need to act coy. You know I've read this script before." She crossed her arms, and my stomach dropped. Was this the moment I was about to be found out? Was this the moment I lost, and in turn, you did too? But then I remembered the hopefully foolproof cover we'd conjured up for this exact moment, and I put it into action.

"Yes, I know. I submitted it last year under a different name," I said.

"Right, right. So why was someone else sitting here instead of you? Go on, I won't bite. This isn't an interrogation. I just need to make sure we're on the same page before we proceed. We don't need any more miscommunication from this point on."

"Okay, okay, you got me." I chuckled, throwing my hands up in surrender. "I chickened out at the last minute before submitting to you. You know, it was just so overwhelming. Being self-taught, and a law school graduate, I just felt out of my element. It was a stupid idea, I know. I didn't think I deserved to make it this far without the credentials. And my friend, Naledi . . . well, she *does* have the credentials. She went to theatre school. She felt like . . . a more fitting contender."

"Hmm." Helen pressed on. She evidently wasn't fully satisfied with my reasoning.

"Well, I mean . . . in this climate, I feel that . . . you know . . . *Great Belonging* is a socio-politically dense piece of work, and in my position of privilege, there could be room for doubt concerning my authentic connection to it. The protagonist, Amali, is a first-generation immigrant, and I . . . I didn't want my own identity to get in the way of that. I wanted her story to be front and centre."

Helen sighed, shaking her head. "Goodness me. It's sad to say, but it seems like white men can't do anything these days anymore, can they? They can't even tell a thought-provoking story! It's almost like we're regressing as a society, isn't it? You should hold your head high and be proud of who you are, no matter how or when the tides change."

I readjusted myself. "Well, I wouldn't say white men can't do *anything*. I'm here after all, aren't I? I won the award." My response could be read as either cockiness or guilt.

Helen looked at me, unblinking. "You're right, you did win. Rightfully so. Plus, I don't think that it's just your identity as a white man that might have been a concern for you. I think there's another reason. I think you and I both know what that reason is."

"We do?"

"So you're saying this ridiculous attempt to hide your true identity has nothing to do with your cousin?" She raised an eyebrow.

I cocked my head, following her interpretation like a cat to a laser beam, almost there, but losing it before I could fully grasp it, then catching it again. "You mean, like I attempted to shy away from that connection? That's one of the reasons, I guess."

"Precisely. That's why you didn't even use your own name. 'Edward Moore,'" she said, sotto voce. "You pulled a Harold Danforth, didn't you? Just like Charlotte. It's genius. It really is." She removed her glasses and laid them on the table. "You wanted the play to have an origin story of its own, not to ride on the coattails of those who have come before you. You didn't want all your . . . privileges, so to speak, to get in the way." She gestured towards me at the word *privileges*. "And yes, considering how *charged* this work is, I *completely* get why you'd want to keep your identity hidden. That's the real answer, correct?"

"Uhhh . . . perhaps?" Well, actually, absolutely not at all.

"It's a shame you got your friend to cover for you. I could smell a fish, you see. I just have this . . . instinct. An instinct for authenticity. I turned down the script the first time around for *that reason alone*. I believe whatever is meant to be will be, and that it's no coincidence you're finally here, as you are." She smiled.

"I . . . umm." I was momentarily stunned, though still holding my composure. I could definitely see where the nickname Smarmy Helen originated from. "Look. It's not that complicated. I just had a bout of imposter syndrome and I was afraid that I was writing something I didn't have the authority to write about."

"Imposter Syndrome begone." She swatted her hand as if to shoo the psychological phenomenon out of the room. "You have a gift. We all know that everybody loves the underdog, and you tried that angle. But Hugo . . . authenticity is key. That is how you unlock doors. Otherwise, congratulations for being the most experimental playwright to ever get your foot in the Wentworth doors. This is a story we can laugh about one day, isn't it?"

"I suppose." I scratched the back of my neck. "I mean . . . what are the chances this whole 'Edward Moore' thing will ever be spoken about? Because I do find it rather embarrassing now, and I'd like to protect my friend's decency. It was never her idea, so she doesn't need it following her."

"You've got nothing to worry about. Our agency doesn't have a reputation for letting talent slip through its fingers. Nobody is to know that this script was once rejected, just as much as you don't want anybody to find out. We're starting afresh, right here, right now. How does that sound?"

I nodded, breathing. "Good," I replied. "Sounds good."

After Helen's insanely presumptuous spiel, she summarised what the next six months were likely to look like and how and when the production of the play would commence. She gave me a breakdown of how the budget would work and how long rehearsals would run. She said she had her eye on the perfect candidate for the director: Nahid Norouzi, a seasoned actress who had shown an interest in making a debut from behind the curtain. If all went as planned, she would be one of the first women to get a directorial position on a Wentworth play in years, and the second-ever woman of colour to boot. Still baby steps, but at least they were getting somewhere. Helen told me it would hopefully be somewhat of a collaborative process between me, the director, the producer, general manager, and so on. With every minute I sat in that office, everything was becoming more and more real to me, and I felt nauseous. What the actual fuck had I got myself into?

I felt dazed after the meeting. I immediately picked my phone up and called you, relaying everything that had just occurred as I walked through the city streets. Despite all this being a clear red alert for a potential case of plagiarism, such a case had not been brought up. Helen must have seen the photos of you and me from the ceremony, and she knew that at the least, you were privy to whatever boundaries this morphing play traversed. Ironically, your attempt to initially submit the play under a different name had helped you in this instance, because Helen was under the impression that it was I who was the rightful owner and that you were the fraud, or at the least, a performer in the show of *Whose Play Is It Anyway?*

"I genuinely don't get this woman's thought process," I said to you over the phone once I'd brought you into the loop. "She thinks the name change is genius. She's rewarding me for the same thing she essentially punished you for. And this whole C. H. Edmonds thing—I haven't even spoken to my cousin in, like two years. We're not even close. She hasn't even reached out to me since the win, for fuck's sake."

"I've got nothing to add. I saw this coming from as far away as Andromeda," you said. "I'm not remotely surprised. It's all so typical. Isn't it just?"

That word, *typical*, was so dismissive, yet weighty with the understanding that you were never going to be as shocked as I was in that moment. *Typical* was shorthand for *life is a zero-sum game, and the winners have already been chosen.*

X

Down to Earth

I had known Belle since we were both around thirteen. We went to the same school and floated around the same social circles, and our fathers were both partners at Pointon & Sumner. Even then, she was not on my radar for the majority of our adolescence. As most people at school did, I saw her as one of the many sought-after girls in our year, always in and out of relationships with one of the many sought-after boys. I was socially awkward for the first two years of secondary school, but things changed in year nine when I was finally integrated into the sports culture à la the rugby team. I'd accrued an appreciable level of notoriety due to my penchant for saying yes to everything—downing an unidentified amalgamation of alcoholic beverages from a shoe at a match after-party, collecting traffic cones as souvenirs, toilet-papering a friend's ex's house—you name it, I'd do it. Come year eleven, it wasn't much of a surprise to find out that I'd been nominated for prom king, and the same could be said for Belle being in the running for prom queen. I rode the high of being the most revered kid in school. It felt great to be seen, and even better to be seen side by side with a gorgeous blonde. It was a golden time in my adolescence, when I learned there was currency in attention. It didn't matter what the attention was for, as long as it was celebratory. I sometimes cringe when I think back to those days. But the jubilant hollers, the pats on the back, the warm embraces, and the everlasting kisses, they remain rose-tinted in my memory. Up until that point, Belle and I had barely shared a conversation that didn't revolve around our maths, history, or chemistry classes for longer than five minutes, but we both found ourselves standing together onstage with our sashes and crowns, winners of the ultimate popularity contest. We ended up at a mutual friend's post-prom celebration, where we shared a series of Jägermeister-flavoured kisses, and the rest was history. We spent two years in sixth-form college walking hand in hand around the hallways, taking the role of the insufferable yet undeniably well-suited and attractive couple who couldn't spend more than one second apart.

The tides turned when it came to picking universities and we realised that we had completely different geographical desires. Durham was her first choice for politics, philosophy, and economics, and I was banking on Oxford for law with UCL as my runner-up and my eventual fate. The following three years were spent long-distance, sewing together our many miles apart with frequent FaceTime conversations and monthly visits on the train to each other's campuses. But it would be a lie to say everything was smooth sailing; there were points in our relationship when object permanence would fall apart for me, and it would take a friend's mention of her in passing or an evening text to snap me back to her. By the time we graduated, she felt a bit more like an old friend than a girlfriend, and the apertures in our relationship started to form. It was a case of people realising before we did, however. People including my closest friend, Damian.

• • •

I rocked up to his house on a quiet August evening, rich in the milieu of a pink-and-blue sky, about a week after the bizarre Wentworth meeting. Even though Damian lived a stone's throw from me over in Fulham, he said he didn't want me to be the first person to turn up to my own celebration drinks. He waited for his girlfriend, Georgia, to arrive and for a small cluster of my university friends to roll through one by one to set up the lounge with balloons and kitsch party decor. Andrew, Damian's housemate, opened the door a few moments after I knocked. I was met with the smell of something piquant cooking in the kitchen, and there was an immediate chorus of "Congratulations" once everyone was made aware of my arrival. Johan, my fellow UCL law comrade, was the first to stand up and greet me with a hug. His sister Klara followed, and then so did Olivia, Matej, James, and Lucas. Emmy, Belle's best friend from Durham, had also made it to the party. Olivia and Matej went to grab some glasses and a bottle of 2011 Taittinger from the kitchen. At this rate, I was convinced my blood would eventually be full of at least 40 percent bubbly. We all gathered in the middle of Damian's lounge just in time for him to raise a toast to me in my brand-new, absolutely bonkers, totally authentic, totally deserved career path.

"I'd like to raise a toast to my best friend. I think it's safe to say we didn't see it coming, but clearly my boy's full of secrets. Next thing you know we'll be celebrating his coming out of the closet." He grinned, grabbing my shoulder with his free hand as a murmur of laughs followed. "He told no one about this play—not even me, the oldest mate he has. I thought we had a deal back in after-school drama club in year five that we'd keep each other in the loop when we eventually climbed the ranks of success, but I think I can forgive him this one time. I'd like to stay in his good books. At least until the prize money runs out." Another laugh from the crowd. "Seriously. Congrats, brother. I'm proud of you. I always knew you were destined for greater things. So, let's drink to that. Cheers."

With that, glasses clinked and our cozy congregation whooped and hollered. Klara grabbed the TV remote to start playing music on Spotify as everyone split into conversations. I floated around the room, dipping into a chat with Matej and James before jumping into Lucas and Klara's one-on-one. Then Georgia suggested we play a drinking game while Andrew ran into the kitchen to get his homemade pizza out of the oven. We sat on all the free sofa spaces and the stragglers got the armrests, balancing their drinks on their knees.

"Let's have a go at Never Have I Ever, shall we?" Georgia declared. "We don't have to explain the rules to that one."

"I wouldn't put it past Lucas. Just a reminder: you take a shot if you *have* done said thing, okay?" James said, followed by a light "Fuck off" from the target of his teasing.

"Okay, okay. Who wants to go first?" Georgia asked.

"I will!" Klara piped up. "Let's start off easy. Never have I ever . . . written a play." She looked at me, beaming with mirth. I took a modest swig of my champagne, which was technically a transgression of the rules of the game. I hoped that wherever you were, your taste buds were awash with a rich carbonated Chardonnay, balanced with notes of peach, cherimoya, and mandarin peel and hinted with almonds.

"All right, my turn," Lucas started. "Never have I ever . . . lost my passport in Chile three days before my flight back to the UK and had to apply for an emergency travel document."

"I think I'm being singled out here a bit," I responded, going in for a second gulp.

"That's sort of the point. It's your party, Hu," he said.

"Well let's switch it up a bit before my whole life story unravels in front of us."

Klara laughed at my joke and rested her head on my shoulder just as Andrew entered the room with a tray of mushroom and truffle oil sourdough slices.

"Oh! I've got one!" Emmy lifted her hand up like a student in class, then used the same hand to grab a portion of pizza from the travelling platter. "Never have I ever . . . gone engagement-ring window-shopping before."

I stayed still, hoping everyone wouldn't think it was something I had to drink to. But Emmy wouldn't stop looking at me, and when she lifted an eyebrow and tilted her head forwards, everybody else caught on. This was no longer a drinking game, but an exposé on the workings of my impulsive life decisions.

"You're going to *propose* to Belle?" Klara gasped, turning to me. "Shit! It's about time."

"We always knew you'd be the first one down the aisle. You're so whipped." Johan laughed.

"I think you mean at the altar, he's not the bride," Lucas said.

"He may not be the bride, but I don't think he wears the trousers either," Johan bantered.

"Hold your horses, you lot. I was just . . . curious. Nothing's set in stone. Emmy, come on." I looked at her, shaking my head.

"Whoops. Sorry. Slip of the tongue," she replied, snickering. "I'm just already planning my maid of honour dress is all."

I saw Damian shoot me a look from across the room. I couldn't help but notice he wasn't as enthused as everyone else. I felt the buzz of my phone in my back trouser pocket and took it out, seeing a push notification from Instagram. With consummate timing, Belle had posted a new photo. It would have been quarter to three in the morning where she was, but she was willing to stay up just to make sure she'd hit peak follower traffic. My thumb hovered over her, hanging midair on the famous rice terrace swing in Bali. I was about to double-tap the screen but was snapped out of it by the sound of Emmy's voice. "You haven't drunk yet, Hugo!" she barked. "Drink!"

And drink I did. Eventually the questions were divvied up between the other participants, so it wasn't just me in the hot seat. It didn't take long for the room to fill with a level of rambunctiousness that almost levelled with our undergrad days. Soon after, Georgia, Olivia, and Lucas were dancing, and Emmy, Klara, and Andrew were having a drunken DMC on the sofa nearby. Johan and James agreed to do a run for more alcohol before the store closed, and Matej called it a night and left with them, giving me a final congratulations on the way out. I sauntered into the kitchen to grab some water to cancel out my blood-champagne levels when I encountered Damian, leaning on one of the counters as he dug into some reheated leftover food. I could tell by his stature that he was a little drunker than I was.

"So when's the wedding, then?" he asked, stuffing a forkful of chicken and rice in between his greased-up lips.

I turned on the tap at the sink, filled a glass three-quarters of the way, and took a cautious swig. "I haven't proposed to her. Emmy just pulled that out of her arse."

"Why did you drink to the prompt?"

"I don't know." I shrugged.

"So you're not going to propose?"

"Maybe one day."

Damian snorted. "Hugo. You can bullshit everyone in the world, but you can't bullshit me."

"What do you mean?"

"I know you don't love her anymore." He placed his Tupperware bowl on the walnut wooden worktop next to him and crossed his arms, looking straight at me.

"Come on, Dame. You know that's not true. We've been together for nearly seven years. It's not going to be a honeymoon at this point, is it?" I was glad to hear a song by the Clash start blaring loudly in the living room, drowning out the potential for any eavesdropping.

"You know that's not what I mean. I've been with George for half that time and it's yet to feel like a chore to be around her."

"My relationship isn't a fucking chore."

"Look. I'm just saying that I know deep down you're not going to marry her. And if you did, it'd probably be for everyone else more than it would be for you or her."

"Damian—"

"Deep down you're relieved that you're not travelling with her, aren't you? I mean, I get it. You're a down-to-earth lad. You're not in it for the Instagram or Twitter followers, or whatever. It's not like you went online and started blasting off about your award, but she did straightaway."

"I think you're being really harsh on her and I don't appreciate it," I rebutted.

"Nah, mate. I'm looking out for you. You've spent the last couple of years on autopilot with Belle, even if you don't realise it. But I think you're moving in the right direction, leaving law and all that. You're figuring out who you really are, which is good to see. I'm hoping that'll bleed into your relationships."

"Oh God. Don't be such a condescending twat."

Damian shook his head, poking the inside of his cheek with his tongue. "I'm just saying. You don't need to fake being in love. You can find the real thing, brother. You're gonna have a line of women at your feet once you hit the West End, you know."

"I highly doubt that."

"See? Down-to-earth." He smirked. Seconds later, the sound of the front door swinging open was accompanied by the crinkle and clinking of bottles in plastic bags and a muffled conversation between Johan and James. "Just think hard about it," Damian said in a low voice as the boys got closer to us. "Fuck weddings, fuck autopilot, and fuck fake love."

I felt the water on my feet before I heard the smash on the tiled flooring. My palm had produced enough sweat for me to lose the grip on my glass. I was standing there like a Pompeii victim, frozen in the pumice from the volcano of my own embarrassment. Johan and James walked into the kitchen at the same time, letting out a big "wheyyy" in unison at the sound of the glass smashing. Damian laughed before offering to help me clean up the mess. Klara and Georgia soon bustled into the room in response to the commotion, followed by Emmy and Olivia.

"Whoa, whoa, whoa, hold on, everyone. There's glass all over the place. Watch your feet," Damian declared, going for the dustpan and brush in the cupboard under the sink.

During the commotion, I was still processing what he had just said to me about Belle. More than anything, I wanted your input on the whole situation; my best friend's words just weren't enough anymore. Who knew—maybe being in a stable relationship with a beautiful blonde borderline social media influencer was a good look for a budding playwright with a burgeoning career. Maybe it was good PR. Maybe you'd appreciate it. Despite finding myself toying with this narrative, it all didn't matter in the end. Soon enough, our master plan might have begun to fall apart, just as it was falling into place.

• • •

"It was love at first sight. It really was. Of course, I'm also terrified, but I'm excited to fall into this," the newly appointed director of *Great Belonging* said to everyone in one of the Wentworth meeting rooms.

"Absolutely amazing. I'm so glad to know how passionate you are about this, and we cannot wait to have you on this project," Helen responded, grinning widely. The primary roster of those who were going to be working on the production, and I, were all assembled under the same roof like some kind of onboarding day. Of course, I didn't recognise any familiar faces; this was despite the lists of features and accolades that prefaced them when they broke the ice by relaying their accomplished backgrounds. One thing was for sure, though—let's just say that most people in this room did not represent the diversity of the cast in any substantial way. As you might say: typical.

I listened intently, trying to absorb as much information as my law-degree-soiled brain could, making sure not to give the impression that I did indeed have absolutely no idea who anyone in this room was by virtue of our supposed shared interests. I had laid my phone face down on the table in front of me on Do Not Disturb mode, covertly recording everything on the voice memo app. For obvious reasons, it was not generally recommended to put the play at risk by potentially leaking its behind-the-scenes processes to the public before it got to the main stage. Still, you wanted to know exactly what was going on, and I didn't think my furious scribbling of every spoken word would be any more practical or less conspicuous. It was clear to me that everyone was genuinely excited to get this show on the road based on their extolling the genius of your work. Meanwhile, I was already counting down the days until we would take our final bow to the crowds at the Regium Theatre, when you and I would storm the stage and reveal the truth. I knew that meant I was also counting down the days until I made a fool out of every single person in this room. It was a heavy feeling that felt tenfold heavier every time I made eye contact with the new director.

She sat opposite me, three seats to my left. Leaning forwards with her elbows propped on the table, she had her hands clasped together in moments of silence. It was like she was conducting her very own personal prayer, hoping to the Gods Above that she was destined for the jackpot with this new project. She was so animated whenever she spoke, her big brown eyes bouncing around every face in the room as she fluctuated between an enrapt expression and an enthused laugh. One of the first things I noticed about her was her crooked grin, accentuated with soft dimples that formed below the corners of her mouth. Her dark shaggy pixie cut framed her face like a portrait and lengthened her slender neck, and her collarbones were adorned with a minimalist gold necklace that swung like a pendulum with every move she made. It was just as much of a convenience for me as it was for you to have my phone recording everything; it was one thing to concentrate with all this information overload, but the categorically stunning woman in front of me wasn't helping either.

It had now been around six weeks since the win, and Helen had recently sent out an email announcing the lucky participants who would help bring this story to life. I forwarded it to you a few days before the meeting, hoping you might have a better understanding of who the new producer, stage manager, and, of course, the director would be. You sent me a text with your two cents not long after scouring the list.

[11:25] **Eddie:** Nahid Norouzi? Isn't she an actress? I'd have preferred a seasoned director, or someone with at least one play under their belt.

[11:25] **Eddie:** Also, she's not black. The fictional country in the play is clearly modelled on an African colony. Does that not mean anything to them?

[11:30] **Hugo:** You never know, she might do it justice. I'm sure they know what they're doing

[11:32] **Eddie:** You have way too much faith in the system for someone helping to shed light on its BS :/

[11:35] **Hugo:** I'm not saying they're right. I don't know. But this woman has been in the industry for nearly ten years apparently, and she's been in a lot of quite political stuff by the looks of it

[11:50] **Eddie:** That's true. She also happens to be married to a big shot theatre director. You don't think that has anything to do with it ???

[12:00] **Hugo:** IDK. I think we should give them the benefit of the doubt.

[12:01] **Eddie:** We're NOT giving them the benefit of the doubt. We're studying them. *You're* studying them. It's in your best interest to look at everything with a sharp eye.

[12:15] **Hugo:** All right! I will. Let's just see how the meeting goes

[12:15] **Eddie:** Lovely. Also, can you do me a huuuge favour when you get in there please?

[12:17] **Hugo:** Uh yeh?

[12:19] **Eddie:** Don't make it obvious, but go on the voice memo app—

After the meeting, Helen caught me in the lobby. She was standing with Owen Kelly, the new general manager; Victor Matthews, the producer; and Nahid. Although I tried my best to slither away once the onboarding process was over, I should have known it wouldn't be that easy.

"How do you feel about everything, Hugo? I'm sure you're just as excited as we are, aren't you?" Helen beamed at me.

"Of course I am. This is something I never saw happening all so quickly." I shook my head. "It's a bit dizzying, if I'm honest."

"Tell me about it," Nahid interjected. "I've spent so much of my time on the stage that the thought of going behind it can feel a little bit overwhelming. I totally get you." She looked up at me sympathetically. "It's also Victor's first time in his role. We're all doing something new here. That's exactly what makes it exciting." She wore a black Bardot-neck jumper that exposed her shoulders. With her arms crossed, the jewel that adorned her ring finger rested on the front of her right biceps. Even from my periphery, it was hard to miss.

"Why don't you get together and pick each other's brains a bit before we start casting and rehearsals? It would definitely help with the creative process," Helen said, addressing the four of us. "You've all got a lot to learn from one another. But we're on a pretty tight timeline, so the sooner you put your heads together, the better. Remember, casting starts in three weeks. Let's jump right into this."

Before leaving, Nahid quickly pulled me aside and asked me if I was free for a lunchtime coffee, where we could properly introduce ourselves and exchange our visions for the play. I didn't have much to do that day besides the meeting, so I took her up on the offer. Any free time I had I usually cherished, but I felt compelled to follow her that day.

We ended up in a café near the Barbican, where she continued to sing your praises, thinking they were mine. She told me how much the idea of turbulent citizenship resonated with her, having herself been banned from ever returning to her home country. Seven years prior, the Iranian government had found out about her role in a play in Scotland about the persecution of women in an unnamed Islamic nation. They saw it as the ultimate transgression of their moral standing and could no longer allow her to set foot on their soil. At that point, she had made a name for herself in the British theatre world, and she had a steadily strengthening platform. Losing her motherland was evidently the price she had to pay for it.

"Did you see what happened last year? When that woman was arrested at the airport in Tehran with her toddler on the way back to the UK?" Nahid asked as she stirred a sachet of brown sugar into her Americano. "Her name's Nazanin . . . I can't remember her surname. She had just been celebrating *Nowruz* with her family, and that was how it ended. It's been a year and a half, and she's still in prison. God knows when she'll make it out. *If* she will. I can't help but feel that . . . that could have easily been me. If I had gone back, they could have made even more of an example of me than they already have. I don't think it's something they should be able to get away with."

"Nazanin Zaghari-Ratcliffe. I remember hearing about that on the news," I responded. "They said she'd attempted to overthrow the government, or something like that, right? It's terrible, I know. I can totally see why this script resonated with you. It's something all too familiar to you."

"Yeah. I hope I do this play justice." She smiled at me. "I just need to know how you came up with this story. It's so wonderful; it feels so vivid, so real. You set the tone perfectly, and the stage direction is so crisp. How you managed to explore the nuances of immigration in such a captivating way is simply phenomenal, considering you aren't an immigrant yourself."

"If I hear one more compliment today, I think my head's going to turn into a helium balloon. Please stop," I said, and my heart sang when she laughed. Any compliment coming from her felt wrong not to embrace, like a warm hug. I tried to forget about the fact that I was a fraud, and that the other shoe was bound to drop at some point. "In all seriousness, though, I just did a lot of research. I read the right books, watched the right movies. I had a bit of help from some of my online writing friends. This one friend, Eddie—she's been particularly help-ful. Especially with the world-building aspects of the colonial island."

"It's nice to collaborate with other writers sometimes. You'll be surprised what can come out of it."

"Definitely. Especially being so new to all this. I think I just fell into the right hands." Or out of the right vagina, you'd opine.

Nahid and I trod deeper and deeper into conversation, weaving personal anecdotes with our opinions on the state of the theatre industry. I learned so much about her on that first day: her father had been a screenwriter who was detained during the Iranian Revolution and held for three years. Once he was a free man again, he met her mother, a schoolteacher from Qarchak. They married, and Nahid came along six years after the country's metamorphosis. She spent her infancy in Germany, where her parents had two more children, Salman and Farid. Then in 1989, they moved to Bristol, where they still resided. Her father became a dentist and her mother became a beautician. It was when she stumbled upon her father's screenplays from back when they were living in Berlin that something clicked inside her brain. This was the life she wanted—the life he couldn't have. Her newfound desire for acting eventually brought her to the Royal Academy of Dramatic Art, and the rest was history.

Before we both knew it, two and a half hours had passed in the café, yet I didn't want the conversation to end. I was vividly aware that we had only just met, and maybe my partiality towards her beauty was getting in the way of what was just a jovial professional rendezvous, but I soaked it in all the same. In the midafternoon we parted ways near Farringdon Station, back into our own daily lives. Upon our sayonara, we moved from our initial handshake greeting territory to a goodbye hug, and even in that gesture I felt like a schoolboy moving up to second base. I had no idea what had got into me, but I didn't want it to get out. With Nahid, it was love at first sight. It really was.

XI

Strictly Professional

That same week, Belle arrived back in London. I picked her up from Heathrow Airport on a Friday afternoon, and I was admittedly over-come with happiness at the sight of her hauling her suitcases out of Arrivals. We embraced each other for what felt like minutes and kissed for what felt like longer. Her hair was brighter, blonder, and wavier than before, and she was glowing with a dewy bronze tan; she was a real-life Barbie, which I guess made me her Ken. As we travelled to her house in Shepherd's Bush, our conversation was interrupted by a third wheel in the form of a GoPro camera. She would turn and speak to me, then to the camera, then to me, and so on. She said it was mainly B-roll for her next vlog upload and she'd be editing out most of what she recorded, and I said that was fine. Lying is too easy sometimes. You and I know that, don't we?

So much had changed in the three and a half months since I'd last seen her. After all, she was coming back to a boyfriend who had de-ferred his legal practice course and was now a man of art and culture. She'd never been a sucker for such—the closest she'd ever been to being a theatre fanatic was when she attended the *Billy Andromeda* spin-off debut with me—but she was willing to give me the benefit of the doubt with my new endeavour, considering how much of a huge deal I'd made of the MBGs. She was elated when she found out that I had actually won; I could hear her excitement over the phone during our subsequent FaceTime call. I knew that whatever happened from this point on, she was bound to be my cheerleader, and it was something I did appreciate. Whether or not it was sincere was neither here nor there for me, and I think it was because I wouldn't feel as bad if it wasn't. Somewhere in my mind Damian's words from the party echoed, and I didn't want him to be right, but I also didn't care if he was. I wanted Belle and me to work regardless, and that was the decision I had come to upon her return.

Later that evening, we went to eat at a sushi restaurant in Soho. It was a Date Night with a capital *D* and *N*, and we both pulled out all the stops in the wardrobe department. She wore a silky cream halterneck camisole that was ruched at the midriff and an ivory-coloured bouclé miniskirt accentuated with gold buttons. On her feet were the rhinestone Steve Madden heels I had got her for her twenty-second birthday. I had fished for my best shirt and suit jacket, slicking my hair back with a touch of gel and donning the small chain necklace she had gifted me for Christmas. As we walked hand in hand through the London streets, everything felt so familiar and all my qualms melted away.

Belle was the love of my life—yes, sometimes there are doubts, but that's all they are, right? We're fine. See, look at us! We're having so much fun with one another, feeding each other tempura shrimp rolls and sashimi with chopsticks she's amusedly teaching me to use. Look at us, laughing and flirting, giggling and making eyes at one another. Look at us, ordering a taxi back to mine and ripping our clothes off the second we shut the front door. Look at us racing to my bedroom and falling onto the bed, writhing all over each other, leaving kisses on every surface of our faces and necks. Look at us, in the midst of reunion sex—arguably the *best* kind of sex—and cherishing every second of it. Look at us, our groans and moans harmonising as we oscillate between the sheets, getting closer to climax. We're fine. See? I've even made her finish before me! That's a rare occurrence, I must admit. I mean, I just haven't finished yet because I want this to last forever. Okay, I know she's over it now, but that's because she's had a long day. I just need a bit more time, I'm getting there, I swear. We're fine, see? She's not sighing because she's annoyed, she's just tired, it's fine! She's not confused at all, or worried that she can't make me come, and neither am I. Ah, look—she's suggesting helping me out with a good old blowie—that always does the trick. I have my eyes closed and I run my hands through her hair, and it's working, it's working! I'm getting there! It's not like in my mind, her hair is darker, shorter, and curlier. It's not like I'm envisioning her eyes as a glimmering black-coffee brown, or her mouth to be accentuated with soft dimples, or her grin to be crooked. It's not like that's why I end up finishing. That would be absurd—fucked up, to be exact. That could never happen. We're fine, see?

• • •

We had hundreds of videotape auditions to sieve through once the casting process was underway in September. As the producer and director, Victor and Nahid got the final word on who got the callbacks. I was still given the chance to add my input, however, so I attended the auditions for the lead role as well as the main supporting cast. I still found a way to record the auditions secretly, but it came with the disadvantage of you only hearing the potential actors' voices and not seeing them. This was fortunately salvageable by way of Victor sending out an email listing the profiles of the top contenders present at the auditions, so I made sure to match the faces to the voices when I got back to you. I worked as a conduit, relaying your justifications for the right selections as best I could. You clearly had your finger on the pulse even with your limitations of not being there—Victor and Nahid agreed with every single choice you made. Additionally, this meant that Nahid was particularly commendatory towards my natural knack for assigning the right actors, and I was swimming in her praise, no matter how undeserved it was.

One day after we had finalised the cast and rehearsals were soon to begin, Nahid, Victor, and I went out for drinks in the London Bridge area, revelling in our anticipation for what was to come. After about ninety minutes, Victor had another commitment to attend and left the two of us inside the warmly lit vaulted cellar bar. We moved over to a booth spot, where it was more comfortable and less exposed. Our conversation continued.

"This . . . sort of feels like a date," I said, after taking a big swig of my craft beer. "I mean, I know it's not, it just feels like it."

Nahid's face fell, then she smiled softly. "It *is* a date. A work date, of course. Strictly professional." She held her wine, rubbing on the glass with her index finger.

"One thousand percent. I don't think I'd take anyone on a date here anyway. This is far too pedestrian."

"Where do you take your girlfriend? The Shard, I bet." She grinned.

My heart jumped at her mention of Belle. "I'd prefer the Collins Room at the Berkeley. It's a tad more regal," I replied.

"But the view from the Shangri-La! How could you ever top that?"

"I guess you're right. London does look really beautiful at night."

"It does," she agreed. "Shall we maybe go for a walk by the river and soak it up for a bit?"

"That's a great idea. Let's do that." I nodded. "We still have quite a bit of our drinks left, though."

Nahid shrugged. "Fuck it. Let's chug them. Are you ready?"

"Readier than I'll ever be," I replied.

"Okay. Three . . . two . . . one . . ."

The chugging definitely worked. As we picked up our pace striding past Borough Market, I could already feel the fuzziness take over me. We got to the embankment and sat on the benches near the rails for another forty minutes or so, watching the boats slowly glide by. We chatted about anything and everything, and I was savouring every moment of it. There was no yesterday or tomorrow, just there and then. She put her hands in her coat pockets as the temperature gradually dipped and the wind from the water started to pick up. It took every bone in my body not to take them into mine to keep them warm. When she rested her head on my shoulder, it was like the whole world had gone silent.

"I should probably head home soon," she mumbled quietly before yawning. "I'm pretty spent."

"That's fair. I'm tired too," I lied. I could have sat there forever.

She lifted her head and looked at me, smiling. "I've really enjoyed today. It was fun. You know, I was so nervous about all this—worried I was going to fumble my first shot at directing, but . . . everyone's made me feel so welcome. *You've* made me feel so welcome. I appreciate it."

"You're going to smash this," I told her. "There's nothing to be worried about."

"Thank you. I think . . . well, obviously my husband's an amazing director, and I didn't want people to think that's the only reason I got this gig. You know, like, he put in a good word for me or something. I guess the public might come to that conclusion, and so be it if they do. But I want to prove myself to everyone involved in the production. I want to prove myself to *you*, the mastermind, the reason I'm even in this position in the first place. Most importantly, I want to prove to myself that I'm capable, too. I want to prove I was right to pursue my dreams of directing."

"I'm not the reason you're here, Nahid. *You* are. I'm a twentysomething who took a risk. You've got a whole scroll of experience."

"Please don't remind me how old you are." She sighed, shaking her head. "I know I was a twentysomething not that long ago, but it's like once you hit your thirties your days are basically numbered."

"If it's any consolation, you don't look a day past twenty-five," I said with a shrug, raising an eyebrow.

She burst into a quick laugh. "I'd have preferred twenty-one, but I'll take the compliment." She stood up, stretching. "Okay, I should head off now. It's been lovely hanging with you. See you at rehearsals, Hugo."

I followed suit, and was subsequently hit with a bout of dizziness. "I'll see you then," I said, going in for a hug. Her warmth was like an envelope I wanted to be folded into. We walked off in opposite directions, and around thirty metres ahead I quickly turned my head to watch her grow smaller and smaller with distance. It was too dark to tell, but I was convinced I saw a flash of her face as she did the same. Maybe it was wishful thinking, but the idea that it was was agonising. Once I was at home in bed, I googled the ever-loving shit out of her like a stalker possessed. She had a Wikipedia page that I'd initially visited when Helen had announced her involvement in the play, but I was now revisiting like a regular. Her Personal Life section was considerably short:

In 2010, Norouzi started a relationship with Scottish-Egyptian theatre director <u>Aaron Yousef</u> during the production of *The*

Adorned. The couple wed in early 2013 in a private ceremony.[67]
She currently resides in North London.[68]

Her husband was the director of the play that got her banned from Iran, and I couldn't help but find that interesting. Had she been willing to put her citizenship at risk for his vision because she loved him? Or was the love just a coincidence? Maybe they were just two like-minded people colliding. I wondered how well their marriage was going, then I mentally scolded myself, because why on earth should I care? It didn't change the fact that she was married, or that she was nine years my senior, or that she was my colleague, or most importantly, that I had a girlfriend. I shouldn't have cared how well her marriage was doing. *Strictly professional,* she had said. Anything otherwise would be wishful thinking, just like the hope that she'd also turned to look back at me upon our farewell at the riverbank. The thought that I was in this feeling alone was maddening. Of course I wanted it to be requited, even if it never went anywhere. I wanted to feel justified in my diversion from Belle, otherwise it was all for nothing. But realistically I knew that my diversion from Belle was independent of my affinity towards Nahid. They ran parallel, yes, but they weren't connected.

To make a long story short, I was screwed.

◆ ◆ ◆

October 2017

"It's the end of the world. What's the last song you're listening to before your demise?"

"'Plastic Love' by Mariya Takeuchi. What about yours?"

"Hmm. Probably 'Georgy Porgy' by Toto."

"Well, that tracks."

"What's that supposed to mean?"

"Your favourite song is a Toto song. It tracks."

"Yeah, and I saw Japanese city pop being up there for you from a mile away."

You looked at me. "No, you didn't."

"You're right," I conceded. "I didn't."

We were walking up Primrose Hill like the first time we had nearly a year prior. Only this time we weren't strangers, but comrades on a mission together. We had ambled up the terrain until we reached the summit and planted ourselves on the grass, balancing our coffees in the process. You started rolling a cigarette as we talked, eventually landing on our music tastes. We had been discussing the logistics of the rehearsals that were due to start in less than a week, when the Regium Theatre would become my second home for a span of two months. I suggested asking the crew to let you join in on some sessions as a close friend who I could trust to keep things quiet, but you were worried that your presence might still be slightly too intrusive. Although it pained you not to get a front-row seat to rehearsals on your own accord, you argued it was better that I continued as the spy, coming back to you with any pertinent information I had. With that understanding, you had to trust me to be honest with how everything was going, and I promised I would be. Everything had to be smooth sailing until the Grand Reveal, when we knew that even if the play was eventually disqualified and the award rescinded, we had managed to hold a mirror up to everyone. As a spy I had to emotionally remove myself from the situation—I was simply just another moving part. There was just one teeny, weeny problem.

A few days prior I had found a filmed recording of *The Adorned* in the Regium Theatre archives online. It was a wonder watching Nahid in her element, commanding the stage. It was no surprise she won Best New Actress at the MBGs that year. The fact that I'd never heard of her up until this point felt criminal, but in my defence I was too busy partaking in initiation challenges for my sixth-form college's sports team at the time. It wasn't until my final year of uni when I decided I missed that world, only for it to be too late. When I met you, I realised I must have been holding on to a glimmer of it, and now I was rediscovering my love for drama from the inside. In a twisted way, I *was* acting.

I wondered what Nahid would think of me when she found out the truth. Would she understand, or would she be revolted by my masquerade? Would she get that it was all for a greater goal, or would she see me as a talentless, attention-seeking con man? I guess we'd cross that bridge when we got to it, even if that bridge was starting to feel more and more like it was made of weathered rope, suspended above disaster.

"We should make a collaborative playlist for our inevitable Armageddon. What do you think?" you asked me, inhaling your roll-up.

"Go ahead. Let's see where we meet in the middle. Maybe there's one song we could both die happy hearing when the asteroid hits."

"Hmm. You like jazz?"

"I dabble."

"I bet you're a classical music fiend."

"Why?"

"You don't want me to answer that question."

"A lot of Labour supporters are middle class, you know. If you think about it, the majority of the working class are probably more likely to vote Conservative than they are to blast Brahms or Debussy on the regular."

"You bring up a good point, Hughey. Now I feel bad for making fun of you."

"It's okay, I'll survive."

After taking a final sip from your coffee, you placed it down beside you and looked out at the horizon. "Look how far we've come. Two years ago, you were staring over at my laptop screen in a café. Now we're besties," you said.

"I prefer the term 'BFFs.'"

"Let's get matching charm bracelets with our initials on them!"

"I say we get matching jumpers and we wear them everywhere."

"Sorted."

I asked you how things were at home now that you had moved back in with your mother. It was going well; you were no longer waitering and had a decent-paying freelance job for an online feminist zine. It wouldn't be a stretch to say that the fifteen thousand pounds I deposited into your account from mine a short while after the awards had made life that little bit easier, too; the immense financial pressure you felt a year ago had been lifted for the meantime. You were still going strong with your girlfriend, who was promoting the release of her band's debut album in December, and I was invited to the launch party. It would be the first time I'd meet Blue in the flesh, which I was excited about. When you asked me about Belle, I feigned comfort in our relationship. I told you that since her return we had been closer than ever. I wasn't completely wrong—outside of my preparation for rehearsals and meeting up with you, I'd committed myself to spending more time with her. It didn't change the fact that every time I closed my eyes, I saw someone else.

After a while at the park, you declared that you had to go and meet with your friend Lydia and her on-and-off boyfriend for a bottomless brunch. I was left wondering what to do, where to go, who to see. As wrong as I knew it was, I found myself messaging that someone else, just on the off chance she was free to hang out—strictly professionally, of course. When I saw the three moving dots pop up under her name on iMessage, I was caught in a limbo of regret and anticipation. But nothing could have prepared me for what was to come.

[12:46] **Nahid:** Hi Hu, how's it going! I'm not free today, unfortunately

[12:46] **Nahid:** it's Aaron's birthday. We're throwing a small get together this evening

[12:46] **Hugo:** Absolutely no worries. Give him my best wishes!

[12:48] **Nahid:** I will, thank you! :)

[22:03] **Nahid:** [voice message] 02 minutes 06 seconds

[22:07] **Nahid:** [voice message] 01 minute 17 seconds

[22:15] **Nahid:** Oh God. sorry for the rant, i've had a few to drink

[22:15] **Nahid:** Ignore those

[22:17] **Nahid:** Long story short, Aaron's going up to Scotland to visit his family for ten days soon

[22:19] **Nahid:** If you want we could maybe hang out then?

[22:30] **Nahid:** Ahh fuck

[22:31] **Nahid:** I'm overstepping my boundaries aren't I

[22:31] **Nahid:** Nvm

[22:32] **Nahid:** I'll see yu at rehearsals

[23:05] **Hugo:** Sorry, I just saw these. I hope you're enjoying yourself!

[23:05] **Hugo:** Hahaha, too late, listening right now

[23:10] **Hugo:** You're not overstepping anything! I asked you first

[23:12] **Hugo:** But maybe see how you feel in the morning?

[23:31] **Nahid:** You're right. I will

[23:32] **Nahid:** But I think I already know how I feel.

• • •

I knocked on her front door a few evenings later. Since our initial message exchange on the night of the party, we'd sort of snowballed into a regular back-and-forth, somehow sidestepping exactly what she'd drunkenly said but still making plans to rendezvous. When the time came I was a jittery mess, but I disguised it as warming myself up from the cold. She opened the door, welcomed me with open arms, and offered to take my jacket to hang in the hallway. I took my shoes off in the foyer and followed her into her kitchen. The house was a modern renovation with cool neutral tones in the interior design. There was something a bit too clinical about the layout for my liking, but I wasn't exactly going to take it up with the homeowner. Salvation came in the form of beguiling ornaments, paintings, and cultural artefacts that were plausibly tied to the Middle East. It was like I was in a museum, but everything on display actually belonged there.

"That smells amazing," I said to Nahid as I leaned over her island counter and watched her walk over to the stove.

"Thanks! It's chicken stew with pomegranate and walnuts. I couldn't be bothered to cook rice, so I've just got the microwave stuff, if that's okay with you." She took the lid off the casserole dish and slowly stirred the contents.

"You've ruined my day," I said, and I watched as she rolled her eyes, smiling. "I brought some wine with me, by the way. A nice white to celebrate the start of rehearsals tomorrow. Exciting times."

"Thank you. I'm shitting this, Hu," she suddenly blurted. "I won't lie. It's going to be so intense; I just know it." She stood leaning next to the stove with her arms crossed.

"Intense is good! People thrive in intense situations."

"I guess." She looked down at the floor, fiddling with her necklace. "I don't know. I just . . . ahhh, fuck. Never mind. Let me get the dinner ready." She jumped into action after a brief moment of desolation.

"You can tell me what's wrong."

"I don't know if I can. If I *should*." She pulled two plates out of one of the cabinets and took some cutlery from a drawer, whizzing past me to lay them on the dining table. I offered to bring the casserole dish and she accepted as she walked to the microwave to heat the rice. It was evident that she was trying her best to avoid whatever it was she wanted to say, and it brought a tense energy to the room.

Once the food was ready to dish up, she let me help myself to a serving before loading her own plate, and we sat opposite one another with our glasses of Chardonnay next to our meals. "This is called Fesenjān. It's usually made on special occasions, so I might have pushed the boat out a little bit. I hope you like it."

I took an exploratory spoonful of the stew and closed my eyes. "Wow. It's so good. I'm in love."

"You don't have to say that if you don't mean it."

"I mean it, Nahid. This is wonderful. It's so warm, and rustic, and zesty. You did an amazing job."

She smiled bashfully. "Thank you. I appreciate it."

"I'm assuming it's a recipe familiar to you?"

"Sort of. My mother does know how to cook it, but I just found a recipe online. I didn't tell you this because it would have been even more of a bummer of a conversation when we first met, but . . . I don't talk to my parents anymore. Not since the whole . . . you know, the ban. I still love them, though. We're just estranged."

I paused my chewing, then slowly resumed. "I'm sorry. That's awful. I hope that changes one day. I'm sure it will."

"God, I'm bringing the mood down again, aren't I?" She grimaced before taking a large swig of her wine. "Let's switch the topic. And after this we can watch something. Maybe a couple of episodes of *Inside No. 9*? I love that show."

"Sounds good to me." I nodded. "Anything you want I'm happy with."

"*Anything*?" She looked at me, suppressing a giggle.

I shrugged, grinning. "Within reason, of course. But I'm a glass of wine down now. Reason might not exactly be my forte."

"What a lightweight. I assumed a man of your stature could handle a drink or two." She smirked.

"A man of my stature?"

"Yes: tall, lean, sturdy. You seem like you can handle a lot."

"I *can* handle a lot. I'm a big boy."

She laughed. "Well, that's reassuring. Do you think you can handle me?" she asked. I found myself tongue-tied, my face starting to heat up and turn red. All I could do was make eye contact, until even that was too much. The tension in the room was stifling. A frown grew across her face. "Shit. Forget I said that."

"No, no. I'm sorry. Truth is . . . I *can* handle a lot, but . . . maybe you're the only exception," I said, smiling softly.

Once our meals were finished, we cleared the table and she washed the dishes while I sat and waited in the living room in an unbearable silence. When she was done, I topped up our glasses of wine before we moved to the living room sofa, where she faced me, resting her biceps on the top of the backrest and leaning her temple on her closed fist. "I'm still violently embarrassed about the messages I sent the other day. I haven't even dared to listen back to the voice notes," she said.

"Oh, I can't even repeat them to you."

"Why not?"

"The voice notes . . . they were interesting. You were very, very forward."

I saw a flash of terror in her eyes. "Fuck off. What did I say?"

"I'm joking." I laughed. "You just told me how the party was going and how you'd have taken up my offer to hang out if you could have. That you would have preferred to." It was true—she had mumbled something about how she wasn't really enjoying herself at the time, but I thought it was probably best to omit that part.

"Oh. Okay. Not too bad. I thought it was something aggressive or just nonsensical. Still, it's embarrassing. I don't consider myself to be a drunk texter, but apparently I am."

"I'm glad you drunk texted me," I admitted. "I felt a bit excited when I saw the notifications, you know. I just like seeing your name pop up on my screen."

"Oh. You do?" She looked at me with hopeful eyes. "Well, I'm glad you're glad I texted you."

"I'm glad you're glad I'm glad you texted me."

She giggled softly before suddenly frowning. "You're so lovely, Hugo. It's a problem. A *huge* problem."

"What do you mean?" I readjusted myself, moving closer to her.

"I don't want to elaborate right now. Just know that it frustrates me."

"I feel the same way about you."

She paused. "Look. *Great Belonging* is my chance to prove myself to everyone; I told you that before. I made it far as an actress, but directing is my life's dream. A part of proving myself is to keep my relationships with everyone on the production cordial and professional. I don't want to step over the line. I mean, I know I'm a massive hypocrite idiot because you're right here in my living room, but I . . . you're just so lovely, and if I'm honest, I wasn't expecting you to be. I thought you'd be an arrogant prick, like most men in the industry are. But now, I . . . I just really enjoy being around you. You're just so sweet, and funny, and charming . . . and—"

"Nahid."

"What?"

"I really want to kiss you," I said. My chest tightened.

She froze before bursting into another one of her nymphlike giggles. "Fucking hell. You don't hang about, do you?"

"If I'm being brutally honest, I fancy the shit out of you. I don't know if I've ever made it obvious, but it's the truth."

"Okay. Wow," she said quietly. "That's a lot to take in."

"The bottom line is that I enjoy being around you, too. And I really, really want to kiss you."

"Hmm. Well. Let's not hang about any longer, then."

EDDIE

Hang It in the Tate

December 2017

The light from the white morning sky flooded through Blue's bedroom, stirring the two of us awake. My head was a heartbeat, throbbing with every move it made, and I was cursed with an unfortunate case of nausea. To say the night prior was fun would be an understatement, but not as much as it would be to say I was now suffering. Suffering didn't even *begin* to cut it. Nonetheless, I felt a bit of solace in the knowledge that I wasn't experiencing a raging hangover on my own; Blue was in the same boat as me, which was made clear by her relentless groaning.

Ego Birth's debut album had finally landed, and we'd celebrated its launch at a venue in Brixton a few streets away from Blue's house. It was an unforgettable affair packed wall-to-wall with friends and family of the band, creatives in the scene, and supporters alike. Alcohol was available on tap for the VIP guests, and I was lucky (or unlucky, depending on which side of the night I was on) to be a recipient of such. Even though I had behind-the-scenes access to the recording and mastering of *Welcome to the Self*, it still sounded all so brand-new and enlightening as a cohesive whole.

By the time of the launch, the band had reached higher levels of exposure off the back of the Renée Sinclair tour, and their collaboration with a handful of notable names in the American jazz scene had pushed them even further. It would be a stretch to say that they were going mainstream just yet, but there was nothing to indicate it wasn't feasible one day. Blue had eventually decided to quit her marketing job to jump into this new world full-force, and I was so proud to show my beautiful, talented, showstopping musician of a girlfriend off to the world. I was in a much better place than I had been just over a year ago. Back then, I couldn't see eye to eye with my mother, and I was brimming with what I could now at least conceive as jealousy towards anyone doing remotely better than me. Now, all I felt was pure bliss. Everything was perfect. Ish.

After a pained rousing into consciousness, the two of us concluded the only tolerable plan of action in our states would be a classic wake-and-bake. The thought of doing anything else was ludicrous. Plus, we deserved it. We'd both been working so hard—me at my editorial position at *BABBLE* magazine, and Blue on her music. I may or may not have also won a Marston B. Greaves award that year and had a production that was soon to debut at the Regium Theatre in less than a month, but hey, it wasn't a competition.

Blue loped out of bed to sit on the desk chair, cracking the window open before gathering the paraphernalia to roll a joint. Once she'd done the honours, she suggested we watch something, and I gladly obliged. We switched sides, her climbing over the bed to grab her laptop from the side table and me getting up from the desk chair to take a few puffs out of the window. In doing so, she happened to get an up-close-and-personal view of the notification that popped up on my phone, lying front side up on the table. She picked it up, grinning at me.

"Well, would you look at that? Your mate just texted. The don from last night."

I perked up, knowing automatically who she was referring to. "What did he say?"

"'Hey, how's your head this morning?'" she read aloud in her best impression of a cast member from *Made in Chelsea*. "'Last night was *amazing*. Thanks for the invite! Ego Birth gained a new fan in me. I haven't stopped listening to the album *all morning*. I'd *kill* for a signed vinyl copy.'" She stressed every other word, overenunciating, embodying her perception of you.

"That's so cute," I replied, relieved it wasn't anything awkward, or worse yet, anything secret. "I told you he'd like it. See?"

"Oh, no, I appreciate it. I'm just taking the piss." She grabbed the laptop and plopped herself back on the bed, putting on *Chewing Gum*. I joined her, bringing the joint and an ashtray along with me. She pushed the screen back so both of us could see it from our respective vantage points and we watched in silence for a while, puffing and passing in between our amused reactions to the scenes from the show. Then she spoke up again. "I don't actually think you've ever told me how you met this guy."

"Who? Hugo?"

"Yeah. He sort of . . . materialised out of nowhere. First he was just Some Rich Guy, now he has a proper name, and he's a proper person that you spend a lot of time with."

"Jealous, are we?" I teased.

She stared at me. "Jealous of what, exactly? Him stealing you from me?"

I snorted. "Good one."

"I'm serious, though. I vaguely remember you texting me from his Halloween party last year, but I thought you went for a laugh. Are you *genuinely* mates? It's just a bit odd."

"He's a writing friend," I said, then took a long toke. "I told you that. Hence why I accompanied him to the MBGs."

"Is he from Kingston as well? I swear I know all your Kingston friends."

If I said yes, my answer could easily be refuted by a quick social media perusal that illustrated the contrary. On the other hand, I also couldn't use the "online writing course" origin story, because Blue would question when and why I was part of an online writing course if I already had a creative writing degree. This left me with having to invent a brand-new backstory in the span of a second.

"I met him on a Facebook group for MBG Award hopefuls. It was a place for people to share their questions and tips on how to get shortlisted. It's super cringe, I know. It wasn't something I necessarily wanted to tell anyone. But . . . yeah. He was in the group, and we formed a smaller group chat. He invited everyone in the chat to the

Halloween party, and I was like, fuck it, why not go? That's why he was just Some Rich Guy for a while at first. But he's decent. And he's super fucking talented. His play is sensational. It's no wonder he won." God. Shoot me.

Blue still looked sceptical. "Right, okay. But *you're* super fucking talented. There's no reason why you shouldn't have won the MBGs yourself. Why does he need your support so much when there are so many other creatives who are probably more deserving but less likely to get the praise?"

"I said he was in the same Facebook group as me. Everyone supports everyone in there."

"Isn't he, like, related to the author of *Billy Andromeda*? What support does he need from some random online group?"

"Not everyone wants to skate by with their privileges, Blue. Some people just want real, authentic help from their peers."

"If you don't think he's skating by, you're getting a bit dizzy."

"Look. Why don't you just stick to all your music friends and I'll stick to my theatre friends, and we don't grill each other for associating with privileged people simply because they're privileged. How does that sound?"

"*Please.* Even *you* know it's weird you're suddenly buddy-buddy with the kind of person who's rewarded for simply existing."

"I thought you knew better than to hate the player and not the game," I rebutted, getting up from the bed to use the toilet.

"It's almost as if hating both the player *and* the game isn't mutually exclusive," Blue remarked snidely upon my exit. The air was now tense and my head had started throbbing again despite my growing buzz. I wasn't expecting an interrogation from her, at least not this early in the day or this soon after such a high from the night before. Even though she'd finally met you in person for the first time, she hadn't necessarily warmed to you. I understood why, because in any other scenario I'd say the same thing as her, and ultimately, I still *believed* the same thing as her. But this belief was ironically the impetus for everything. So once the truth was eventually exposed, Blue would finally understand that this game was chess, and the player was also the pawn.

I silently got back into bed next to her and we resumed the show like we hadn't just been bickering. After a few minutes, I broke the silence. "Are you gonna sign the vinyl for him, then?"

• • •

With the opening night of *Great Belonging* edging closer each day, I was internally growing slightly more neurotic. My inclination towards a state of disquietude begs the question as to why I'd ever put myself in a position where I'd be in the least control of everything, so personally connected yet so situationally distant. All the control I ever had was when I wrote the play in the first place, figuring out the plot, building the world, crafting the characters, working out the stage direction and so on. I was the god of my own universe, but it was all out of my hands once I put the pen down. That's the plight of a writer: to be in full control of what you choose to give, but completely at the mercy of what the world chooses to take. I knew this loss of control would have been the same had I been the one who put the play forward. Regardless of the circumstance, I would have been controlled by my desire to be in control. I was like a ventriloquist with a hand up my own arse, I suppose.

I knew you wouldn't get it, but I also knew that your lack of an emotional attachment to the body of work made things easier. You did as I said, and you told me what I needed to know in order for me to hover around undetected, a fly on the wall of the Regium. Of course a part of me wanted even more access—that was only natural. Even more so when I could tell I was wearing you down with questions, but I was grateful for your willingness to divulge every detail. I'd ask you how the blocking process was going, or which creative direction the set designers went in, or what colour palette the costume team decided on, or how the sound design was determined, or if the actors were making headway in rehearsals, and I always, without fail, got an answer from you. Whether it was the whole truth was something I'd never be sure of until the Big Day, and this probably fed into my growing neuroticism.

Nevertheless, it was evident that in many ways, the director had the same vision for the play as I did. I got the chance to attend two rehearsals in the first couple of weeks, and that was when I met Nahid for the first time. She vaguely knew of me already; she was aware of your and my friendship, based on your occasional reference to me in your conversations. We enjoyed jovial small talk in our first few encounters, and I feigned fascination with the play, acting as though I were a mere spectator to it. I was surprised by the contrast between Nahid's affable and demure demeanour off the stage and her ardent, assertive approach behind it. It was quite jarring but also comforting. This realisation made me feel bad for having ever doubted her, and it eventually levelled out some of my qualms to know that the director was doing a much better job than I'd initially wanted to give her credit for. The two of you worked in tandem, responsible for lifting this motherfucker off the ground. Consequently, it was in the two of you I trusted.

Once our hangovers were bearable enough for us to get out of bed in the late afternoon, Blue and I decided to quell our lingering hunger the best way we knew how: a visit to our favourite Korean barbecue spot in Paddington. Before I knew it I was almost back to normal, and all that was left were the psychological consequences, the dawning realisation that I had most definitely been acting a fool at the launch party. I just hoped that most people were drunk enough for it not to mean much in the grand scheme of things, even though however drunk they were had no impact on the grand scheme of things.

By the time we'd gorged ourselves with an unhealthy portion of lightly scorched bulgogi and galbi pieces, we could call our hangover recovery a success. The early evening had crept up on us once we parted ways outside the restaurant. Instead of going home together, I made the last-minute decision to take a quick visit to see you. It seemed efficient enough, as I was closer to your neighbourhood than my own, and it had been a little harder to catch you in person since the rehearsals amped up. After you gushed about the previous night in your earlier texts, you asked me what my plans were for the day, and after answering, I returned the question. I was at least confident that you were home, and I wanted to see your face light up as I stood outside your front door, holding the signed vinyl copy of *Welcome to the Self* that you had so politely asked for.

Half an hour after kissing Blue goodbye, I was walking up the path to your house. Your living room curtains were drawn, but I could see the lights were on and I could hear signs of life via the faint sound of music. I confidently rapped the brass knocker and waited for a few moments. The music stopped, followed by the sound of approaching footsteps. My heart jumped at the voice I heard when I realised it wasn't yours. It was a female voice, but it wasn't Belle's.

"You're back already?" the voice asked, at the exact same time the door opened, and then both of our voices harmonised in startled squeals when our eyes met. Nahid was standing in front of me, wearing nothing but one of your unbuttoned shirts over a lace bra and a pair of matching lace briefs. She slammed the door closed reflexively, and then there were a few seconds of unbearable silence. During those few seconds, I was thinking of different ways to kill you. Perhaps a bludgeoning, or a strangling if I had the strength. I had the fury for it.

"Umm . . . I can come back at a better time," I finally said.

"Wait! Wait, don't leave. Give me a second," Nahid replied through the door, sounding both urgent and mousy. I heard her brisk footsteps move further away, and as I waited, I went back to brainstorming how many different ways I could make you suffer. I'd run you over if I could drive or push you off the roof of a high-rise building if I could get us both up there, but the logistics didn't matter in my imagination. I just wanted to kill you. You were supposed to stay focused and keep all your energy on the play, *my* play. You were supposed to take this seriously. I couldn't believe how stupid you could be to risk everything we'd worked on—*I'd* worked on—with the *director*, of all people. *Jesus Christ.*

Nahid eventually returned some forty seconds later, opening the door slowly this time. She had hastily changed back into her clothes, and she was visibly flustered. We stared at each other for another few seconds.

"So . . . ?" I prompted her.

"Oh. Shit, sorry. Just come in," she replied, beckoning to me with her hand. I stepped into the foyer, hit with the faint smell of dinner from the kitchen. "He just went to the shop to grab a drink and some dessert. He won't be long." Her act of referring to you without mentioning your name didn't just allude to the fact that it was self-explanatory—it was also how she hid away from saying your name out loud in front of me, like it was an ominous curse. She led us into the living room, where we sat on adjacent sofas. In that moment, I was trying to figure out what I had missed. Where I had failed to connect the dots. To be this blindsided left me uneasy, with a pit in my stomach. I never had any inkling; you had acted normally and never hinted at any interest in Nahid. I wondered why you hadn't just told me. Did *you* not trust *me*? Rich of you, if that were the case. I looked down at the hardwood floor, tapping my foot incessantly while she sat leaning forwards with her face in her hands.

"One of us has to say something," I started after a while. "We can't just sit here in silence and act like that didn't just happen."

She looked at me. "I don't know what to say."

"I'll help. When did this start?"

"Just before rehearsals began."

I paused. "*Six* weeks ago?" When she nodded, I shook my head. "You've got to be joking."

"I know, I know. It's not great," she said, pulling a frustrated grimace. "I can't justify it."

"Who made the first move?"

"I . . . I don't know. It was a one-thing-led-to-another sort of thing."

"Someone still had to lead it."

"Well, I'd grown a liking to him. I just tried to play it off and get it out of my mind. It was hard, though, because we were spending more and more time together. Then one day, he . . . he told me he liked me. I was surprised, but I welcomed it. I know I shouldn't have." She looked down. She was already so small, standing at around five foot two, but in that moment she somehow looked even smaller. She was curled up and hunched in, like all she wanted to do was shrink into the size of an atom. "We told each other we'd end things once the play was wrapped up, when we had no reason to be around each other."

"Ahhh. So it's just a cute little production fling, then?" I remarked caustically.

"Don't put it like that." She looked up at me, and for the first time since speaking, she sounded a bit more assertive. "It's not . . . just a *fling*. I know it's bad, but it's not frivolous. Also—why are you so bothered? What bearing does this have on you? Aren't you and Hu just friends?"

I paused, realising that I'd come in way too hot, which was understandably a tad confusing to her. Being interrogated this harshly by a woman she'd only met a couple of times was probably not something she could process. Of course she couldn't know the real reason I cared, so I played the morality card. "If you and your husband are open, power to you. I honestly couldn't give a fuck. But the last time I checked, Hugo had a girlfriend. Something tells me she isn't exactly polyamorous."

Nahid stood up, sighing. She slowly ran her hands down her face. "I'm an idiot, I know. I shouldn't have accepted his advances. I was just so out of my element when I first got this directing job, and he was the only person who encouraged me and affirmed my potential. He was just so welcoming."

"So you return the favour by shagging him? Jesus Christ. He's welcoming to *everyone*. That's just how he is."

"Don't make me out to be naive. It wasn't that simple."

"Yeah, no. You're not young enough for that excuse," I retorted, but I immediately felt a little bad. I was well aware that she was nearly a decade older than us, but she had a nimble youthfulness to her. She was beautiful, I could admit that. It just wasn't necessarily the kind of beauty I saw you gravitating towards. Up until that moment, I didn't even really expect you to be attracted to anyone who wasn't Belle-esque, even if it wasn't Belle. Also, the age difference between you wasn't exactly subtle, but I couldn't act like it was entirely immoral. It sort of just left me wondering what the two of you talked about when all was said and done.

"Look, Eddie. Please, just listen. I really, *really* don't need this getting out. It could put the play's publicity in jeopardy, and that's the last thing we need right now." She stood with her hands clasped together on top of her head, like a football coach watching their team lose. Deep down I knew I wasn't ever going to tell anyone. Ultimately, it wasn't any of my business. I wasn't the one being cheated on, nor did I have any loyalties to those who *were* being cheated on. I also knew Nahid was right: if this affair was exposed, it could potentially get in the way of everything. That was not what I had signed up for. It was not what *Great Belonging* deserved.

"What if Belle had knocked on the door and not me?" I asked.

"She's out of town." Nahid looked away.

"I could always tell her." I shrugged. I was bluffing. If I knew only one thing about Belle, it was that privacy was basically an alien concept to her. As curated as her social media presence might have been, the fact of the matter was that her relationship was her top priority. There was no way she'd stay silent about this.

"*Don't.* Please." She looked at me with pleading eyes, and that twinge of guilt I had earlier came rushing back.

"You both need to stop what you're doing."

She nodded quickly and sat back down. I realised she was trying her best not to cry. A few seconds later, the front door opened. I could hear the rustle of the bags you were carrying and the shuffling of your feet. You called Nahid's name from the foyer, and she hesitantly hollered her whereabouts. You dashed to the kitchen to park the food and drink, and then you made your way to the living room. If I could freeze time and capture the drastic change in your facial expression the moment you realised Nahid was not alone, I would, and I'd hang it in the Tate.

"Oh. Shit. Naledi. What are you doing here?" You took a step into the room, perturbed, your eyes flitting between the two of us.

I got up from the sofa, grabbed my tote bag, and marched towards you. "You *said* you weren't doing anything today," I hissed. Technically, you didn't say you weren't doing any*one*.

"You could have at least given me a heads-up, though."

"To give you some time to come up with a lie, right?" I crossed my arms. You clenched your jaw. I could feel the anxiety ripple off your skin, but I was too angry to sympathise. Up until that point I'd trusted you to tell me everything, but this was the first secret you had kept from me, and from then on I couldn't be sure it would be your last. "You have until the end of this week to break up with Belle. If you don't, I'll tell her." Although I was lying about the blackmail, I needed Belle out of the equation. A YouTuber who spilled most of her personal life online was dangerously close to this situation for my liking.

You and Nahid both yelped, "No," in unison, and I thought about the power I had over you in that moment, how I could turn everything upside down. But at the end of the day, I really had about as much power as a hero aiming for a villain who was taking cover behind a human shield. The situation was precarious, and collateral damage was a high possibility.

"I'll do it. I will. Please. Just give me some time," you pleaded.

"The time I give you is the time you take away from her." I barely knew the girl, but what I did know was that she deserved to be with someone who loved her. Everyone does. I guess that also applied to Nahid's husband, but I wouldn't go there. Nahid wasn't my responsibility. You were.

"You're right," you murmured, chewing on the inside of your cheek. "I'm sorry."

"I almost forgot why I came here," I said, taking the signed vinyl out of my bag. A part of me didn't want to give it to you at all, considering I'd rather have gifted you with a shiner, but I wanted to be the bigger person. I didn't want to hate you. "Here you go. Enjoy."

"Thank you. I appreciate it."

"You have one week, Hugo. I'm not joking. If you don't, you'll regret it."

In hindsight, I wish I could say I had made the best judgement call with that ultimatum, but I hadn't. There was just *one* thing in the way.

Somehow, that thing was me.

A Very Close Friend

January 2018

The tears started forming around the same time that the cast bowed to the deafening standing ovation. Blue, Lydia, and I were in the second row, close enough to see everything in its perfection. A wave of emotion had taken over me and I was a mess. I had finally seen my play, and it was the most beautiful thing. So, so, so beautiful.

If I could have helped it, I'd have made less of a palaver of everything, because it immediately made Blue suspicious. However, judging from her effort to console me, she saw that I was upset for different reasons. She knew that I probably wasn't just overjoyed, I was also devastated, because it was my dream to be up on that stage bowing to this thunderous whooping and hollering. She knew I wanted this more than anyone else in the world, and that watching someone else live that dream must have been agonising for me. In reality I was devastated because I had been proven right, and this was just as much salt in the wound as it was vindication. I was still trying to figure out if this was enough, just seeing my work in front of me. Did I really need more? The answer was already becoming less clear.

You decided to do a quick curtain speech once all the applause was over, with Nahid and the cast standing behind you.

"I wanted to say a word or two before we all disperse tonight. There's someone here in the audience who I have to shout out," you said, looking at me. Blue turned to me at the same time, catching your line of sight. In that moment I felt her confusion, but I wasn't focused on it. I needed to know what you were going to say. "*Great Belonging* would not have happened without every single person in this hall, including all you bloody phenomenal audience members who have come to support the opening. But I don't think the script would have come to fruition without my main inspiration: my talented friend, Eddie. I was a fish out of water when we met, and in many ways, she showed me the ropes. She's one of the most talented writers I've ever met, and it's a no-brainer that I dedicate *Great Belonging* to her. It also goes without saying that I have to give a *monumental* special thanks to the incredible Nahid Norouzi, who animated this to its full potential. I can't forget to thank the Wentworth Agency for seeing something in me. I just hope that one day, more voices, like those of Eddie or Nahid, can be uplifted. I hope other people's stories can be told, and not just those of the ones who look an awful lot like me. Thank you."

The crowd erupted into applause once again, but from my periphery I could practically see Blue's eyes rolling into the back of her head. Every word you said left a lump in my throat that grew bigger and bigger until I thought I'd never stop crying. I was floating, stuck in a space between pride and pain. But once I finally took my phone off airplane mode as the theatre was slowly emptying out, that space turned into one of confusion and horror.

I went to the bathroom and sat in one of the toilet stalls. I had a flurry of message requests, primarily on Instagram, but also some on my other social media accounts, Facebook included. Shit—even some on LinkedIn. When I decided to open the messages, my heart caught in my throat.

[18:08] **rachelfickel182:** U dirty homewrecking slag

I stared at my phone screen, astounded. Without thinking, I checked the next message request, then the next, then the next.

[18:29] **beckaswindonxx:** Ewww! Why would anyone even touch you
with a pole u fckin specimen > :(

[18:35] **kfhhsyt225:** Go back to the jungle U gold digging monkey

[19:17] **sofiexoroseox:** OMG. what a fucking downgrade :/

[20:37] **positivv_energy_princess:** TEAM GRIFFY FOREVER, BURN IN
HELL U SKET!!!

[21:13] **xbrionyamylouise:** what a heartless bitch, stealing another
girls man . . .

[22:02] **useridrfk:** N I G G E R

"What the actual fuck?" I remarked, feeling dazed. I had absolutely no idea what was going on, and I didn't want to know. But the messages were crawling in one by one, and they weren't stopping.

I was snapped out of my trance by the sound of Blue's voice as she entered the bathroom, calling for me. "Babe, are you all right? You've been in there for a hot minute."

"Uhhh . . . I'm fine. Just give me a sec." I stood up, flushed the toilet, and sorted myself out. As I walked briskly towards the sink, Blue caught me.

"Are you okay? You seem quite frantic."

"I'm okay. I promise I'm fine." I washed my hands, looking ahead at myself in the mirror, and tensed up at the buzz of my phone in my pocket. "Let's just follow everyone to the pub."

"Ed, you know that'll be you one day? Up there? Winning all the awards? You're the star. It's in your name. Don't be upset. I hate to see you like this." She put a hand around my neck.

"I'm not upset, Blue! I'm allowed to show emotion without just being some sorry nobody," I snapped, and I watched her retreat as I went to dry my hands. "Where's Lydia?" I asked afterwards.

Blue stared at me. "She's . . . waiting for us outside. Eddie, something's not right. I don't know what it is, but you're acting strange. It's either that or you're taking your jealousy out on me."

"I'm not taking anything out on you. I'm sorry," I responded, deflated.

"Stop acting weird, then," she replied. "I don't like it. You're scaring me."

We left the theatre and made our way to the Old Brewery, where there was a private function booked for everyone to let loose after the showing. Not everyone had arrived yet, so we beelined towards the bar while there was still less of a queue. The whole time, I was trying to connect the dots to figure out why I was suddenly receiving a flurry of hate messages, and why those hate messages were coming from a drove of white teenage girls who were on a mission to avenge their leader at all costs. Their leader being Annabelle. Fucking. Griffiths. *Belle*.

By the time you arrived, your entire demeanour had shifted. Your expression was etched with trepidation that levelled with mine. You, Nahid, her husband, and a couple of her friends had joined Blue and Lydia and me for a chat among the throng of the other pub-goers, but all the while I sensed this restless energy from you. Eventually, I interrupted the conversation to announce a smoke break, which I practically scampered outside for. I walked onto the wide pathway that cut through the Cutty Sark Gardens, looking out at the twinkling lights and the water in between the towering Canary Wharf high-rises. I took my phone out of my pocket again, hoping this was all just some weird hallucination. It wasn't.

I heard your voice behind me when I was halfway through my cigarette. You'd stumbled out of the doors and jogged towards me. "Hey. Are you okay?" you asked, standing a few feet away.

"That was a lovely speech you gave tonight," I said.

"Naledi, I've got something to tell you. I'm not sure if this has happened to you too, but I . . . I started getting a ton of vile messages earlier that I only saw after the play. Then I realised they were all about Belle. So I checked her YouTube channel, and she uploaded a video a few hours ago. I'm really sorry, but . . . shit."

"Say it!" I hissed, feeling myself bubble up with anger. "What happened?"

"I swear to God I never said anything about you. I'd never do that."

"Stop speaking so *cryptically*, you prick! Spit it out."

"She . . . she sort of insinuated that . . . that I left her for you. In her video, I mean. I know she's just angry. She just wants to spite me, which is understandable. But she got the wrong end of the stick."

"Wait a minute." I shook my head. "How did she even come to that conclusion?"

"When I ended things with her last month, she just couldn't comprehend it. It was painful to watch. She just sort of . . . spiralled. She was adamant that something had to have happened while she was away—that I'd started seeing someone else. You were the only person she could think of. You stood out to her. No matter how much I tried to tell her that wasn't the case, she wouldn't budge." You shrugged. "It wasn't something I could easily explain away, either."

My heart sank and my breathing shallowed. "What are you saying? That you implicated me in your breakup?"

You shook your head incessantly. "No, I swear I didn't tell her it was you. But I obviously wasn't going to say it was Nahid, either. You know, for the play's sake." You said this more quietly, leaning in closer to me. We both looked around to see if there were any potential eavesdroppers, but the brewery's well-lit glass doors would have alerted us of such.

"This is insane. I just wanted to enjoy tonight, but now I'm getting racial slurs hurled at me by a wave of randoms on the internet." I dropped my head back and looked up at the light-polluted sky.

"Oh my God, Naledi, I'm so sorry."

"*Stop* calling me Naledi. It's fucking Eddie."

"Okay. Sorry."

"Shit. Why is this happening to me? Why now?" I agonised.

"I tried to tell you I needed more time. That I couldn't just dump Belle on a whim. That was never going to look good."

"What do you mean 'look good'? Is looking good all you care about? Do you not have a moral fucking compass? I was the *only* person who was considerate of her feelings. Yet *I'm* facing her wrath. Because of you, the bottom of the barrel of humanity has been dredged up and into *my* DMs. Even on my LinkedIn, for fuck's sake! I don't even use LinkedIn!"

You looked away. "I've asked her to take the video down, but she hasn't responded yet. She must have purposefully uploaded it today to draw more attention. I don't know if she'll take it down, but the damage is already done. I am so sorry."

I took deep breaths as I paced back and forth, wondering what the hell we were going to do. Picking up my phone again, I frantically searched for the video and found it. It was titled "WE BROKE UP (NOT CLICKBAIT) (HE CHEATED) | Vlog #60" and the thumbnail was a picture of her sitting in her bedroom, visibly distraught. The views had climbed exponentially just in the last six hours alone. She had over half a million subscribers; in a quarter of a day, an army of them had managed to sleuth their way into my life. "We should tell the truth about the play. Like, as soon as possible. To take back control of the narrative," I said. When you didn't respond, I instantly knew you were hesitant, and I knew why. "You don't want to, do you?"

"It's not that I don't want to. It's just that—"

"It's Nahid. You don't know how she'll react. You're afraid."

You sighed, rubbing your face. "I just need a moment to make sure I don't look like any more of a phoney prick than I already do. That's all."

"You never stopped sleeping with her, did you?"

"Naledi—"

"*Eddie.* When was the last time you shagged the married director of *my play*?" When you stayed silent, I pressed on. "I deserve to know. Forget Belle—there's this guy, I don't know, it's not like he's a big deal in the industry right now—his name's Aaron Yousef. Does that name ring a bell? He's actually here tonight! How wonderful is that? There's a chance he could find out that his wife's cheating on him, and then word could get out. Everyone loves a good cheating scandal, after all. But wait, no! Now because of your scorned ex-girlfriend's sixtieth vlog post, Nahid's in the clear. Everyone's just going to assume *I'm* a home-wrecker! That'll look great for me, won't it? Chances are, you're going to get off scot-free and I'll be hung out to dry."

"Look, I just need to get my bearings and think of a way out of this for both of us."

"Well, *I* need to know if you're still seeing Nahid. Because if you are, you're already making things more difficult. Please, just tell me."

You sighed again, looking away. "Yes. But we're *very* careful not to . . . you know . . . get caught. Especially after what happened with you."

"Oh my God. Oh my God." I laughed in disbelief. "This can't be happening."

"I'm sorry, I . . . we can figure this out, I promise. It's just that seeing how proud she is of all of this . . . of *me* . . . seeing how well it went tonight, and how amazingly everyone did . . . I don't want to make a mockery of her. I want her to be in the know before we tell everyone else."

"No, you just don't want your affair with her to end. It's one thing to have your ex think you're a liar, but you don't want Nahid to think so either."

"I *did* just say I don't want to look like more of a phoney prick than I already do, didn't I?" you cracked, sobering me.

"We have to tell the truth eventually," I said quietly, even if I was unsure when.

"We will," you said, moving closer and resting your hands on my shoulders reassuringly. "I promise we will. Everything's going to be fine."

We'd both been so engrossed in our confrontation that we hadn't paid attention to the silhouette across the path from us, right at the entrance of the pub.

"Tell the truth about what?" Blue interrupted us from afar, and our heads snapped towards her in unison.

Fuck.

Fuck.

"Fuck," I hissed, throwing your hands off me. We both froze, looking at each other and then back at Blue. In that moment, I wasn't in my own body. I was just looking down at the three of us from a bird's-eye view.

"This isn't what it looks like," you piped up. "There's just been a huge misunderstanding, and—"

"I'm not talking to you. I'm talking to my girlfriend," she remarked cuttingly. "Eddie, what the fuck is happening?" When I failed to respond, she shook her head, chuckling incredulously. "Why are we *actually* here? Why do I have this god-awful feeling you're hiding something really bad from me?"

I felt so lightheaded in that moment. I couldn't speak or move. I remember you looking at me, just as desperate for an exit plan as I was. I could have told more than just the truth only you and I shared. I could have opened Pandora's box if I wanted to. But I didn't. I couldn't. It was like you said: the damage was already done.

"Hugo, can we have a moment, please? Can you leave?" I prompted you. Without skipping a beat, you walked briskly back inside. I looked at Blue until my vision blurred. I was trying to hold back tears, but they fell anyway.

"I . . . I feel like I don't know who you are anymore, you know?" she said, walking up to me until we were face-to-face. I could feel her sense of betrayal. It choked me like a noxious gas.

"I'm sorry. I don't know what to say."

"Are you seeing him?" she asked me quietly, her voice wavering. I wanted to vomit. Instead, I wiped a tear and looked up at the tree behind her. "Because if you are, you're not being subtle about it. Ever since you met him you've changed. I don't know who you are anymore. I'm losing you. His speech earlier . . . what was that all about? Why did he dedicate the play to you? It's all so . . . *bizarre*. I don't care if you supported him in a group chat or whatever, it's still fucking *weird*. If you *are* seeing him, please just tell me. I mean, you're going to 'tell the truth eventually' anyway, right? There's no time like the present."

I sighed shakily, feeling like a deer in headlights. I had no idea what to say. Just as you were afraid to come clean to Nahid, I didn't know how *Blue* would respond, either. She always had too much faith in me, and I was afraid to face her disappointment. Even if I painted it as a big *gotcha* moment, she'd want to know why she'd been left in the dark for so long. Our argument back in December was still weighing heavily on my mind; I couldn't trust that she wouldn't prematurely blow the lid off against my wishes if she found out the truth, even if she did it for a righteous cause. It was also feasible to assume she would eventually find out about Belle's video, and considering how suspicious she already was of my association with you, it wasn't a reach to conclude that she'd believe it. Hell, the sooner we announced the truth, the less believable it might be, as if we were trying to cover our tracks somehow. It was probably more feasible to conclude that I *was* a home-wrecker. Any other explanation would feel like we were already lying. The truth felt more ludicrous.

The fact of the matter was that we just couldn't be sure how everyone would receive our "experiment." I thought back to how I was sobbing in that crowd earlier, watching my one dream become a reality. I didn't want that feeling to end yet. The more real things became, the harder it was to let go. People's reputations were on the line, actors' incomes were on the line, the production team's jobs were there, just straddling the line. All because of what? Me. Me and my *evidently* foolproof master plan. The relentless yet convoluted pursual of hopes and dreams, so glaringly out of reach. Ultimately, I was backed into a corner of my own doing, and I had never felt more hopeless. So in that moment, I had to choose between being honest with Blue, or keeping my play alive. I made a decision that I knew I'd regret. A decision that would instantly change the trajectory of everything.

"I need you to know that I love you so, so much. You mean the absolute world to me. But I . . ." I choked on my words, in between my tears. "I fucked up big-time. I made some stupid decisions, and . . . I don't know if this will work."

"If *what* will work? What the fuck are you saying?" Blue's voice rose by a few decibels.

"God, shit," I muttered, sniffing. I closed my eyes, holding my breath for a moment before exhaling. "I just can't be with you anymore."

As I uttered those words, I felt the universe collapse in on me. Time and space were futile; a silly joke, a worthless measurement of existence.

"This isn't happening," Blue said, pressing her fingers on both of her temples, squeezing her eyes shut. "You're not doing this."

"I love you—"

"Fuck off! Just stop—"

"I'm so fucking sorry, I swear to God—"

"Please, stop. I don't know you! I don't know you. The person I know would never do this to me."

"I'm a fucking idiot. I really am."

Blue composed herself, wiping her tears and stepping back from me. "You've broken my heart, Eddie," she murmured. "You might as well have just died in front of me."

"Please don't say that."

"You don't get to tell me what to say. I'm leaving now. I hope you enjoy the rest of your evening. I hope you enjoy the rest of your life." She turned away, taking her phone out of her bag to make a call. Her chunky boot heels clicked on the tarmac as she marched in the direction of the park's entrance. Just like that, she disappeared into the night. She was gone. From my bird's-eye view, three had become two, had become one.

• • •

I went back into the pub and beelined for the bathroom, determined to keep myself together. I had basically walked in as a shell of whoever I was before, but it didn't matter to me. If I was a stranger to Blue, I might as well have been a stranger to myself. I stood in front of the mirror, trying to make sure my eyes weren't too bloodshot, but I soon realised I didn't recognise myself anymore. Most of my makeup had melted off in the midst of all my blubbering that evening, so I quickly splashed my face and freshened up a bit, wiping away the moisture with a paper towel.

I had the impulse to go into one of the stalls and watch Belle's video properly, to see what she had actually said. I took my Bluetooth earphones out of my bag, put them in, and listened. The first half of the video was pretty standard: she showed off her morning routine and her gym session, then showed a snippet of a day in the life of her consulting job. I skipped through to the second half of the video, where it got juicy. She was sitting in her warmly lit bedroom with the camera panning up to her on her bed. She started off composed, but as she continued speaking, she began to fall apart, becoming more and more aggrieved. When I looked at her, I saw a pain that mirrored Blue's in a lot of ways. It was hard to watch.

"... I was travelling for a few months, just, like, enjoying myself and living in the moment. He started writing plays and stuff, which was cool or whatever. I was so supportive. But he ... he sort of changed. I could feel him pulling away. We've had our ups and downs, but I was always under the impression that there was basically *nothing* we couldn't get through, you know? I guess that was too naive and optimistic of me.

"There's this *one* girl. He told me she was just a friend he met in the theatre world. Well, she was a very 'close' friend, if you ask me," she said, lifting her fingers in quotation marks and grimacing in contempt. "Still, I believed him. Even when she accompanied him to the awards ceremony, which he won, or when they'd always hang out in their free time, going to parks and such. There's no way I'd have suspected anything. For one, I didn't think she'd be his type—he's always been into blondes. Let's just say . . . she's *definitely* not blonde. Oh, and the last time I checked, she was a lesbian. I don't know, sexuality is so fluid these days anyway, isn't it? You can be gay one day and latching on to someone's boyfriend the next." She shrugged, frowning. "Not to speculate too much, but it seems pretty convenient for her that this happened after he won a big cash prize. But whatever. It is what it is. I just wanted to update you guys on my personal life. And please, whatever you do, do *not* send any hate to anyone. I wish my ex the best of luck, and ultimately I hope he's happy." She wiped away a tear. The video jump-cut, and she had composed herself again. "Anyway, I'm going to end this here, I need my beauty sleep. Next week I'll be skiing, so expect a vacation vlog at some point! Also, don't forget to use the code GRIFFY for a ten percent discount on glamgarmz.com! Love you lots! Mwah."

Just as the video ended, I received another message request—probably the millionth racist tirade from one of her disciples. I was frazzled, trying to process the roller coaster of a night I'd had. In the space of a few hours, I'd gone from seeing my script come to life at the Regium, to becoming an online pariah, to breaking up with my fucking girlfriend. Something must have shifted in the universe that night. It was the only explanation. All I knew for sure was that I hadn't prepared myself to become a spectacle in any way, shape, or form, let alone in *this* way, shape, and form. But then I thought to myself, *If you can't beat them, join them.* So that's exactly what I decided to do.

◆ ◆ ◆

The private function had got busier in my absence. Most of the actors were there now and spirits were beautifully high. It warmed my heart, but also had me feeling incredibly alone. I was too frigid and anguished to properly enjoy myself, but re-entering the building as a freshly single person gave me the want to thaw, so I headed straight to the bar.

Nahid had broken off from a group conversation and was

approaching me. "Hey, Eddie. I heard something went on outside. Is everything okay?" she asked.

"Blue and I just broke up," I said. The nonchalance of my delivery even shocked me a little bit.

Nahid's eyes widened and she placed a hand on her chest. "Oh my God. I'm so sorry—wow. Just *now*?"

"Yes, just now."

"Holy shit. That's intense. I can't imagine what you're going through. Just know I'm here for you." She leaned closer, putting a hand on my back.

The bartender handed me my beer, and I took three swallows before wiping my lips. I turned to Nahid. "You know, you're very brave. Having your boyfriend and your husband here together and not batting an eye. It's impressive how well you hide it. Does it make you feel powerful? To know there's more than one person in the world, in this room, who wants you to themselves? Because personally, I was satisfied with just the one."

She slowly recoiled, looking away sheepishly. "Did . . . did Hugo tell you something out there?"

"I don't know how you even have the time. You're a busy woman. Juggling *Great Belonging* and two relationships. That's real girlboss behaviour, I suppose." She looked down at the floor in response, shrinking like she had when I first caught you two together.

A few moments later, you joined us. I guess our argument outside had been interrupted by the breakdown of my relationship, so it was imperative you circled back. Of course Nahid's presence was a bit of a tricky obstacle, but it was only right that you checked in on me.

"Hey. Where did Blue go? Is she still here?" you asked me.

I gritted my teeth, looking ahead. "No. She's gone."

"Oh. Did you manage to, uhhh . . . clear everything up?"

"I told her about the video, and she didn't believe that it was a misunderstanding," I lied. It felt better than admitting I'd actively pushed her away. "She obviously wasn't happy about it. So when I say she's gone, I mean she's gone. For good." I looked at you.

You stared back, stunned. "Shit. Eddie, I cannot stress how sorry I am. This is all my fault."

"What video?" Nahid interrupted, looking at both of us.

You turned to her. "Belle thinks I left her for Eddie, and she posted a video about it. She doesn't explicitly call her out, but she still made it pretty obvious."

"But you *did* leave her for me, didn't you? She's not wrong." I shrugged. You and Nahid both screwed up your faces in confusion. "What? It's true. The whole world knows now. We're madly in love. We might as well come clean."

Your mouth hung agape as you tried to process what I was saying. Nahid looked at you and then at me, and I could see the stress building up in her eyes. "What's going on here?" she asked.

I pulled the two of you in closer. "Look. Despite the dirt I've got on you, I'm not in the business of ending any more relationships tonight. Belle did you two a favour. So it's in your best interest to go along with everything I say right now, unless you'd rather I blew your cover." Although there was still an electric tension in the air, the both of you let out a breath, finally picking up what I was putting down. You both ordered your own drinks, making an effort not to make eye contact with each other, like you were role-playing as strangers.

A minute later, Nahid's husband wandered away from the raucous exchange he was having with some of the actors and headed towards us, still laughing and smiling. He put an arm around Nahid's waist, kissing her on the cheek. You and I stood next to each other, wired from our veiled knowledge of their unstable coupledom. If you looked close enough, you could almost see the charade. Or perhaps it was just because we were aware of it.

"I was just telling Celeste how unreal she was tonight. She hit the lead role right out of the park," Aaron said to her before moving closer to the bar, waiting for his opening to order a drink, which he did. He had sort of bulldozed his way into our three-way discussion, completely oblivious to the awkwardness floating between us.

"She was an amazing lead, you're right," Nahid replied, smiling. "She's definitely a contender for awards season. I can feel it."

"As she should be. You did a mint job with casting. Pat yourself on the back."

She jokingly did so, chuckling. Then she looked over at me. "By the way, I don't think I've ever properly introduced you to Eddie," she said, gesturing towards me.

Aaron turned to face me and smiled. "How's it going! A pleasure to meet you. Aaron." He put a hand out for me to shake and I reciprocated. "The show was just absolutely incredible, wasn't it? I haven't seen something this thought-provoking onstage in years. I can guarantee you it's gonna be on everyone's lips by tomorrow morning. I'll make sure of it myself. Hugo, my man, you're a genius." He turned to you.

"Thank you. I try," you replied.

"Yeah, it was amazing. It was breathtaking." I nodded. I couldn't control the sudden quivering of my lips, or the cracking of my voice, or the welling of tears in my eyes in that moment. Aaron looked at me with concern, as did you and Nahid.

"Is everything all right?" he asked.

I wiped my eyes, shaking my head. "I've just had a long night. I broke up with my girlfriend."

"Holy shit, that's awful. My condolences. At least you're in the right place for a breakup!" he said, gesturing to our environment.

"Aaron, come on," Nahid murmured.

"Just a wee bit of comedic relief, that's all." He grabbed his drink from the counter and took a sip. "Apologies if you're not comfortable answering this, but why did youse break up so suddenly? I could've sworn you looked all right when you walked in here."

I froze, then I looked at you. This was it—the cue to set our new fiction in motion.

You paused, clearing your throat before speaking up. "Uhhh . . . because she found out that Eddie and I . . . have feelings for each other. It all came to the fore this evening," you said in a marginally stilted tone. I watched as Nahid looked at us, fiddling anxiously with her necklace.

"Wow. Well, the heart cannae help what it wants, can it?" Aaron said.

"Exactly," I remarked. "You can't help who you love. Even if they're with someone else." It wasn't visible to the eye, but I could feel you squirming slightly, and I could only assume Nahid was probably doing the same.

"Aye. On the bright side, it could have been worse. It's not like you were married. A breakup is easy. Way less paperwork. You can just crack on." Aaron chuckled. I was delirious enough to burst into laughter at the unfortunate irony of the conversation, but I held myself together. "You've bagged yourself a very talented chap, Eddie. I wish you two all the luck."

You and I both said, "Thank you" in unison. Nahid smiled softly at us, but I could see the mixture of guilt and relief in her eyes. I had covered for her, and I think it was because I felt indebted to her. If she'd done a shit job at directing my play, who knows if I'd have been as considerate. This was the space where the personal bled into the professional; the better she was at her job, the more mercy I felt I could give to her off the stage, even if it meant helping her hide her affair. We were all hiding behind something at the end of the day, whether it was personal or professional, or in your case, both. We were all acting. *This* was true theatre.

• • •

I decided it was my cue to leave. I downed the rest of my glass and announced my departure, hugging Nahid and Aaron goodbye. Before you escorted me out, I remembered Lydia. She was piss drunk, cavorting around the room with some strangers she'd become best friends with in the span of an hour or so. I grabbed her, linking her arm with mine, and we walked to the entrance together. I was supposed to have gone home with Blue that night, but that obviously wasn't a possibility anymore. Lydia was too inebriated to question Blue's absence or why I asked if I could crash with her instead. It was probably for the best that we went home together, considering her state.

I ordered our Uber to Mile End and then hugged you goodbye at the door. "Don't get it twisted," I stopped to whisper in your ear. "This is just a new plan of action. I'm not doing this for you or Nahid. I'm doing it for my play. You get that?"

I felt your nodding. "Understood. I've got you."

"No, you *need* me," I replied.

Once Lydia and I got into the Uber, I deflated with exhaustion. She demanded that the driver put on some banging tunes. When he said he didn't have a Bluetooth connection, she groaned and leaned her head on the window. She suddenly remembered the baggie of ketamine she had at home and got excited again. "We should do a few keys and put on some Jamie xx," she said. I found myself smiling at her obliviousness to the dramas of the evening. I was a little bit jealous of it. I nestled my head on her shoulder, closed my eyes, and tried not to think about what I'd lost. *Who* I'd lost. It was too much to take in. But it couldn't be in vain. In the end, it would be worth it. It had to be.

An Ideal World

March 2018

"Look who's here! If it isn't Baby Suga herself!"

"Morning, peasant." I strolled into the *BABBLE* office on a Monday, pain au chocolat and coffee in hand.

"Every day I ask myself why you're still here." My desk neighbour Franki sighed, spinning her chair to face me as I sat down. "You know damn well you could be in Dubai right now."

"With their human rights record? Never."

"Point is, you could be anywhere but here. If I had a meal ticket like you, I would."

"You may find it hard to believe, but true love can prevail!"

"Not in *this* economy."

"We're working at a feminist publication. Where *is* your integrity, Frances Gao?"

"She comes and goes as she pleases," she said with a shrug, and I laughed in response. The banter between us was seamless and easy, and from the moment I started working here it had been this way. Like a moth to a flame, I was drawn to her. It was a relief to finally have something to show for myself in the form of a nine-to-five, but even more of a relief that it was something I enjoyed, and with people I could tolerate.

A week after Blue and I broke up, she came to my house in Woolwich to bring me an IKEA bag of all the stuff I had left at hers. I found myself bawling in my room as I sifted through it. Not only had I broken her heart, but I had broken my own. I thought back to the times when I'd shut her out, afraid of how she'd see me if she knew what I genuinely thought of my chances at success. How I hid the play from her in the hopes that I could keep the evil eye at bay, or how I failed to tell her about the moniker changes. I wondered if patience and faith would have taken me just as far, with Blue championing me all the way through. In an ideal world, they would have. But the world isn't ideal—not for everyone. In a less-than-ideal world, we make less-than-ideal compromises.

It was safe to say that a fair number of the people in my life were left scratching their heads at my new "relationship." When Nick found out, he was confused, but he wasn't nosy enough to investigate any further. He was the type of person to ask a question and just smile and nod at the answer, however out of left field it might be. My mother's initial reaction was, "*Ao! Ke monna wa lekgoa, ga se mosadi! Waitseee!*" which translates roughly to, *Wow, so you're in love with an Englishman now! I didn't see that coming, but hey, at least you're not a homosexual anymore! I can tell the family back home you're less of a disappointment!* I'm being a little hyperbolic, but you get the gist.

Even Lydia was taken aback. But seeing as she was a working-class Northerner, I guess it made sense. If there was anything we had in common, it was how far removed the upper-middle-class life was to us. To her, things didn't quite add up. This was also the reaction at *BABBLE*; I'd prided myself not only on my unapologetic queerness when I joined the force, but also on my never-ending love for my girlfriend. Blue had basically become integrated into my work life, visiting me at the office on occasion and joining in on social events. When she suddenly disappeared two months prior and was replaced by a cookie-cutter cisgender straight white male overnight, questions did arise. No matter how much I tried convincing my colleagues that you and I had naturally grown close to one another, bonding over our love for theatre, it had become a running joke that I was taking advantage of your social standing. Franki, along with almost everyone else in the office, had given me the name Baby Suga, and I went along with it. Taking it on the chin was the best way to go about it because it was only temporary, after all. And honestly, there was some truth to it. Our relationship was entirely transactional.

When I first started at *BABBLE*, I worked on an ad hoc basis in the art and culture section, proofreading and editing articles and short stories for pay. Tahlia Wilson, the head of the magazine, was notably impressed with my technical writing skills and my input, eventually offering me a proper position, adding another head to the fifteen-person office. I felt a sense of pride to be in a place primarily operated by women of colour, from the managerial positions down to the free-lancers. The magazine was still a fairly new creation, eighteen months into being a crowdfunded startup. It focused primarily on contemporary social issues that surrounded intersectional womanhood, queer-ness, race, and general politics. There was an online issue published every six weeks on a Friday, and articles came out frequently. Photo shoots with creatives and interviews with people from different in-dustries were a regular part of the experience, and we were delegated to whatever work suited us the most. It was a well-oiled machine that paid adequately, but the money didn't matter to me. I don't think it mattered to most of us, as there were clearly easier ways to make a living. Like having a sugar daddy, I guess.

I switched on my computer, setting it up for a long day of sieving through submissions and editing articles. Franki edged closer to me and grabbed my pastry to take a cheeky bite out of it. She'd got into the habit of doing that every morning, like she was an indulged little sister.

"How was the gala the other night? It looked so fancy," she asked me through her chews.

"It *was* fancy. I felt like a sore thumb. But I did look good."

"You *slayed*, darling. From the mug to the shoes."

"And the purse!"

"We can't forget the purse," she said.

The annual Regium gala had just taken place, and everyone in-volved in *Great Belonging* had an invite and could bring a plus-one. With a seat at the table coming up to fifteen hundred pounds a head, it was a star-studded affair that was teeming with rich and famous people from all over theatre, TV, and film. It was our first public appearance together. It was also one of those moments that had snuck up on me, reminding me that you were teetering on the edge of notability. It wasn't even a year ago when we were still waiting to see if you were a contender for the MBGs, but now you had essentially been catapulted into breakout status. If you were still with Belle and me with Blue, it would have been harder for me to follow the play's ascension. Now we were a team walking hand in hand, beaming at the lenses of photographers on a red carpet.

The night was a whirlwind. We bumped into many big theatre names, and I tried my best to hide my awe. I'd spent some time trying to give you more of an understanding of who the big players were. We would watch various productions together in our spare time, and I would rant your ear off about the societal implications of one play or the cultural impact of another, just so you were not completely clueless. You had the charm and the affect to play the part, and your background in law gave you a bit of an excuse not to get everything, but you still had more to learn. By the time the gala came around, you were shaking hands and complimenting the right people on the right roles they played in the right works. It was a balancing act of knowledge and curiosity, self-assuredness and humility, and you were doing a pretty good job.

Smarmy Helen also made an appearance at the gala, much to my dismay. She joked about how she was in on our little secret, and a split second after my heart jumped, I realised she was referring to the Edward Moore incident. I hated the fact that she gained anything from this. If there was anyone I was close to blurting the truth to, it was her, but I needed to keep my cool. She was merely a cog in the machine of prejudice, a player in the game. I knew she was also probably happy that she'd managed to nab Nahid and use her as a symbol of progress at the agency, along with the multiple actors of colour who were involved in *Great Belonging*. Celeste Adebayo, the lead actress, was British-Nigerian, and the traction she gained at a rapid speed for her jaw-dropping performance looked doubly as good for optics. Helen was probably rubbing her hands together at what was merely just a cash grab to her, despite the fact that nearly two years ago, and under my name, she had not seen it as such. I couldn't wait to expose her one day for the disingenuous sod she was. But for now, I'd let her laugh and wink and think she knew what she didn't know at all.

• • •

Since the production ended, Nahid had had her fair share of recognition and was swept into the media junket. You saw less of her, which was expected, but you were put on a couple of panel talks together along with some of the lead actors. Shortly after Blue gave me back my things, you suggested I take up the spare room in your house so that we could coordinate things more smoothly, and I wasn't opposed to the idea. Even though your stay was initially limited to a gap year, you made a deal with your father that you'd start paying discounted rent after a certain point, and my moving in helped to further discount it. It also worked as a cock-blocking of sorts, because you were more reluctant to have Nahid around with my condemnatory presence looming over everything. It meant that you'd sometimes spend the odd night away, or occasionally turn up home in the small hours of the morning. You explained away these disappearances, usually by saying you were spending time with your friends, but it got to the point where I didn't think you could possibly like your friends *that* much.

The night after the gala, I overheard you on the phone in your bedroom. It was safe to assume that Nahid was on the other end of the line based on the tone of your voice—a soft saccharine lilt, coupled with the odd chuckle. I know I shouldn't have, but I leaned my ear on the door to get a better listen. From what I gauged, you were praising how beautiful she'd looked the night before, and when you were met with a slight protest from her, you emphasised it. When you told her you missed her, I stepped back and my heart caught in my throat. There really was something there between you, even if I didn't quite understand it. Just as you had found love, I had lost it. A less-than-ideal compromise for a less-than-ideal world.

One balmy April afternoon I took a trip to the Columbia Road Flower Market. I was lost in my own world, blasting seventies Brazilian popular music in my ears, trying to choose between a laceleaf and a dragon plant, when I felt a tapping on my shoulder. "Cavalo-Ferro" by Quarteto em Cy was replaced with the sound of my busy surroundings as I swiftly whipped out my earphones and turned to see Nahid standing there, clutching a waxy bromeliad saturated in hues of magenta and orange. The front of her hair was pinned back with mini butterfly-claw clips, and she wore a denim dress over a plain white tee. I rarely saw her outside of her professional duties, so I almost didn't recognise her and assumed it was some girl who wanted dibs on the last laceleaf. I was ready to stand my ground, but then I clocked her husband Aaron standing next to her, and I began to put two and two together.

"Fancy seeing you here!" Aaron greeted me. "I thought I noticed you. How's it going?"

"Hey! I'm good, I'm good. How're you guys?" I asked, putting on my best cordial-conversation-with-an-acquaintance voice.

"We're all right. I guess we all had the same idea in mind," Nahid chuckled. "Flowers and all."

"We did. I'm still deciding, but I think I'm going to nab this anthurium."

"Oh, don't let us stop you! Go ahead," she prompted.

As I turned to get it, Aaron continued the conversation. "So, Nahid told me a while ago that you also write plays, like Hu. That's dead impressive. You kept that secret, didn't you?"

I faced them again, plant in hand. "Oh, uhhh . . . well, I went to uni for it. I haven't really written anything of substance since I graduated. I feel like I'm still honing my craft."

"I'm sure you're all right. It's easy to fall into perfectionism. Nothing's ever good enough when it's yours, is it?"

"No, not when it's mine. If anything has my name on it, I doubt it'll get far. It's a curse." I shrugged. "I heard you're branching into film. Now *that's* dead impressive."

"Aye. I'm in talks to direct a period drama, but it's early days. I'm trying to get the missus an acting role in it, too, but she's not too keen," he said, nudging her.

"I'm not *not* keen, I'm just so busy with other things. I want to prioritise my projects a bit more, you know?" Nahid said, addressing me.

"It'll be your first role on the big screen. That could take you places."

"First doesn't mean only," she responded in a strained singsongy tone through gritted teeth. "Anyway, sorry for holding you up, Eddie. We'll let you go."

"Don't apologise, it's all Gucci. This was a lovely coincidence! I'll let Hu know I saw you," I said, smiling at her. She bit her bottom lip, nodding. It was like we were speaking to each other in code.

I waved them goodbye as they walked off into the bustling market crowd, and I mentally analysed our interaction, taking notice of her demeanour. At that point I felt like I knew her well enough to know that like me, she was putting on her best cordial-conversation-with-an-acquaintance voice. I'm pretty sure I was the last person she wanted to bump into while she was with her husband. She seemed slightly irked about his film role suggestion, and to be honest, the curiosity was getting the better of me. I wanted to know more. I *needed* to know more. I wanted to know why she had strayed from her marriage, or how her marriage even came to be in the first place. I wanted to know how such a revered woman of colour in the industry somehow seemed so . . . stuck. What was holding her back? Why was it that the more I got to know her, the less self-assured she appeared? I walked up to the vendor to pay for my new plant and then put my earphones back in, drowning everything out again with "Abre Alas" by Ivan Lins. All the while I was ruminating on all the above questions, unaware that I was to find out the answers much sooner than I realised.

• • •

Considering my relationship with you wasn't real, it meant that it also had an expiration date. We would eventually have to have a fake breakup, too. The question was when, and it was sort of contingent on how long we could ride the *Great Belonging* wave, which wasn't something we could predict. One could argue that technically there was no real reason for us to still pretend to be together, but as long as you were in the public eye, I couldn't risk you misrepresenting my art. I had to have an ear to the ground at all times, and our partnership made that easier. Although you balanced knowledge, curiosity, self-assuredness, and humility well, you *were* still a fraud. I didn't want you to put your foot in your mouth, and it was evident that this was also becoming more and more of a worry of your own. There was one panel event that went relatively smoothly, but there were times where I caught you faltering, searching for an adequate, educated response to one of the moderator's questions. From the outside it could have just looked like plain nerves, but we had spent that morning rehearsing potential panel scenarios, making a list of answers and studying the play's themes like we were back in school. I was the director and you were the actor, and every prep session for a press commitment was a rehearsal of our own.

On the same evening that I saw Nahid at the flower market, I decided to sit down with you and ask how you were feeling about everything. You had the tendency to nod and smile, but even in my proximity to you, I didn't necessarily feel like you were allowing yourself to stress in the same way that came so easily to me. I was the emotional wreck and you were an anchor, but I knew deep down, you worried like I did. I just needed to know what about. That's what relationships are for after all, right?

"I'll be honest. Things have been getting quite intense. I constantly feel like I'm going to say the wrong thing. I've literally been waking up from dreams about it. I know that's unlikely—I know *Great Belonging* like the back of my hand. I was the first person to read it, besides Helen. It's imprinted in my DNA at this point. But that doesn't change the fact that it's not mine." We were sitting in your living room as you spoke, watching a zany black comedy anthology series on the BBC. The same four or five actors were in every episode, playing different characters, and it had distinctly odd plot twists.

"I get that. I do. It's a sticky situation. I guess there's nothing stopping you from becoming more reclusive, right? There are some creatives who make amazing shit, then avoid the media. Like Stanley Kubrick, or . . . Enya."

"Enya! What a legend. Thanks for reminding me of her."

"See? I told you. A talented recluse. You can do the same thing."

"I guess I could, you're right. Helen has a string of appearances lined up for me, though. Should I just turn them all down?"

"Why not? You did what you were supposed to do. It's all about the play now. I just don't want you to feel pressured to perform for the masses. That wasn't exactly the main point."

"I know," you said, nodding. "But if I were to turn down public appearances . . . wouldn't that mean we don't need to keep playing house? We can just live our lives and watch the fruits of your labour play out in front of you. I could call this bad boy my magnum opus, 'quit' playwriting, and then switch careers. Get actual acting training and whatnot."

"Wow, you've already got this all mapped out! There's just one thing. I have this feeling I'm not quite done yet. It started after the play ended its run at the Regium, and seeing how well it did . . . I don't know. I just feel like I haven't quite reached my ultimate goal, which is to prove everyone who ever doubted me wrong. To reveal the farce this industry truly is. The truth needs to come out in the end, but I also want something to show for *myself*.

"I've been thinking about working on something new and getting it out there. A 'round two,' if you will. This time, I'd be in a much better position. Maybe that's when we could start to phase out of this."

You nodded slowly. "That sounds like a decent idea. So . . . eventually we'll reveal everything, then?"

"Definitely. Ideally, I'll have my next play completed before we reveal the truth. It'll wow everyone and further prove what I'm capable of, if anyone still has their doubts. They'll never be able to deny me a seat at the table. How could they? But we're already playing the long game now, so I think we should just wait until then."

You looked at me hesitantly. "Do you know how long that could be?"

I paused, looking straight ahead. I couldn't give a definitive answer. That dawning uncertainty stopped me in my tracks. "It won't be too long, I promise. I'll start writing something soon. Whatever it is, it will be even better than *Great Belonging*. It will be tectonic-plate-shifting. That I know for sure."

"I'd expect nothing less from you," you replied.

After watching a bit more of an episode of the TV series, the one where a man becomes fixated on a shoe he finds on the pavement on his morning run, I thought to bring up that I had seen Nahid earlier. Your energy shifted immediately.

"You did? Where?"

"At the flower market. It's where I got Rio de Janeiro from."

"What?"

"The plant. That's what I named it."

"Okay. Did you speak to her?"

"Yeah, I did. She was with Aaron. You know. The man she walked down the aisle and said her vows to."

I saw you cringe. "How was she?"

"Well, you'd know, wouldn't you?"

"God. Please stop holding this over my head, Eddie. I'm begging you."

"She looked very pretty. She was dressed well and her hair was done up all lovely. If she was gay, I'd go for her." You stared at me, unamused. "*Kidding.* She was all right. Basically, I just wanted you to know that I get that you're still involved with her, and . . . it's whatever. As fucked up as the whole Belle situation was, I get it. You don't need to sneak around me. It is what it is."

You relaxed, sinking into the sofa a little bit. "If I'm honest, I don't care if the whole world found out tomorrow that I was lying about the play. Okay, that's a lie, I'd obviously care a little bit. But Nahid . . . her opinion matters so much to me. The longer I keep this from her, the more it eats me up inside. I don't want her to feel like she's throwing her marriage away for a fake."

"Well, something's got to give, then, right? You can't keep seeing her under false pretences. I mean, you can if you want. But it seems like that's what's really bothering you."

You nodded and then sighed. "I'm in awe of her. She has so much to give. So, so much. But I can't give that back, at least not properly."

"You could just tell her the truth."

"Shit. You think so?"

"Yeah. Just because I don't want us to tell the truth to everyone yet doesn't mean I'm opposed to telling *anyone* else. It just depends who it is. Think about it: Nahid's the common link between our lie. She's one of the reasons we're faking this relationship. If you genuinely care about her, you should just let her in." My chest tightened as I momentarily thought of Blue.

I watched as you readjusted yourself, contemplating. "What if she blows the lid off? Would you be okay with that?"

"She could, theoretically. But surely if you just tell her not to, she won't. At the end of the day, you're her biggest weakness. What reason does she have to out you without outing herself?"

"Okay. I know she probably wouldn't say anything if she found out. I don't know for sure, but that's not my main concern. I just worry it will change how she sees me. The only reason she knows me is through all this. It's kind of like, I don't know, a woman finding out her husband is gay. It's a tad hard to move forward, isn't it?"

"Erm, it's not like that at all." I screwed up my face. "You're both still straight. No?"

"Touché."

"I think this would be the ultimate test. To see if it's even worth still doing whatever it is you're doing with her. If she can't accept you as you are, then that's that. We can all move on. But I just don't think she'd want to reveal the true origins of the one thing that's jump-started her directorial career. She has a horse in the race. And I'm not trying to play Cupid here, but it's evident to me that you love her, and I do think she must love you, too."

"I *do* love her. I don't want to lose her."

"You should just come clean. If she's the one person whose opinion you truly care about—besides mine, of course—then nothing else should matter."

You paused, taking some time to ruminate on the situation. It was a risky proposal, I got that. But by telling her you weren't the mastermind, you'd be telling her that *I* was, and I couldn't imagine her feeling the need to out me against my wishes, considering the lengths I was willing to go to to not expose her. I felt that it was a safe bet. When you're this far out into the ocean with no wind in sight, it's sometimes worth trying to get the albatross off your neck.

"Can you be the one to tell her? I don't know if I can. It will sound better coming from you. I can't bear to see how she'll react."

"Belle was right, you really *are* such a Libra. Why don't I call Nahid now? See if she's free, then invite her over?"

"You can't do it now!"

"Why not? Let's rip the plaster off."

You shook your head. "If you want to do it tonight, I can't be here. I just can't."

"Okay, you can find something to do. Go play darts or bingo or whatever." I took my phone from the coffee table. Once it started ringing, you were practically rocking back and forth. Fifteen seconds later, she picked up.

"Hello?"

"Hey, how's it going? It was lovely seeing you earlier. Great plant choice, by the way. Anyway, this might be a tad short notice, but Hu's gone out to the Flight Club and I've got nothing but wine and my own excruciating thoughts. I was thinking maybe we could shoot the shit? Perhaps discuss botanics?"

"Oh, really? I've literally just left the Flight Club! Which one's he going to?"

"Uhhh . . . ," I stalled. Wow, what were the chances? "I don't know. What am I, his girlfriend?" I snorted. "Anyway. Where are you going now?"

"I think my friends and I are heading off to Slug and Lett—"

"Okay, so nowhere important. Just call it an evening out there and split some red with me."

"Eddie, I can't just derail my plans to hang out with you. Where's this all coming from?" I had failed to consider that my impulsive reaching out to her might have come off as jarring, considering we technically weren't that close. She wasn't Lydia, or Franki, or anyone in my frequent social circle, so as familiar as we were with one another, it didn't mean we were particularly chummy. You were our common ground, so my next angle was to use you as bait.

"I have something to tell you. It's about Hugo. I think you ought to come." The silence on the phone went on for too long. You and I looked at each other in trepidation.

"Oh. Right," she eventually said, clearing her throat. "Fine. Give me a second to split."

"No worries. I'll see you in a bit!" I said before hanging up. I turned to you. "It worked. She's coming over. Go and find something to do."

You shot up and paced around the room. "Are you sure this will work?"

"Trust me, it will. I'm telling you."

"Okay." You nodded. "Okay. I'll call Damian and see if he's about."

"Nice one. Let me get started on the wine. I think I'll need some Dutch courage."

When you finally left, the nerves started setting in. With Enya's greatest hits playing on the Alexa and a glass of wine in my hand, I braced myself for what was to come—for the moment our little secret would no longer be just ours.

XV

Adorned

I chickened out when she first arrived. I wasn't drunk enough yet, and although she was lightly buzzed on a couple of cocktails from her night out, it was clear to me she too had some loosening up to do. She looked just as nervous as I did, and this invisible wall between us made me almost regret my impetuous invitation. But she was here now, and there was no point in turning her away. I just needed time to rip the plaster off.

I told her the real reason I wanted her company was because I was still reeling from my breakup with Blue. This was technically true—although it had been three months since I last saw her, the longing hadn't got any less intense. In a way, I was distracting myself with this circus I was a part of. I explained that most of my friends had also been Blue's, so I was existing in isolation from my old social life and was in need of some downtime with another feminine presence. She immediately sympathised, and I guess it was because she felt partly responsible. She had previously said she would be there for me if I needed her, and she was evidently a woman of her word.

We primarily hung out in your kitchen, sitting on the island counter stools with a Malbec in hand, and I spent the first half hour pouring my heart out about my relationship. I told her how Blue and I had met and ranted and raved about her inspiring musical journey. I even told her about my strained relationship with my family upon my coming out of the closet, and how it was something I was willing to sacrifice for true love. After all, not everyone gets that chance to feel existential gratitude towards sharing a little corner of a relatively inconsequential galaxy among an infinity of other galaxies with that one special person. In telling Nahid all of this, I could feel her wanting to open up to me about her own experiences, which was what eventually happened.

• • •

She began with the genesis of her acting journey, from when she had started at fifteen to when she decided it was her life's dream. She didn't know if this relentless desire was something that lived inherently within her, passed down from her father and his creative streak, or if it was something that she serendipitously stumbled onto. Either way, she was determined to chase it. After a gruelling multistage application process, she was one of only thirty hopefuls who were accepted into the 2002 cohort for an acting degree at the RADA. She started off as a meek but determined student, gradually working to strip away her strong West Country accent in exchange for a more agreeable Southern one. As someone of Middle Eastern heritage, she was often typecast and othered, and this was only heightened in a newly post-9/11 environment. Although she initially took pride in her background and bilingual proficiency, she eventually grew tired of constantly being cornered into it. At a time when she was still trying to discover who she truly was, the world already had an answer.

She fell in love for the first time in her final year of drama school. It was with a graduate who she had been paired with as part of the school's buddy programme, which was meant to help soon-to-be graduates get some intel on the harsh acting world ahead of them. As her mentor, he was entrusted to show her the ropes and hand down invaluable information, which he initially did. He was four years her senior and had a string of theatre work behind him, so it had come in handy. But soon their mentorship had traversed any semblance of professionalism, and they were locked into a relationship so intense she couldn't make sense of it. It only lasted four months, but when it fell apart, it fell hard. It turned toxic and borderline abusive on his part, and it had broken her down into smithereens. It was like the previous three years she had spent trying to build herself up had all been for nothing. That was a feeling I could unfortunately relate to. However, in a sick and twisted way, it strengthened her acting skills. She could pour out her anguish into her roles intuitively. Despite the fact that she had stopped eating and started drinking and only left her university accommodation for production rehearsals and exams, she was smashing her final-year grades. The first person in her life who was essentially tasked to be her cheerleader was nothing of the sort, but it somehow worked. That was how she entered into her career— with this awfully skewed understanding of her worth.

"I needed a break from the stage after I graduated," she told me. "I was sick of it. Even though I had done so well, I had become disillusioned by it. I just wanted to live a simple life for a bit. I moved back to my parents' house in Bristol and just worked in restaurants. I'd go and get wrecked with my hometown friends every other weekend. I'd date around to keep myself occupied. It wasn't necessarily healthy, but it was what I needed at the time. To only have to think about what I was going to wear at pre-drinks and not where my life was heading."

Eventually the latter question began to nag at her. She was on the fence about her return to theatre, but she still wanted a purpose. Feminist activism had slowly started creeping into her interests, especially concerning the oppression of women in her home nation. She was grateful for the opportunities afforded to her being raised in a more liberal country and wished the same for others elsewhere. She tried thinking of ways to make an impact the best way she could—the best way she knew how. That in turn brought her back to acting.

She moved back to London on a whim and auditioned for plays left, right, and centre, nabbing supporting acts and small roles in anything she could get her hands on just to build a stronger portfolio. Her golden ticket came in the form of a lead role in a production up in Edinburgh, spearheaded by a charming and driven up-and-comer in the thespian community who hailed from Glasgow but had roots in Cairo. *The Adorned* seemed like the perfect opportunity for her to make her voice heard and her name known. Her character had a harrowing ten-minute monologue in which she was to slowly remove all items of her clothing, most controversially her hijab, until she was left standing bare in her underwear. Even though she knew this would cause a stir, she felt that it was a stir worth causing, and she was right. The awards instantly came pouring in, and a tour was scheduled at the same time that she won an MBG.

"I felt so grateful, and somewhat indebted to Aaron. A part of me thought that our connection during the rehearsals had been a catalyst for my performance. It was fucked up, I know, but it was hard for me to think that I just had it in me. I guess I also wanted to shift some of the heavy weight of the potential consequences. If he was the mastermind and I was merely helping him execute it, the repercussions couldn't all fall on me.

"It helped me get through the citizenship ban, too. I wasn't Iranian anymore. I was just British, and that was okay. It was more than enough. If I hadn't been British, I'd have been . . . a subjugated nobody from a totalitarian society. I was better off, you know? This is why I loved *Great Belonging* so much. I really see myself in Amali, the main character. I relate to her struggle of wanting to be safe from harm and judgement, of wanting a fruitful life, be it in her homeland, or elsewhere—whatever it takes." My heart sank a little when she said this. Amali was an amalgamation of my own experiences, but she was also a mirror for those who understood her plight as an immigrant. To know that Nahid saw her as someone she could relate to was sobering. In many ways, she and I were just one and the same.

"I told myself I'd done the right thing with *The Adorned*," she continued. "Aaron had done the right thing. We did it together, as a unit. It was all a huge blur, but before I knew it, I was getting my makeup done and slipping on this *gorgeous* cream-white wedding dress in the Scottish Highlands. I was no longer lost in the world. I'd found someone, and I'd found myself in the process. Or so I thought."

She couldn't pinpoint exactly when her feelings began to change. It was a gradual process. She started to see Aaron as more of a paternal figure in her life who couldn't envision her as more than her role as an actress. It became evident that he never seemed to truly rally for her branching out into more creative positions in the industry. She started to realise how few female theatre directors there were, and this was something she wanted to change. Her father had once been persecuted for his creativity, and she was lucky enough not to have that as a reality for her. She wanted to take the bull by the horns, but instead she felt she was just living in the shadow of her successful director husband. Like the title of his play, she was nothing more than an adornment to him. That was what it looked like to everyone else, too. That was what it had looked like to me. In that moment, I hated myself for it.

She had been relaying all this information to me as she drank, getting more intoxicated in the process. Eventually, there came a revelation that turned my heart inside out and compelled me to take her by the hand and squeeze it as she spoke.

"Not a lot of people know this, but . . . I had a miscarriage. It was a year ago to the week before I got the script for *Great Belonging*. I had absolutely no idea I was even pregnant." She looked down at the glossy surface of the counter. Her voice had got quieter and her eyes were rimmed with moisture. "When it happened, I was acting in a gruelling production in Wales. When I'm stressed, I usually get nauseous to the point of vomiting, and I sometimes miss cycles. So I guess I just chalked it up to that. Maybe there was also denial, I don't know. Aaron was out of the country for a work commitment at the time. I called my best friend and she drove me to the hospital, and that was where my world basically shattered around me." She closed her eyes, trying to stabilise her shaking voice. "I was eight weeks along at the time. Eight weeks of going about my days, blissfully unaware. Eight weeks of drinking what I wanted, eating what I wanted, living carefree—or carelessly, as I came to think. Maybe if I hadn't, it wouldn't have happened.

"But then . . . there was this deplorable part of me that was sort of . . . *relieved*. Aaron and I were at our most distant. I couldn't imagine a baby would have changed that. I would have just become a stay-at-home mother; I was sure of it. I felt guilty for feeling relieved, but I also grieved for what could have been. It's frankly something I wouldn't wish on my worst enemy." She wiped away a tear.

It was only inevitable for her to fall into a depression shortly after that, she told me. Once the shame and the anger subsided, she felt nothing for a long time. She would have felt guilty about feeling nothing if she could even muster up the intensity of an emotion such as guilt.

"Did you . . . ever tell Aaron?" I asked her, softly rubbing the back of her hand with my thumb.

She looked at me, then away, shaking her head. "I didn't know how to. I know, it's awful. We were three years into the marriage, but I felt like he stopped caring about me long before then. So I just didn't have the heart to. I was too traumatised, quite frankly. I just wanted to forget it had happened and move on. I couldn't unearth it with someone who put his career before everything. It almost felt like telling my boss, in a way. And . . . if I'm being honest with myself, I think once I realised I could hide something like that from him, it sort of . . . just made it easier for me to hide other things, you know. I'm not saying that's good, but that's just my shitty excuse."

The Royal Central School of Speech and Drama ran an eight-week evening course on theatre directing. When the fog had lifted from her vision and she could see the possibilities the future held, she decided to sign up for it. Getting any help from Aaron was not an option in her mind; their lives essentially ran parallel to one another. When she told him she had got her first gig, and that it happened to be for that year's MBG playwright award winner, he was initially supportive, but he remained emotionally distant. She felt cast aside, and it took her back to her twenty-one-year-old self, a past self who struggled to believe that internal approval was the only kind needed. She had the fame, the fortune, the looks, and the acting accolades, but was she enough? Would she ever be? She had what it took. There was just something missing. What was it? Love? Maybe. Maybe that was what it all came back to.

By the time the play's rehearsals were in full swing, she had completely disassociated from him, and the empty corner of her heart was slowly becoming fully occupied by someone else. Her sex life with Aaron wasn't nonexistent by that point, but it was a ghost of what it used to be. It was a clinical and bathetic routine. Instead of fireworks, there were party blowers. With you, she told me, there were more than even fireworks; there were little supernovas. Once she was reminded that her body was still capable of harbouring such carnal pleasure—

that someone was capable of giving her that luxury—it was all she wanted. Of course she felt violent shame at the beginning of your trysts with her, but her taste of unmarred intimacy superseded that shame. So, no, it wasn't just a production fling; it wasn't frivolous. It was serious. To make a long story short, everything was fucked.

"A couple of weeks ago we spent a night at the Shard." She said after finishing off the rest of her wineglass. Her lips were tinted burgundy and some of her mascara had smudged. She looked worn down, but it was impossible not to notice her eyes brighten when you were the subject of conversation. "The view from the top was beautiful. If I could, I'd live the rest of my days up there with him, just watching the sun rise and set over the city." She smiled softly, propping her chin up with her elbow on the table. At this point it wasn't just the copious alcohol I'd consumed that was making me nauseous.

"Nahid. You know what I'm about to ask you, right?"

She quickly stripped her smile away, and her head dramatically fell forwards. "Ugh. It's the dreaded *D* word, isn't it," she murmured. "Why I haven't done it yet."

"Exactly that. You know better than to keep living like this."

"I know that. I obviously will."

"Oh! It's obvious, is it?"

"I'm just waiting for the right time. Everything has been such a whirlwind since I picked up *Great Belonging*. My life went from being in a complete standstill for a year to . . . all of this. It's not like I went out of my way to be with Hu—that was entirely unexpected. I told you that before. He was . . . a complication. A beautiful one, though."

"I'm literally going to vom, babe. Please stop."

"Sorry. I also just think I might be stalling the divorce out of spite. I want Aaron to see me do better than him. Maybe it's like some sort of power play. I can be just as successful as him, if not more. I want him to have to look me in the eye and squirm at my triumph. But I realise all of that means nothing if no matter how close he is to me, he's still so distant. I'm getting that now."

"*Yes.* Right on. Get out of his shadow and get out of his life. End of story."

By that point, I remembered why I had lured her over to your house in the first place. I checked the time on the kitchen wall clock: it was nearly eleven. I assumed you were still somewhere out there waiting with bated breath for the outcome, and I realised it was now or never. Nahid had bared her absolute all to me in just under two hours. It was enlightening, but also pretty gut-wrenching. My compassion for her had grown tenfold. I admired her now more than ever, which was why it hurt more than anything to do what I was about to do. My heart started palpitating and I straightened my posture, clearing my throat before I spoke up again after a few moments of silence.

"Okay, so. The actual reason I brought you over here was to tell you something about Hu."

Nahid's head snapped towards me instantaneously. "Oh God. He's seeing someone else, isn't he? You two are *actually* together, aren't you?" she near whimpered. "Fuck. Fuck."

"No, relax. He's not seeing anyone else, and *definitely* not me. It's a little weirder. See, I lied earlier at the flower market. I *have* written something of substance since leaving uni. Long story short, I also went through a dark time in my life. In the same way you came to the realisation that some of us just aren't taken seriously, I did too. The only difference was . . . I was too exhausted to fight for myself—to prove everyone wrong. So one day I thought, if you can't beat them, you might as well join them. And . . . that's where Hugo comes into play."

Nahid looked at me, puzzled. "I'm sorry, I'm not following."

"I saw a lot of the same qualities in him that you do. His likeable character, his good looks, his charisma, all that. I latched on to it, too. But for different reasons. I latched on to the ease with which he moved through the world. I wanted that for myself, but it was a dream far-fetched. So, let's just say that if you've ever got the impression that Hu's just *way* too humble about his playwriting skills, it's because he can't afford not to be. He can afford everything else, obviously. Just not arrogance."

"Eddie. What are you trying to say?"

I took a long exhalation. "The first play I wrote out of uni was pretty interesting. I wanted to reconceptualise the idea of an immigrant and what it means to be one. I wanted to explore questions about national identity because I've struggled with mine at times. It's even more of a mindfuck when I consider the history of colonialism and how I'm inextricably tied to it as someone from a Commonwealth nation. I thought a dystopia would be fitting, because I think that dystopias force you to hold a mirror to society and point out its hypocrisies. So, that's what I did. I wrote a play. It was originally called *The Worthy*, but I think you're more familiar with its current title."

Her face fell as I spoke. The penny had finally dropped. "Are you trying to say . . . are you saying that you wrote *Great Belonging*? Am I hearing that correctly?" she asked me. I nodded, staying silent. I could hear the blood rushing through my ears. "Oh my God," she whispered.

"He didn't steal it from me. It was all my idea. I'd tried under my own name and didn't get anywhere, so this was my desperate ploy, and it worked. So just know that I'm not faking this thing with Hu purely to cover for you two. It's just more convenient.

"I'm sorry you didn't know any sooner, but you're the only other person I've told. I need it to stay that way for now. It'll all come out at some point, but I thought it would be wise to let you in on it, considering . . . how entangled you are in everything. Considering how much Hu means to you, and how much you mean to him. It's hard to deny it. It's definitely thrown things off course; I'll give you that."

She stared at the ceiling. "So Hugo's been lying to me? He's been lying to everyone?"

"I put him up to it. I wanted to prove a point, and he was willing to help. But then he met you, and it complicated things. Like you said."

She shook her head, chuckling in shock. "There's no way this is real. I feel like I'm being pranked. I don't know what to think."

"If it's any consolation, you've done an amazing job with the play. You executed it perfectly. I was so scared that it was going to end up in the wrong hands, and all my work would have been for nothing in the end. You're such a talent, Nahid. You're going to go far."

"It *did* end up in the wrong hands! It's all a sham. I'm part of a sham."

"It's not a sham! It's real. It's mine. I'm just not the face of it. And it's opened the door for you. You got the chance to prove yourself."

"I can't really process this right now. I'll deal with Hu later, trust me. Just know this is the most *batshit* thing I've ever heard."

"I totally get that. It is." I nodded. "But I just need to know that you won't tell anyone else. It took a lot for me to get to the point of telling you."

"Of *course* I'm not going to tell anyone else. But you can't either. Ever. Not now, not in the future. Never."

"Sorry?" I stared at her.

"I know I've made some morally inept choices, and I'm not saying I'm void of any responsibility, but this . . . this is a whole new level. This is my career we're talking about. I feel blindsided. I'll have to hear Hugo's side of things too, because he *has* been lying to me, even if it was for you."

"Hold on. You've been lying for *him*. I've been lying for *you*. Nobody's innocent here."

"Exactly. This is all so convoluted. Regardless, nobody can ever find out about this. You can figure out your next steps and I'll figure out mine, but none of those steps involve telling anyone else. I swear to God, Eddie, I'm not getting swept up in your scheme. This can *never* get out. You can't do this to me. I never asked to be a part of this." She had her arms crossed, looking straight into me.

Fuck, I thought.

Fuck.

Dropping my face into my hands, I sighed. "Fuck."

XVI

The Canvas

June 2018

THE WRITER AND HIS MUSE: HUGO LAWRENCE SMITH TALKS ART, IDENTITY, AND INSPIRATION

―――――

The twenty-three-year-old playwright has burst
onto the scene with his groundbreaking political
dystopia, and he sits down with us for an exclusive
exploration of his creativity and sense of self

―――――

MARCUS EASENER

Sprightly, he welcomes us into his garden on a warm June afternoon, although there is a noticeable undercurrent of nerves in his body language. This is the first one-on-one sit-down interview he has conducted since the string of showings of *Great Belonging* at the top of the year, and he has admitted to trying his best to shy away from the intense media scrutiny. His grass is neatly mowed and the framing rosebushes are saturated with colour, as is the apple tree at the far end of the yard. "Whenever my mother visits, she does a lot of upkeep out here, even though it's actually my father's garden. I really appreciate it; I've never been much of a gardener myself. This would be a jungle if it was left up to me." He chuckles.

I start our conversation by further probing his relationship with his mother, which is evidently one of importance based on his mention of her before we've even sat down. His self-effacing smile morphs into a confident grin as he dotes on her. Penelope Smith-Murray spent twenty years teaching English literature at Magdalen College, Oxford, before her retirement in 2013. It is safe to assume that her connection with the discipline must have rubbed off on her son.

"There was always a part of me that I felt I was suppressing. Maybe 'suppressing' isn't the right choice of word, actually—I'm aware that I had the freedom to delve into something more creative. But in that freedom, I felt confined. With law there is room for interpretation, but the ultimate goal is to seek truth. Whether it be my truth or yours. It's formulaic in that way. Art isn't formulaic at all. There is technique and there are general rules, but that doesn't mean people see it all the same. It's the ultimate Rorschach test. I guess I was afraid to have my imagination tested for such a long time. I took what I thought was the easy way out, but in the process, I locked my dreams in."

I'm absorbed by Smith's earnest portrayal of his internal battle, and I note his posture as he speaks—initially sitting forwards, elbows resting on knees as he looks down. Then, as he continues, he loosens up, straightening his posture and making more eye contact. He mentions how his love for theatre doesn't end with the pen but extends to the stage. He plans to start acting once he has completed the training for it. "This experience has not only opened up my eyes to the boundlessness of my imagination, but watching the amazing actors who helped to bring my dream to light has encouraged me to want to do that for someone else. The fluidity that comes with being able to bend emotion at will and captivate an audience is something that fascinates me. I admit that I regret not delving into this at a younger age, but I know that regret should be a fuel and not a blockage. I'll appreciate what I have and I will make the most of it."

We start to tread into deeper discussions of *Great Belonging*, the play that put him on the map. He tells me he came up with the concept of families ruptured by a draconian law that aims to uphold, in his words, the "myth of meritocracy," after a conversation with partner and *BABBLE* magazine editor Eddie Moruakgomo. "I think I just wanted to pose the question as to what actually makes someone British. In the play, the postcolonial island, Taniba, is a representation of a good chunk of the planet that was once under our rule. I say 'our' not to take full responsibility, but to acknowledge that when we take pride in our country, we have to do that with full awareness of the warts and all that make Great Britain so . . . great. Taniba has been independent for a couple of decades, but just by association, Britain is the primary destination for many of the citizens when there are economic and environmental hardships. Are they entitled to that?" he asks rhetorically. "Once the National Sweeps become a part of the system, are the Brits entitled to flee to these distant nations that were technically once theirs? It's a case of raising the question, but not the assumption of a clear-cut answer.

"People are so quick to point out differences between one an-other. We're quick to categorise, to say who belongs where, and rationalise these beliefs to the nth degree. If we're honest with our-selves, we realise that we've never stuck to our own rationalisations. Colonisation is a glaring manifestation of that. Ultimately, we're so much more alike than we'd like to think," he continues, his initial reticence replaced with a more impassioned flow of words. He lands on an interesting analogy.

"Think of it this way: my surname is one of the most prevalent names in the English-speaking world. It started off as occupational— you know, a job label. Then it became so commonly used that it even-tually had nothing to do with occupation but everything to do with social mobility. It's one of the most common names about, I'm aware of that, but it's not often we ask ourselves why. Its utilisation basi-cally ensured a safe blending into the populace. Germans switched out 'Schmidt' to avoid discrimination during the world wars. Polish people did the same with the equivalent 'Kowalski.'

"I don't mean to give you a history lesson. I just wanted to make a point: my partner, Eddie—her surname is also occupational. It means 'cattle farmer' or 'herdsman' in her native language. The roots of our names are the same—they're occupational. They represent social mobility. If I'm a blacksmith, she's a farmer. Obviously we're neither of those things, but we are people trying to earn a living; that's the point. I feel like that's lost on a lot of us sometimes, and that's what I try to remind people with *Great Belonging*. No matter where we are, we're all trying to survive. Whether we're able to or not is not entirely up to us. Sometimes it's a case of being born in England, or Poland, or . . . 'Taniba,'" he says, pulling up air quotes. "That's the thing. That's our fate."

Although it is clear that Smith is smitten with Moruakgomo, he shies away from the personal details of his newfound relationship with her, instead emphasising the value her worldview has brought into his life and art. He praises the Kingston drama graduate on her artistic ability, insisting on her right to one day expose her work at her own time. "I don't want to speak for her. But I can assure you that her work I've had the pleasure of reading blows mine out of the water. I'm not even being humble—it's just the truth. She's phenomenal. She's my muse, in a lot of ways, although I think I've reached my peak in her presence. I'll happily switch to acting and never turn back, just to spare me the comparison. Who knows, I could be the lead in her debut. She can call the shots and I'll just put on my best show." He smiles.

"Okay. It's actually not that bad," I said to you once I'd got to the end of the article. "It's a little bit 'we're all one race—the human race,' but that's palatable enough, I guess." I shrugged. "It'll do." We were sitting in the same place where you took the interview a week or so prior. I balanced my laptop on my lap and held a cigarette in my free hand, staring out at the very roses tended to by your mother.

"It better do. I've already done it now," you said.

"You love sneaking these innuendos in there, don't you?"

"What innuendos?"

"'She can call the shots and I'll put on my best show.'"

"I'm just having a bit of fun with it, aren't I?" you replied, grinning. "Might as well."

"You've put the pressure on. You're telling the *Guardian* that I'm sitting on a treasure trove of plays, and I'm still only on the outline of a new script."

"It's what you wanted, though, right? I'm just sticking the batteries in your back. I wouldn't say any of that if I didn't mean it. I'm soft-launching your success."

"In vain, perhaps." I took a deep toke of my cigarette before crushing the butt in the glass ashtray on the table next to me. Wary of my nicotine addiction, you had gone out of your way to buy it for me at a secondhand antique shop at some point shortly after I'd moved in. I spent more time than I should have in the garden for that reason alone.

"Remember, it was you who wrote the play, not me. You can certainly replicate its quality, or do something better. Just don't get in your head about it."

"I'd probably be less in my head if there weren't so many sceptics."

You paused, looking at me. "Sceptics? Of what?"

"Oh, please. People don't like me. It didn't just end with Belle's army, you know. Don't act like you haven't noticed it. I know you have."

"There's hate on every corner of the internet. So be it." You shrugged. "It'll suck the life out of you to care about every one of them."

"I'm not one to care about hate comments. The fallout from Belle just became a nuisance if anything. But there's something about these. They're just *so* presumptive; reading them feels like an itch I can't scratch. Listen." I took out my phone and went into my photo gallery to bring up screenshots of opinions I'd seen on various online platforms. "'I don't think they're actually together. She gets access to his money and fame and he gets to appear 'woke.' 'Quite suspicious how he dumped his other missus for her once the play got rolling. I bet she's turned him into a proper lefty, I can't see how else this would work.' 'He just wants to seem more politically correct, so he's prancing about with an immigrant.' Should I go on?"

"Eddie. Those are just a few smart arses. If anything, more people are intrigued by you, which should be a boost. Hell, even the sceptics should boost you. Otherwise, you shouldn't pay it any mind." Granted, there were also comments directed towards your authenticity (or lack thereof), and how you were the last person who should get to have a say on whether meritocracy was a myth. Ironically, this would also make you the last person who got to deny that it was.

"You can see why it would piss me off, though, can't you? They're so misguided. Just imagine if I had been the one who put out *Great Belonging*. These idiots would be like, 'Ah, she's just a typical woke lefty.' It's not even like they're explicitly saying that about you—they're saying that you are because you're with me. Do you not understand how frustrating that is? I'm just this nefarious agent of 'wokeness' to them. You have the privilege of being a blank canvas, and I'm just the paint that taints you."

Your face fell as I spoke, and you looked out into the garden, sighing. Then you turned to me. "Do you think that's maybe one of the reasons you were willing to give away ownership? You know . . . because, I guess I'm just a blank canvas . . . ?"

"I don't mean it with spite. You know that. I just knew if you had a greater chance of success, that meant you had a lesser chance of critique. Nobody will look at you with scepticism like they do with me. If you weren't associated with me, what would they attribute your ideologies to? They'd call you an independent, progressive, a freethinker. But I'm part of the equation, so you're none of those things. I'm not your muse, I'm the chip in your brain."

This had always been something that rubbed me the wrong way, although I'd never found a way to vocalise it. White artists and writers have the freedom to traverse all spectrums of thought, to hold fringe ideologies and to openly campaign an array of political worldviews, but they are seldom held to those standards on the basis of their race. On the other hand, just by virtue of being a black writer, I entered into the arena with a glaring label pinned to my forehead like a game of Who Am I? I'm expected to approach art from a very specific angle, with a very specific mindset, with very specific political ideals. I'm expected to bring my blackness to the table. If I write a script with an all-white cast, people will wonder why, or assume I'm out of touch with my identity. If I write a script with an all-black cast, people won't question it, or they won't question why there aren't any white people. As if it's okay, because my art isn't relatable to them, as if art is even supposed to be relatable.

Alexander McCall Smith, a white British writer who was raised in Zimbabwe, got to write a bestselling series set in Botswana with an all-African cast and have it become the most prolific fictional depiction of my native country. Norman Rush, a white American writer from California, was shortlisted for the Pulitzer Prize for Fiction and won numerous awards for his novels, which were set in—you guessed it—my native country. On the other hand, there is no conceivable reality where any depiction of England I write about isn't pigeonholed into an outlying category, despite my undeniable familiarity with the place. See, I don't get to just be a writer. I'm also a walking agenda, whether I like it or not.

This realisation was growing harder to ignore. It gradually made me feel like I was compromising the play's purity by merely existing in proximity to it. It's twisted, I know. It's like one of my fears come true—the tainting of my work's reception, just by the public's osmosis of me. I was in the way of my work when it was my own, and I was in the way of my work when it was yours. As the pool of sceptics grew, I felt more compelled to "well, actually" them, just as I felt towards Smarmy Helen. But I had already resigned myself to secrecy, not even for my own sake or yours, but for the only other person who knew our secret and wanted it to stay that way.

• • •

When I had dropped the bomb on Nahid on that wine-fuelled evening a couple of months prior, I wasn't sure how she'd react. I was right that she'd probably want to protect her reputation, but I guess a part of me thought she'd get the bigger picture, that she'd possibly rally behind us. Behind *me*. Well, she hadn't taken well to it: she didn't speak to either of us for days, prefacing her silence with a text about how she needed time to figure things out. I'd questioned whether she'd want anything to do with us ever again. My anxiety had been at a new high in that silence, and I'd never seen you so anguished about anything. But then around two weeks later, she called you. You spoke for just over an hour on the phone, and all I could do was hope the conversation didn't turn left. With relief, it hadn't. She was still dead set on her stance regarding the exposure of our master plan, but even then, remarkably, she had come around. She had forgiven us. She had forgiven *you*.

I met up with her in a bustling café on Tottenham Court Road a couple of days after her phone call with you. I was weirdly more nervous than I thought I'd be; it felt like I was preparing for a bollocking. When I first saw her, there was still a glimmer of disbelief etched in the lines of her face, like a shadow of an expression frozen in time. Eventually I felt her deflate with repose as she emptied a sachet of demerara sugar into her coffee and let me in on where her thoughts had settled.

"I'm sorry I went dark, but I needed to. This is all a lot to process," she said, looking down at her beverage.

"No, I get that. It's not often you find out about something like this," I replied. "I realised it was a batshit idea when my ex-girlfriend became collateral damage. I'm surprised it even took me that long." I shrugged, then leaned forwards to prop my chin up with my hand. "I always ask myself what I'd have done if Hugo never won the MBG. Would I have kept trying? Would *he* have been willing to keep trying? There wasn't really a whole lot of foresight into all the possibilities. This is where we ended up, but I'm struggling with it. If 'what is meant to be will be,' is this it?" I was looking away from Nahid at this point, speaking more to myself than anyone in particular.

"I guess we'll never know how else it would have turned out, will we?" She shook her head sympathetically. "You shouldn't keep thinking of what could have been. Just figure out what you're going to do next."

I paused. "But you still don't want me to expose *Great Belonging*, do you? That's the problem. That's what I want to do eventually. When the timing is right."

"Eddie, the timing will never be right. It just won't go the way you think you want it to. Yes, we know there's a representation problem in theatre, but this was not the way to go about it. People can see it one of two ways: that you accepted that fact and just found a willing participant to take ownership of your work, or that you don't care enough about your work to attribute it to yourself."

"Yes, that would be the case if I never told the truth. That's the point—I just have to angle this in a way that puts me in the driver's seat. *Great Belonging* wasn't stolen from me, I gave it away. I'm the one in control."

"You're not in control. It's an *illusion*. You can't sway the future. You don't know what will happen if you go back on this."

I tutted. "God. If only Hugo wasn't so obsessed with you. I'd probably have just done it anyway."

She sighed, shaking her head. She didn't speak for a few moments, but when she did, her voice grew softer, more forlorn. "I hate that I can't get him out of my head. Even with all this, I . . . I can't shake him. It scares me sometimes. I feel like he could have more to hide, and I'd still brush it aside. It's . . . insanity. I don't know what else to call it."

"As far as I'm aware, he doesn't have anything else to hide. He's an open book in that way. Look, I know what it feels like to love someone and not want to let them go. I just think that . . . where you and I differ is that I find it a bit too easy to let go of the people I love, but . . . I also couldn't spend a sliver of a second with someone I don't."

She jerked her eyes towards me, jarred by my allusion to her marriage. If I was resentful about anything, it was her cheating on Aaron. I didn't let you get away with carrying on with Belle, and the more time went on, the more hypocritical it felt to let her string her husband along, too. She was afraid of her directorial debut becoming marred by the revelation that her lover boy didn't write it, yet not afraid of her directorial debut becoming marred by a potentially exposable affair with the lover boy who she now knew didn't write it. It was absurd, and I didn't want to keep covering for her. Like I said before, she wasn't my responsibility. My play was my responsibility, and so was figuring out a way to bring everything to light. But your life became mine, mine became yours, and Nahid's became ours.

"God, you're making me out to be like some sort of slag," she responded sharply. "I hardly even interact with Aaron anymore—at least not intimately. We rarely share the same bed. Not that you're entitled to this information, anyway. You don't understand that I can't just waltz out of a marriage if and when you demand it; I have to play my cards right. It's a whole process. Just because you don't get that doesn't mean you get the moral high ground. I'm not speeding my separation up for you."

"I'm not asking you to speed anything up. I just think you should reprioritise things. Hu isn't going anywhere, so you should hold off on your sleepovers at the Shard or wherever. You can't risk getting caught." I lowered my voice and leaned in closer. "Remember, this is my play. It's not running at any other venues at the moment and the press junket is slowing down. You'll start running out of excuses to sneak out. I care just as much about reputation as you do. This is bigger than your love life."

She looked away, frowning. Then her bottom lip started to tremble. *Oh God,* I thought. How someone could be so steadfast yet so sensitive fascinated me. "These last couple of weeks without Hu have been so empty. He's the most comforting thing in my life right now. My family don't speak to me. My husband's a drain on my morale. My friends see my life on the outside and think it's picture perfect. Things are going so well with my career and I'm getting offers for more work, which is so amazing—I don't take that for granted at all. But . . . I can't help but wonder how things would have gone if Hu hadn't been by my side this whole time." She closed her eyes. "He's always been there for me. He's never made me feel the sense of dread I usually feel in the pit of my stomach, like everything is a competition and I constantly have to prove myself. As an actor, a director, a woman, a *brown* woman, all of it. He's fascinated by everything I do. I know he's not a playwright, but I don't care. He's a breath of fresh air. I don't know if I can just . . . cut him off completely."

I looked at her. "God. You're so insecure for someone who's so talented. Stop relying on him."

Her face curled into an expression of disbelief and amusement. "*Wow.* That's rich coming from you."

"What on earth does that mean?"

"*I'm* relying on him? *Me?* Eddie, come on. Listen to yourself."

"It's not the same—"

"It's exactly the same, if not worse. You don't even love him. He's just your little lackey," she remarked woundingly, and it worked. I knew she knew how to hold her own, but it was unpredictable. Her opposing forms, affable and demure, ardent and assertive, morphed in and out of one another.

"He's my *friend.* He's been my friend for longer than he's even known you. I told you, this was an experiment that got out of hand.

I'm not insecure, I just know the system and I'm using it to my advantage."

"Ahhh. The advantage of living in someone else's shadow? Of not putting your real, authentic self on the line? Sounds like a solid deal." She stared at me as though she had won the war of words. I stayed silent, sitting dumbly, feeling heat prickle my skin. She continued. "If you get cut, it's not Hugo who will bleed. It's you and you only. You told me I should get out of Aaron's shadow, and you were right. I don't want to share my successes with anyone anymore. I want my accomplishments to hold up on their own. If I were you, I'd start thinking harder about what to work on next. There's no turning back with this play, but you and I both know you're capable of more. Hugo knows it, too, or else he'd not have done this for you. If you want me to take a step back from him"—she sighed—"I'll do it. I think the takeaway here is that we both just need to fight for ourselves that little bit more.

"When I was younger, all I wanted was to see more girls and women like me getting substantial screen time and holding up awards, so that I didn't feel like I was just spitting in the wind if I bothered striving for the same thing. I've always hoped that I could pave the way for someone else. Surely there's a part of you that wishes for that, too."

It pained me to hear it, but I saw where she was coming from. Everything she said was just confirmation of how I'd already started feeling. Yes, you were a means to an end, but what I'd failed to realise was that you had *become* the end. That wasn't quite what I wanted. I had to step out of your shadow. I had to let everyone know I was here, and that I was here to stay.

• • •

This was made all the more clear as I now sat in your garden, whining about the scrutiny I was receiving as a result of our fake coupledom. I'd also received a slight influx of emails over the last few months from the same literary agencies I'd sent my play to a few years back; I failed to consider the potential outcome of them going back to their slush piles once you started mentioning my name every chance you got. I'd given them the same excuse we had conjured up for the Wentworth Agency, immediately shutting their suspicions down about the eerily similar script for *The Worthy*. If I was willing to draw a line in the sand and completely separate myself from *Great Belonging*, it was time to set the wheels in motion with something new. I had to strike while the iron was still hot. Of course, negative attention was something nobody wanted. If I was going to get it regardless, then so be it.

"Eddie. You're not the chip in my brain. You are my muse," you said to me, standing up from the garden chair. "I mean it when I say that. You're right—maybe I am a blank canvas. But I'm also trying my best for you. I want you to win. I'll keep yelling it from the rooftops for as long as I do this. The next script you write has to be under your name. My job here is done."

I stood up, following suit. "You're too good to me," I said. "Come here. Give me a hug. And well done with the interview. You did do a good job."

You took a couple of steps towards me and we wrapped our arms around one another. "Thanks, Eddie. I appreciate it." As you stepped back, you grinned, crossing your arms. Then you paused, suddenly frowning. "Oh, shit. I feel a bit funny," you said, and grimaced.

"What? What's wrong?"

You tugged at your collar and squirmed a little bit. "I don't think I should have hugged you. Something's happening to me. I think I'm . . . turning into a woke lefty."

"You prick." I shoved your shoulder as you laughed.

"To hell with the sceptics. They don't know the half of it. They don't have a clue," you said, before making your way into the house.

XVII

Because You Love Me

When my father left England, that was the first summer we didn't spend in Botswana. My parents' separation had initially caused a huge rift in the family, and on top of that, my mother now had to financially recalibrate. Even though my father promised to send money over to help us out once he got settled, it was never going to be enough for us to live prosperously. My mother tried her best to hide the progressing bleakness of our situation from us at every step, but when we down-sized from a three-bed to a two-bed flat in a rougher estate in Wool-wich, that bleakness was difficult to conceal. We thankfully never got to the point of rationing food or heat, but I noticed the diminishing arrival of new clothes and the shrinking of birthday gifts in size and value. It was also the summer before my first year of secondary school, the summer I suddenly sprouted in height and grew out of my pri-mary school uniforms in the span of the six weeks since I'd last worn them. I started caring more about how I'd be perceived by my peers. I feared I'd enter year seven without the newest schoolbag for class or trainers to boast in PE, or that our Freeview channels limited the op-tions I had to keep up with what everyone was watching every week. These were never worries I vocalised to my mother, because even then I had an understanding that they were probably pipe dreams. My fa-ther's absence was replaced with a low, vibrating hum of resignation, and it was much harder to ignore than the tinnitus of the hankering I had for a comfortable life.

To make up for not going back to our home country, my mother took Nick and me to Brighton instead. It was less than two hours away on two trains, and the hotels weren't as exorbitant as other seaside destinations. I loved every moment of that holiday: the pier was a wonderland that levelled with the Vegas Strip in my eleven-year-old mind. The arcades and the fair rides were mesmerising and exhilarating, the ice cream was addictive, and the endless expanse of ocean was something you'd never find in a landlocked semidesert in Southern Africa. My mother would split cones of fish and chips with us that we dodged from predatory gulls after we'd dipped our legs into the glacial frothy waves, swaying above pebbly terrain. I remember floating with my brother in the ocean, staying completely still in the water until I no longer felt tangible. I had melted into the sea, only sure I still existed by my sight of Nick's bobbing head, silhouetted by the pier lights. I remember the salt of the water and the sound of music in the distance tuning in and out from clear to muted as my ears traversed the boundary between liquid and air.

By the time I was back in London, I was grateful for the time I'd spent away from it, even if it wasn't longer than usual or with extended family. But when I found out Molly McKinney in chemistry had gone to Magaluf and Joshua Bush in maths had spent three weeks in Florida and Khalil Montero in English language had just got back from Saint Lucia and Avery Sanders in design tech got a sunburn in Ankara, that vibrating hum of resignation hit me again, and again and again. *I've only been to England,* I'd thought to myself. Not locked by land, but by water. The only place I could escape to was the only place I knew.

◆ ◆ ◆

One day in June, you told me you were planning a trip to Italy with your friends in six weeks, and that you wanted me to come along. Your father had purchased an apartment overlooking Lake Como in the late seventies after falling in love with Northern Italy on a work visit. Before you were born, your immediate family had enjoyed summer after summer hopping back and forth across the Italian-Swiss border, the illustrious choice between swimming and skiing. Your older brother inherited the apartment once your father had exhausted his experiences there, but was often too busy working to take full advantage of it. Since the explosion of Airbnb, it had turned into a temporarily rented homestay for tourists, but during uni, you managed to convince your brother to give you a designated slot that you and your friends would happily chip in for every summer. As you explained all this to me, I was extremely lucid to the fact that in my nearly twenty-four years of existence, this would be my first time holidaying somewhere that wasn't Botswana or England. I pretended to ruminate on your offer, already envisioning the holiday in my head.

We flew business class to Milan in mid-July, splitting a chicken, bacon, and celery brioche sandwich between us. I had been adamant that economy was more than enough and that I'd rather save my money for the actual trip, but you reminded me of the fact that a healthy amount of play royalties were rolling into my account by way of yours and that it wouldn't bankrupt me to stretch my legs out a little bit. I told you that when planes crash, they usually nose-dive, so the business class are paying to die first. You smiled and said, "If it's inevitable, then that's the best way to go, don't you think?"

When we disembarked the plane, I was immediately hit by the heat. It was the primary sensory indication that I was somewhere different. You rented a car and we made the hour-ish journey from Malpensa airport to Menaggio, weaving through the scenic countryside. I had a childlike fascination with my view and I kept my eyes on the road ahead, concealing my all-consuming excitement at the fact that my footprint on the world was growing bigger, yet was still nanoscopic in comparison to yours.

"God. I've been to quite a few places, now that I think about it. I almost christened Asia before you came along," you told me on the drive to our destination as we talked about our travelling history.

"That's unfortunate. Columbus would have been so proud."

"Oh, stop it. It's only human nature to want to explore. There's a reason we have the means to travel. It's because we want to."

"It's also out of *necessity*. I'm not an immigrant because my parents wanted to try some authentic bangers and mash."

"Hey, bangers and mash aren't bad."

"I'm not doubting that. My palate has grown attuned to it. For better or for worse—I don't know."

The apartment sat among a cluster of others of varying sizes and heights on a hill that faced the lake. All the buildings were a mixture of pastoral and suburban, ornate yet simple, painted with overlapping layers of aged mustard, coral, camel, and milky yellow. The interior of your abode was upgraded for the modern age (and the appeal of the multitude of homestay tourists it now hosted), but it maintained its rustic ambience. I took in the tiled floors, the artwork, the furniture, and the sculptures peppered in every corner and archway. There were two bedrooms and a pullout sofa in the lounge, so the place could house six people in total. The lounge and the kitchen shared one space, and a floor-to-ceiling sliding glass door gave us a sight to behold: the foliage-swathed mountains splitting below the sky in a jagged fashion and slicing above the deep teal water in a straight line. It almost distracted me from the swimming pool situated a few feet ahead of the patio.

"This place isn't half-bad," I said to you after my reconnaissance of our new temporary dwelling. "It'll suffice."

"I think that's Eddie speak for 'I bloody love it,'" you said, smiling.

Once we settled down and unpacked everything, we decided to grab a meal at a restaurant nearby. I let you lead the way through the curved hilly neighbourhood roads as the sunlight dimmed. We eventually reached the muted bustle of the main streets that holidaymakers and locals frequented. There was a small restaurant on the corner of one of the roads you beelined towards, and I followed suit, trying my hardest to ignore the already-forming blisters that were a result of breaking in my new leather sandals. Your Italian was self-admittedly pitiful, but it sufficed when it came to getting us a table. You ordered a roasted fennel, burrata, and Parma ham bruschetta for starters, and I went with a light caprese salad. Don't get me wrong, I've had Italian food plenty of times before, so it wasn't like I was a fish out of water or anything. But there was something about my being there that evening that made it feel like the first time. There was something in the milky richness of the mozzarella, hinted with a floral tang, coalescing with the sweetness of the tomatoes and the peppery basil, drizzled in the herbal, fruity kick from the olive oil. Something in the ambience of the establishment, the mellow murmurs of the patrons, and the subtle classical music in the background. There was something that made the concept of this place feel so novel, like I'd never even heard of the country before. It was beautifully overwhelming. I made a mental note to call my mother before bed.

We came back to the apartment in the opaque dusk, full to the brim from our tagliatelle ragù and Milanese risotto mains and our tiramisu desserts, slightly fuzzy from the alcohol accompanying each plate. We were both exhausted from a long day of travelling, and the restaurant feast had nearly finished us off. Your friends were due to arrive the next day. This would be the first time I had properly met the social circle that kept you company throughout your young adult life. Although we had been performing our relationship masquerade for the last six months, I had always been evasive when it came to meeting your friends. I didn't see the point in integrating myself into your social life in the same way that I wasn't exactly quick to invite you to hang out with my friends. As a duo, we existed in our own bubble—a mechanism for access and infiltration into the theatre world and nothing more. But now here we were, and I couldn't shake the feeling that I was entering the lion's den. I guess it was only natural to want approval from the associates of someone you respect. The fact that such associates were under the impression that we were an item made things a tad more nail-biting.

I started thinking about Belle, and what it must have been like when you two were together. Did she fit in with your circle? I supposed she would have. I had done my fair share of sleuthing, trying to get a vibe of your friends, namely the ones that I'd be meeting, and it all made sense. On a superficial level, nobody seemed out of place. It was all loafers, Lululemon, and Lacoste, peacoats and navy gilets; trips with skis, trips with surfboards, trips to places I barely remembered existed. Belle was easily one of you. This year would be the first time she wouldn't be joining you in Italy, and I was hyperaware of that fact. I was aware that I was her successor. The real question was whether *I'd* fit in.

We got comfortable in the lounge, keeping only two lamps on and yawning periodically in between our conversation. You sat back on one end of the sofa and I had my head on the other end, lying across with one leg stacked above the other and my calves settled on your lap. My feet ended on the armrest where you had your elbow as you leaned your head on your hand.

"Can I ask you something?" I started.

"Fire away."

"Did you ever think Belle was your soulmate?"

You looked up, pausing. "I did once, yes. I don't know if I'd use those exact words, but . . . I suppose I did. She was my whole world once, and I was hers. Is that what a soulmate is?"

"I guess it's what you make it," I replied. "When you thought of the future, was she all you saw?" *Like how I once saw Blue*, I wanted to add but didn't.

"Of course. For a long time. She meant everything to me. But meeting Nahid changed things. I mean, I did love Belle—I can't deny that. I cared for her deeply, and I still do. I'd never want to hurt her, so it's a shame I ever did.

"I won't lie: sometimes I still check on her. To see how she's getting on. I think about her and I hope she's doing well. There definitely was a time when I thought we were meant for one another. That might not be the case anymore, but I still have love for her."

"Wow," I tutted. "I remember when I first met you in that café. I had a cheeky perusal of your Facebook profile afterwards, as one does. When I saw you with Belle, I thought you looked like a poster couple. I thought you had the life people dreamt of. You looked like you were made for one another. I guess 'look' is the key word. Things can seem so perfect from the outside."

You lifted your hands behind your head and weaved your fingers together. "It's scary how easy it is to make things look how you want. I worry that . . . if my life hadn't changed so drastically—with all this— that I'd still be fooling everyone else, but in a different way. In a way that only I was in on."

I wondered if I would ever live up to Belle—in relation to you, or in any way—from the outside. "Do you think your friends will buy this?" I asked, pointing back and forth at us.

"I've been thinking about this, to be fair. I take it you have, too."

"Of course."

"I'm sure they'll buy it."

"But they'll compare me to Belle. I know they will."

"There's nothing to compare. You're two *completely* different people."

Emphasise the "completely" a little more, why don't you? "Exactly."

"No, I mean—if I started seeing someone who was more like my ex, my friends would wonder what the difference was and try to suss out every little thing. They can't do that with you. You're so different from Belle that there's no point in trying that. Besides, we'll be 'over' by the end of the year, won't we? You know, when Play Number Two is complete?" You raised an eyebrow.

Oh God, I thought. Play Number Two. Our facade somehow hung on this (slightly arbitrary) determination of my solo triumph in the theatre world. If at the least, I could be ready to hand something over at a close enough point to the timeline of our coupledom, whether it was over or not, people would maybe be more receptive to it. I could try the Wentworth Agency again, this time on my terms but with your association. I could see it already: *Eddie Moruakgomo debuts with a groundbreaking drama at the Regium off the back of her amicable split with Hugo Lawrence Smith.* I'd probably have to dodge all the typical questions that weren't related to my own skill and talent and were focused on your influence or whatever, but eventually I'd make a big enough name for myself. This was all in theory, because I was still penning the stupid fucking script that had to get me there first. Tragically, in order to be successful, you actually have to do something. *Successfully.*

"Let's just hope I finish this shit sooner rather than later. But I do think that regardless, we need to be able to sell ourselves in the meantime. People have only seen us interact with one another from afar. This—this is more intimate. Living in a house with four of your closest mates? We can't give the game away. We need to prove this to them."

You readjusted yourself, sitting up straight. I pulled my legs down, switching positions so that my feet were tucked behind me.

You stared at me. "Prove it how?"

"We need to show genuine romantic chemistry. Don't get it twisted—it's the last thing I want to do." I placed a hand on my chest, closing my eyes and grimacing wryly. "But it has to be done."

"What do you suggest?"

"We just need to amp up some interactions. You know, do some straight couple shit. Maybe stupid nicknames, or, God forbid, hold hands. Throw in a 'babe' here and there. We still need to sell it. We need to sell *love*. We have to play the part a little bit more on this vacation. You have to put your acting chops in top gear."

"Okay. Gotcha." You nodded. "I think we should do a bit of a rehearsal. So it seems more . . . natural."

"Hmm. I guess so. Should we try now?"

"I think we should, yes. I'm knackered, but it's worth it before Damian and company arrive in the morning," you replied, rising from the sofa and loosening up like you were hyping yourself up for a match. I got up too, and we stood a metre apart—silent, awkward, and waiting for the other person to make the first move, like non-player characters in a video game.

"So, what do we do?" I asked.

"I don't know. I thought you knew."

"*You* were the one who suggested we rehearse."

"I didn't think much further than that, to be honest."

"If you're so desperate to become a thespian in your own right, now's your chance to practise. Just pretend you're in love with me. It can't be that hard, jeez. Pretend it's an audition."

You crossed your arms and stared at me for too long, like you were trying to solve a puzzle. Then, without warning, you took a few steps forwards and slowly took my hands.

"I . . . love . . . you," you said. Your delivery was wooden enough to put Pinocchio out of business.

I plastered on my best poker face; laughter was the last thing we needed in that moment. "Is the gun to your head in the room with us right now?" I said, looking around.

You rolled your eyes and then tried again, clearing your throat. "I *love* you."

"You *love* me?"

"Yes. I love *you*."

"You love me?"

"Indeed. *I* love you."

"Say it with a bit more passion."

"I *love you*."

"Tone it down a bit."

"I love you," you murmured.

"It should still be audible."

"I love you," you said.

"Why?" I asked. "Why do you love me?"

Your face fell for a moment, as though you were earnestly considering this. You took my hands and pulled them up to your chest. "I've never met anyone like you. You excite me but ground me at the same time. You . . . complete me. I don't know who I'd be without you."

"A bit too dramatic. Doesn't feel authentic."

"I love you because . . . because . . . you're unique."

"Not 'unique.' I hate that word."

You sighed, closed your eyes, then opened them again. You let go of my hands and weaved yours around my neck. "I love you, and I don't know why. If there was a reason, it would imply a condition. There isn't one. That's the beauty of it. I love you because you exist. That's it. That's my reason."

I don't know what you channelled in your final answer—maybe Nahid was bouncing around between your ears—but it was convincing enough. I grinned, grabbing your face like a politician about to kiss a baby. "That's more like it," I said. "I love you too. I love you because you love me."

"Haha. Of course that's why."

We let go of one another and I crossed my arms. "You believe in me, and that was all I ever needed," I replied.

We slept in separate rooms on the first night, but we planned to claim the twin bedroom once your friends arrived. I found it so difficult to sleep; my anxiety climbed with each second that rolled by, and it was worsened by my cyclical urge to deep-dive into the rabbit hole of your social network. Your friends were all so beautiful. I didn't necessarily consider myself to be of the contrary, but it was hard to situate myself in this context. I just hated that creeping feeling that I was already starting to see myself differently, like I was looking at a fun-house mirror. I felt inadequate; my braids weren't fresh enough, my septum piercing needed to be hidden, I needed a bit more makeup, I had to dress well, I had to break into my shitting leather sandals whether I liked it or not because they showed off my pedicured toes, for fuck's sake.

You and I had to play our roles perfectly, because if we didn't, I'd be more of a sore thumb than I was already bound to be. Love is supposed to conquer all at the end of the day; love is blind. But *people* aren't blind, are they, Hugo? They aren't. Your friends certainly weren't, were they?

◆ ◆ ◆

"Hugo, my man! Good to see you, brother!" Damian cheered as you went in for a bear hug at the front door.

"Hey, I'm glad you could make it!" you responded, echoing his cadence. Once you'd let up your embrace, Damian hugged me, his girlfriend Georgia hugged you, then I hugged Georgia, a systematic group convergence.

"Eddie! The main man's main squeeze," Damian said to me. "It's a pleasure to finally meet you."

"Well, I hope it's a pleasure to know me," I replied bashfully.

Just as I'd expected, the couple were gorgeous in person. Damian was lofty and lean with floppy dark hair and a lopsided grin. He funnily bore a loose likeness to a young John Travolta. Georgia was a tanned brunette with olive-green eyes—a Mediterranean quintessence. Her wavy tresses were pulled back from her face with black Prada sunglasses. They both presented as casually expensive, looking good without trying. We helped them bring their suitcases in from the foyer of the apartment and showed them to their bedroom. I had on my cordial-conversation-with-an-acquaintance voice as we filled our time with a mixture of small talk and catch-ups. It took me a while to fully loosen up, but the Campari-heavy negroni Damian whipped up for us after a quick trip to the local supermarket was a great help. We milled around on the back patio and I leaned over the balcony by the pool, taking in the stunning view of the lake, acquainting myself with the opulence of it all.

The hugging ritual was repeated when Klara and Lucas arrived a couple of hours later, and, gladly, I was less frigid this time around. Georgia suggested we cool off from the heat of the July air in the swimming pool once everyone had settled in. I'd packed a couple of swimsuits and bikinis, but I groaned internally at the thought of having to wear them. It was daunting to basically have to strip down in front of a group of strangers, and insecurity made itself at home in my mind. I wanted to enjoy my time here, but as I stared at myself in my nylon two-piece in the mirror, I worried that my enjoyment would be just as much of a subterfuge as our romance.

"Wow, Eddie, you look gorgeous! That colour really complements your skin tone," Georgia said to me when I joined everyone at the pool. She was leaning on the balcony in a white triangle bikini set that displayed her willowy build. You were gliding inside the water aimlessly, but made it a point to throw me a "Ciao, bella" when I made my presence known.

"Aww, thanks. Just what I hoped," I lied, lowering myself to sit on the pool's edge. I'm all for colour coordination, but it didn't come to mind when I was picking out skimpy fabric to swim in. I wondered why she had to mention my skin tone. I questioned whether she meant what she said, or if she just thought I'd appreciate it more. Then I wondered if I appreciated it less because I thought she thought I'd appreciate it more. I wondered why she felt the need to compliment me in my scantily clad form in the first place—if she was trying to make me feel more welcome or more exposed. Then I wondered if I was just overthinking, and I concluded that I probably was. Was I?

Klara was lying on one of the sun loungers. Her eyes were closed and she looked peaceful. I noted how her strawberry-blonde bob appeared to glow around her face in the sunlight, like a silly halo. You told me she was the sister of a uni friend called Johan. He couldn't make the trip this year, but she was more than happy to fill in. When Johan left Sweden to study law in London six years ago, he and Klara kept in constant communication. She purported to stay in Stockholm so she could pursue architecture, but she would fly to the UK whenever she could to spend some time with him. There being only a year's age difference, the siblings were super close. She had integrated easily into his university social life on the occasional visits she made, and she very quickly got the knack of all the connections, hierarchies, and tittle-tattle between her brother and his comrades.

She had supposedly just moved to London from Stockholm after an impulsive career change and needed a getaway before she settled into her new job. I was surprised to find out she and Lucas weren't together, which theoretically made them the single ones in our holidaying group. When I watched him appear seemingly out of nowhere and hoist her off her resting position into the pool, I had assumed it was amorous horseplay, but I came to find out that it was all platonic. In fact, Lucas had briefly dated *Georgia* years ago before Damian nabbed her, and rumour had it he still secretly had a thing for her. Damian didn't even attend UCL, but as your closest friend, he was around often enough to still be considered one of the gang. Klara divulged a lot of this to me a few days later, but until then I settled into my newcomer status, familiarising myself with everyone from a distance.

You swam up to the spot beside me, resting your arms on the edge of the pool. "Coming in?" you asked.

I swirled my feet around in the water. "Yeah, I will. I just don't want to get my hair wet. The chlorine shows no mercy."

"Belle used to hate it when it turned her hair green. I thought it was funny."

I chuckled. "I think it's safe to say that I won't have that problem. Whatever the case, if anyone throws me in here at any point, I'll make them wish they had a time machine."

"Noted." You pushed yourself from the pool wall and glided backwards, throwing me a daft salute before the splashing water engulfed you.

The rest of the day consisted of us drinking, eating, and faffing around the apartment. I quickly grew accustomed to the company and found it relatively easy to involve myself in group repartee, which helped me to bring my guard down. As much as there were some conversations I didn't gel with, I just chalked it up to the fact that I was an outsider to this inner circle, and I wasn't necessarily privy to all the deep friendship-level lore.

But then, at around two in the morning, I woke up choking for a glass of icy cold water, after drunkenly passing out a few hours earlier. I turned on the lamp beside me to see you on the other side of the room, deep in the abyss of slumber, one arm hanging limply off the bed. I turned the lamp off, crept up to the door, and stealthily opened it. The small crack I made was enough for me to hear a faint conversation, confirming that some of your friends were still awake in the lounge, although I initially wasn't sure who. What I overheard stopped me in my tracks and left me with an awful pit in the base of my stomach. I thought to myself, *The water can wait*, and I crawled back into bed.

XVIII

Gentlemen Prefer Blondes

We rented a boat to take us down the lake the following morning. We left Menaggio and passed Varenna, Bellagio, Lenno, and Nesso, as the lake's perimeters widened and narrowed, until we reached the banks of Como a few hours later. The clusters of surrounding villages were a vibrant foreground to the monumental dark green hills. As sublime as the sights were, I couldn't shake the discomfort I felt that had carried on from the early hours of that morning. I was noticeably quieter, but our varying stages of hangovers gave my silence more grounds. After a stop for dinner on land, we got back in the boat to relax and get group photos. We went around in turns: Damian and Georgia got their couple's pics as they posed on the upper deck, the boys got a trio shot and so did the girls. We all had a self-timed group photo, and then Georgia excitedly offered to get some shots of me and you as the sun set. By this point we were back on the drinks as if we had never stopped. You and I clutched on to champagne flutes as we beamed for the camera. I leaned into you as you draped your free arm around my shoulder. My heart started racing in my chest at the realisation that the photos of us would be posted on social media for everyone to gawk at and speculate about. Questions about how we met, what we had in common, if we even liked each other at all, if it was all just for show. Obviously it was, but that wasn't the point. I didn't want to be perceived in this way, as nothing more than your exotic arm candy. Even if all of this was temporary, the magnifying glass felt eternal.

"Ugh. You two are *such* a gorgeous couple," Georgia said a while later, once we were sitting down. The evening had crawled its way in as we slowly U-turned back to our home base.

"Well, isn't that a relief?" I responded, sipping on my drink.

I could tell by her face that she didn't know whether to take it as a joke, but she continued. "Seriously, your children will look out of this world."

Ugh, yawn. "Oh. Like aliens?" I responded obtusely.

"No. I mean beautiful."

You were sitting beside me, and I could feel your want for words. I don't know if you understood just as well as me that it wasn't a compliment, but you definitely sensed I didn't see it as one.

"I don't know." I shook my head. "Not necessarily. They could look quite unsightly."

Lucas and Damian both snickered at my comment. Georgia looked puzzled, but Klara was amused.

"That's a bit pessimistic, isn't it?" Georgia remarked.

"No, it's not. It's just a probability. Not every biracial child is beautiful. Because that's what you mean, right? That's why they would be beautiful."

"Of course not. I never said anything about race. I mean they would be because *you* are," she responded, scrambling onto the high road. First the bikini comment, now this. I was tired of her backhanded arse-kissing.

"Well, sometimes two positives make a negative," you interjected, clearly trying to defuse the growing friction with a silly jest.

I turned to you, then back to Georgia. "Exactly. Besides, beauty is subjective. One could argue we're *not* a gorgeous couple. Maybe one of us is punching above our weight. Maybe it depends on who you ask. For example, Hu, I think your friends here might have a thing or two to say on the topic." I gestured towards Damian and Lucas. "You know . . . something along the lines of how you've 'gone rogue' this time around?" I pulled up air quotes as I spoke, watching their faces fall.

"What do you mean?" you asked with a mixture of confusion and trepidation.

"Hmm. I don't know, what *do* I mean? Lads, would you like to clarify?" I looked directly at them, watching them cower.

"I think you got the wrong idea," Damian replied, readjusting himself. "We didn't mean any of that as an insult."

Georgia piped up. "What on earth are you guys on about?"

"I . . . I'm guessing Eddie might have heard us talking last night. I barely remember what we even said, to be honest." He shook his head, pining for damage control. I knew I'd opened a can of worms at the worst time, when none of us could escape from the confined space in which we were huddled, but it didn't bother me. I felt powerful in that moment, even if that power came from a place of hurt.

"Oh, fuck off. Your lack of memory doesn't take away from what you said," I retorted.

"I think you're reading too much into things, Eddie." Lucas entered into the conversation, presumably trying to dissipate the tension. "We were just having a laugh. Hu's always had a type, and you're just . . . not that type. It's that simple."

"No, it's not that simple. I think you should elaborate," I said, shrugging. I wanted to push your friends into a corner of their own making; the boat we were in wasn't small enough. "What's Hugo's usual type?"

"Guys, guys, come on," you butted in, chuckling nervously. "I've not exactly been on the market until recently. We're all a bit too grown-up for this talk about types, now, aren't we?" You sat forwards. I watched Damian shoot you a look; it was subtle, but it read to me as *you're full of shit*. I saw Klara look out onto the lake, potentially signifying a wish to jump in it. Even Georgia had fallen quiet. Something was clearly amiss. It was like there was an elephant in the room—or on the deck—threatening to bring the boat down. Regardless, I didn't appreciate being turned into shallow gossip fodder between a bunch of your entitled toff mates.

"Let's change the subject, shall we?" Damian urged. "I think there's been a bit of a misunderstanding. We weren't trying to demean you, Eddie. It was just . . . an inside thing, you know. A bit of banter between us. I'm sorry you had to hear that."

"Ahhh. So you're not sorry you said it."

Lucas jumped in again. "With all due respect, we didn't say anything out of line, and we didn't say it to you. You're blowing things out of proportion."

"I'm blowing things out of proportion? *Really*? So you think I'm not allowed to take offence at being spoken about like I'm some sort of . . . specimen? Give me a break."

He scoffed, shaking his head and looking at you. "You got yourself a sassy one, didn't you, Hu?"

"'Sassy'? *Wow*. The audacity."

"Jesus, I can't say anything around you, can I?" Lucas riposted, his voice climbing up a few octaves like someone had just twisted his bollocks. I already thought he had a punchable face, but he had officially confirmed it. At this point the two of us were battling it out amid a disinclined audience. It was either you struggled to get a word in edgeways, didn't know what to say, or both. Ultimately, your taciturnity wasn't lost on me.

"You know what, I surrender. You're in the right and I'm in the wrong. Congratulations." I put my hands up before rising from my seat. I dug through my handbag, fished out the cheap Italian cigarettes I'd picked up earlier that day, and walked to the other side of the boat behind the stern cockpit. I could hear a trail of concerned murmurs from the group, but I was far enough not to clearly hear what they were saying. I sat slouched forwards with my elbow on my knee, barely allowing a breath between each toke of my cigarette. All the energy I had before had deflated and I was suddenly hit with a wave of misery.

After a minute or so, you made your way to my side of the boat and sat next to me. "Eddie. Why didn't you tell me what happened?" you asked.

"I drank too much tonight. I should have just kept quiet."

"No, you're well within your rights to be upset. I'm just saying, you could have told me. I had no idea."

"If I had told you, what would you have done?" I turned to you. "You wouldn't have said anything. It's not like you're obligated to."

"Look. My mates were being stupid and crass. But . . . that's just how they are to everyone. They never gave Belle a break, either. I'm sure they like you."

"Hmm. Do you know what else they said last night? They said that you'd wandered off onto the 'wrong side of the tracks'. Sounds like a statement from people who 'like' me."

You sighed, muttering, "For fuck's sake" under your breath. "Eddie, I'm so sorry. I'll talk to them, okay? I really didn't expect this from them."

"If I'm being honest, you're winding me up by acting like you thought any of this was beyond them. I told you I was afraid of being compared to Belle, and clearly I was right to be."

"They're pricks sometimes. Men are."

"I don't like Georgia, either."

You let out a quick puff of air. "That just leaves Klara, I suppose."

"Funnily enough, she's the only one who hasn't said much. So that makes sense."

You spluttered a quick chortle before sobering up. "Please, let's just try to get along for the remainder of the vacation. Italy's a beautiful place and I want you to enjoy it."

I threw the butt of my cigarette overboard, looking out into the water that glinted against the illuminated villages in the night like crude oil. "Your friends aren't just pricks, Hugo. It's more insidious than that. If you can't see that, it worries me. But I can't expect too much from you. I can fend for myself, at the end of the day." It wasn't your job to come to the rescue, but if you put assuaging the discomfort of your longtime friends before quelling the alienation of your new relationships, I wondered what that really meant. What it really said about you. I briefly thought about Nahid, and questioned your ability to fight her corner if something like this ever occurred with her. It could have been another case of me overthinking, but I ultimately concluded that it was a case of me just doing enough thinking for the both of us. You were more than just a blank canvas in these moments; you were a lenticular portrait that switched between harmless and passive, depending on the angle. There was harm in that passivity, noise in that silence. It left me with a bad taste in my mouth.

"I know. I'm sorry. I am," you said, rubbing your forehead. "I promise I'll talk to the lads. What they said was out of order. We all just need to get along and treat each other with respect. That can't be too much to ask."

"It's fine," I said, standing up. I leaned on the railing of the boat's hull. "You're right, it's my first time in Italy. It is a beautiful place. I see the appeal. I should focus on making the most of it."

"That sounds like a plan," you said, nodding. "So, what do you think so far? Does Lombardy suffice?"

"I mean, it's no *Brighton*, but . . . sure."

◆ ◆ ◆

I dreamt of Blue that night. It was so vivid, like it hadn't been six months since I last saw her. There was a visceral realness to her, and I was convinced it was how people felt when they thought they'd seen a ghost. My heartbreak was paranormal in that sense. In the dream, we were on a cruise ship in the middle of the ocean. It was late at night, the moon was full, and there was a party on the upper deck. The DJ was playing the popular upbeat edit of "Missing" by Everything but the Girl, and the two of us were dancing like our lives depended on it. It was one of her favourite songs, and it had eventually grown on me. The lyrics about missing someone like a desert missing the rain were so on the nose that when I woke up from my dream, I felt like smothering myself with my pillow.

I realised that my knack for stalking people online conveniently didn't go as far as checking on Blue. I thought I'd take a leaf out of your book the next morning and do just that. I knew that in reality, whatever I saw was never going to tell me the full story, because social media is the showreel of life. But I wanted to see hers, or at the least, my subconscious mind wanted to. She primarily posted pictures of London in all its forms—night and day, the urban and the suburban. Ego Birth appeared to be touring during festival season, and they had put out their first high-budget music video in the last month. I kept scrolling down Blue's feed until I recognised the photos from when we were still together. I expected my presence in her life to be wiped clean, but my chest still ached all the same when this was confirmed.

I decided to click on the feed of posts she was tagged in to see if there was a chance I could find out anything new. My heart sank when I saw a photo, dated around two weeks prior, of her kissing a woman on the cheek. She had her arm around her, and the caption read: *I'm the luckiest girl in the world.* A sheet of moisture swept across my vision, obscuring what I so desperately didn't want to see yet so desperately did. Once my brain was ready to fully take in the information, I realised she was with Arianna, her bandmate. *Arianna the pretentious saxophonist.* Maybe they had bonded while spending so much time together on music, or over their shared Jamaican heritage. Maybe Arianna was just a shoulder to cry on, or maybe they were destined to be together. Either way, I lay on my side in bed, feeling like something had just been brutally ripped out of me. I felt naked and stupid, awkward and alone. I held off on my crying until I went to brush my teeth, letting my tears mix with the saliva-diluted toothpaste in my mouth. I sat on the toilet bowl and sobbed silently, subsumed by the sound of morning activity just a few metres behind the locked bathroom door.

• • •

Later, we all went for a two-hour hike through the hills to a smaller, more secluded lake you had discovered a few years prior. There was a café and car park nearby, and at its busiest it was peppered with families off from work and school. It wasn't a tourist hot spot, which was the reprieve we needed. The lake had a small pier that worked as a nice diving point. I didn't have a fear of swimming, but more of an aversion to dunking myself in a relatively opaque body of water that worked as a biosphere for unfamiliar organisms. Small lakes felt like dirty bathtubs, and I wanted no part of it. Instead, I let you and your friends push each other into the water and take turns diving while I sat on the bank, reading.

I was still silently reeling from my self-inflicted discovery of Blue's new relationship, but the last thing I wanted to do was tip anyone off about my heartbreak. I was stoic and mysterious in my comportment, keeping my vocalisations minimal outside of appropriately timed quips in group conversations. I think you had picked up on my dim mood on the hike, but you didn't do too much pressing. You must have also picked up on my desire for my dim mood not to be further investigated. I was appreciative of your ability to read every iota of my body language, especially in a place where I was so out of my element.

You were racing Damian and Lucas in the water while Georgia stood on the pier taking photos and videos of the whole ordeal, when Klara climbed out of the lake and walked towards me. She picked up a towel, quickly scrubbed herself down, and rubbed her hair with it. She towered over me, looking down at the book I was reading. Then she straightened the towel out on the ground below her, sat on it, and wrapped her arms around her tucked knees.

"Zadie Smith?" she said. "I love her. I've been meaning to read *On Beauty*. Is it any good?"

"It's quite interesting. There's a lot going on. But in a good way."

"I've only read *White Teeth*. The Swedish edition. Maybe I don't love her, then." She grinned, catching herself as she spoke.

"I've only read her work in English, and I haven't read *White Teeth*. Maybe *I'm* the fake fan," I responded.

"Haha, perhaps. I recommend it. I was hooked to every page of that book. It made London seem so lively. It was maybe, like, twenty percent of the reason I wanted to move there."

"Oh, cool. What was the other eighty percent?"

"I don't know . . . maybe, reinvention."

"Reinvention. I like that." I put a dog-ear in my book and leaned back on my elbows, stretching my legs out. Over at the pier, Georgia was now sitting with her legs swinging off the side. Damian was climbing out while you and Lucas were having a battle for the fastest breaststroke.

"Are you the reinventing type?" Klara asked.

"I'm not sure. Maybe during a crisis. But who isn't?" I was already thinking of all the colours I could braid my hair once I touched back down in London, purely on the basis of my meltdown earlier that morning.

"Tell me about it. I had a shitty breakup last year and I gave myself a buzz cut. My hair was so long before. But I like it short." I realised that even though this conversation had barely started, it was already the longest amount of time I had spent talking to Klara one-on-one since the start of the trip. She was more on the quiet side, but it left a lot to the imagination. I didn't expect her to be so conversational. I was pleasantly surprised.

"Short hair looks good on you," I told her.

She smiled and thanked me. But then she looked out to the lake for a few moments and then down, twiddling her fingers. "I have a question. What is it that you like about Hugo?" she asked me, which took me by surprise.

"Hmm. Well . . . that's—that's quite the question."

"It is, I guess. What do you see in him?" She looked at me.

I shifted around. "I'm not good at this kind of stuff. You know, being all mawkish about my relationships."

"Right. Okay." She nodded slowly.

"Why are you asking me this, anyway?"

I could tell she had something pressing to say, and she eventually did. "I don't know if I should tell you this, because I don't want to . . . get involved in your relationship, but . . . ahhh, I think I should."

"Say what?"

She quickly looked towards the lake again and then at me. "When we got back to the house after the boat ride and everyone went to sleep, I think . . . shit, this feels so wrong to say. Maybe I should just let you know after the holiday."

"Are you joking? You've *got* to tell me now."

"So, Hugo snuck out onto the patio. He woke me up, going through the living room, but Lucas stayed asleep. He was talking on the phone to someone. It sounded . . . let's just say, it wouldn't be a leap to assume he might be seeing someone else. I know I've only just met you, but I . . . don't know. I think I was the only person who heard. It feels wrong not to tell you."

I looked at her. "What made you think that? What was he saying?"

She looked out as she spoke, as if to keep watch. "He was saying stuff like, 'I miss you' and 'We just need to wait a little longer,' you know, stuff like that. He also said something kind of like, 'I know it was crazy, but I just wanted to be there for her at the time.' He also said he felt oddly 'flattered' that you chose him," she said, pulling up air quotes, "but that you two won't last much longer and it's just a case of when. None of that sounded good to me. Call me crazy, but I think he might secretly be trying to get back together with Belle."

"Oh," I said quietly. It didn't take me long to realise that she'd overheard you speaking to Nahid, even if she was mistaken. "Fucking *idiot*," I hissed to myself.

"I mean, he's more than just an idiot." Klara narrowed her eyes. "He's cheating on you. I just thought you should know that."

"Well, thanks for the . . . heads-up," I said.

She cocked her head to the side. "You don't actually seem upset. Did you already know? I'm not too convinced you didn't."

"You don't know me. I don't need to prove anything to you."

"No, I don't. But I know *him*," she said. "We all do."

"What is that supposed to mean?"

"Never mind. They're coming back," she said, readjusting herself. "We can talk about it later if we get the chance. I'm sorry to bring this onto you so suddenly. I just think you ought to know," she said in a hushed manner as you and the other three got closer to us.

"Well, I appreciate it," I said, picking my book back up. She nodded at me before looking away.

It was hard for me to tell exactly how close Klara was to you or your friendship group. She was clearly close enough to be invited here, but I guess that didn't stop her from having morals. It seemed that maybe there was at least one person here I could trust.

• • •

After the lake swim, we all hitched a taxi on the main road back to our apartment. Everyone took turns showering and freshening up so that we could go out for dinner in a neighbouring town. My mood was still fairly sour, but I felt a vibe of camaraderie forming between me and Klara. I was itching to continue the conversation with her, to unravel whatever thread she had started pulling. The fact that you were imbecilic enough to potentially foil our plan so brazenly was playing on my mind, because it meant there was someone who might have more of a reason not to believe we actually had feelings for one another. It wouldn't have been the worst thing in the world for Klara to think you secretly weren't that interested in me, but the doubt extended further than that. Klara knew the lack of romantic interest went both ways; she could see through it. It wasn't exactly in the same way that other people might doubt us—it wasn't in a way that I resented. She could see through us respectively, not as a unit. This was made more clear after the group dinner, when she pulled me aside. She concocted a plan to pretend she had unexpectedly started her period and needed to get to the nearest pharmacist or supermarket for tampons, and I would volunteer to accompany her. We walked casually through the bustling streets and piazzas once we were out of the group's eyeline.

"So, what's your deal?" she asked me.

"What deal?"

"You and Hugo."

"Not sure how you expect me to answer that," I responded, crossing my arms as we ambled along.

"You don't sleep in the same bed. Me and Lucas took the pullout, but we're not even together. We could have taken the twin room. It's a bit odd, no?"

"I chose the twin room because it's too hot and I didn't want to share my bed with anyone. Nothing odd about that."

"We left the patio door open. There was a breeze, it was fine."

"Good for you."

"I haven't seen you kiss each other. At all. Even on the cheek, or anything."

"That's a bit voyeuristic."

"No, it's just an interesting observation." She tilted her head. "You're bisexual, right? You had a girlfriend before?"

I turned towards her, furrowing my brows. "I'm queer. And yes, I did. What's your point? Have you been stalking me?"

She shrugged nonchalantly. "Nope. I just feel that something is off."

I didn't know what to say for a moment. I was too tired to act defensively. Now that she had heard you babbling sweet nothings to someone else, there was no point in dying on that hill. A sudden and sharp melancholy hit me, and I thought to myself, *What am I even doing here?*

"Why do you care so much?" I asked her.

"I don't know. I just thought Hugo had changed his ways, you know. I thought he was a new person, but I guess he's still up to the same old tricks. That is, of course, if it doesn't bother you."

"Tricks? What the hell are you talking about?"

She shook her head. "I supposed he wouldn't have told you this. So, I guess I will."

She told me that you and Belle had been long-distance throughout university. There were times when you withdrew from your social life because you were consumed by your romantic life. But there were also times where the opposite happened, where it was sometimes easy for people to forget you were even in a committed relationship. These phases waxed and waned, but eventually came to an end by the time you had graduated.

Whenever Klara would join Johan and his friends on nights out, you were usually in attendance. You'd have your arm around a girl at the bar, very evidently flirting, until you decided to end the night early. You would say goodbye to your friends and make your way home, but you'd never go alone. Klara couldn't put a number on how often this happened, but she knew it was a regular occurrence at one point. And it wasn't just you who did this; most of the guys in your group were guilty of nefarious hookups. Damian was already with someone when he first slept with Georgia; Johan's other friend James was quite dramatically and publicly dumped in the middle of Covent Garden after his girlfriend caught on to his mischief. You had it a little easier; Belle was 270 miles up north, and you never left a paper trail of your conquests, so she almost never found out. Your group debauchery even got to the point of having a running joke: Damian went for the Anne Hathaways, and you went for the Margot Robbies. The brunettes versus the blondes.

Klara was aware of all this, but she just watched from a distance. *Judged* from a distance. She was the silent spectator, someone with no skin in the game. This all changed when you took a sudden liking to her one summer. She was naive enough to flirt back at first, but she usually didn't take it further than flirting. Then the unimaginable happened: she caved. After a few drinks and lines of coke at a house party, she lost her inhibitions. You didn't do anything more than heavy petting, but it was egregious enough. Before, it had just been strangers, one-off encounters with hookups whose numbers you'd delete posthaste—not that that made it any less immoral. But this was different. It was too close to home. It was a line you'd never crossed before.

Ridden with guilt, Klara blew the lid off the whole operation and told Belle everything, and it was the biggest scandal in your group thus far. Of course Belle was heartbroken when she found out, but she forgave you. She gave ridiculous excuses for you: the long distance must have been hard, you only went for blondes because they looked more like her, and so on and so forth. They were coping mechanisms for her—a way to rationalise your careless actions. It sounded silly, but I could see how she got to that point. When she subliminally called me out in her YouTube vlog, it started to make a little more sense. *Let's just say . . . she's* definitely *not blonde.* What I saw as an immature, slightly racist microaggression apparently went way deeper. For her, I was a confirmation that you were well and truly over her. I was the actual line you were willing to cross. Whether it was true or just some university in-joke was beside the point. It spoke to your character. It gave you more substance, but in the worst way.

You and Klara stopped speaking for a while after the incident, but things neutralised over time. She had left it all behind her, but bearing witness to your secret phone call brought it all back. It left her feeling as guilty as she had done. She couldn't keep it to herself; she had to warn me, like she tried to warn Belle. As she told me all this, my heart caught in my chest, because I realised that everything you told me on our first night in Italy couldn't have been true. You never loved Belle. No fucking way. Did you even really love Nahid? Had you ever really loved at all? Were you capable of it? Was there a chance you had potentially put my play at risk out of fickle lust, and nothing more?

"Wow. Shit. That's . . . a lot," I said to Klara. We had been lapping a half-mile radius for over twenty minutes at this point. I was afraid to return to the group; I didn't know if I could hold something this big so close to my chest.

"Again, apologies. I don't want to cause drama. I really thought this kind of bullshit was left at university," she said.

"You haven't caused anything, don't worry. I really appreciate you telling me all this. You didn't have to. It's . . . putting things into perspective for me. So, thank you."

I now understood why Damian shot you that look on the boat and why the air felt heavy with unease. The only time you had the energy to speak up during the disagreement was when you were lying. When you were saving your own arse. Ultimately, you knew your friends would judge me. Not just for any reason, either. You knew they'd judge me because I was black. You told me they wouldn't even bat an eyelid. They did, actually. It was you who didn't.

Klara smiled sympathetically, shaking her head. "No need to thank me. I appreciate how you don't really take bullshit. It's refreshing."

"That's not something I hear often."

"Exactly. You're not afraid to make enemies. You made the boat trip a little bit more entertaining."

I paused and did a fake stage bow. "Thank you, thank you. Critics call it the *sassiest* performance of the year. Do you agree?"

She snorted, covering her grin with her hand. "Not at all. I thought it was supercool, though. I think *you're* pretty cool, too. I'd love to hang out with you after this, when we're back in London. I'll give you the Swedish version of *White Teeth*. You can give me *On Beauty*. Or whatever you want."

I chuckled. "Of course. It's a deal."

When I checked my phone, I had a couple of missed calls and texts from you. You asked me if we'd managed to find a pharmacy or if we'd got lost. We decided it was probably wise to head back. Klara turned around and led the way, linking my hand in hers as we stepped up our pace.

At that point, the last place I wanted to be was in the middle of Northern Italy. I wanted to be at home. My home, not yours. I wanted to be with Blue; Arianna could kick fucking rocks for all I cared. I wanted nothing to do with you. But because of our pact, I still needed you. Nothing in this world was more agonising than needing the one person you so desperately wished to wash your hands of.

That night before bed, I decided to call Nick. I kept the

conversation short and sweet, stripping the holiday down to its bare bones and trimming out all the shambles. I tried my utmost to hide any hint of desolation in my voice, but I wouldn't have been surprised if he could still detect it. If there was one thing I could be truthful about, it was the beauty of the world I had found myself in. I relayed this to him, telling him how beautiful the water was here, and how much he'd love it.

HUGO

XIX

A Romantic Tragedy

September 2018

With near-comical timing, a cacophonous boom of music blasted through the walls of the house. The few seconds that it took me to realise that the bass thumping along the floors was in fact not a violent ambush, and that danger wasn't imminent, felt painfully long. I sighed, apologetically holding a finger up to the webcam before dashing out of the study. I popped my head into the room from where the source of the nightmarishly loud sounds had emanated, and I silently and impatiently signalled that I was in the middle of a call. An eye roll later, the music was turned down but not switched off completely. I sighed, pulling my head out of the room and gliding back to the study.

"I'm so sorry about that, Helen. It's a common occurrence at this point. I should have warned beforehand that I had a meeting," I said as I sat down, slightly flustered.

"Oh, no worries! Think of this as more of a chitchat than a meeting. Nothing too formal."

"Ahhh, okay. Gotcha. Still, apologies for the interruption. Living with a younger sibling comes with its obvious challenges."

Helen sat forwards. "I didn't know you had a younger sibling. That's interesting. I always took you for an only child."

"I might as well be." I chuckled. "I'm a middle child. I have a brother, but he's nearly twenty years older than me. My sister's from Hong Kong. Well, she's half Hong Kongese. She's always lived there, but she moved in with me last month. She got into . . . I think it's Central Saint Martins, for fashion. She's been making the most of living here, as you can tell."

"Indeed, I can. It might be a nice bonding experience for you. Especially if you don't see her often. Family is *everything*," she remarked.

I nodded slowly, then quickly. "Sure. I mean, I don't think we'll be best friends anytime soon, but it's worth a try. It might be nice to have the company, too."

"Of course. How's Eddie, by the way? Is everything all good on that front?"

"Oh, uhhh . . . it's fine. But we did break up recently. She moved out of my house a while back."

"Goodness! That's a shame; you two were a great pair. Do you mind me asking why?" She spoke with a level of seemingly artificial curiosity. It was hard to tell if she actually cared, or just wanted to seem like she did. She was a hard one to read.

"No reason in particular. It was an amicable split. We've both just been so busy. Her more than me. It wasn't working out schedule-wise."

"It happens, I suppose," she sighed, shrugging. Then she narrowed her eyes and looked intently at me through the screen, raising an eyebrow. "I can keep a secret. Was it *really* amicable?"

"Yes, of course. She recently got promoted at *BABBLE* and wanted to focus on her job a bit more. She's also actually just finished the script for a new play. It's her first project since leaving uni. So we just didn't have as much time together. All's well that ends well, though."

"*All's Well That Ends Well*. Shakespeare. So, this isn't a romantic tragedy, then?"

I shifted in my seat. "Not at all. No hard feelings. We're . . . good. Great. Fine."

"Okay. That's good to know." She smiled, staring long enough for me to think that the laptop screen had frozen. I blinked, waiting for reanimation. Eventually, it came. She leaned on her elbows on the desk in front of her, resting her chin on clasped hands. "Now, back to why I even called you in the first place. I've got some *amazing* news, Hugo. The agency is currently in talks to take *Great Belonging* on tour around the country!" She beamed. "*Great Belonging* does Great

Britain. We're thinking Bristol, Swansea, Birmingham, Manchester, and Edinburgh, all over the next year or so. How marvellous is that!"

"Oh. Wow! That sounds . . . that sounds . . . yeah. Wow." I did something with my head that was a mix between shaking it and nodding.

Her smile stayed frozen in place, but she furrowed her eyebrows. "That wasn't the reaction I was expecting. Where's the excitement?"

"I'm . . . just taking it in, I guess. It's all still quite daunting."

"Oh, don't worry. You don't need to be as involved this time around. I know the Regium was a huge commitment. The agency will be sorting everything out. You should just keep yourself busy. Maybe start on something new? That'll surely do the trick." She raised her eyebrows suggestively.

I shrugged. "I wish I could. I've had writer's block since I won the MBG, to be quite frank. Nothing's coming out of me anymore. It feels like . . . like I never wrote *Great Belonging* in the first place, you know? It feels like a fluke. I don't think I'm capable of ever writing anything that good again."

Helen shook her head. "What did I tell you, Hugo? Trust and believe in yourself. You got here through *you* and *you* alone. You're amazingly talented. Don't doubt yourself. You're robbing the world of great things."

I swallowed. "Potentially. You know . . . I . . . I think you're putting too much faith in me, Helen. If you're expecting a new project, it'll probably be a while. But I do have a suggestion. Actually, it's more of a request. You see, I was hoping you, or the agency, would . . . be open to having a look at Eddie's new script. No pressure, of course—I'm just throwing it out there."

She stayed silent for a moment, her expression impenetrable. Then she smiled. "Hugo: the Wentworth Agency prides itself on finding talent through fair and accessible avenues. We have so many writers and creatives here, all part of the theatre world, who also have budding playwright friends. So it's a bit of a slippery slope if we start some sort of . . . internal referral system. Our culture will lose range; it will turn into an echo chamber. I'm sure Eddie is very talented, but I would encourage her to take the usual avenue of submitting an enquiry letter and her script to a chosen agent. We'll eventually get to it."

I nodded, heart stammering. "I—I completely get what you mean. Of course you don't want to create a stale environment, and I do appreciate that. But I can assure you that Eddie's work would definitely not do that. In fact, it would do the opposite. I think it could potentially breathe new life into the agency. Not that it's dying, per se. I just mean, in terms of the diversity of ideas, you know?"

"First off, I'd like to point out how *Great Belonging* is one of the most diverse and broad-thinking productions we've birthed in years. Celeste Adebayo won an MBG for Best New Actress this year, which *definitely* means *something*. The entire cast was a *beautiful* mishmash of creeds and cultures. This play has put a female director of colour on the map. You've managed to capture the cultural consciousness in a fascinating way. You don't shy away from intersectional discussions of class, race, immigration, and so on. It's commendable. You're selling yourself short.

"My second point is that . . . Eddie is probably more sought-after than she might imagine. What's important is that she continues to work on her craft and cast her net far and wide. The Wentworth Agency might not be the perfect fit for her, just as her work may not necessarily fit in with what our agents are currently looking for. It's a Goldilocks situation, you see—it's all about finding the right home for her work, not the most accessible home. Nepotism can only take you so far, I'm afraid."

I creased my eyebrows instinctively. "Helen, again, I completely understand what you're saying. But don't you think that two things can be true at once—that the right home could be the most opportunistic one? Don't you think that maybe her work should speak for itself? And that . . . that the agency's current roster of playwrights is a little . . . stale—not necessarily in its diversity of ideas, but . . . you know . . . background-wise?" I started off timid, like a shy child asking their mother for a later curfew. But I was becoming more of an impatient one who dared to ask, *But why not?*

"What I'm saying, Hugo, is exactly that. Her work will speak for itself. Neither you, nor anyone else, can speak for it. That's all." She shrugged matter-of-factly. I could tell she was trying to shut down the conversation, or at the least, take back control of it. I slowly nodded again, looking down at my desk. "We don't just choose people purely because they're minorities. That would be even more insulting. This isn't the United Nations. We're trying our best to take steps in the right direction, however, and I appreciate that it's something you care about. I assume it's because of your association with someone like Eddie. But, you know . . . I feel that you're unusually obsessed with her. It almost seems . . . slightly compensatory."

My eyes shot back up at the screen. "I'm not sure what you mean."

"You want to give her a platform, I get that. But this . . . it's all a bit too much. There's something afoot here. There's a reason you're going to great lengths for her, isn't there?"

"Not at all. I admire and respect her. I want the best for her."

She shot me a look so subtle, yet so loud. "Hugo, I believe there's something you're not telling me. Whatever it is, it has clearly left you indebted to your . . . now-ex-partner. It's getting in the way of your professionalism, and I want you to stay on track. I can only hope that the two of you are at the least on good terms."

"You believe there's something I'm not telling you? Could you elaborate?" I felt the skin on the back of my neck and under my arms heat and prickle.

"If I think it's important enough to tell you, I will. It could also just be me and my suspicions, who knows? It would be irresponsible for me to open up a can of worms so . . . *unnecessarily*." Oh, the irony. I could practically see the worms writhing around in front of her. "Ultimately, the Wentworth Agency has to act and appear impartial. We can't look like we have favourites. The theatre world is small, yet big. I can understand that you want to support Eddie, and she is more than welcome to send her script over. If she's talented enough, she will easily find success in no time, whether here or elsewhere. I can assure you of that. Like you said, all's well that ends well."

"All right, Helen." I chuckled anxiously. "I'm not sure how we ended up here. I just wanted to help enrich the agency's roster by putting in a good word for someone who I know is extremely talented. I don't appreciate you talking in riddles, if I'm being honest."

"That's not my aim at all! I just don't want you to let any potential *guilt* you've harboured from any *decisions* you might have made eat you up. Sometimes, when you make your bed, you just have to lie in it. We live and learn and we move on. Most importantly, we keep the agency's *reputation* in mind at all times." She plastered on a tight-lipped smile. "Well, would you look at the time! I have another meeting in ten minutes I need to prepare for, and I can't do that without another Americano. Long day. We'll have to wrap up now." She frowned. "I'll be in touch with more information about the tour, all right? I'll add another meeting to the calendar."

"Wait, hold on—"

"I really do have to go, Hugo, sorry. I can't overrun. You know what, tell Eddie to send her little passion project over. I'll put it at the top of the pile, *just* for her. We only take on the best of the best, so nothing's guaranteed. But if this is what she's asked of you, it doesn't hurt to give her a chance, I suppose. Chat later!"

When the screen went blank, I was staring back at my dumbfounded reflection. What on *earth* had just happened? Why was she dancing around the topic like a floor gymnast? Why did she think I felt indebted to you, or that I was harbouring guilt? Did she know the truth? Maybe she did, but if that was the case, she wouldn't have been gushing excitedly to me about the play going on tour if she knew it wasn't my play to begin with. She wouldn't have been telling me that I got to where I was through me and me alone—unless that was her point. Perhaps she wanted me to know that she knew I hadn't, that she was one step ahead.

But then, if she had an inkling that *you* were the original author, why would she be so hesitant to take you on? Why would she act like she didn't know what you were capable of? Did she actually care about what she purported to care about? None of it made any sense. Just when I thought I knew what she knew, I felt that I didn't. I was dizzy with confusion, subdued into discomposure. All I wanted to do was slowly back away from *Great Belonging*. I was feeling more and more out of my element. All the questions, the demands, the press and publicity, it was a beast that kept growing bigger, that was harder to wrangle and contain. I could no longer handle being celebrated for being someone else. I could no longer have what I didn't deserve.

I stepped out of the study, sighing loudly. My thoughts were everywhere, bouncing around my head like ricocheting bullets. My heart was racing at a million miles an hour. The inside of my mouth was dry and my tongue felt like rubber, so I ambled downstairs to the kitchen to pour myself a glass of water. I glugged it ferociously, and then poured myself another one. I drank the second glass until it was half-empty, and then I stood there, holding on to it as I tried to gather my thoughts. Instantaneously, the cacophonous music from Luna's bedroom started blaring again, causing me to flinch. The glass slid right out of my hand and onto the tiled floor below me, smashing into pieces. I looked down at the mess I'd made and stared at it for at least ten seconds. Then, all I could do was laugh. At this point it was either a clumsy coincidence or something of an omen.

• • •

I called you a few days later. It had been months since you and I had held a proper conversation that didn't just consist of terse text messages or read receipts. It was a quiet Sunday morning; Luna was out somewhere, most likely exploring the city with new uni friends. I wavered somewhere between savouring the silence and hating it. On any other day, I don't think I'd have bothered clicking on the phone icon next to your name, but on this day, it felt like the right course of action. I sat in the back garden, counting each phone ring as they echoed in my ear. A part of me expected you not to answer. But then the rings stopped, and there was a fuzzy silence.

"Hello?" you muttered, voice hoarse. I guessed I must have been your alarm clock.

"Happy birthday to you, happy birthday to you, happy birthday, dear Eddie . . . happy birthday to you." I was shamefully out of tune, but when I heard your dispersed chuckles, I knew my mission had been accomplished.

"God. Cringe. Thank you, though," you said, yawning. "I'm half-asleep right now, sorry if I sound dead. I really do appreciate that."

"It had to be done. How does it feel being one year older?"

"It feels a lot like being one day older. Fuck, I'm so hungover."

"I bet. I saw you had a party last night. It looked like a time. Clearly it was," I said. I hoped I didn't sound sarcastic or wounded. I hoped it didn't feel like I was drawing more attention to the fact that you didn't invite me to the party, or even tell me you were having one.

It was like you read my mind. "The *BABBLE* lot organised it for me. It felt more like a work function, to be honest. Also, it was a very No Boys Allowed kind of vibe. It was basically a femme and nonbinary orgy. I don't think you'd have enjoyed it."

"An orgy, was it?"

"In the most platonic sense, of course. No actual shagging. A couple of snogs, though. A *lot* of drinking games. I'm paying the price now."

"See, that's the thing about alcohol. It's just consequence wrapped in a bow."

"Preach, brother."

"Speaking of things wrapped in bows: I have a gift for you," I said, segueing us into a new topic.

"You do?"

"Actually, it's a metaphorical bow. I got two tickets to *Light as a Tonne of Feathers*. You know—that play that's on at the Regium until the end of October."

"Oh. Wow. You did?"

"Yup. I booked the showing that's a couple of weeks from now. I thought it would interest you. Got the seats with the best view, too."

"Hu. That's so kind of you. You didn't have to do that."

"Of course I did. I knew you'd probably want to see it." The play-wright, Zayani Chimbalanga, was a poet and English literature gradu-ate who had spent years frequenting London's slam poetry scene and writing script after script until she hit the jackpot. Her latest play had been scooped up by Sonder Words, a less-established agency on the rise with promising new talent. *Light as a Tonne of Feathers* was one of the few productions that had made it inside the Regium's walls with-out going through one of the usual agencies, Wentworth included. I'd seen her at some panels and talks in the theatre world over the last year, so it was great that she was finally making a splash. I knew there was no way you'd not have known about her new play. I'd hoped it meant something to you.

"You were right, I did want to see it. So I went, like, four days ago. Ugh. Now I feel like shit."

My heart dropped. I was surprised at how visceral my disappoint-ment felt. "Oh, wow. Great minds think alike, I guess." I chuckled. "Absolutely no worries. I can find someone else to go with, or what-ever. It's fine."

"I'm sorry. I honestly wasn't expecting a gift of any sort from you."

"Why not? It's your birthday. I'm your friend."

"I know, but . . . I don't know. Whatever."

"Honestly. Don't worry about it. Just enjoy your birthday. You only turn twenty-four once."

"Sometimes it's harder to enjoy the things that'll only ever happen once."

"Hmm. That's an interesting take. Ever the optimist. I miss you a lot, Eddie."

"Oh. You do?"

"I can't stress how much I do." It was true. Ever since our trip to Italy, I felt the shift in your energy. The day after our swim in Lago di Piano, we all took a day trip to the Villa del Balbianello in Lenno, touring the topiary grounds and capturing memories on our cameras with the ornate stucco mansion painting the background. It was our penultimate day in the country before we headed back home. You'd barely said a word to me all day, and I couldn't figure out why. When I asked you what was wrong, you said you had a headache. If your silence was any indication, your headache was apparently perennial.

Once we got back to England, you decided it was probably best if you moved out and made living arrangements with your friend Lydia, over in the east of the city. You said you'd be closer to the *BAB-BLE* office, and that you needed more distance and concentration to work on your next project. You also said you wanted to be closer to your family—your brother Nick was a quick journey away in Canary Wharf, so you'd get to spend more time with him. I remember watch-ing you lug your belongings out of my house with Lydia's assistance. I couldn't help but think back to my Halloween party, when I was just a boozy postgrad student dressed in a Julius Caesar salad costume, escorting the two of you out into an Uber to the best of my ability, as you stumbled messily onto the front lawn. Now as I watched you hail your own taxi and wave me goodbye, I was overwhelmed with a myriad of feelings. Awe at how far we'd come since then; warmth towards the trajectory of our friendship; guilt, because as much as I wanted to help you when you drunkenly opened up to me that night, I knew now that I'd failed.

Lydia had been dragging your suitcase down the pathway when she tripped and fell into the same hedge she had once vomited in, and I laughed when you laughed. But when you were finally gone and I closed my front door behind me, I was alone, and not by way of solitude. It was more like a misplaced memory; knowing something was now different, but not knowing how. I really did miss you, Eddie. I felt your absence. I could only hope you felt mine. I could only hope you still wanted me around, regardless of the circumstances.

"You don't need to miss me. We live in the same city," you replied.

"Yes, I know, but we both know that we don't see each other as much anymore."

"I told you, I've been hard at work."

"Do you miss *me*?" I heard myself ask. It sounded more pathetic out loud than it did in my head.

You paused. "You know I'm not the soppy kind, Hu. I'll be caught dead before I tell you that."

"That's not true. You were always soppy with me. It was hugs galore with you." I was well aware of my speaking in the past tense, and I hated it.

"I appreciate people when they're around, but I gain nothing from missing them."

"I understand that. But I was just hoping that two years into our friendship, I'd be an exception to that rule."

"Frankly speaking, you're not an exception to *any* rule," you said.

I frowned. "What do you mean by that?"

"Never mind. I'm just being a prick, sorry. My headache is getting worse and I need to smoke a joint. Can we talk later?"

"Sure. I'll leave you now. I hope you have a great day."

"Thanks."

"By the way, before you go: I spoke to Helen. I told her about your new play."

"Oh. Really?"

"Yeah. You told me you're finished, right? I told her." Granted, you didn't give me a sliver of more information about it; it was a few weeks back when I sent over a check-in text, and you sent me a quick response of *Finished already. Sending it around.* That was when it sank in that something had truly changed between us.

"Well, what did she say?" you asked. Despite the lethargy in your general tone, I could hear the intrigue and hope peek through your voice like a slit of sunlight through a curtain. Admittedly, it fuelled my ruse.

"She said you should send it over. She's very, very interested. She said she'd put it right at the top of her pile."

You paused for a second. "She really said that? She's interested in my work?"

"Yes, she did. She was super keen. Especially after all the championing I've done for you. I couldn't give her much information about it, obviously, as you've kept it close to your chest, but she's expecting it. So send it as soon as you can." I instinctively lifted my free hand and started biting on my pinky fingernail.

"This sounds too easy to be true. It's pretty laughable if I was playing the long game and this ends up working. I guess I already knew that, though."

"I guarantee you, if it works it's because the agency doesn't mess about. It's because you're great."

"If you were right, I wouldn't be in this position in the first place. I wouldn't need your help."

"I *know.* But I'm not helping you just for the sake of helping you. That would be even more insulting," I found myself saying, parroting Helen. "I believe in you. That's what matters. Remember?"

You sighed. "I don't know. I'm just hungover and hungry and it's making me angry. *Hangrovy.* Thanks for telling her. I don't like the bitch, but, whatever. I'll send it over. I guess we'll see how it goes."

"We will indeed," I said. My chest felt tight. You were a sceptical person, but people were only sceptical because they didn't want to be pissed on and told it was raining. You were sceptical because you had to be. By the time you hung up, I fully understood that. I understood, because even though I had no way of knowing for sure if Smarmy

Helen would take you on, I still couldn't help but feel that ultimately, I was just telling you it was raining.

◆ ◆ ◆

I went to watch *Light as a Tonne of Feathers* by myself when the time came. It was early October, and the late summer heat had finally withered away, replaced with a prematurely refrigerant atmosphere. I sat with a clear view of the stage, marvelling at the play in all its exquisite glory. I was enamoured with the way the actors worked so fluidly together, a cohesive whole like a living, breathing body. Their words echoed and pulsated like a heartbeat, their movements were seamless and vulnerable, their voices torrid, yet controlled. The story was just beautiful. No other word was needed. Beautiful. I couldn't turn my eyes away. I didn't want to. As I soaked it all in, I felt more and more out of touch with myself. I knew I was a fraud, but the feeling doused me like a scalding-hot shower.

I ambled into the foyer of the theatre along with the rest of the audience once the applause had ended and the curtains were drawn. Even in the dimness of the room, I could feel the odd glance from people I assumed might have recognised me. I was close to exiting the building when I made eye contact with two women, one of whom was talking dotingly to the other. Admittedly, I didn't initially realise I was staring at the creator of the play I had just watched, but it was made evident based on my tuning in to the compliments and praise she was getting. When the second woman finally slunk away, I looked down at my phone, feigning preoccupation. My head shot back up when I heard my name.

"Hugo? Hugo Lawrence Smith?"

"Yes! Hello. Zayani, right?" I closed the gap between the two of us as we hung on the perimeter of the foyer. "What a pleasure to meet you." I put out my hand for her to shake.

She shook it. "Thank you. Feels good to bump into another playwright! I wasn't supposed to come to today's showing, but my cousin's in town and I wanted to sneak him backstage." She chuckled. Although I'd heard her speak before, her strong, jovial Black Country accent always took me by surprise.

"Totally fair. If I had written a play like that, I'd be here every night. Congratulations, it was amazing."

She smiled, but her eyes narrowed ever so slightly. "Thank you. I mean, you have written something like this, I reckon. *Feathers* is a sociopolitical think piece, but *Great Belonging* is basically a . . . sociopolitical soap opera."

I nodded and shrugged simultaneously. "I'm just a very passionate . . . observant person. I saw what Brexit was doing to this country, and I had to throw my two cents in. But enough about me—I came here to see your play. I'm surprised all the seats weren't filled."

"I don't pay too much attention to the ticket sales, 'cause it ain't why I write, but I can still tell it's not doing as well as it could," she said, pursing her lips.

"Oh. Really?"

She beckoned me aside a bit more so we were closer to the wall and farther from the bustle of the other people. "The first week was quite good, to be fair. It's still filling some seats—I guess it depends on the day. But I'm sure you know that your play was a sellout from the moment the opening week was over, don't you? It feels a bit silly even telling you that." She chortled. "On the other hand, mine's doing . . . fine. For the Regium, pretty lackluster, but . . . it's fine."

I clasped my hands together behind my back. "Well, I stand by what I said. I'm surprised that's the case."

She moved a step closer to me, lowering her voice a bit. "I'll be brutally honest. Everyone kept telling me to watch your play, and I held off it for so bloody long, because I thought, you don't need my support! But eventually, I thought, why not. It looks like it's on the right side of history at least.

"I loved the final act so much. You know, the scenes with the National Sweep interviews of that family from North Yorkshire. I loved how you contrasted it with the interviews of Amali and her mother coming in from Taniba. It was so *scary* how well-done and true to life it was. I moved here to Wolverhampton from Malawi when I was seven. I've had my ups and downs, but I've struggled to put it into words, y'know. Deep down, I found it hard to believe that someone like you could ever capture the immigrant experience so accurately."

She shook her head, her eyes wide. "I was seriously in denial. I came out of the play with so many mixed emotions. I was amazed, but . . . I was also resentful, if I'm honest. I'm sure you understand. I guess that's the point, isn't it? You understand your privilege. So you speak on it. But when you speak, nobody listens to anyone else. It's like a dog eating its own tail," she said, smiling dolefully.

I looked down at the carpet, then back at her. "I know. It's . . . a never-ending cycle that needs to be broken. We just need to keep spotlighting plays like yours."

She straightened her posture. "Serious question: What are 'plays like mine'? And how do they differ from 'plays like yours'? Because, I wonder, is it really about the plays, or the *playwrights*? The art, or the artist?"

"Hmm. I suppose it's a mixture of both, don't you think?" That's what I wanted to tell myself during this exchange, but I knew it wasn't as easy as that. Admittedly, my response was a bit of a cop-out. Art didn't exist in a vacuum, and I knew that.

"In theory it's a mixture, yes, but in practice, that's not the case." She paused, hesitating before speaking again. "You're signed to Wentworth, aren't you? I know all the MBG winners go there now."

I tilted my head up slightly. "Yeah, I am. Why?"

"I heard they have close ties with the awards and control the nominations and the wins. Is that true? I applied so many times but never made it to the short lists. I might just be a sore loser, but I doubt it. They don't have a great track record for inclusion."

"Oh. Well, that's the first I'm hearing about it."

"They've always got flack for being too elitist, especially recently. I'm sure this year's playwright winner is talented, but bloody hell, it's all very much of a muchness, if you ask me."

I grimaced. "I'm well aware of the discrepancies. It's a tricky one. Everyone's deserving of recognition, but not everyone gets it. I care a lot about equity in this arena, I really do."

"I see that. But does *Wentworth*? Or is it just some . . . performative schtick? Personally, I'm leaning more towards that theory. Don't take this the wrong way, but I doubt they'd have taken *Great Belonging* on if, you know, an actual immigrant wrote it."

"Huh." I chuckled anxiously. "I'm sure that's not true." I wanted to turn around, bolt for the door, and run endlessly through the London city night.

Zayani shrugged. "Either way, it's all probably a blessing in disguise. Sonder is a much better agency for my work, personally. It is what it is. Anyway, I think my cousin's probably waiting for me, so I'll dash. Thanks for coming out tonight. Every seat counts. As a . . . reluctant fan of your work, I'm glad you enjoyed mine."

"Of course. Of course." I nodded, shifting my weight. "It was breathtaking, it really was. I was just wondering, before I let you go: I'd love some more information on the agency you're currently signed to. I've only heard good things about them."

She shot me an investigative glare. "Sonder?"

"Exactly, yes. It's housing some good talent, clearly."

"Respectfully, Sonder is for the underrepresented, not the overrepresented. I don't think it would be fair for me to signpost you in that direction."

"Oh, no, of course not. I'm pretty close to quitting playwriting, honestly. I'd consider it a bit of a flash in the pan. But I know someone who I think would be a great fit for your agency. She's"—I paused for way too long—"a . . . woman of colour. Well, she's . . . black. A black . . . woman. Immigrant. Like you. As underrepresented as they come! Sonder would be so lucky." *What the fuck, Hugo.* I cleared my throat, trying to hide my mortified wince. "Not because she's underrepresented—I mean, because I know she'd contribute positively to your collective."

Zayani stared at me with a leery expression as I fumbled through my words. Then I saw a lightbulb go off behind her eyes. "Wait. Don't tell me. It's Eddie Moruakgomo, isn't it? The writer at *BABBLE*? I *love* her work." When I said yes, she tutted, putting a hand to her forehead. "I knew it, she's your bloody partner! I remember your *Guardian* interview. She went to the gala with you as well, didn't she? She looked gorgeous."

"You're right. She's my ex-partner now. But we're on good terms. She's looking for representation for her more creative projects."

"Ahhh, okay. That article she put out last month about Meghan Markle was just too good. She's right—British people *love* to tiptoe around racism. The *Daily Mail* won't call a black American woman the N-word, but they'll say she was brought up in Compton." She snorted. "Even if they're dead wrong, it doesn't matter! She's not from around here—she's from the wrong side of the tracks." She shook her head incredulously, and I followed suit, huffing in impassioned agreement. Internally, my chest tightened. I felt like I knew where you were potentially drawing some of your inspiration for that article from. I felt bad for not having kept up with your *BABBLE* work as much as I should have. As someone who wasn't necessarily the primary target audience of your magazine, and considering how distant we had been in recent times, it had slipped my mind. If only I had understood then how sometimes things are just as important for the people who aren't the primary audience as they are for the people who are. Then again, is a delineation between audiences even necessary? Is this world not too big, and this life not too short? "I don't know how closely you two work, but I can see a bit of a crossover in themes you explore," Zayani continued. "Is she really the inspiration for your work, like you said?"

I nodded. "I often wonder what kind of stuff I'd have written if I'd never met her. The immigrant experience is something I got a good understanding of through her. She opened my eyes in many ways."

"I find that quite fascinating. Well, it's a shame about Wentworth." I could hear a thin layer of judgement in her tone. "It'd be nice to see them shake things up a bit, y'know? But anyway, if Eddie's work is anything to go by, I'm quite intrigued to see what else she has up her sleeve. I can let my agent know. She has to send something over first, but yeah. Go on. We're always looking for new talent. The more the merrier."

I left the theatre feeling much more perturbed by everything, certain that I had to cut ties with Wentworth somehow. I had tried to tell myself that this was just society as a whole, this was just the way the world worked, so if you needed my back, you had it. But if this was society, then it also meant this was the industry, and if this was the industry, it also meant this was the agencies. Of course, all's well that ends well when you're bringing in crazy dividends, and Smarmy Helen was rolling in it. After all, *Great Belonging* was her sellout, and I was her cash cow. You were a financial risk she wasn't willing to take. A historically successful agency wasn't going to budge anytime soon, but something had to give. It was only a matter of time.

XX

Chef's Kiss

October 2018

I practically leapt from the living room sofa the second I heard the sound of a car slowing down to a stop outside. I made my way to the front door, then swung it open and stared out into the night-covered street. The Uber drove away, and its disembarked passenger strode towards me. If I had tried my utmost to wipe my grin away, it would have been an impossible task.

"Hello, stranger," I said, leaning on the doorframe.

"Salam eshgham!" Nahid responded, stepping into my arms.

"Is that a direct translation?" I muttered into her ear, squeezing her tight. She smelled like she always had, a perfect fusion of her favourite Jo Malone scent and a natural redolence that was wonderfully unique to her.

"Something like that," she said. I kissed her on the cheek, then she turned her head and we kissed properly, pressing our lips together like they were stamps running out of ink. It had only been around six weeks since we last saw one another, but time has a funny way of making the days feel like lifetimes. Luna's trip to Paris during Reading Week was the perfect opportunity for us to reunite, albeit briefly. I led her into the hallway, hung her coat up, and took the weight of her belongings off her. I ushered her into the kitchen before bringing her bag up to my room, where I stood alone for a moment, taking a deep breath. My heart was racing, and for once, it was because I was happy.

I was elated, in fact. I could have started doing push-ups right there and then, just to disperse the buzz I could feel in the core of my being. Instead, I rolled my shoulders and made my way back downstairs.

"I bought something to wash dinner down with," Nahid said, fishing through the carrier bag she had brought with her. "A lovely red."

"Thinking ahead, I like it." I walked towards her and took the bottle from her hands. "Wow. Château d'Angludet. I love this kind. It's perfect, thank you." I put my hand on her forearm and squeezed it softly. "I'm so hungry. Shall we get started?"

The dimples at the corners of her mouth deepened when she grinned, and I could never get enough of it. "We shall," she said.

I stuck my speaker on and shuffled some music for us to cook to before getting all the ingredients out from their designated storage places. The steaks had been marinating in the fridge for a few hours, so it was just a case of getting the vegetables in order. I delegated Nahid to the potatoes and carrots while I sautéed the button mushrooms and spinach with chopped garlic and rosemary, and hopefully showed off my flash-frying skills with the steak when the time came. Somewhere in the midst of our conversation, diluted by preoccupation with our respective cooking tasks, the song on the speaker changed. I grabbed a wooden spoon with my garlicky fingers to use as a mic while I belted along to "Everybody Wants to Rule the World" by Tears for Fears. Nahid stood and watched, laughing into her hands. During the bridge of the song, I took her hand and twirled her around, much to her further amusement. When I got to the guitar solo, my fingers slid along an invisible fret, hitting every chord with precision. Then the song finished and I caught my breath, thanking my audience of one.

"You're ridiculous," Nahid said, shaking her head. I noted how much longer her hair had got. It was now a curly and buoyant bob, and it made her look younger, fresher.

"It's a song for the ages," I replied, returning to crush more garlic.

"It is. It came out the same year I was born, I think," she said, drizzling the roasting tray of vegetables with olive oil.

"Ahhh. Those were the days. I remember it like it was yesterday," I jested.

"Oh, stop it." She rolled her eyes before placing the tray in the oven.

"To be fair, I don't even know what came out when I was born. You've got a good memory."

"Hmm . . . you were born in ninety-four, right? Well, I always remember my birthday was on a Saturday that year, because I played that 'Saturday Night' song at my party. I think there was a lot of Take That and East 17 in ninety-four. What else . . . ?" She paused, ruminating. Then she gasped. "Oh my God. How could I forget 'Love Is All Around'? That was inescapable."

"Wow. To be fair, it was *very* romantic of me to come into existence in the same year of *Four Weddings and a Funeral*. Would you agree?"

Nahid stared at me coquettishly, crossing her arms and rolling her tongue inside her cheek. "Ridiculous. That's what you are."

I had a near-miss with arson by way of my inept flambéing of the steak, but everything else ran smoothly. We soon set up the dining table and tucked into our meal, which was wonderful. I did a chef's kiss with my fingers, and Nahid did the same with hers.

We swapped life updates with one another as we ate. It was safe to say that a lot had happened in the last few weeks since I'd seen her. For one, she was currently hard at work co-directing a new play at the Soho Theatre set to premiere in less than a month. It was her first gig since *Great Belonging*, and it was definitely a step up. The cast was full of notable actors from around the country, and she was working alongside the renowned Parisian theatre director Clotilde Belmont, who was known for her formidable, no-nonsense approach to the stage. Nahid knew how to curb a rowdy crew of performers, but Belmont struck the fear of the guillotine into the hearts of anyone she instructed. Nahid told me she felt a lot more confident this time around, but that the hours were somehow more demanding despite her input technically being halved. Most of the time, both directors still had to attend rehearsals at the same time for the sake of efficient communication. It was a tiring job, but it was obvious that Nahid thoroughly enjoyed it. It was almost all she ever talked about, and it imbued me with warmth to see the passion in her eyes.

She told me that up until then, only three out of the nearly forty winners of the Laurence Olivier Award for Best Director had been women. All three of those women were white. She said that she would change that statistic one day, come hell or high water. As long as she had a functioning brain and a beating heart, she'd prove to the world that she was just as worthy, if not more. I admired her tenacity so much; she deserved the whole world. It was only a matter of time before she had her dreams in the palm of her hands. I just hoped the same for you.

"What worth are these awards to men if they're always getting them?" she asked me rhetorically. "Surely, it dilutes its value. There's a reason you got away with taking credit for Eddie's work. It's all superficial. It's like: say you only ever date one kind of person. Like, you have a super-specific type. How special is each individual person to you, really? If someone different comes along and you see something in them, that *has* to mean more. They're actually special. That's what I want to be. I want to be special. I *am* special."

I didn't know if it was worth challenging this notion, because I wanted to believe that every winner was equally as deserving as the next. If every winner looked the same, it shouldn't have mattered, but *because* every winner looked the same, it did. Did that mean that if the statistics started to skew in some freak event and all the winners became non-white non-men overnight, they'd not be as special anymore? Where was the line drawn? Where was the real value found? It was unquantifiable. Then again, her dating analogy sort of made sense to me, especially as it pertained to my personal history. I told Nahid that she *was* indeed special, because she was. In more ways than one.

She then asked me how life was on my end, and I gave her a quick rundown. I told her that since Luna had moved in after you moved out, I was a little less lonely. But only in the sense that my thoughts were drowned out by the music she'd constantly play in her bedroom. She would be back in five days from Paris, so I was going to cherish the time I had with Nahid, and to drown out my thoughts with the music *I'd* constantly play instead. Tears for Fears included.

Otherwise, life had been much of the same. Except that along with Luna's arrival came the annual reminder of my father's presence. He had told me that he expected me to be able to accommodate for both myself and my sister if I had to, considering I was technically still living under his roof. He had been putting the pressure on, asking how my theatre stuff was going, and I told him that it was a gig economy. I could tell he was sceptical.

"I told him I'm fine. I mean, I'm lying—I've essentially been unemployed for the last . . . oh . . . well, I've never had a proper job. I had uni, and then master's, then a gap year, and then I did the MBG thing halfway through my gap year, and the rest was history."

Nahid took a sip of her wine. "Wow. *Never* had a job? Not even as a barista or something like that? I don't miss my time as a waitress, but I had no other choice."

I shook my head. "It's quite embarrassing, to be honest." I *did* once work at this family's restaurant in Colombia in exchange for shelter, but I doubted that really counted. It was definitely not something worth relaying to Nahid. "I have to start properly thinking about what I'm going to do. My father thinks I should be reaping the fruits of my labour by now. Except it's not my labour, or my fruit."

"Ugh. Figures." She frowned. "You need to get a job. A proper one. For your own sake. How are you even surviving right now?"

"I've been dipping into my trust fund."

"I should have guessed you had something like that. How long have you had access to it?"

"I got access to a certain amount when I turned twenty-one, and then my next installment is when I'm twenty-five. So, in a year's time." Nahid asked me how much I had in there, and when I told her, her jaw dropped. "I know it seems like a lot, but I can't keep using it for my daily life. I can't rely on it forever, I need to save it for the future. I mean, I'll most likely get an inheritance when the old man finally croaks. He is in his seventies, so it's not necessarily a distant future. But there's no way he'll be splitting it equally between all three of his kids. I'll probably get peanuts."

"By the looks of it, your peanuts are probably the average person's coco de mer nut." She snickered before taking a bite of her steak. "Why wouldn't he split it equally, anyway?"

"Well, my brother Dominic already has the house in Lombardy, for one. Also, he's done pretty well for himself. He's probably making way more than what my dad was making in his day, inflation considered. Luna will most likely get the lion's share, if not everything. I might get *something*, but I'm telling you, there's no way it'll be equal."

"What's the difference between you and Luna? You're pretty close in age. I don't get why he wouldn't give you the same amount."

I sighed through loose lips, a long *pfft*. "I don't know. I think there are a few factors at play. First of all, Luna's his only daughter. She's also his youngest child. He probably just cares more about her well-being than he does about mine. I'm just the classic middle child. What can I say?" I shrugged before digging into the last of my vegetables.

I didn't feel like elaborating on the fact that I knew I was ultimately the result of an attempt to fix a crumbling marriage. Aged forty-one and desperate not to become a lonely divorcée whose only child had already fled the nest, my mother had convinced my father to make things work for a while. There was a renaissance period after Dominic left for uni where things actually went smoothly again, and somewhere in that calmness, I was born. But then the toxicity leaked back into my parents' relationship, although there's room for debate as to whether it had ever really left. Instead, my father eventually abandoned my mother and me, taking a one-way flight to Hong Kong to start a new life and family. Maybe she didn't see it coming. Maybe it was her ignorance towards the inevitable.

"If it makes you feel any better, it's not like my parents love *me*. The last thing my mother told me was that I was dead to her," Nahid said.

"That's *awful*, Nahid."

She shrugged. "It's okay, honestly. I understand why they feel the way they feel. I don't hold anything against them. And on the bright side, my father's slowly warming up to me again. I spoke to him for the first time in a long time recently. We talked about my directing and stuff like that. It was quite overwhelming, to be honest. I never thought I'd see the day."

"You're a really strong person. I admire that about you."

"I'm not that strong. I just care a lot. Maybe too much, who knows?"

"You can never care too much."

"Maybe, maybe not." She lifted her glass. "Let's cheers to our shitty families."

I looked at her. "Don't get me wrong, my family might be shitty, but it's not the same. You've been through way more than I have."

"That goes without saying," she responded quietly. "Okay. Let's cheers to something else. Something more fun."

"Hmm . . . let's cheers to . . . Tears for Fears. Can't go wrong there," I said, holding my glass up towards her.

She tilted her head back, laughing, lifting her glass again. "Cheers to Tears for Fears."

• • •

We were cuddled up on the living room sofa eating bowls of Häagen-Dazs ice cream after we cleared up dinner. The TV was on, but it was just background noise. We were too busy sustaining conversation. She eventually decided to bring up a topic we had yet to cover: you. Although she had some idea of our waning camaraderie, we'd never gone into depth about it. I could tell she had her opinions, though. She made it clear soon enough.

"When was the last time you spoke?" she asked me.

"Uhhh . . . well, over the phone, about three weeks ago. I wished her happy birthday. I tried to surprise her with tickets to this play, but she had already seen it."

"Do you know why she didn't invite you?"

"Honestly, I didn't bother prying. I just went alone last week. It was great; I'm glad I went. I managed to catch the playwright after the show. I told her about Eddie. You know, a bit of networking on her behalf."

"If I didn't know ninety percent of the people in the theatre scene, I'd have gone with you." She licked the ice cream off the back of her spoon. "Seriously, I don't get Eddie. The only reason she knows you is because you enjoy theatre. Why has she just iced you out like that?"

"I don't know. I assumed she needed her space for her work."

Nahid looked at me. "She was *obviously* finished with her new script by the time she went to see the play. Don't act so naive."

"I'm not being naive. I just can't beg for answers to everything. Sometimes people grow distant. There's nothing bigger at play."

She was quiet for a moment, then she told me, "It's more than just growing distant. At this point, she is actively avoiding you. Surely you can see that."

"I think you're just reading into things, Nahid."

"I'm not. She gets to live in your house and go on holiday with you, and then she does a runner and gives you the cold shoulder. You're out there promoting her new work without even thinking twice. Have you even read it? Do you even know what it's about?"

"Uhhh . . ." I looked up at the ceiling, my mouth half-open. "I haven't. I have no idea what it's about. I did ask her for updates on the script, but she never actually told me. Honestly speaking, I assume it must be good, since she wrote *Great Belonging*."

Nahid shook her head. "That's not true. It's not necessarily good. I think you should stop trying to help her. You've done as much as you can. If she wants to succeed, she has to do it on her own," she said, placing her bowl on the coffee table and then leaning back on the sofa. "I'm so proud of my achievements. I made some pretty life-changing decisions, not knowing the outcome, or if it would even be worth it in the end. I got banned from my home country, for fuck's sake. I'm not saying that's a valid sacrifice, but that's my cross to bear. At least I have a shelf of awards to show for it.

"You know, sometimes, Hu . . . I think you think that being someone's friend is trying to keep them happy all the time. Even if you know deep down that you don't have to."

I looked at the television, attempting to hide how stung I felt by her brutal honesty. "I don't think that's true."

"You were willing to do anything for someone who doesn't give you the time of day anymore. It's not fair to you."

I looked at her. "You know why we pretended to be together. She wanted better access to the play. She was covering for us. You know that."

"You never had to take it as far as you did. You didn't have to make it such a . . . thing. Taking her to the Regium gala and all. To be honest, I don't know if pretending to be together was even that foolproof of a cover. Who's to say you couldn't have been messing around with the both of us?

"You could have just remained platonic. But the way I see it is that she wanted more from you. She wanted more access to your *life*, not the play. Who knows? Maybe she felt like she deserved it; I guess I can sort of see why. But then she decided to jump ship after she spent Italy sulking because she hates all your friends. Deep down, she probably thinks she's better than them. She probably even thinks she's better than *you*. She's always on some sort of high horse."

I shook my head, clenching my jaw. "You're not being very fair. She's a great person. She was the only one who knew about us for a long time, and she kept our secret. She had every reason to tell Aaron on that opening night of *her* play. She could have said something at any time, but she didn't. You can't discount that."

She groaned, lolling her head back and staring at the ceiling. "God. This is all so ridiculous. You just can't make any of this up." She closed her eyes. "One day I just want an MBG or Olivier for directing. That's why I took on *Great Belonging*. That's why I do anything I do. I don't need all this drama," she lamented.

I chuckled, loosening up once I realised she had let go of the topic. "You're a drama grad who doesn't enjoy drama. That's a new one."

"You're a playwright who doesn't write plays."

"Touché."

She twisted from her seated position and turned 180 degrees, then mounted my lap. She cupped my face in her hands. "All right. I'll give Eddie a break. Let's just hope she leaves *Great Belonging* alone. Besides, it's true: without her, I'd never have known you. And what a wonder it is to know you."

I put my ice cream bowl aside and wrapped my arms around her waist. "This is the part when we snog, isn't it?"

"Yes. It's also the part when we have sex," she said.

• • •

We woke up earlier than usual the next morning. It was a Monday and she had rehearsals with Clotilde. I just had another day of figuring out what I was going to do with my life. I toyed with the possibility of getting proper acting classes now that I had already made a name for myself in theatre, though I wasn't sure how common writer-to-actor transitions were. Did I *really* want to become an actor? Did I enjoy the attention? Was I up for the gruelling memorisation of lines and taking on different personas all the time? I *had* been practising for nearly a year and a half now. I must have been somewhat good at it. But then again, there was a difference between looking the part and embodying it. I didn't know if I had the chops to do both. The fact of the matter was that I didn't know what my true calling was, and it pained me to come to that realisation.

Nahid snapped me out of my existential crisis, turning on her side to face me in bed. She placed a hand on my bare torso and kissed my shoulder. Then she kissed my neck and slowly slid her hand down my abdomen. She edged farther under the duvet until she had positioned herself near the bottom of the bed. Her kisses travelled down my chest and past my navel like little footsteps, getting closer and closer to my groin. I released a shudder once she had me in her mouth, and I softly gripped her mess of coiled locks. After a while, I beckoned her out from under the duvet and she lay on her back. I turned around and got between her legs. She gazed deeply into my eyes, and I kissed her hard. She clasped her hands around my neck, and we fucked, mouths open, speechless. Usually, there was barely ever much silence between us; we could talk to each other for hours. But it was times like these that were the exception that proved the rule. It was times like these that left us both lost for words, and with no intention of finding them.

Afterwards, we lay on our backs and took a moment to bring our heart rates back down. This was when I decided to bring up the elephant in the room. "Does Sophie know you're with me?" I asked her. Sophie, being her best friend who came to the rescue when she'd finally mustered the courage to leave Aaron a couple of months ago. It was never going to be easy, and it sure wasn't. It was the first time Nahid had ever seen him bawl. He begged her to stay, told her he'd change. When she said there was no turning back, he picked up a vase and smashed it against the wall, right in front of her. He went from disbelief, to sorrow, to denial, to pleading, to rage, all in one sitting.

He then suspected she might have met someone else. She assured him she hadn't, that they'd just grown apart, that it didn't have to take someone else coming into the picture for her to realise they were no longer compatible with one another. I guess two things could be true.

Nahid took a moment to answer. "She does know I'm with you, yes. She isn't too happy about it. But, whatever." She brought a fingernail to her teeth.

Sophie had provided her refuge at her flat in King's Cross when everything transpired, and this was when Nahid broke down and told her everything about us, from start to finish. That was when it was no longer just you who held our secret. Sophie had insisted that Nahid keep her distance from me during the initial fallout, especially since Nahid decided to omit the affair to Aaron. It wouldn't look great if she was seen around with me so soon. Sophie was like you in the scenario, the voice of reason who tried to keep us apart for our own good. The fact of the matter was that I was more in love with her now than I ever had been; it didn't matter to me that her divorce was yet to be finalised and that her friend had her reservations about me. Every moment I spent with Nahid I cherished. I waited for the day it could be done under the wide-open sky.

I playfully ran my finger down the centre of her forehead and along the bridge of her nose. She laughed, pulling my hand away. "Why did you do that?"

"Why not?"

"I thought you'd finally clocked onto it." She looked away.

"Clocked onto what?"

She sighed, grimacing. Then she sat up straight, bringing me upright with her. "That I've had a nose job."

My eyes widened for a moment. "Oh. You have?"

She nodded. "It was a long time ago. I got it when I was seventeen. We went back to Iran one summer when I decided I wanted one. It's not as outlandish as it sounds. I'm from the nose job capital of the world." She shrugged.

"Did you think you needed it?" I asked.

"At the time, yes. I also knew I wanted to be an actress, so I wanted to look as 'appealing' as possible." She pulled up air quotes. "I was so naive, but it was also just so ingrained in me that I was going to get one as soon as I could."

I fiddled with the duvet on my lap. "Do you regret it?"

"Sometimes I do, sometimes I don't. Sometimes I wish I had accepted myself as I was so everyone else would have no choice but to do the same. It would have been a big 'fuck you' to the world. But it's complicated. I didn't know who I was yet. I just knew who I wanted to be, and what I wanted to look like. Apparently, that meant conforming to Western beauty ideals."

"Nobody knows who they are or who they want to be when they're that young, anyway. I know I certainly didn't, and I still don't now. I'm glad I don't have beauty standards to go up against."

"What a feminist you are," she teased before sobering up again. "If I ever have kids, I'll make sure they love themselves more than anything or anyone else. They don't need to inherit my insecurity."

"You want kids?" I asked. It was seldom something I thought about for myself, and surprisingly, it was a topic that had never come up for us until now.

"Sometimes I do. But I'm only getting older. I'm turning thirty-four soon. Biological clock, yada yada yada." She rolled her eyes. But then I saw her stare straight ahead, suddenly dark and distant. She brought her knees under her chin. "Knowing my luck, I probably can't even have kids."

"What makes you think that?"

"Oh, nothing. I'm just being dramatic," she said, but she was already wiping a tear away. I put an arm around her. "I'm just desperate for a successful career. But sometimes I also want a family. Maybe I can only have one thing or the other."

I shook my head. "You know that's irrational."

"Is it? Explain to me why there are loads more successful male theatre directors. I don't think they have to worry about pushing a human being out of one of their . . . *orifices*. They don't have to worry about raising a child and working at the same time." She scowled.

I couldn't help but burst into a snicker at her use of the word *orifice*. She glared at me, but I could tell her melancholy was slowly easing away. "I love you," I said to her. "I love you very much."

She smiled. "I love you too, Hugo. I love you very, very, very much."

• • •

It was time for us to break out of our cocoon and meet the new day. She went to take a shower while I made the bed and lounged around. Ten minutes after she left the room, my phone started ringing. I saw it was you who was calling. Naturally, I was slightly confused, but I answered anyway.

"Hey, Eddie! How's it go—"

You didn't even give me time to finish my sentence before you spoke. "Helen rejected my script, Hugo. She fucking rejected it."

My heart plummeted. "Are you serious?"

"Yes, I'm serious! That stupid smarmy bitch rejected me! *Again*. I can't believe this. I'm going to lose my mind."

"Shit. Eddie, just relax. Relax."

"*Don't* tell me to relax!"

"I'm sorry. Where are you right now? What are you going to do?"

"I'm at my office. What do you *think* I'm going to do? I'm going to tell her the truth about *Great Belonging*."

Shit. "Whoa, whoa, whoa. Hold on a second. Just give yourself a moment to think about this."

"Fuck off, Hugo! Don't talk to me like I'm a child. *You're* going to tell her, too. We're both going to."

I felt dizzy. "Wait. Please, just wait."

"Wait for *what*?"

Nahid entered the room instantaneously, dewy from the shower and wrapped in a towel. When she saw the look in my eyes, the smile she walked in with vanished.

"Who are you on the phone to?" she asked.

XXI

Losing the Plot

I was walking towards the entrance of the *BABBLE* office building in Shoreditch an hour later. You were standing outside, and you crushed the butt of your cigarette when you saw me. I noted how colourful and sophisticated you looked, in a hot-pink blazer over a lime-green blouse. You had on flared blue jeans and chunky brown boots. Your eye makeup was vibrant, and your nails were manicured in different shades of pastel. Your hair was the most astonishing to me; it was the first time I'd seen you without braids. Instead, you had immaculately cornrowed hair that exploded into a big, puffy ponytail. I wanted to compliment you in that moment, but the thunder etched on your face told me it would have been a doltish idea.

You silently led me into the lobby of the building. Once we got into the lift, you spoke. "I told my colleagues that I'm having 'personal relationship' problems. It's fine; the vibe's pretty casual here. So that's what we're talking about. Got it?"

I nodded. "Okay. I take it that I'm the personal relationship?"

"No shit. They all think you're my ex." You crossed your arms.

"Fair enough. I'm glad you're willing to talk about this."

You scoffed. "That's one way to put it."

Once we were on your floor and the lift door opened, you flounced out and I followed behind you. I was markedly impressed by the interior design of the office: it was a multicoloured coordination of eighties funky-style decor. It matched the aesthetic of the magazine, and so did everyone there. As we walked through the open space, all I could see were zany haircuts and kaleidoscopic outfits. It was impossible for me not to notice the glares I got from everyone in the room. As groovy as the vibes were, I couldn't help but sense that I was entering the lion's den. It's an interesting feeling, to be in a space and know you aren't welcome.

We walked through an opaque glass door at the back of the open office labelled QUIET ROOM. Although the primary scent was incense, a woman sat lazing on a beanbag smoking a joint with the window open, and the smell was noticeable. You glared at her, prompting her to kill the joint in a marble ashtray on the table beside her and leave the room. We were finally alone to talk, but I was hyperaware that the only thing dividing us from everyone was a glass wall, three-quarters of which was opaque and the top quarter transparent. With my height, and depending on where we stood, I could still see the people outside, which meant they could still see us.

"The wall's soundproof," you said, almost reading my mind. "You know, 'cause this is the quiet room. They're not going to hear us. Unless things start to get heated." You plopped yourself on one of the beanbags, sinking into it.

"This place looks so cool. Everyone seems quite close-knit," I said, sitting down on the beanbag opposite you. "It must be nice to work here."

"So, why did you tell me Helen wanted to read my work?" you asked. I guess there was no time for small talk.

I hesitated. "Because . . . she *did*. She said she would. I don't know what happened."

"Her email was *so* condescending. She showed absolutely no indication that she even thought I had any talent. In fact, I'm pretty sure she insinuated that I was just trying to ride your coattails. She was just like, 'The script is *too rushed* and doesn't have a strong foundation. It's not *quite* at the level Wentworth is looking for, but I wish you the best on your *journey* for representation.' What kind of a response is that?"

I shook my head and shrugged. "I'm sorry, Eddie. I really did vouch for you. I'm just as shocked as you are." I swallowed.

You narrowed your eyes. "I don't believe you."

"Why not? Why would I tell you she put your work at the top of the pile if she didn't? She got back to you in a few weeks. Usually agents don't respond for months. I'm sure she was interested." I could feel the heat rise on the back of my neck and the helices of my ears as I spoke.

You sat forward. "You're lying to me. I can tell. I've known you long enough to know when you're lying."

"Eddie, come on. I gain nothing from lying to you. Besides, I don't think Wentworth is a good agency for you. I spoke to Zayani Chimbalanga—you know, the woman who wrote *Light as a Tonne of Feathers*. She said Sonder Words is a much better agency, and that she'd put in a good word for you if you sent something over. She's a big fan of your *BABBLE* work."

"Why should I believe you? You're only telling me this now, when shit's hitting the fan."

"Respectfully, you've been quite distant, so it hasn't been easy to reach you. Also, Sonder is a much more inclusive agency. They actually platform underrepresented stories. Trust me, Eddie, you don't want to be under Wentworth."

"What makes you think that I want to be pigeonholed into a little box where all the black and brown writers are relegated to, either? Why do we always have to be pitted against each other? Why do we have to be pushed aside and given our own category? I'm *not* a black writer. I'm a writer who is black. There is a difference."

"I get that."

"No, you don't. You don't get anything. You just say what people want to hear."

"That's just not true."

"Not being funny, Hugo, but I wasn't in my right mind when I asked you to do what you did for me. If you were in your right mind, too, you'd not have said yes."

I screwed up my face. "Hold on, are you blaming me for saying yes?"

"I'm not blaming you for saying yes. I'm just kicking myself, because I didn't know you then like I know you now. I didn't know you were a pathological liar."

"What are you talking about? Why would you say that?"

You got up from your beanbag and stood towering over me, arms crossed. "For one, you kept your thing with Nahid from me at the beginning. Second of all . . . you *loved* Belle, did you? She was your *soulmate*? She meant *everything* to you? You'd *never* want to hurt her?"

I got up, standing level with you. From my vantage point, I was reminded that anyone walking past could see our disembodied heads bobbing about, and I felt exposed. "I was telling the truth. If you think it makes me a pathological liar because I fell in love with someone else, then so be it." I shrugged.

"Oh, you're in love with Nahid. Right. Sure."

"Of course I am! It's been a year. I think I'd know by now if I didn't love her."

"Hmm. I don't know. It's hard for me to believe you when you failed to inform me that you fucked half of London while you were still in a relationship."

I stood there, stunned. "What are you *talking* about?"

"I mean, you *fucked* half of *London* while you were in a *relationship*," you said louder. "You're a man-whore! You wouldn't know love if it slapped you across the face. You just think with your prick, like all men do!"

"Could you . . . maybe . . . speak a tad quieter?" I muttered, shifting around. Even if the room was soundproof, there was no way the office dwellers would not have heard that. But then I realised, maybe that was the point. You wanted to unleash your anger on me in a way that could work as a double entendre to any eavesdropping party. You were having "personal relationship problems," after all.

"Why shouldn't I yell? You're a serial cheater! Why should I believe you? You only like blondes anyway. In the words of your ex, let's just say Nahid's *definitely* not blonde."

"Eddie, you've lost the plot."

"You hooked up with Klara and you never told me!"

My face fell. "Sorry?"

"She told me you got with her at uni. She told me you only ever hooked up with blonde girls who looked like Barbie, or . . . fucking Marilyn Monroe. Is that why Belle dressed like her at your Halloween party when we first met? To keep you interested? Are women of colour just an experiment to you? Are you going to have a taster of every corner of the world? Where's next, Japan? Brazil? Turkey? Ethiopia? Columbus would be *so* proud."

I could have sworn I heard a couple of snickers coming from the office space. If it was possible for the floor to swallow me into an abyss, I'd jump in without a second thought. "Is this why you've been off with me since Italy? Because Klara started a rumour about me?"

"A *rumour*? How is it a rumour when your friends basically confirmed it? Is it also a rumour that you went on the balcony and started basically having phone sex with Nahid while I was asleep? Was Klara lying about that as well?"

"Oh shit," I muttered. I didn't know you knew that.

"You sabotaged everything. You sabotaged *us*, and put my play, my one life's dream, in jeopardy. You made me look like a mug in front of your friend. You had your chance to tell me about Klara, but you didn't. You acted like Nahid was the first and only time you'd ever turned your head. God knows why. I don't know if I can trust you, Hugo. You're making it hard to believe it."

"So you believe Klara? You believe a girl you met once more than me?"

"Why would she lie about you?"

"I don't know, do I? I barely know her. She's my friend's tagalong sister, for Christ's sake."

"Is it true or not? Did you get with her?"

"Eddie, my life before I met you has nothing to do with you."

"So it *is* true."

"I'm not going to let you interrogate me like this."

"It's because you have no integrity," you replied frostily. "You have no spine."

I was taken aback. I'd never been the recipient of this much vitriol from you. But sometimes, vitriol was just a way to communicate pain. Regardless, I wanted to stick up for myself. "With all due respect, Eddie, I think you're misdirecting your anger at Helen towards me. You can't even tell me that *you* have integrity. You don't. If you had any integrity, you would have never put yourself in this position."

"We were going to tell the truth on opening week!" you hissed. "Don't you fucking *dare* forget that. I moved the goalpost for you and Nahid."

"I'm not denying that. But I've always been there for you. I've done everything I can to help you."

You stared at me. "You've always been there for me. Really."

"I have! I constantly talked about you during public engagements. I let you live with me. I tried my best for you," I said. I could feel a lump growing in my throat. "I really wanted you to succeed. I still do."

"You did everything short of defending me when it mattered the most. You didn't stand up for me in front of Lucas and Damian in Italy, remember? Any slight towards me was never a big deal to you. You were never as vulnerable as me. You never could be."

"I didn't want you to wallow in self-pity! You're one of the strongest people I know. I didn't want to make you feel like you're doomed for perpetual victimhood."

"Oh, so me being upset about being treated like a second-class citizen is me succumbing to 'perpetual victimhood', is it?"

"That's not what I'm saying. I'm saying I want you to stick it to everyone who's ever treated you like a second-class citizen."

"You don't realise that by minimising my frustrations, *you* are treating me like one."

"What else am I supposed to do? I know people are bad, I know the world is unfair, I know all of this. I don't want to keep reminding you. You don't need a reminder from me. I'm pretty much a walking reminder, as is."

You looked away. "That's the first honest thing you've said in a while."

"I'm not a dishonest person, Eddie."

"I *thought* you weren't."

"You put me in a position to lie because you thought I was an honest person? Does that make any sense to you?" I frowned. "Granted, I'm not perfect. I'm not a saint. I try my best, but I don't always hit the mark. You just can't expect total honesty when everything started from a dishonest place."

"You're right. I shouldn't have, I guess."

I bit my bottom lip. "I'm sorry. I'm sorry you couldn't rely on me. I'm sorry I wasn't a good enough friend to you."

Your eyes watered and your lips trembled as you looked up at the ceiling. "I made it this far, but I'm back at square one. Worse yet, I'm at square minus one hundred. I'm successful, and nobody even knows it." You cried, not even bothering to wipe your tears. They landed as little dark streaks on your shirt. It wasn't long before you were sobbing, and you lowered yourself into a crouching position, resting your elbows on your thighs and covering your face. It was a tragic sight to behold. It was painful. To think that I had caused the pain made it hurt even more, because that was never my intention. I'd have never agreed to help you if I knew it would cause more harm than good. But the trade-off would have been living a mundane existence. The trade-off would be never meeting my soulmate. You changed my life for the better. In that moment, I wished I could have done the same.

I lowered myself back onto the beanbag opposite you, and I sighed. "Screw it. I'll tell Helen. I'll tell her the truth."

You looked at me, pausing mid-sob. "You will?"

"I will. I'll draft an email, detailing everything. You can go over it with me, if that works. *You* can draft it, even. I'll CC you in the email so you know I sent it."

You planted yourself back on the beanbag. "What about Nahid?" you asked.

"Let me talk to her." When I left my house that morning, I told her you were on the phone, but I didn't tell her that you had threatened to unleash the beast. Considering she was on her way to rehearsals for her next big break, I didn't think that was something she would take kindly to at the time. Or ever, to be honest.

You shook your head, sniffling and wiping your remaining tears. "I don't want Helen to know so I can get signed to the Shitworth Agency, anyway. I just want her to know she's wrong about me and that she's a fucking racist."

I nodded. "Of course. That's what matters. We'll send the email. Honestly, best-case scenario is that I get dropped, or they even offer to take you on. The ball will be in your court at that point. I'll talk to Nahid and give her a heads-up. She might feel a bit blindsided, but it doesn't matter. You're my top priority right now."

You stood up, blew out air from your lips, and relaxed your shoulders. Then you turned to the table near the window, picked the abandoned joint up, and lit it. You took a long toke before blowing the smoke up towards the open slit in the window. "Let's sort this smarmy bitch out," you said.

Although you'd calmed down by the time we left the room, the walk through the office felt even more humiliating than it had on the way in. I could hear the light murmurs from people at their seats, and I could feel the hot stares. One woman slowly spun to face me on her desk chair, framed her mouth with her hands, and mouthed what was most definitely *wanker* at me. In the lobby, a tall woman of East Asian descent with a bleached buzz cut walked up to you and asked if you were all right, throwing me a look. You said you were fine, and you introduced her properly to me. She told me her name was Franki, and she kept her arms crossed as she spoke. You both said goodbye to me at the lift. As the door closed and you walked back into the office, I overheard Franki laugh. "I can't believe white men are real," she said.

• • •

If I was going to tell the agency the truth, I needed to prepare myself for all possible outcomes. There was just one outcome I didn't want to face, however. It hurt me the most to think about. As I walked through the East London streets, I texted Nahid and told her that I needed to speak to her as soon as possible. Almost immediately, she called me back.

"I'm on an early lunch break. What's going on?" she asked.

I hesitated, and then cleared my throat. "Eddie wants to tell Helen Hunter the truth about *Great Belonging*."

"That's not going to happen," she scoffed. "She told me she wouldn't tell anyone."

"The agency rejected her second script. She's upset, and she rightfully wants them to know she's clearly worthy of being signed."

Nahid was silent for a moment. "What if her second script is terrible? She made her bed. There's no point in going backwards."

"Nahid, come on."

"*What?*"

"I'm going to have to do it. I'm sorry. It's neither my nor your place to tell Eddie what to do with her art."

"Oh, stop it! She used you as a little pawn in her game and now she's throwing a hissy fit because it's not going her way! She's going to screw everything up if she does this. She won't make things any easier for herself."

"I can't deny her the chance to tell the truth. It's her decision to make."

"No, it's *not*. She already made her decision. I made sure *Great Belonging* was the best it could have been. I put my *all* into that production. I don't want to be roped into this stupid bullshit." I could hear the desperation leaking into her voice.

"You won't be roped in, babe. Eddie and I will make it very clear that you had nothing to do with this."

"It doesn't matter! I knew about it for a long time. I'm basically a complicit party." She paused, and said quietly, "I'm leaving Aaron for you. If we go public with our relationship, the speculation will be relentless. If this goes tits up, my career is going tits up with it."

"It won't. Plus, it doesn't take away from the fact that you're an amazing director."

"That's all I want to be. Not one that was linked to some weird theatre scandal."

"I think you're kind of letting your ego get in the way of things right now," I said, and I instantly regretted it.

"My ego? My *ego*? Did you just call me *egotistical*?"

"I didn't mean it like that—"

"What will happen here is that this will catch wind in the worst way possible. It's going to end up looking like a racist fucking ghost-writing situation. Spin it how you want, but that's the bottom line. You and Eddie are idiots. You had no idea what you were getting yourself into, and now you're about to make it everyone else's problem."

I stopped in the street, sighing. I couldn't win. There was nothing I could do right. I didn't want to lose Nahid, and I didn't want to betray you. But you and Nahid were at odds with each other. She rooted for individualism, and you saw the system as a bigger fish to fry. The odds were stacked against the both of you, but you sought different solutions. No matter what decision I made, I was going to hurt someone. I had to accept that. There was just no turning back.

It meant that I desperately needed something to fall back on. I wasn't prepared for what would happen if the truth got out. It was only earlier that morning when I was thinking of what to do with my life. When I got home, I sat in the living room. After at least twenty minutes of incessant rumination, I sighed, picking up my phone. I remembered that I had deferred my legal practice course a year ago, and the September term had already started, but there was also a starting period for the following spring. I called my father and told him that I was going to start it, and I asked if it was possible for him to land me a vacation scheme at Pointon & Sumner, his old stomping grounds. At the end of the day, I wasn't cut out for the theatre world, and I was running away from that. I wasn't worthy of the fanfare. I heard the delight in my father's voice in reaction to my change of heart; he said he was glad I was done experimenting with the arts, and that he'd get me a space at the firm as soon as he could. I thanked him and hung up. You said you felt you were back at square one; that made two of us. Actually, I was always set for life with law. I had that road paved out for me since before I was born. It's just that my suffocating fate also happened to be my lifeline.

• • •

The next day, I drafted an email to send to Helen. When I was finished, I ran it by you. You made a couple of edits here and there, but it stayed relatively the same. I was charged with anxiety in the moments before I pressed send. I could already hear the betrayal in Nahid's voice. When she got back to mine later that evening after her rehearsals, she asked me if I had told the agency, and I said I hadn't. She seemed relieved but exhausted. She didn't finish her meal that evening, and she looked slightly washed out. I wondered if I had cursed her with stress after our phone call, and I felt as guilty as ever.

At around three in the morning, I was on my side facing away from Nahid when she woke up to go to the toilet. I don't think she realised I was awake and heard her retching for a while before she flushed the en suite bathroom toilet. She slid back into bed quietly, trying not to wake me. All I could think about was Helen's potential response to my email, and Nahid's reaction, when she eventually found out. All the while, I hadn't slept. By the time I did, I heard the birds chirping outside.

XXII

Commendable Behaviour

You and I were sitting in Helen's office two days later. She had her hands clasped together, leaning forwards on the table. Her smile was uncanny. If she moved a muscle in her cheek, her face might crack like stone and fall apart.

"I'm so glad you two could make it on such short notice. I'm quite busy with my current roster of talent; it can be hard to get any free time." She pursed her lips. "Now, as you can imagine, I was quite *shocked* by your email. It took me by surprise. I'd like you to just . . . run me through it, if that's okay."

"What's there to run through? We laid it all out in the email," you said.

"Right." She gave a half nod in your direction, and then squinted her eyes. "Well, it's a shame you feel that the Wentworth Agency is not representative enough of other creeds and backgrounds, and I do applaud your efforts. But I have a couple of questions: What exactly was the end goal here? Why has it taken the both of you so long to finally reveal this?"

You looked at me, and I spoke. "The production went so well. I think it was just . . . hard for Eddie to call it off so soon after. It was all she ever wanted, to see it in real life. She had never told anyone about this play, even when she was writing it. I was the only person she let read it. For that, I'm grateful." I smiled at you and you smiled back. I could see a forlornness in your eyes.

Helen nodded slowly. Then she began to laugh. "Wow! See, I had this all wrong, Eddie. I thought you were trying to gain a platform through your more successful counterpart. Silly me! But now, I've got a bit of a conundrum on my hands, because it means that technically, the MBG doesn't belong to you, Hugo." She turned to me. "Which means that *technically*, you're ineligible for it, and that would result in a disqualification, wouldn't it?"

"I suppose it would, yes," I said.

"It'd be *my* MBG," you said. "You can just change the names. It's really not that hard."

"Eddie, Eddie, Eddie. What a determined little lady you are. Unfortunately, we can't do such a thing. In fact, I don't think it would be very wise for us to endorse this . . . narrative."

"What narrative?" you pushed back.

"One where we have to publicly announce that the winner of the 2017 Marston B. Greaves Award for Best New Playwright is not a playwright at all, and in fact got his . . . black girlfriend to write his play for him. That would not look good, would it?"

"We're not actually together, and she wrote the play before she even met me. We said that in the email," I responded.

"Right, right. But the general public don't know this, do they? They think you *are* together, because you made us believe that you are. Or were. Whatever. Which, honestly speaking, has made things a tad more complicated, hasn't it? Because if we were to rescind the award and give it to you, Eddie, there could be room for speculation that there are some . . . dishonest dealings going on at the agency. You know—that there are no checks and balances. It will just be an all-in-all very *bizarre* story. You've put us right in a pickle, you two. Haven't you?" She laughed again. It was uncomfortable to watch.

"I'm done caring about whether it 'looks good' anymore," you replied. "Whether your biases are implicit or not doesn't matter. At the end of the day, Hugo faked his way into Wentworth, and he succeeded where I failed. Yet he can't write for shit!"

"It's true, I can't." I shook my head, shrugging.

"You were blinded by the money you could make off him, Helen. Just admit it."

Her smile vanished. "Oh. Is that your understanding of the situation? What a shame. I'd hoped you didn't see me that way. I've been here for nearly two decades. I'm motivated by my desire to find the best *talent*, not money. I'm not exactly equipped to keep my eyes peeled for the odd deceitful person who wanders into my office."

"Why didn't you take on *Great Belonging* when it was *The Worthy*?" I asked. "And when I won the award, why weren't you more suspicious of me, considering you'd already seen the script before?"

Helen looked at me. "Did Eddie not tell you? We had budget cuts that year. We couldn't afford to take it on when it was *The Worthy*. See, if she had submitted the play again under her *own* name at the MBGs, that could have been her chance. There's submitting directly to the agent, and there's applying to the competitions. There's no rule that says you can't do both." I questioned this, considering what Zayani had told me after her play—that the agency may have had some sort of covert hand in the MBG nominations and wins. If they really were separate processes, it may have been understandable. I couldn't trust that they were. "To your second point: it's not often you come across conspiring on this level. You had every moment between now and when you won the award to speak up. I saw that the two of you had attended the ceremony, and in our first meeting, you concocted some *bizarre* backstory about how because you went to law school, you felt like you weren't a fitting contender. What was I supposed to believe?"

I shook my head. "No. You saw that I was C. H. Edmonds's cousin and you clung to it. The alarm bells should have started ringing once the script made its way back into the MBGs under a new name and title. But they didn't, because you certainly looked me up and saw who I was related to. You knew my name could produce headlines. That was the bottom line."

"It's not my job to understand why people make the choices they make." Helen leaned back in her chair. "We turned Eddie's play down because we had budget cuts. It was out of our control. It's as simple as that, really. We never expected her to Trojan horse her way back into the agency when she could have just tried again."

"'Budget cuts' my arse," you retorted. "You said my play was too 'politically sensitive.' I wonder why? Just admit it, Helen. I was never going to win an MBG under my own name."

"But you never tried, dear. How could you know for sure?"

"You had something good, and you binned it the second I walked into this office and you saw I wasn't really an Edward Moore. Admit it. Admit that you'd rather play it safe. I never stood a chance. You wrote me off a long time ago."

"Eddie. The last thing I'd want is animosity from you. Either of you, to be honest. That's what I feel I'm getting. You see . . . the theatre world is fairly small. But it's also pretty *big*." Helen gestured the size with her hands. "Animosity can translate into a lack of professionalism. You wouldn't want to *hinder* your chances at working with other agents in the future, would you?"

"Is that a threat?"

"I don't make threats. You know, I don't think we got off on the right foot, and I think it's been a bit rocky ever since. Would you say the same?"

I intervened. "If anyone is acting unprofessional here, it's you, Helen. You're clearly applying intimidation tactics to get us not to speak out about the truth. If we received an ounce of self-reflection from you at the least, this conversation would start making headway. None of this is about me. It's about your lack of regard for talented people who can't guarantee you success."

I saw her lip twitch as she looked at me. Then she laughed. "See, this is . . . this is all quite a lot for me to absorb, to be frank. I got it *completely* wrong when I had that video meeting with you last month. I thought you wanted me to take Eddie on because of your terrible breakup, and it was mostly your fault. However, I told you that this agency has to be *impartial*. It would be wrong for me to bring on your girlfriend just because you asked me to, you see? Now, it might seem like a *big* conclusion to leap to—that you're compensating for whatever . . . romantic shortcomings you had by giving her a leg up here. But I had a little bit more of a reason to come to the conclusion I came to. I'm not sure if you're aware of this widely *renowned* theatre director. His name is Aaron Yousef."

When she mentioned that name, I felt my blood run cold. I shifted in my seat. "I do know of him, yes."

"He's a big name. *Awfully* talented. He's directing something in New York at the moment, how delightful! I hate to bring this up, but . . . he's currently going through a lot in his personal life." She frowned. "Keep this between you and me." She leaned farther into the desk and dropped her voice to a loud whisper. "*His wife is divorcing him.*"

"Oh. That's . . . that's a shame," I said, trying to mask my sheer mortification. I had a feeling I knew where this was heading, but I didn't quite know how we'd get there.

"It really is a shame. He was *beside* himself. See, Aaron's a good friend of mine, and when he told me his wife was planning on getting into directing, we were intrigued. We were more than happy to give her a project; she had apparently been taking classes, so we knew she wouldn't be *completely* inexperienced. We thought the new MBG-award-winning play would be a good springboard. We never expected it to gain as much success as it did, contrary to your suspicions, so it was a pleasant surprise.

"I was sorry to hear their marriage started falling apart around the same time that *Great Belonging* was peaking in popularity. I felt for the both of them; it's hard trying to sustain a relationship and work so hard on your career. I'd know—I've been married twice." She shook her head, sighing. "I've also been cheated on in both of my marriages. So, when I found out that Aaron had an inkling Nahid wasn't being faithful, it's safe to say that he was probably right. Except he couldn't prove it. Then she decided to leave him, and there were still dozens of questions left unanswered." With each word Helen uttered, I felt more and more nauseous. I could also feel the tension radiating from you. I had my focus on her pen on the desk, never breaking my stony expression.

She continued. "Poor Aaron was *heartbroken*. He wanted answers. So he did something he probably shouldn't have, in hindsight. He hired a private investigator to see what his beloved ex-wife was getting up to. He wanted to know how she was faring after the brutal separation. The results were . . . interesting." She looked at me. "She was spending some time around different parts of London, primarily North. But sometimes . . . she'd end up in South West. Hammersmith, to be exact. Isn't that funny?

"This is all to say that Aaron only recently started putting the pieces together. To find out that not only was Nahid potentially unfaithful, but that she also failed to disclose it, is pretty unfortunate. To find out that this is her *second* relationship formed with a work colleague paints a not-so-great picture of her. It seems . . . potentially habitual.

"Now, I'm willing to look past personal relationships in theatre—they happen *all* the time. It's only fair to point out that Aaron and Nahid met on set, too. But Aaron is worried that this is behaviour that might be getting in the way of Nahid's professionalism. Having an affair with someone so many years your junior is *never* a good look. Especially someone who is essentially a fledgling in the industry. There are some potential power dynamics at play, which isn't ideal. So . . . it's probably best that we try to cut any more of this palaver short before there are further consequences for not only you, but Miss Norouzi."

I was lost for words, and I could feel my heart sink slowly like a brick in molasses. We had hit a wall; telling the truth had got us nowhere. Nahid was absolutely right about this whole situation. Little did she know that she never had to worry about the play's truth getting out there. That was the *least* of her worries. She was at risk of being blacklisted from theatre by her powerful scorned husband. Even if this play *had* always been mine, the problems wouldn't end there for her. From the moment we met, we fell into a kamikaze entanglement. Her directing career was potentially over just as it was beginning, and she had no clue.

You snorted. "Oh, I see. So now you're blackmailing Nahid. Commendable behaviour." You slow-clapped.

"I'm not blackmailing anyone, darling. Aaron gave her this opportunity, so you can understand how upset he might feel about this. Now, if he also found out what you've just told me, it would just . . . add fuel to the fire. It would be a *shame* for Nahid to garner any negative publicity if the ugly truth behind the play she directed ever came out, on top of the *illicit* affair she had during its production. We wouldn't want that, would we? We wouldn't want her not to be taken seriously in this industry. It's already a steep hill to climb for us women, isn't it? Women of colour, especially." Helen raised an eyebrow. "Well. Anyhoo, I need to wrap this up. You know me, so busy with my many meetings," she chirped, smiling. "I'm more than happy to pencil in another chat with you two if you need any further discussion. But as it stands, it would be wise to let you go from the agency, Hugo. There will be no harm and no foul. If you want to get the one-hit-wonder framing, that's perfectly fine. We'll just . . . let you be. That is *if* and only *if* what was discussed in this room stays in this room. Furthermore, we've already set the wheels in motion with the *Great Belonging* tour. It'd be unfortunate to have to bring it to a halt and put people out of work because of all this."

"Are we going to gloss over the fact that this is *my* play?" you said.

She pursed her lips for a moment. Then her eyes widened. "Tell you what, why don't we . . . provide you with a nice lump sum for your troubles? We can talk more about this another time, but . . . we're no longer in a budget deficit, so we can afford to sprinkle some compensation in your direction." She beamed. "I'm thinking, a one-off payment of around . . . two hundred."

"Two hundred?"

"*Thousand*, of course. We're not *that* stingy." She chuckled.

I saw you freeze, and then look at me, before looking back at Helen. "That's . . . that's a lot of money, I suppose. But it's on the condition that nobody can know I'm the real mastermind behind one of your most successful productions in recent years. It's on the condition that Hugo remains a winner in the public eye, despite the fact that Wentworth now knows that's not the case."

"It's *your* fault Hugo is a winner in the public eye, not ours. The MBGs take their awards *very* seriously. The fallout from this revelation could be its downfall. This would tarnish every past, present, and future award winner's legacy. *And* you'd be two hundred thousand pounds less rich." She stood up from her chair, straightening out the creases in her pencil dress. "As I said before, I've got to run. It was an absolute pleasure talking to the both of you. We learned a lot today, didn't we?" She put a hand out for you to shake and you ignored it, turning to the door. She then pivoted her hand towards me and

I shook it reluctantly. "I wish you and Nahid the best," she said, winking at me before I left the room.

When we got into the lift for the ground-floor lobby, I noticed that you didn't look as frustrated or forlorn as I thought you would. In fact, you looked pretty smug.

"Are you taking the money?" I asked you. "She's a piece of work. It might seem like a lot, but you're worth way more than that." Accepting the money was not a win by any means. You could never really win. At the end of the day, I was just a name; that was all I was selling. Your name wasn't enough, you thought. But it was always enough. You were always enough.

"Of *course* I'm not taking the money," you said. You pulled out your phone from your back pocket. You leaned in closer to me, showing me the unlocked screen. You had the voice memo app open. "I had my phone face down on the table. I recorded the entire meeting. Every single minute of it."

My mouth dropped open before morphing into a wide grin. "Oh my God, Eddie. You fucking legend!"

"I knew she wasn't going to want the news to ever get out—she has a reputation to uphold for being the 'savviest' agent at Wentworth, after all. So I came prepared. When the time comes, we'll get the truth out on our own terms. It will be their undoing."

• • •

Nahid was visibly alarmed to find you with me upon our return to the house a couple of hours later. She was still under the impression that we'd not been on good terms, especially considering what had occurred a few days prior. She slowly rose from the living room sofa when we entered the room, and she crossed her arms, her eyes flitting between us in suspicion.

"What's going on, Hu?" she asked as if she already knew what we had done. "Why's she here?"

"I'm standing right here, you can ask me," you quickly rebutted.

I shot you a look before turning back to Nahid. "Right. I think . . . I think we should all sit down for this," I said to her.

As everything unravelled, I could see the disbelief in her eyes. She was at a loss for words and was holding back tears as we explained everything, from Helen's blackmail to Aaron's vengeful mission to sabotage her career. When she finally spoke, she sounded meek and tired. Her lips trembled as she sank into the sofa and looked up at the ceiling. It broke my heart to see her this way.

"This whole time, I thought *Great Belonging* was mine," she began. "I had no idea that Aaron had told Helen to give it to me. I thought I got it on my own. I didn't even know they were *friends*. I barely knew anything about him at all." Her voice rose into a whimper as she wiped a tear away. "Oh God, I feel like such a fucking idiot." She groaned, cupping her face in her hands.

"Don't feel that way, Nahid. Please, don't," I replied. You and I were sitting on the sofa adjacent to her, and I leaned forward so I could address her more directly. "You are immensely talented. Aaron had no idea who he was dealing with. He's just scorned. You'll make it through this, I promise you that. *We* will, together."

She collected herself, straightening her posture and letting out a long, meditative exhale. Then she looked at you. "Eddie. I'm so sorry about Helen. I really am. I tried to warn you that it wouldn't work in your favour. I guess some things are worth finding out on your own terms."

You shook your head. "No. It's fine. I can't fault you for your stance. You wanted to protect your image, I get that. Who wouldn't want that? Ultimately, though . . . it's a good thing we told the truth. Had we not, you might have never known about Aaron. The fact that he thought it was perfectly fine to hire someone to stalk you is frankly . . . obscene. He obviously just saw you as his property. All the right things came to light in the end."

"Ugh, I feel so violated. Why did I ever marry that bastard?" she agonised, holding back tears again until there were too many. I moved to sit with her as she sobbed, wrapping my arms around her. You and I knew in that moment to just remain silent, to let her ride her emotions. After about a minute and a half, she wriggled out of my embrace and composed herself, leaving for the kitchen to grab a glass of water. She soon returned, and she placed the glass on the coffee table and leaned back on the sofa, crossing her arms. "So, is that everything?

Are there any more bombshells left? Because . . . I actually kind of have one of my own."

I looked at her. "You do? What is it?"

"Wait, wait," you interrupted. "There *is* something else, Nahid. I actually recorded the meeting with Helen. I have the whole thing on my phone. I also had a feeling things might not go as planned, so I needed leverage. I have proof of her blackmail and bribery. It's just a case of what I'm going to do with it." You shrugged.

"Shit," Nahid breathed. "Okay. Well, that was clever. It's great that you're one step ahead at least. God, aren't you tenacious?" She shook her head, teasing a smile.

"You and me both," you quipped in response. "I want to do a *BABBLE* exposé on Wentworth and include the leaked recording in the online article. I can get some of my colleagues to do some thorough research on the history of the agency, dig up more solid evidence of corruption, that kind of stuff. We could interview former and current clients and get a feel for what people *really* think about Smarmy Helen and the rest of the agency. God only knows what will come of it, but it's worth trying."

Nahid paused, seemingly hesitant to get on board with the plan. "Okay. Right. When exactly were you thinking of releasing this exposé? It seems like it might take a while to gather everything, cross your *T*'s and dot your *I*'s, all that. It's crucial not to rush anything. The article must be completely infallible. I know Helen's hanging a big lump sum of money over your head, and she'll probably throw an NDA at you any moment now, but don't let that spook you."

"For sure." You nodded. "We'll work on it for as long as it takes. Your input would be great, too. You've got some good insights." Seeing how the two of you had warmed to one another in the space of an afternoon was dizzying, but ultimately gratifying. It felt like everything was coming together. Things were heading in the right direction, and I felt nothing but relief in that moment. The intensity of the last year or so was slowly drawing to a close. I could recalibrate and think harder about my own future. About *myself*. It was about time I did.

Not too long later, you decided to make your way home, hugging us goodbye at the front door. Once you were gone, I remembered that

Nahid mentioned having a bombshell of her own to drop. I brought it back into the conversation when we returned to the living room. "What was it that you were going to say earlier?" I turned to her.

It felt like an eternity before she finally spoke. When she did, I heard the blood rush into my ears like white noise. "I'm not one hundred percent sure just yet, but . . . I think I might be pregnant," she said.

NALEDI

Love and Ego

June 2019

I was sitting by the window in a café in Bow, charged with anticipation. I tried to focus on anything but my nerves, from swirling my tea around with my spoon to going on my phone, aimlessly clicking on different apps. Eventually, from the corner of my eye, I saw Blue through the window, walking across the road in my direction. She was on her phone until she reached the door and pushed it open, then scoured the room until she saw me. Then she smiled, approaching me. I stood up to hug her. She hugged back, but I felt the reluctance. She sat down opposite me, and I took everything in. She had bleached her hair blonde and sported multiple new tattoos. She had always been stylish, but her fashion sense was more elevated now. Everything she wore complemented her perfectly. She looked so beautiful, just as she always was.

I didn't say anything for a few moments, and neither did she. Eventually, she broke the silence.

"It's been a minute, hasn't it?" she said. "How are things?"

"Wait. I should have asked first." I put my hand up in front of me. "Let's start again. How have you been?"

She let out a *pfft* before responding. "That's a loaded question. Well, I've been great, actually. But so much has happened since I last saw you."

"I'm aware. Congrats on your award! Fucking incredible. I called it, didn't I?"

"Thank you! It still doesn't feel real, honestly. I'm waiting for the moment I wake up and realise it's all a dream. And . . . sure, you did call it." She grinned softly. Ego Birth had won Best Jazz at the Ivor Novello Awards a month earlier, following the release of their critically acclaimed sophomore album, *Love and Ego*. It was highly collaborative, packed with features from established and up-and-coming artists in London's jazz scene. I remembered listening to it when it first came out, in awe of how extraordinary it was. I didn't get to celebrate the release with her at her launch party like last time, but I still took comfort in its familiar yet elevated sound. I tuned in to the piano, absorbing every note, knowing she was playing it.

"You looked beautiful at the ceremony. You all looked great, but you looked the best. That's not just ex-girlfriend bias, by the way. Well, maybe just a little bit."

She chuckled and then frowned, looking down, struggling to find an apt response. "What about you? I'm sure you've got a lot of interesting shit to tell me about," she said.

"That'd be an understatement. The reason I reached out to you wasn't just for a lunchtime catch-up. I actually have to come clean about something. There's an article coming out on *BABBLE* in the next week or so, but I owe it to you to let you know everything first."

I could see her face morph from intrigue to fear to confusion in seconds. I took a deep breath before finally opening up to the one person who should have known everything from the start. Once I was done, I watched her stare in disbelief. She shook her head slowly, letting out an incredulous laugh.

"What the fuck? So, you essentially pretended to cheat on me?" I was amused that out of everything I had just told her, that was what stood out to her the most. Ironic, considering I'd done it out of fear of her finding out the actual truth.

"When you put it *that* way . . ."

"That's literally what happened!"

"All right, all right. But yes. I never actually cheated on you. I would have never done that. Everything just turned into a shitshow, to be honest."

"You really are something else, Ed. Your mind works in mysterious ways."

"It does, I guess. But on a serious note, I can't stress enough how sorry I am for everything. For leaving without an explanation. I hurt you really badly. I ran away instead of fighting for us, and it was wrong of me. You were my biggest fan, and I discounted that. I want you to know that I appreciate everything you've ever done for me. I really do."

Her face fell. "It's okay. Thanks for apologising. I've healed, though. A lot of things got me through it. The band, family, friends. Arianna, too."

My heart sank at the reminder that *her* heart belonged to someone else. "I'm so happy for you. I'm sure she's a better partner than I was."

"You know, I was still so fucked up for months when we broke up, Eddie. Even when I got serious with Arianna. I saw those photos of you and Hugo in Italy, and it sent me over the edge. I didn't know if I had it in me to move on, but I did eventually. It feels so good to not be heartbroken anymore."

I told her the irony was that *I* was crying over pictures of her new relationship when I was in Italy. We had become two ships passing in the night, but it was all my doing. She had no fault in any of it. She always had my back. Maybe my fears of being so close to someone who I saw with so much potential for success had subconsciously hindered my willingness to open up to her. Who knows? The fact of the matter was that she was no longer my past, present, and future. She was just my past. A beautiful one, at least.

We soon brought the conversation back to the main topic at hand. I told her that the reason we were publishing the article soon was because Nahid had made an express request for the exposé to be published after she gave birth. She wanted to make sure her pregnancy went without a hitch before subjecting herself to a deluge of publicity, which was understandable, considering what she'd once told me about her previous miscarriage. She'd had her baby about a week ago. A girl, Soraya Smith. Seven pounds, happy and healthy. When you'd told me you had given her the middle name Edie, I was lost for words. You dropped a *D* for a more feminine touch, but I appreciated it all the same.

I was also nervous at the prospect of the article coming out; after all, I didn't know what to expect. Would it go viral overnight, with *Great*

Belonging's long con making international headlines and stirring a larger conversation about the industry? Or maybe it would just backfire, resulting in unwanted controversy. There would be camps of people who commended me for bringing to light a long-standing problem that permeated almost every sector of late-stage capitalist society: the belief that some people's ideas were worth more than others. The belief that some people's names, and faces, and genders, and races, were more profitable than others. Other camps of people might just see it as a farce or an attention-seeking ploy. There might even be a camp of people who still believed *you* were the real playwright. There might be people of colour praising my actions and calling me a genius, and people of colour who thought that I lacked integrity. It was scary being confronted with the truths that people could be willing to hold on to. I guess I could say that none of it mattered in the end. I didn't need the whole world to believe in me. I just wanted to love what I did and do what I loved.

After we had finished the bulk of our conversation, I took in the full spectrum of emotions painting Blue's big brown eyes. It was hard for me to read.

"What's up?" I asked her.

She didn't say anything for a while. Then she took my hand in hers, over the table. "See? I told you. You're a star. It's in your name. Granted, this wasn't exactly what I meant when I said you were destined for fame." She chuckled softly. "But I'll take what I can get at this point."

◆ ◆ ◆

I found myself standing at my mother's doorstep in Woolwich that evening. It was a gamble, because I hadn't actually checked beforehand if she was home. To my relief, not only was she, but Nick was there too. When she opened the door, I just stood there and burst into a torrent of tears. I let her bring me into a hug. I blubbered about how much I'd missed her. All the anger and fear that had occupied me for so long felt null and void, especially since the meeting with you and Helen. All I had wanted to do for the last few months was reconnect. After getting closure with Blue, I knew I had to do the same with my mother. Things had never been perfect with her, but I had to give her some credit. She took a risk all those years ago, when she stood her ground on keeping us in this country against my father's wishes. Frankly, I couldn't say it hadn't paid off. She did her best with what she had. I wanted her to know that she was appreciated.

Nick soon followed behind, joining in on the hug. The three of us held tight in a soft embrace, with no words needing to be exchanged. The smell of dinner permeated the flat, and I had never felt hungrier. Luckily for me, my mother always made enough food for leftovers.

A Bright Future

July 2023

A GRAND OPENING: HUGO LAWRENCE SMITH LIGHTS UP THE REGIUM IN GRIPPING STAGE DEBUT

———

Four years after the scathing *BABBLE* magazine article
that rocked the West End, the newfound actor puts
on a hypnotic performance in *Dreams of Elsewhere*, a
semi-autobiographical play directed by his wife

———

EMILY FAIRFAX

Although this is the twenty-eight-year-old's first acting gig, it most definitely won't be his last. *Dreams of Elsewhere* is the gripping new play directed by accomplished actress-turned-director Nahid Norouzi that opened to a sold-out box office at the Regium Theatre in London earlier this week. Norouzi co-wrote the script with London-based playwright Leila Abedini, with whom she shares a Persian background. The play is an allegedly loose retelling of Norouzi's time at the Royal Academy of Dramatic Art in the early 2000s. It follows Yasmin, a budding actress who is finding her voice in an industry dominated by privilege and lacking in substantial representation for women of colour. Smith only takes up twenty minutes of the production's two-hour run time, playing the role of a toxic love interest who mentors the protagonist in her final year. However, his performance is striking and memorable, leaving the audience and critics alike with anticipation for his future endeavours.

Smith first entered the scene parading as a playwright at the behest of his friend, black British writer and journalist Naledi Moruakgomo (formerly known as Eddie). Moruakgomo's play *Great Belonging* was an instant success after its run at the Regium in early 2018, though it remains hotly contested as to whether its deceptive accreditation had much to do with it. Once she published the article "Why I Gave My Play Away: An Exposé of the Dark Side of the Theatre Industry" in social justice, art, and culture magazine *BABBLE* in 2019, Smith, Moruakgomo, and Norouzi were catapulted into instant notoriety. *Great Belonging* was retroactively disqualified from the Marston B. Greaves Awards, and Moruakgomo and Smith were required to give back the trophy and the £15,000 cash prize. Moruakgomo then declared her plans to quit playwriting and focus on her new role as editor-in-chief at *BABBLE*. The magazine had garnered an international audience in a matter of weeks, and its headquarters eventually spread to Manchester, and then New York, where Moruakgomo would settle after COVID restrictions were phased out in 2021.

Renowned talent agent Helen Hunter was subsequently fired from Wentworth following an enquiry into the agency's diversity and inclusion initiatives, based on shocking revelations from the *BABBLE* article. Wentworth pledged to foster a more inclusive and diverse environment "rich with talent from all walks of life," with plans to implement initiatives that would "ensure that anyone and everyone feels comfortable submitting work to us." Conversely, the disgraced Hunter fell down a similar pipeline to beloved *Billy Andromeda* author C. H. Edmonds, who had begun espousing controversial beliefs aligned with those of trans-exclusionary radical feminists, commonly abbreviated as TERFs, around the same time. Edmonds spent weeks firing off gender-critical tweets in defence of the biological differences between the sexes. Hunter soon decried what she considered to be a growing wave of political correctness and cancel culture, with Edmonds among a pool of staunch defenders of her campaign.

Although Smith is related to Edmonds, he has vocalised on various occasions that his political views in no way align with those of his first cousin. This line of enquiry was rehashed during the reignition of the Black Lives Matter movement following the murder of George Floyd, after old pictures of Smith from his A-level days had resurfaced that appeared to show him dressed in racially offensive attire at a costume party. He has since publicly apologised, crediting ignorance and peer pressure from his rugby friends at the time and vowing to continue to grow and learn from his past mistakes.

What also caught everyone's attention after the *BABBLE* exposé was the announcement made in the same week that Norouzi had separated from award-winning director husband Aaron Yousef and had given birth to her and Smith's first child. The pair's love affair became the subject of intense online speculation, inadvertently eclipsing Moruakgomo and Smith's initial aim to highlight unconscious bias in theatre. They welcomed their second child in 2020, six months into the pandemic. The couple wed in a private ceremony in July 2021, two years after the article's publication.

It was late last year when thirty-seven-year-old Norouzi voiced plans to direct her first play since the critically acclaimed drama *Roses Are Red*, which she had co-directed with Parisian theatre powerhouse Clotilde Belmont following *Great Belonging*. A cast of actors were announced to star in *Dreams of Elsewhere* earlier this year, with up-and-comer Zara El-Khoury set to take on the lead role. What caught everyone's attention, however, was the announcement that Smith would also be taking to the stage in his debut performance, directed by none other than his wife. Following years of dazzling publicity from drama pundits who considered his fabricated infiltration into playwriting to be one of the most convincing performances in contemporary history, it seemed he finally caved into requests to take a dedicated leap into the profession. *Dreams of Elsewhere* has not only affirmed Norouzi's impressive directing talents, but Smith's acting abilities. Chemistry between the debut actor and his co-star El-Khoury was electric on the opening night, and it is reported that he readily and eagerly integrated with the cast and production crew during rehearsals. His riveting performance is enough to silence the sceptics, and it appears that he has a bright future in theatre, or even on the big screen, ahead of him.

"Holy *shit*. This is pure drivel," Nahid said, staring at the laptop screen in disbelief. She shot me an incredulous look, as if to say, *Can you believe this?*

"I told you it was bad," I replied, leaning on the island counter where she stood in the kitchen. It was just the two of us in your house; you were out somewhere in the city, and little Soraya and Kamran were in Kent with your mother for the week. I had flown to London from New York to catch the play a few days prior, acquiring a front-row seat on the opening night. It was spectacular; the story was vivid, moving, and it felt surreal to see her hardships, which she'd once opened up to me about, play out in front of me. I was sure it was a cathartic process for her. There was not one weak link in the cast, and that was most definitely due to her. Regardless, I wouldn't have said you were the *strongest* link by any stretch of a mile. Your performance reeked of first-time jitters, and there was the odd stumble here and there. It was nothing substantially distracting, but it wasn't necessarily MBG-worthy.

"Twice. *Two times* in this article I'm referred to as a *wife*," Nahid went on. "That's what they reduced me to. They spent way too much time harping on about my personal life and not enough about my play. And Hugo . . . fuck." She laughed. "He was onstage for *fifteen* minutes, not twenty. Trust me, I made sure of that myself for this reason. I didn't want him to distract from the play. Not because he's shit, but because he's . . . just *not bad*. That's all it takes for him to receive a puff piece from the *Guardian*, apparently." She slammed her laptop closed and reached into the fridge for a bottle of wine before pouring it into a glass. She offered me one and I accepted, watching her pour another serving.

"I doubt this Emily Fairfax woman is a reputable journalist or critic," I replied. "She's just trying to get the most views on her article. If she focuses on Hugo, then she's already got a wide-reaching story. She isn't worth taking seriously."

"Well, I *am* taking her seriously, because everyone else will be.

There was no mention of my history as an actress or my experiences that brought me to where I am. They don't even talk about Leila, or any of *her* recent accomplishments. She's an amazing playwright, and I owe a lot of this to her. We carried this show on our backs, but they haven't given us our dues. This was nothing but tabloid fodder. And don't get me started on this 'electric' chemistry Hugo had with Zara. Is it *that* obvious to everyone? Fuck me." She took a long swig of her wine.

I narrowed my eyes. "It is?"

"He's definitely sleeping with her," she said matter-of-factly.

I snorted. "No way. Surely not. Do you have any proof?"

She shook her head. "Nothing concrete. But I just know. I see it in the way he looks at her." Her voice trembled. "How could he not? She's gorgeous. And she's twenty-five. She's basically just a younger, hotter version of me. He's going to leave me for her, I'm sure of it." She fiddled with her wedding ring as if itching to take it off. "I only cast him in this role because I felt sorry for him. He hated his legal training contract. He constantly complained about how boring it was, and I wanted to shut him up a bit. I also wanted an excuse to spend more time with him, frankly. We were drifting apart before this. I really didn't think it'd backfire in this way. I just want to be respected and revered for my work. But I'm just the wife of a breakout star." She frowned, and my heart sank for her.

After a moment of silence, I spoke. "We never needed Hu. He needed *us*. He was nothing before us. We made him. Always remember that. And don't let this take away from the fact that you've just sold out the fucking *Regium* with such a vulnerable, inspiring story. So many women are going to look up to you. So many already do."

She smiled softly, then crossed her arms. "You're right, we did make him. There's not one bloody article about him that can even be written without reference to us. That says it all." She rolled her eyes. "God, I wish you still wrote plays. We could have worked on something together. That would have been worthwhile."

"Don't give me any ideas. I've put it all behind me," I replied.

"I totally get that. It's hard out here." She sighed, taking another long swig of her wine.

I paused before speaking again. "But . . . I still have my second script lying around somewhere. You know, the one I wrote after *Great Belonging* that Wentworth turned down. Maybe I could wipe the dust off it. I could switch to *BABBLE*'s London HQ for a couple of months, and we can perfect it and get it stage-ready. You can take the helm with directing it? I don't know, it's just an idea."

Nahid raised an eyebrow. "It sounds like you're already considering it."

"Honestly, it's only just popped into my mind. I'd need to give it more thought."

But by then, the idea was already lodged in my brain. The cogs were whirring. London's streets were calling me back. I could see it already: my magnum opus, Nahid's best project yet. Queues of theatregoers snaking around the building on opening week and for weeks to come. Awards left, right, and centre. MBGs, Oliviers, you name it. An undeniable masterpiece. Something that was just ours.

Something that was just mine.

Acknowledgements

I'd like to thank Emma Leong, Marya Spence and everyone at Janklow & Nesbit for their unending enthusiasm and support. Thank you to Rose Green, Jade Hui and Serena Arthur, for helping me shape this novel into what it became. Flora Willis, Rachel Quin, Lucy Richardson, Grace Harrison, Fritha Saunders, Vidisha Biswas, Robyn Haque and the rest of the Footnote/Bonnier team I am forever grateful to for championing *Grand Scheme* and platforming stories of immigration. It isn't lost on me that these are all women, which makes me smugly proud, all things considered. I'd like to thank my UK/US copy-editors, Ross Jamieson and Valerie Shea for helping me cross my *T*'s and dot my *I*'s. Of course, a big thank you to Washington Square Press/Atria/ Simon & Schuster.

I started writing *Grand Scheme* as part of a creative writing PhD at Brunel University London, and my supervisor Dr. Sarah Penny was the first pair of eyes on this project. I'm very thankful for her guidance and confidence in my work. Thanks so much to the other staff at Brunel who I came into contact with, including Professor Nick Hubble, Dr. Kate Houlden, Dr. Emma Filtness, Dr. Max Kinnings, Helen Cullen, and the formidable Bernardine Evaristo, whom I had the pleasure of being given encouragement and advice from towards the end of my PhD.

Thank you to Emma, Daniel, Sakina, Lauren, Maddy, Jasmine, Hasan, Ely, Melanie, Vanessa, Molly and Philline, and many other friends and family who have supported me during this process and over the years. Finally, thank you Mum and Dad for everything.

About the Author

Born in Botswana, raised in the West Midlands, UK and living in London, Warona Jay studied law at the University of Kent and King's College London before switching to a creative writing PhD at Brunel. She was shortlisted for the Sony Young Movellist of the Year Award judged by Malorie Blackman and longlisted for Penguin Random House's WriteNow Scheme in 2020.

The Grand Scheme of Things is her debut novel.